Axel

An MC Romance

Charlotte McGinlay

Copyright © 2023 Charlotte McGinlay

All rights reserved.

ISBN: 979-8-3972-8313-7

DESCRIPTION

Axel

I'm the president of our club, making my father proud every day.
I love my life of freedom, booze, girls, brothers, and family.
Nothing else mattered to me.
But then she walks into my world.
She takes my breath away and she's all I see.
But she's in danger and I'll do anything to save her.
Even take a life if I have too.
Because she's mine. And I protect what is mine.

Annalise

I haven't had an easy start to life.
But with help of the people who love me, I managed to get to where I want to be.
I live for baking and had opened my own bakery.
I didn't want a relationship or the hassle of heartbreak I'd rather just settle.
I didn't count on him though or how he makes me feel.
I fall for him without realizing.
He's all I want; all I think about.
But then I'm in danger and I can't let him get hurt because of me.
I try to push him away, but it doesn't work.
Because he's mine as much as I'm his.

This can be read as a standalone. It is book 1 of 7 of Untamed Hell's fire MC series, with a HEA. Due to mature content and themes this book is recommended for readers aged 18+, this novel may contain triggers.

Prologue

Axel – 8 years old

I huff and kick a rock. I was comfortable lying on my bed, playing my video games, when my momma told me I had to go get my dad from the clubhouse for dinner in the Texan heat.

I grumble.

Why couldn't she just call him like a normal person? But no, not my Momma. Sending your child into this heat should be classified as child abuse. Granted, it's not as hot now as it was at lunchtime, and the clubhouse is only down the hill on the same land, but still. It's 39 degrees, which is stupidly hot, especially in the height of June, where the summer months are even hotter and the evenings are only a smidge cooler than now. I shake my head while rubbing the bump there, and I sigh.

Once I reach the back of the clubhouse, I can hear the music booming as I head inside. I blink a couple of times because of the smoke and light difference and walk towards my dad's office when Jewels, a club sweet butt, shouts over from where she's sitting on a club brother's lap, her big boobs squishing his face, "Hey Logan, your dads in the basement." I sighed again just wanting to get back to my game, I was so close to beating Travis's high score.

I wave at her,

"Thanks, Jewels."

She smiles and goes back to the brother while I continue heading towards the basement of our huge clubhouse, ignoring the brothers who are busy with the sweet butts—not something an 8-year-old should see.

It's only 6:30 in the evening, so technically they shouldn't be having sex in the open yet, but with momma at home today, the brothers have decided to say screw it. I shake my head because momma will find out; she knows all and sees all, and there will be hell to pay when she does.

My momma is not one you want to anger.

When I make it to the stairs in the basement, I stomp down the stairs and reach the metal door. I open it with a shove and come to a stop when I notice my dad, his VP, Stormy, and his enforcer butch standing near a man who is only in his boxers, dangling by his arms from the ceiling covered in blood.

I raise both my brows.

All three men quickly turn, paling when they see me.

"Fuck, shit, Logan. What are you doing here?" My dad booms while I tilt my head and say,

"Dad, wouldn't it be easier to use an axe to chop off his toes instead of that knife? Less messy?"

My dad's mouth hangs open while I look at the man's toes. They're hanging off only slightly attached, but I'm pretty sure axing them would be less messy, right? I mean, it'll just cut through them. Hmm, maybe not less messy, just easier. I nod to myself. Yeah, definitely easier.

Butch clears his throat.

"Well, Axel, that's a great idea."

Both my dad and Stormy look at Butch and grin, while my dad states,

"It looks like you just earned your road name, son." I smile wide. I've wanted one for years, probably since I was like four, yeah, four.

The brothers smirk while my dad continues.

"Ok, son, first of all, that's a brilliant idea, probably not less messy but definitely a lot fucking easier, and secondly, don't tell your mother you saw this." The look he's giving me would scare most men away, but all I can do is slowly smirk and tilt my head again. I'm not scared of my dad; he may be president of an MC, but he's still my dad—my momma is scarier than him, and he knows it too. The back of my head knows it from the smack she gave me when I complained about coming down here. This is going to cost him more than he realizes.

He sighs, "I'll get you that Call of Duty game you've been crazing your momma about."

I nod, like I'm agreeing but wanting to push my luck a little bit more. I state,

"I'm guessing you also don't want me to let momma know about the brothers having sex before 9 p.m. out in the common room too? Hey, Dad, how does Jiggles fit three men inside her like that?"

Butch and Stormy's eyes widen, then they try to hold their laughter in while my dad slowly closes his eyes and takes a deep breath, wishing for patience he's never going to get when he has me as a son and is married to momma. Their 'guest' looks on in confusion, mouth gagged, hands going purple. I wave at him, making him struggle against the ties. He's obviously done something bad; otherwise, he wouldn't be here, so why not antagonize him?

The men lose it, laughing their asses off, while my dad says,

"I'll also up your allowance by $10."

I smile smugly and nod, then turn around while stating over my shoulder,

"Oh, and dad, momma said you have 10 minutes to get home for dinner or you're on the couch tonight, which was roughly 10 minutes ago; you may want to hurry before she comes down here herself and sees the common room."

My dad's mouth hangs open, then he curses up a storm while I mutter,

"Maybe being forced out in Texan heat isn't child abuse, after all—I got myself a road name, more money, and a game. Good day for me."

As I walk out the door, I hear all three men laugh their butts off while Stormy states, "Fuck, he's going to be a good pres one day." I grin wide because yes, yes, I will be.

Annalise – age 3

I'm lying under my bed with my hands over my ears, tears streaming down my face where Mommy screamed at me to run. I don't know what I did to make Daddy so mad at Mommy; he says it's all my fault. What did I do? I don't know what I did. Mommy was giving me my favorite nuggies, and he came in and hit Mommy; she had so much color coming from her nose. More tears roll down my cheeks.

I want my mommy.

I hear more screaming, and my body shakes.

"You s-stupid bitch-h, I to-told you to c-cook me t-tea. You know the b-brat doesn't eat until a-after I do, and-and I don't c-care what time it is."

I hear him growl, his words sounding funny, while Mommy cries harder, screaming for him to stop. There's more banging and screaming, with Mommy begging for Daddy to stop. He always hurts her, makes funny colored stuff come out of her, and puts funny color marks on her.

I sniffle.

After a little while, the noises stopped, but I don't move. The last time I did, Daddy snapped my arm; it hurt a lot. I had to go to the big doctor. Mommy told them I fell. I don't know why she lied, though; she told me to never lie.

My bedroom door slams open, and I jump. Tears run down my face.

"A-Annalise, come out right f-fucking no-now." Daddy growls funnily, but I don't move. I don't like it when he comes into my room; he hits me hard. I scream when his hand grabs my foot, and he drags me out from under the bed. He looks down at me and grins wide.

"There y-you are y-you little b-bitch. Think you c-can eat b-before me. T-This is a-all you-your fault; she's dead b-because o-of you." His brown eyes look black as he stares at me with hatred, and his black hair is all over the place and greasy. I try to move away from him to run, but his hand comes down and hits me hard in the face. I feel dizzy as I scream. He hits me again and again, kicking me in the back over and over when there's a loud bang. "SHERRIFF'S OFFICE, PUT YOUR HANDS UP, NOW." My daddy freezes his hits. Fury and rage cross his face as I look up to him with blurry eyes. Why can't I see properly?

Daddy places both of his hands up, and the policemen put something around his hands as they say,

"Grant Lawrence, you are under arrest for the murder of Lucy Lawrence and the attempted murder of Annalise Jessica Lawrence. You don't have to say anything, but anything you do say will be used as evidence in court." Someone leans over me while my daddy is being dragged out cursing badly; mommy doesn't like it when he says bad words. My head hurts and my tummy aches. I can't move my legs. Why can't I move my legs?

I want Mommy.

I slowly start to close my eyes when I hear someone shout.

"WE'RE GOING TO LOSE HER; SHE'S CODING."

And everything goes black while I wish for my mommy. I want my mommy.

MOMMY.

Chapter 1

Axel - age 30 – present day

I grunt as a sweet butt deep-throats my cock. Bubbles knows what she's doing, and fuck does it feel good.

She's my main girl.

Well, she and Ginger, especially together, fuck they're hot when they eat each other out. Bubbles brings me back out of my head when she licks under my cock on the triangle. Fuck, yes. I grab a hold of her dyed blue hair and fist it, holding her still. I thrust my cock deep down her throat, making her gag. Tears run down her face, her brown eyes glistening, but it doesn't deter her; she moves her hands up my thighs. One hand grabs my ass while the other fondles my heavy ball sack. I grunt and fuck her face harder and faster while she sucks hard, just the way I like it. My balls start to tighten, and cum spurts out from my tip. I thrust to the back of her throat and keep her there as she swallows me down. I never come in a sweet butt's ass or pussy or any woman really; it's either down her throat or in a condom after I've quickly pulled out of her that I then dispose of myself.

You can never be too careful.

Just as I finish cuming, the door to my office slams open, and I sigh, knowing who's just ruined my bliss. "Momma, what have I told you about not knocking?"

I remove my cock from Bubbles' mouth and quickly put it away, so momma doesn't get a full view of my package. I look at her and see she's scowling at me hard. Her brown eyes are throwing daggers at me. My momma's a beautiful woman.

Brown eyes, light brown hair, curvy but short as fuck at 5"2, I'm literally a foot taller than her. Though you wouldn't catch me calling her short to her face, she'd beat my ass like last week when I left the date that she set me up on at the restaurant without even telling me. My head still fucking hurts where she hit me with a fucking frying pan when I told her it was her fault in the first place.

"Don't you talk back to me, boy; it's bad enough. I have to deal with your father's flipping lip, and I'm your mother; I shouldn't have to knock." I snort and cough to cover it up, then she turns her daggers to Bubbles, who's also scowling, realizing she's not getting any.

She points at the sweet butt,

"You out. I need a word with my son before he goes into church. Go and find another brother to satisfy you before they have to go in." Bubbles looks to me like I'm going to deny my mother over her. I just raise a brow, and she huffs, storming out of the room.

I turn my attention back to my mother.

"What's up, momma? You seem stressed."

She sighs and goes to take a seat on my black couch that I have on the side wall. She looks around and says, "Baby boy, you really need some color in here; it's too dark." I shake my head and also look around. dark gray walls that have box-squared white shelving behind my dark mahogany desk and black chair. There are two black chairs sitting in front of my desk that match the couch.

I look back at Momma.

"We both know you didn't walk in here to complain about my office; what's going on?" She leans back and just shrugs.

"I want to hold a luncheon here in two days with my book club ladies, but your father says you won't go for it."

I just stared at her for a minute because I clearly didn't hear her right. There's no way she wants to hold a fucking luncheon with her book club buddies at our smoke-filled clubhouse that's full of half-naked women, right?

She doesn't blink, keeping eye contact.

Ah, fuck.

I quickly get my phone out, about to ream my father's ass for not preparing me, making her growl at me. I shake my head. 5 years—that's how long I've taken over from him since he handed the gavel to me—and I have ensured to make him proud that I've managed to double our profits. The least he could of fucking done was give me a heads-up about his wife.

I sigh and close my eyes when I see I have a message. Fuck.

Dad- incoming, lock your office door, run, hide, and turn into a ghost—the bulldogs loose.

Then I snort at her nickname, which she has no idea about and will never find out about either; we all value our fucking lives. How my dad is still kicking is beyond me. I put my phone away and tilted my head. Her brown eyes look all sweet and angelic when I definitely know better. I sigh again, not fucking wanting a bunch of civilian women here.

"Ok, fine." She squeals—yes, my mother—the bulldog fucking squeals in delight, then jumps up, ready to hug me. I go to catch her when she stops herself, her face twisting into a disgusted grimace, making me frown at her. "Yeah, I'll hug you when you don't smell of that harpy son. I love you though." Then she turns to walk out while I laugh at her and shake my head until she turns around and says,

"Your father and I know a lovely woman who's just opened a bakery shop early this year, have known her for years actually. I think I'll order her cakes and see if she wants to come too. I think you'll like her. You actually know her grandmother, Rosie Lawrence."

I scowl at her, causing her to grin, knowing I'm onto her. For fucks sake,

Then I state, realizing what she said,

"I didn't know Rosie had a granddaughter." My mother nods her head.

"Yes, she's 5 years younger than you and was homeschooled; we have dinner with them once a week. She struggled growing up and doesn't go out all that much, but I still believe you two will get along nicely. I'll just have to double-check with Rosie to see if she's still with that idiot. She's way out of his league." I furrow my brows, not knowing whether to be pissed at being set up again or whether to ask more questions about her, like her fucking name, while my mother just smiles, happy that she got my fucking attention. Rosie's always been a nice lady, but I've never seen her with anyone growing up. I mean, there were stories of her idiotic son, but I just thought they were that; stories.

Shaking my head at her relentlessness, I leave my office, ensuring I lock the door and head towards the common room. Brothers lounge around waiting for me to call church or play pool while the sweet butts lean against the dark brown walls, sulking that they're not getting any attention or are sitting on the light brown leather furniture that surrounds the TV when they should be fucking cleaning. The prospects are busy filling the bar, ready for after our club meeting.

I sigh, bang the wall twice, and shout,

"CHURCH."

Then I hand my phone to Liam, our prospect, who's nearly ready for his patch, and head inside the room. The walls are just like the ones in the common room, dark brown and littered with memorabilia and pictures of our generations in black and white frames, and a big wooden circular table sits in the middle of the room with our logo carved in it. A massive hawk with its wings on fire looks like a fucking badass, and our name circles it in. I take the head of the seat, while Dagger takes a seat next to me as my VP. His blood brother Ink takes a seat next to him as our secretary, while Gunner, our enforcer, sits to my left, then our treasurer, Slicer, sits next to him, and Flame, our road caption, and Tech Guru sit down next before Hawk, our sergeant at arms, takes a seat.

                      The rest of the table is filled out with the old timers who were counsel before we took over. The rest of the brothers don't attend these meetings. We only inform them when necessary, plus we have roughly another 15 brothers outside these doors; we won't fit them all in here, and most of them don't want these jobs, even if we do get more money than them.

I bang the gavel.

"Alright fuckers, church is in session."

My father raises a brow at me, knowing I'm irritated, and I sigh.

"It seems momma has found another taker for me." All the men burst out laughing while I glare at my father, who's trying to hide his smirk.

He lifts his hands up in an innocent gesture.

"Hey, I texted you, son."

My glare hardens. "I was a little busy getting my dick sucked, dad. Now we all have to deal with momma's busy body book club friends and some woman she seems to think I'll 'like'." The men's laughter goes louder while my father's face goes red as he tries to hold his in.

I scowl harder and shout over the idiots.

"INK, HOW IS THE TATTOO PARLOUR?"

Ink clears his throat, trying to get himself under control, while the men chuckle like fucking hyenas.

"It's g-good, Pres.; we're making a p-profit." He stutters over his words, trying to get himself together, and I scowl and growl out,

"It isn't fucking funny. Remember a few weeks ago when she set me up with Lindsey? The fucking woman wouldn't stop staring at me, giggling without fucking blinking. And let's not forget about crazy Masie, who screamed the restaurant down last week when I didn't want to bring her home. She caused a grand amount of damage, then bullshitted Momma, who then proceeded to whack me over the head with a fucking frying pan.

Ooh, and how about Samantha Freckle, how she's so different from high school. How she's changed her ways and no longer drops to her knees for anyone walking past, except for when I show up at the blind fucking date; I thought I was meeting my mother too, and she tries to suck me off in front of the fucking town's pastor."

My father loses it with the rest of the brothers while I lean back and wait for them to calm down.

Then I smirked. "Just think, brother's, once she's finally found the 'one' who I don't fucking want because I like loose pussy, she'll get onto you lot."

They all shut up and looked at me wide-eyed.

Dagger and Ink shout at my dad at the same time.

"SORT YOUR FUCKING OLD LADY OUT."

Their dad Storm bursts out in laughter, along with Gunner's dad Butch, as I bang the gavel to get everyone to quiet down and point to my dad.

"Tell her to stop, Dad; I don't want to meet this next crazy woman. I like my life just as it is; she can fucking wait for grandchildren. Got it."

He chuckles, "Son, this is your mother we're talking about here."

I sigh and look towards Dagger, who nods at me. "I didn't want to do this, Dad, brothers, but I will if I have to."

They all straightened at my words.

"Dad, either tell her to back off or I'll ensure momma's aware of all the times you let the brothers break her rules about no sex in the common room before 9 p.m.—in front of her young son, no less. I mean, you saw what she did the one time she caught everyone when I was 8, remember? Or how about when Star walked in on one of the brothers getting sucked when she was only 11?"

My father pales while all the brothers look at him with pleading eyes. Yeah, my momma is one mean bulldog when pissed off.

My dad clears his throat. "Ok, I'll talk to her."

I nod, then bang the gavel again. "Alright, back to business, Gunner, Slicer, how's the bar?"

Slicer is the one who says, "We're up 65% in profits; things are going well; no trouble is happening."

I nod and Dagger states, "The strip club is doing good profit-wise. But we're going to have to start drug testing the women again. Silver overdosed in the changing rooms last week. Looks like the devil's gear."

I scowl.

"They're getting too comfortable around us despite having a truce. We need to send a message."

I look to my SGT at arms, Hawk, and he nods, "I'll make sure to find their drug runners. If they're in our territory, I'll question them before sending parts of them back to Snake. I'll make sure to take a couple of brothers."

I nod, then look towards Flame, and he states, "The garage is increasing more each day; there are no problems on our end."

I nod and ask, "When is Stars exhibition?"

                        He smiles wide at the mention of his long-time friend. She's 8 years younger than most of us, but we've known her all our lives, especially since her dad was a brother before a Devil ran her and her dad off the road when she was 10. She was shot and found nearly a mile away from the bike; she nearly died while her dad was missing on-site, presumably dead. That's the year she fell for Flame; he was her person through all of it. He loves her back but believes she deserves better, so he fucks around to ensure he doesn't try anything with her, which is fucking stupid if you ask me.

"In five months, the shows sold out, but I made sure the brothers had unlimited access."

We all nod and clap, happy for our club princess.

I smile and ask, "How's our road plan coming for our next run to Wincher?"

He grabs his paperwork. "The route is all set, mainly back roads on the way there, and much easier than going to Winchester. There's less chance of bumping into cops while we're delivering the merchandise over to the Rebels MC. Four patched brothers and two prospects should be enough."

I nod. "Ok, so Liam and Elvis will go in the truck while Slicer, Flame, Dagger, and Butch go on their bikes."

They all nod, and Flame continues,

"It's a 5-hour, 20-minute drive from here in Dallas to Louisiana, where we'll be meeting Anchor, their road captain; we should be able to get it done in one day." I look around, and all the men nod.

"Alright, fuckers, anything else?" My dad sighs and stands up, knocking on the table twice. We all look at him, and I tense. He never speaks out in meetings anymore.

"Apparently some of the sweet butts are poking holes in the condoms. I'm just not sure who. My old lady has gone to all the brother's rooms, including the ones that do have old ladies, and has placed them all in the water. More than half of them were faulty." All the brothers shout in outrage, and some pale. Fuck. I bang my gavel and look toward my enforcer, Ink. I don't even need to tell him what I want; we're one and the same. He nods and gets up, going into the common room.

He whistles loudly.

"All sweet butts in here right fucking now."

My dad sits back down as Ink returns, and the ladies all come in and line up against the wall. They all smile, pulling their tops or lack thereof down some more, showing more tit, or pulling their short shorts higher up, and I shake my head. They obviously think they're here to serve us, which is fucking ridiculous because we have never and will never fuck a sweet butt in this room.

Fuck I'm pissed.

We took them in and gave them food, clothes, and a roof over their heads. They don't have to fuck us; just clean the clubhouse and do the shopping. The fucking is completely consensual, so this takes the fucking piss.

I stand getting their attention. "Does someone want to explain why more than half of the brother's condoms are faulty?" half of them pale while the other half look at me confused, which is mainly the ones who don't fuck around with the brothers often and actually wear clothes. Only a couple sleep with a certain brother hoping to be patched in as an old lady, which is never going to happen; otherwise, they focus on what they get paid to do, unlike the other half.

I sigh.

"Here's what's going to happen: we're going to replace all the condoms and place them in locked-up cupboards, and the next time you ladies decide to trap us men, you'll not only be on the streets, but I'll ensure I ruin your fucking lives. I may not be able to identify which one of you is guilty, but I don't mind starting afresh with new pussies who want to earn their keep cleaning and cooking in the clubhouse; if this is the route you all want to take, especially after we put a roof over all your heads, then I will make it possible. Do I make myself clear?" I say it in a menacing voice, void of emotion, making the women shiver in fear.

They all nod frantically, and I say,

"Don't disappear from the common room; Doc will be giving you all pregnancy tests. Now fuck off." They pale again and scurry out, with Ink following them out to ensure they all stay where I told them to, and I look to Doc, who, without having to say a word, nods and heads out too. I look around the room at the pissed-off brothers.

"Anything else."

They all shake their heads, and I bang the gavel.

"Meeting adjourned, fuck off."

They chuckle and head out, and I follow. As we get into the common room, I hear a screech of happiness.

"ZAYNE."

Star shouts and jumps into Flame's awaiting arms, and we all stand back and watch, smiling. She's the only one who calls him by his given name, the only one who can get away with it. I look at Dad and shake my head while he chuckles. Flame really needs to pull his head out of his ass before someone realizes how fucking special she actually is.

Flame puts her down and raises both his eyebrows, and she states,

"Guess who just sold her painting for $4,500?" Flame's grin widens, and he picks her up again, twirling her around and making her laugh while Clitter, one of the sweet butts, glares at them. She's been after Flame's patch for years but knows Star comes before anyone, including the brotherhood. All of us brothers and some of the old ladies that are around cheer loudly, and I shout,

"CELEBRATORY DRINKS."

Making the brothers cheer louder, I walk over to Star and Flame as he puts her down, putting his arm around her shoulders, and I push him away playfully and grab Star, hugging her tight.

"Proud of you, little star." She sniffles and squishes me tightly, causing Flame to growl. I let her go and looked at him with a raised brow, and he just cleared his throat like he didn't just fucking growl at me like a dog. I shake my head; he knows all of us brothers see her as a sister, but one day soon, someone won't. I give him a pointed stare, and he sighs. He then holds Star in his arms again, kissing her head, and she grins at him, holding him tighter, making me smile. He knows what he's got but is still not willing to risk it.

I go to the bar and order a beer when Bubbles comes back towards me. I raise a brow, and she shows me her pregnancy test.

"Doc made sure to watch us all pee on them, which is gross by the way; all of our tests came back negative, and he'll be doing more tests in two weeks; can we fuck now?" I chuckle and grin at her, then drag her back to the room I have here. I do have a plot to build as well as several other brothers. Dagger, Ink, Slicer, Hawk, and Gunner have already built theirs, but that'll give momma more reason to nag me. I like loose pussy on tap and don't want to settle down.

I drag Bubbles into my room and shove her against the door, ramming my tongue down her throat. I won't fuck her cunt until we get new condoms, but I will fuck her ass and make her swallow my cum.

Axel: An MC Romance

Chapter 2

Annalise – age 25 – current day

I sigh and rub the back of my hand on my forehead, probably spreading flour all over my face. I look at the clock. I've been in here baking for about 4 hours, and my feet are killing me. I quickly take the triple chocolate brownies—my mama's recipe—out of the oven and put the biscuits in when the door opens, and Sandy, the 40-something wonderful woman who I employed straight away when I opened a year ago, comes in with a bright smile on her face, her brownish green eyes sparkling while her reddish hair is pinned up in a bun on the top of her head.

"Hey, Annie, Cammy Ramirez is asking for you." I nod, quickly wash my hands, and make sure everything is looking okay before going out front. I go through the door and look around. Half of my dark red tables are full of customers, and I smile. It took me a while, but with the help of my grandma, who took me in at just 3 years old when my father killed my mama and nearly killed me—the Ramirez—and the inheritance my mother left me, I've finally opened my own bakery, 'Sweet Treats', they were all extremely supportive, and I wouldn't be here without them.

The walls are light red at the bottom and white at the top, with a dark red border separating them, with painted pictures in black and white frames covering the back wall that range from sunsets to forests to loved-up couples that my friend Star painted. I help her sell them, and no, I don't take any of the profits; it's all for her because she's that good. I'm also teaching her to bake and cook because her mom turned into a drunk after her father was killed.

The windows are stained glass looking out on Meadow Street with double glass doors and I smile. I am so grateful for everything my grandma and family have helped me achieve. After getting my high school diploma at home, I went straight into culinary school and haven't looked back.

I round the glass counter that displays all of my sweet treats, which range from brownies, cupcakes, sausage rolls, cookies, Danishes, cheesecakes, pastries, and many more, to see the beautiful Cammy waiting for me. She's in her usual leather pants and a tank top with her cut on too; it says property of Dead Shot on the back as well as the club's name, Untamed Hell Fire's, on the front. Her light brown hair is loose in curls just past her shoulders, and her brown eyes twinkle when she notices me.

"Annalise, finally."

I smile, and she comes to hug me lightly, minding the flour over my outfit.

"How are you, Mrs. Ramirez?"

She huffs, then scowls at me, making Sandy chuckle. "How many times do I have to tell you it? It's Cammy, sweetheart; you call my husband Dead Shot; you have done so since you were 4 years old, so it's no different. You'd think after knowing you since you were a little girl basically raising you half the time, you'd get used to it."

I just shake my head at her. I love messing with her. Truthfully, I'd prefer to call her something else, but I just don't have the courage to—one day.

"You know my grandma taught me to be polite, plus remember when I called him Mr. Ramirez just to see his reaction? The look he gave me scared me for life."

She just laughs, "You were only 6 years old; Rosie said you had nightmares for weeks; he felt so bad. It's why he bought you the princess house. How is the old bat today anyway?"

This time, I laughed, especially at the memories. The Ramirezs are like a second family to me, they're my parents through and through.

"Crazy as ever."

She shakes her head, then looks at the cakes, then at Sandy. "Could I have 3 brownies and a few cookies, Sandy?" Nodding her head, Sandy gets her treats before she sets her attention back on me.

"I was wondering if you could make me some things for my luncheon in two days. Rosie will be there, and I would love to have you there as well."

I smile and nod. "I'll try my hardest to come, but I will make the goodies for you if you have a list for me." She smiles wide and hands me a piece of paper, then kisses my cheek.

"Thank you, sweetheart."

I nod. "Of course, anything for you. Just message me the time and place."

She nods, pays for her baked goods after I tried telling her not to, waves bye to Sandy, then nods her head towards the door to me and turns to leave, where a big, scary biker with black short hair and bright blue eyes that's waiting for her stands just outside of the door in his biker outfit with a smile aimed at me, and I smile wide—Dead Shot. He's been like a father to me over the years, and I haven't seen him since dinner last week.

I quickly head out of the bakery, passing a chuckling Cammy into his waiting arms that he's spread wide for me, and he hugs me tightly, not caring about the flour on my clothes, and kisses my head. "Missed you, sweet girl."

I mumble into his chest, "I missed you too."

He kisses my head again and lets me go. "We'll see you tomorrow night for dinner, sweetheart, and we'll set up a day for us to spend together." He says, and I nod, then kiss his cheek and then Cammy's before waving and heading to the back of my bakery again and going through the list of stuff she would like before pulling the rest of my baked goods out of the oven-ready for the display case out front all while smiling feeling grateful.

Life is good.

A couple of hours later, after finishing up the wedding cake someone had ordered, I cleaned the bakery with Sandy's help, then dropped the cake off before I headed to see my grandma before going back to the bakery, where I had a flat over the top of it. She wasn't too happy about me moving out, but like I said to her, I have to learn to spread my wings at some point.

My father is still locked up as far as we know, so he won't be able to get me. Dead Shot has been keeping an eye on him. For years after he was sent to prison, he would request a visit from my grandma, wanting her to bring me, but she refused. As I got older, he got more relentless, even sending people he knew over to her house, and it got to the point that my grandma told him I no longer lived with her. He's been trying to find me for years; that's why I was home-schooled and why no one knows I even exist, including the Ramirez's son Axel. We don't know if my father wants to find me because he wants to finish the job or if he is generally concerned about me, but I think it is the first one. I don't care how long he's been inside; once a psycho, always a psycho. That's why I've been practicing self-defense since I was 10.

And I would bet anything that he wants—the inheritance Mama left me, which unfortunately for him is now all gone.

I pull up outside of my grandma's yellow bungalow 5 minutes later and get out of my old Ford, making sure to grab the box on the passenger seat and head to her white front door.

I put my key in and went in.

"Grams?"

I was walking through the flowered wallpaper hallway when she shouted,

"In here, pumpkin." I smile at the nickname and head towards her kitchen, where we have shared many memories together. I mean, she is the sole reason why I love to bake, well that, and I have my mama's genes. According to Grams, before my father tainted her, she used to love to bake and cook. She dreamed of owning a restaurant. I just don't understand how she gave it all up for a nasty man like my father. I shake my head at my thinking; I wasn't there at the time, so I wouldn't know and can't judge, plus you can't change the past.

When I walk in, I see her standing at the stove wearing her 'best Granny' apron. I bought her one when I was 8 years old with my saved-up pocket money for Mother's Day. I bought

Cammy a matching one, but it said 'best mommy' which made her cry, confusing me until she said they were happy tears.

Grams is stirring something in a saucepan, and I smile.

"Whatcha making Grams?"

I walk over to her and hand her the tub of brownies, kissing her cheek. She smiles wide. "Hot chocolate sauce with a little bit of brandy for these amazing brownies I just knew you were going to bring me." I grin wide and get a couple of bowls out of the cupboard and place a brownie in each, then Grams pours the sauce.

I sit next to her at the kitchen breakfast bar, and we dig in, smiling. I turn to look at her.

"Mrs. Ramirez came to see me today. She lectured me again about not using her name; it was funny."

Grams hums, "You know how much it would mean to her for you to not be so formal with her, even if it is a running joke now. She's known you for years, Pumpkin; heck, she basically raised you as well."

I sigh while prodding my spoon into my brownie.

"She's always been more of a mother to me growing up; I continue the joke because calling her Cammy just seems..." I shrug, not completing my sentence, while my Grams smiles. "It would feel too impersonal because, in your mind, she's your mom. I know, darling, I do; if you were upset, you'd call her.

You got your first period, you called her, your hamster died, you called her. You love her like a mother, and when you're ready, I think she'd love that title from you, just like Dead Shot would too. Heck, he taught you how to drive and has ensured you know your self-defense; he loves you like you are his blood daughter."

I smile because I know she's right, but they have a son, a son I've never met because Grams feared for my life; they don't need me as well, and they don't need my drama. Plus, I have my Grams, who've brought me up as well.

Grams pats my hand. "She has a luncheon in a few days; she's invited me and you to it. Could you maybe make your famous raspberry swirl cheesecake for me?"

I chuckle, "Anything for you, Grams, I'll add it to the list of things she wants me to bake for her."

She grins and takes a bite of her brownie.

"How's David?"

I put my spoon down and sighed. I was hoping she wouldn't bring this up, and now I'm really hoping she doesn't go for her shotgun, or worse, call Dead Shot, because then I'll have to help hide the body or, worse, burn it, and I don't want to do that. David and I met about six months ago when he came into the bakery. He was about 5"6 and stodgy, but I didn't mind; he was sweet to me, and being home-schooled meant I didn't have any dating history or experience, and I wanted to change that. I also wanted someone who wouldn't be like my father.

I take a breath and bite the bullet.

"We broke up last night."

Her spoon pauses in her mouth, and she slowly looks at me. Shit, not good.

She has her killer look; it's the look I usually have to hide the knives from, so she doesn't kill anyone.

"What happened?"

Oh, double shit, her voice is void of emotion.

I clear my throat. "Well, you see, um, I.. um"

I stutter, and Grams slowly gets up from her seat and grabs her phone.

Oh, not good. Definitely not good.

"Just spit it out, pumpkin, before I call Dead Shot; what happened?"

I swallow hard and say it in one word, hoping she doesn't understand me, "Icaughthimlastnightwithanotherwoman," but my hopes are dashed when she shouts,

"THAT SON OF A BITCH, I'M GOING TO KILL HIM."

She goes for the door.

"How dare he cheat on you, you were way out of his league; what does he think he'll do better?"

Oh shit, I quickly run after her and jump in front of the front door, putting both my hands up.

"It's ok, Grams; I'm not exactly heartbroken. Did I give him my virginity and now regret it? Yes, but it doesn't matter. At least now I can honestly say I've tried dating, and it stinks; all men are clearly just like my father, well, except Dead Shot." Her eyes go wide with my words, and I nibble my lip. Shit, I know I said too much when she states,

"Oh, no, this will not do; this will definitely not do." She gets her phone out of her apron, where she shoved it on the way to the door, and my eyes widen.

"Grams?"

She puts her finger up to me, and my brows raise to my hairline. Seriously, my 5-foot-nothing Grandma with white hair did not just put her finger up to me like I'm 10 years old again. I scowl at her, and she just smiles sweetly at me.

"Cammy, it's Rosie."

Oh shit. I went to take the phone. I do not want someone's death on my hands. Even if he was a lying piece of...

"About our talk this morning, there's been a new development; the weasel cheated on her."

I blink several times in shock. What conversation?

"Yep, I know, she was way out of his league, the pompous idiot."

Ok, seriously, why didn't I call him that to his face instead of walking away without being seen?

Dammit.

"Yes, I believe your plan should go ahead; she's already talking about men all being like her father; yep, ok, see you in a few days, lovely; oh, and make sure you inform Dead Shot."

Then Grams hangs up while I go pale and shriek.

"GRAMS, I'M NOT CUT OUT FOR HIDING A BODY." knowing he's going to go on a hunt and kill the guy.

She just smiles at me sweetly, and nothing good comes from that smile. I should know; it's her "I'm about to make waves" smile. She's up to something. She shrugs and turns around, going back to the kitchen, and states, "Nothing to worry about, my darling girl, absolutely nothing."

My gut sinks. I have a bad feeling about this.

The next morning, I'm bent under the counter, adding some more brownies because we're sold out when a woman comes in. She's in a tight, short leather dress with the sides cut out, stripper heels, and her face heavily done up with make-up while her blue, yes, blue hair is up in a high ponytail. What on earth?

I hear Sandy growl, and I look at her with a raised brow because the woman sounds like a flipping dog.

She shakes her head and murmurs. "That's Bubbles; she's a sweet butt at the clubhouse and thinks she owns the town because she fucks the Pres, Cammy's son. I cannot stand her; she kicked Tizzy in the head last week."

That makes my eyes narrow. Tizzy is Sandy's 8-year-old corgi who is sick. He has cancer, and it's not fixable. When the woman, 'Bubbles' walks over to the counter, curling her lip at

Sandy I intervene before a brawl starts in my establishment because, let's face it, I'll be backing Sandy.

No one kicks Tizzy.

"Sandy, can you go check on the Danishes, please? Then you can have your break; I'll serve for a little while." Sandy nods while scowling at the woman, then heads out back. The woman looks down at me, not because she's clearly taller than me even without the heels, but because in her mind, I'm beneath her, and she states in a nasal voice,

"You really should look into the people you hire at this place."

That instantly pisses me off, and I put my hands on my hips and say, "And people really shouldn't kick animals that have cancer." Her face starts to get red. "Now, are you here to buy something? Or try to get me to fire an amazing woman who doesn't deserve your negative attitude?"

She narrows her eyes at me. "A triple chocolate brownie and four white chocolate macadamia nut cookies are there for my old man." I nod and collect the goodies, wondering what the hell Cammy's son sees in this woman.

I shake my head and place them neatly in the box, then ring her up.

"That'll be $8.25,"

She furrows her brows. "Isn't this place under the protection of the MC? This should be free."

Then she goes to grab the box. I shake my head and pull the box back. "$8.25 or get out." She goes red again and grabs

$10 from her bra. I roll my eyes and quickly get her change, passing it over to her as she sneers at me and storms out, but she halts when I say,

"Don't you want your purchases?"

Her body trembles with anger, and she turns back, snatches the box, and storms out, making me chuckle. I go into a full-blown laugh when I hear Sandy shout,

"Yeah, bitch, that's what I'm talking about."

You have to love good staff nowadays, unlike my other baker. I go back to placing the other cakes in the display case and smile.

That was fun.

Chapter 3

Axel

I'm at our strip club, Untamed Girls, sitting at the bar going over the inventory. I hear a moan, roll my eyes, and look to the left. Slicer is currently fucking one of the girls in the ass against the wall, where it's a little bit darker.

I shake my head; he's been on a fuck fest for a few years now since coming back from one of our club runs. It turns out he met someone, but she was gone when he woke up the next morning. He's been trying to find her since, but with no luck, so he uses sex as a way to forget her for just a little while, but he's now known as the club's biggest whore.

I shake my head again, fucking glad we're not open for another hour yet. I don't need the public to think this is a brothel. I get back to the paperwork. The prospect behind the bar places a bottle of water in front of me when the door slams open, and I sigh. I'm really not going to get this done at this rate.

I internally wince when my name is whined.

"Axel baby, you are not going to believe what just happened to me." fucking Bubbles. She may be good in the sack, but that's where it ends with her. She's one of the clingiest fucking sweet butts going, and because she's my main girl, she thinks she's queen bee. She places a box in front of me, and I instantly fucking drool. Fuck yes. I open the box and grab one of my favorite cookies that momma keeps bringing to the clubhouse—white chocolate macadamia nut cookies—while Bubbles kisses my cheek. As a reward, I place my arm around her waist, my hand moving to her ass, where I squeeze it while biting into the cookie.

"The owner of the cake shop I got these from was disrespectful to me Axel. She told me to get out of her shop. Is it my dress?" Tears fall from her eyes, and I stiffen, swallowing the cookie, and ask,

"What are you talking about, Bubbles?" She's got my attention now; no one disrespects one of our people, sweet butts too. She sniffles, and makeup spreads down her face.

"I went to buy you these as a surprise, and she told me I wasn't welcome in her shop. Why would someone do that?"

I raise my brow in suspicion, she seems genuine, but I can't be too sure, she can be a good fucking actress when she wants something. I look towards Slicer, who is already zipping up his pants. He nods to me and heads towards the door to check things out while I pull Bubbles tighter to me to placate her until I get the full story.

"Why don't you head back to the clubhouse, and I'll meet you there in a few hours, baby?" She smiles wide and nods, then kisses me gently before turning and walking out the door.

I shake my head; she recovered quickly. That's why I don't think she's telling me the whole truth. I get back to my paperwork and wait to hear from Slicer. Bubbles can be dramatic, and I don't want to punish anyone without the whole story; it's one of the things my dad taught me.

Always get the full information before acting, and my gut is saying she's lying and is trying to cause shit.

An hour later, I've moved into my office because the doors have opened for clients. Slicer walks into my office, biting into what looks like a chocolate cake ball thing. I tilt my head as he takes a seat, passing me the other one.

"On the house." I nod and bite into it, groaning. Fuck, that's good. You can taste the hazelnuts before hitting the gooey chocolate in the center. Fuck me.

"So, Pres, you know Sandy Houston, right?"

I nod, chuckling, ignoring the Pres title. He knows I prefer my childhood friends not to call me that; even after 5 years, it feels weird. "Of course, she babysat most of us growing up; she still got that bloody Corgi? I think I was 22 when her momma bought him for her."

Slicer smiles and says, "Yeah, Tizzy isn't doing so well; she has cancer. She's devastated."

                        I frown, feeling bad for Sandy, that dog was the last thing her mother bought her before she passed away, "I'll give her a call, and make sure she's good. But shall we stay on topic, brother?"

He just grins as he states, "Did you know she works at Sweet Treats, the same bakery where Bubbles got you your goodies from?" I chuckled darkly.

See gut instinct.

"Turns out Bubbles walked into the place as she owned it, and the owner, who I didn't see—she went to deliver some cakes—let Sandy go into the back on a break because Bubbles, being Bubbles, looked down on Sandy and was lucky she didn't get a black eye from our old babysitter." I smile. Sandy could throw a mean punch. Slicer smirks, and he continues. "Turns out Bubbles booted Tizzy in the head last week and hasn't been the same since, so the owner wanted to make sure there wasn't a brawl in her bakery, something about probably joining Sandy in the brawl if it started, so she served our sweet butt, who then tried to take the cakes without paying for them, something about the shop being under our protection, so she shouldn't have to pay."

Oh, for fucks sake, I sigh while he nods.

"Yeah, the owner told her to either pay up or get out of her shop. Bubbles paid, then left with the goodies for you."

I sigh. "How much did she try to save by basically stealing using our name?"

He full-blown laughs, "$8.25." I sigh again. Seriously, she tried to swindle 8 fucking bucks, then turned the waterworks on over it. I shake my head.

"Bubbles seems to think she's got you wrapped around her finger, Pres., and I know that's not the case, but she knows no one fucks with ours and we'll retaliate for disrespect. She tried to play on that, knowing we'd destroy that shop, and for what? Over 8 fucking bucks. It's not on; those fucking cakes are amazing. I would have been pissed if I'd trashed that bakery."

I nod, fucking pissed, and pull my phone out, sending out a group text to all the council brothers.

Me - church 20 minutes.

I look back at Slicer and say, "Let's get back to the clubhouse; this shit ends now. The sweet butts are taking the piss, and an example needs to be made, or we'll end up banning sweet butts from the clubhouse full stop and just hire a cleaning service and cook because I'm fucking done with this shit."

He nods and goes to head out while I shut down everything and lock the office up, following him outside to our Harleys.

Ten minutes later we're pulling into the clubhouse. The prospect opens the gate, closing it behind us as we park up near the front before walking inside. When we get inside, all the brothers stand, and we head into church. When I look around, everyone except for Ink is here, and Hawk speaks up.

"He's with a client, full back piece; it's roughly 6 hours today and another 6 hours in a month's time. High profit."

I nod. Ink's missed church before for high-paying clients.

"Then we'll fill him in." I bang the gavel and look towards Slicer, and he stands, explaining what happened with Bubbles today. The men in this room all scowl and frown, not liking the ballsy move from the sweet butt, thinking we wouldn't look into it, especially with the whole condom fiasco. My father jumps up and kicks the chair. I raise a brow at him, confused by his reaction. I mean, we're all upset, but this takes it to a new level, so it must mean that he knows the owner. The brothers look at him in shock, and I tilt my head. "I take it you know the owner?" He clears his throat and nods his head.

Looking around the room, he sighs. "Not one word to my old lady; hear me? She hears about this, and she'll burn the clubhouse to the ground with the sweet butts inside."

We all nod because no one wants the bulldog loose,

"The owner is Annalise Lawrence." The brothers look at him in shock while I nod. I knew Rosie had a granddaughter recently, but that's about it. My father continues, "Her father is Grant Lawrence, Rosie's son, who is currently serving time for beating his wife to death 23 years ago. He also nearly beat Annie to death too when she was only 3.

Rosie took her granddaughter in and raised her. I and my old lady have been having dinner with them ever since, once a week, while you Axel were at Butches. Cammy and I were great friends with Lucy, but as soon as she got with Grant, she changed."

We all look at him speechless. We all heard the rumors, but we never realized they were true.

"For years, Grant tried to get in contact with his daughter, but Rosie wouldn't allow it, and when he started getting more relentless, she told him Annie no longer lived with her. When I last checked on him two months ago, he was still locked up, and he's still looking for his daughter."

Gunner speaks up, "Does he want to finish the job he started?"

My father shakes his head. "His wife's family was wealthy before they died in a car accident right after he married Lucy, which is believed not to be a coincidence. You see, Grant wanted her money; he has a gambling problem that Rosie refused to pay off, so he married Lucy but could never access the money. He thought if he got her pregnant, she would become more willing so to speak, but it never happened, and the more controlling he got, the less she was willing to hand him a penny. Then he started using his fists. We all saw the bruises, but she didn't want us to get involved." My father looks at Stormy and Butch, who nod. They obviously knew too, and I sigh as he continues. "She had decided to sign all the inheritance over to her daughter and then sign all the legal rights of her daughter over to me and my old lady when Annie was only 6 months old. Grant was never placed on the birth certificate, so if anything ever happened to her, then she knew Grant couldn't get her daughter or the money."

My eyes widen in shock. Why in the fuck have I never heard this before or of Annalise?

"The night Grant killed Lucy was an accident. He was drinking and took it too far. Lucy had fed Annie first because he was out past 9 p.m. and she was hungry, but unfortunately, it made him snap, and he killed her with his fists. He beat her to death before he went after Annie. Thankfully, the police got there just in time after some neighbors reported a domestic abuse disturbance. Annie had suffered a broken back and a severe concussion. She's lucky not to be paralyzed to this day; one more blow and she would have been killed too."

I tense at each word and growl out, "This is the woman who owns sweet treats."

Dad clears his throat and nods his head.

"She's worked hard to get that bakery open. It was her dream. Her mama loved to bake, and she wanted to help keep the memory alive, so along with Rosie, your momma, and me, we helped that dream become a reality. She used her inheritance to open it, then she gave $100,000 to Rosie and $100,000 to your mother and me, which is what we gave you, Axel, when you turned 25, which Annie was happy with; even at 18, she had a level head on her shoulders because, for the rest, she donated it all to a women's abused shelter."

We all stare at him with our mouths open while I'm fucking gobsmacked that that's where my inheritance came from. It built up over the years, and I have roughly over $160,000 in my savings now while placing $500 here and there myself.

My dad continues, "And the only reason why she never came to live with us after her mother was killed was because Rosie begged us to let her have her. Me and your mother agreed on the condition that we have a meal every week and are up-to-date with her. We had 24-hour access to her when we wanted; she is our daughter in every way but blood. We always left you with Butch because Rosie was worried about the repercussions of Grant being locked up. I nodded, knowing Rosie would have been worried about myself and her granddaughter. I sigh, rubbing a hand down my face. For fucks sake, fucking Bubbles starting shit.

Dad clears his throat, and the men tense. Ah, fuck, what now?

"Son, your mother, when she finds out about this," He shakes his head, and most of us pale, fuck, "She'll go full bulldog, worse than the time she beat a sweet butt up with a frying pan for flirting with me, she loves this girl like a daughter, for years she's been wishing she'd call her mom and I would be lying if I didn't want her to call me dad.

We can see the love she has for us in her eyes, but she's holding back. I'm actually surprised she hasn't tried to set you both up yet, to be fair; it's one of the main reasons why she agreed not to bring you around her growing up. She didn't want you to see her as a sister."

The men chuckle at that while I scowl.

Not fucking happening. I like my life. Momma might not have wanted me to see her as a sister, but I fucking will, I guarantee it. I bang the gavel to get the men to quiet down.

"Alright, Bubbles has been banned from all sexual activity for 4 weeks and is on bathroom and bar cleaning duty. Another problem like this again, and she's kicked out. If we have any more problems like this with any of the sweet butts, then the next plan of action would be banning them from the clubhouse, and we'll hire a cleaning service, and the brothers can go to bars to find pussy.

All in favor, say aye." The whole room bangs the table, saying aye, and I look toward Dagger, my VP. He grimaces before sighing and nods.

"I'll go inform her."

We all chuckle, happy not to have the pleasure of that meltdown, and I dismiss the brothers, scrubbing a hand down my face. Fucking bitch drama, I shake my head and stand, but before we can exit the room, a loud wail and shriek echo through the doorway, and we all laugh. I guess she took the news well.

Fuck I need a drink.

Two days later, I'm sitting at one of the tables in the common room with Ginger in my lap, rubbing her peachy ass over my hardening cock. My mother and Rosie keep looking over towards me, scowling, then whispering to each other, making me frown, while the rest of my mother's friends chat with each other. Fucks sake, there goes my hardening cock to the flaccid cock. What are those two up to now?

Ginger gets my attention when she slides her tongue down my neck causing my cock to jump, waking him up again. I squeeze my hand on her ass and smirk. I look towards the women again when I hear my mother's hiss,

"Where the hell is she, Rosie?"

Then they both look at me again, and I sigh, slowly closing my eyes and placing my forehead on Ginger's shoulder as Dagger and Slicer both snort when they realize the same thing as me: They're setting me up with someone.

For fucks sake,

I lift my head, shaking it as Bubbles stomps past, taking empties to the bar and scowling at Ginger. I really need a vacation from all these women. I look towards Hawk, who's sitting at the next table with Misty, one of the brother's old ladies.

"Please tell me I'm wrong and they're not trying to set me up in my own fucking clubhouse."

The fucker just laughs while Misty bites her bottom lip, and Dagger and Slicer pretend to be looking elsewhere.

I sigh. Fuck.

I'm about to remove Ginger from my lap and get up to tell them to call whoever they're setting me up with off when the clubhouse door opens and this beautiful, curvy, blonde bombshell walks in carrying a massive box full of baked goodies.

Fuck me, she is stunning.

I look from her feet that are in canvases, going up her jean-covered lean legs, past her great thick thighs to her waist that curves from her wide hips to show her flat stomach that's hidden behind the red collar shirt that has a logo on it, her tits pressing against the material that must be a handful, my heart rate picks up, and I sit up straighter, nearly knocking Ginger off of my lap, making her look at me in confusion.

The bombshell eyes scan the room, and ours connect after I trace every inch of her beautiful heart-shaped face. I feel like I've been punched in the chest.

Violet, she has fucking violet eyes.

She looks away quickly, looking around the room again, then smiles when she looks at the women and goes to head towards them. I stand, making Ginger stumble off my lap as she squeals and moves a little away from me. She pouts, then sits on Slicer's lap, who's looking at me with raised brows, while Dagger is looking between me and the bombshell of a woman who's walked into my clubhouse. I hear Hawk snort, but I ignore them while watching this gorgeous creature.

Just before she can get to the table where my mom is sitting, Bubbles stands in her way, scowling. She sneers, "What the fuck are you doing here, you fat bitch?"

Rage instantly takes over. Possessive, territorial, and protective feelings build up in my chest, but it's not me who puts Bubbles in her place; nope, it's sweet old lady Rosie. "WHAT THE FUCK DID YOU JUST SAY TO MY GRANDDAUGHTER?" She shouts as she stands.

That's Rosie's granddaughter; fuck me.

Bubbles looks at Rosie in shock while our new guest, who I'm going to take a guess and say is Annalise, looks at her grandmother with wide eyes and then mumbles,

"Fuck," making me smirk.

Why did that sound so hot coming from her mouth?

Bubbles opens her mouth stupidly again, not realizing her danger because Rosie is looking for a kill and her eyes are blazing,

"I asked what the fat bitch is doing here; she's not welcome here, old woman."

Oh fuck.

I sigh and drop my head when I hear my mother growl and my father mutter, "Shit bull dogs awake."

He moves and stands next to Annalise, taking the box from her and kissing her cheek. She gives him a wide smile, and her love for a father shines through her eyes, and it does something to me; the love she has for him is so genuine, and now I'm jealous of my father for having her attention, I want it back on me. Bubbles looks at them in confusion, and I walk over to the chaos that's about to erupt. Right now, I don't know who's more dangerous: my mother, whose face has gone red, the first sign of the bulldog appearing, making the brothers quietly slide away from her vicinity, or Rosie, who's just grabbed a pool stick; shit.

"Oh, that's it, you two-bit tart."

I snort along with the rest of the brothers when an angel's voice floats to my ears. Fuck, she sounds so sweet despite being stressed.

"Mrs. Ramirez, stop her."

          Her hand is clutching my father's arm, and my mother only scowls harder and says, "Why, if she doesn't do it, then I will; no one calls my daughter fat, and what have I told you, young lady, it's Cammy for the last time?"

Annalise sighs and drops her head, and I have to bite my lip to stop laughing, which my father is also struggling with while the brothers' mouths drop open, but then she says,

"Seriously, that's what you focus on when the old bat's about to beat this woman with a pool stick."

Then she looks at Rosie.

"Grams, put that fucking stick down and breathe before you give yourself a heart attack."

And that does. We all burst out in laughter as my dad wrapped his arm around Annalise and kissed her head. She smiles at him, then turns to her grandmother and scowls, putting her hands on her hips. Fuck, she's tiny; she can't be any taller than 5"4. She looks my way, and our eyes connect again, and I can't help it. I smirk, making her look away, a blush coating her cheeks.

Fuck yes.

I lock eyes with Momma and smile wide; her eyes sparkle when she recognizes my look, and she starts bouncing in her seat, excited because I'm claiming her.

She's mine!

Axel: An MC Romance

Chapter 4

Annalise

I can feel the blush on my cheeks as I look away from the Greek god. Black hair, short back and sides, long on top, roughly 6"2 and bright blue eyes, with a body made of sin and full of tattoos showing on his neck and arms; he should be in a magazine or on the cover, not in a clubhouse.

I feel Dead Shot's body shake with silent laughter. He saw my blush. Dammit, I'm never going to live this down. I narrow my eyes at him, making him smile. He leans down and whispers,

"That would be Axel, sweetheart."

My eyes widen, then I blush harder. Shit, he is really hot and a fucking playboy. I heard the rumors, and now I feel sad, dammit, again. Dead Shot bursts out in laughter again, so I shove him, not that it does anything anyway because he's like a fricking brick, and I look back at my crazy grandmother.

Placing my hands back on my hips, I state,

"Grams, you either put that fucking stick down or I'm taking your cheesecakes back with me to the bakery."

Hers and Cammy's eyes widen, and my Grams throws the stick on the floor like it burned her in a dramatic act. "Pumpkin, do not threaten my goodies." She gasps, and I close my eyes in a sigh as the whole room erupts in laughter again while I shake my head and look back at the blue-haired woman who's still glaring at me, and I state,

"Annalise Lawrence. I'm Rosie's granddaughter, and I'm also here with the baked goods. That ok with you?"

Her face goes red while everyone around me smirks, obviously realizing I have sass and spunk. Thank you, Cammy and Grams, for that, and just because I love pissing not only this woman off because it's become a new favorite after the other day, but also the woman I see as a mother.

I smirk as I state,

"Also, Dead Shot and Mrs. Ramirez are like my parents; they basically brought me up with my Grams."

Her face goes redder, which I didn't think was possible, and I bite my lip to stop my laughter when I hear Cammy shout, "I SWEAR TO GOD ANNALISE JESSICA LAWRENCE. IF I HAVE TO TELL YOU ONE MORE TIME TO CALL ME CAMMY, I'M GOING TO SPANK YOUR FUCKING ASS."

Everyone in the room freezes, looking a little scared, but I just smirk while Dead Shot chuckles silently. This woman basically raised me and made me a mini-her, and he knows that. I think I might be the only one in this room with big enough balls to answer back.

Now only if I could get the guts to call her what I actually want without feeling like I'm burdening her.

I turn toward her and raise a brow. "You couldn't spank me when I was 10 years old, and I spat out your nasty broccoli back on my plate at the dinner table, and you can't do it now." Everyone's eyes widen in shock at me for talking back while Cammy huffs and sits down, muttering,

"Dammit, the girl knows me too well, and why the hell did I have to make sure she had my traits?" making me and Grams giggle.

I turn back towards the man who I see as a father and go to grab the box back, which makes him give me the look while he grips the box tighter. It's the look that gave me nightmares. My eyes widen, and I shove it back into his chest, making him chuckle while Grams full-blown laughs as Cammy states,

"That's not fair; why is she scared of him with just that fucking look and not me?"

I shake my head with a smile at her outburst and place a kiss on Dead Shot's cheek before he takes the box to the other table to set it up for me as I walk over to my Grams while all the men stare at me openly. I fidget a little, not liking the attention. Grams pulls me in for a hug, then points at blue-haired Barbie, who's still standing in the same place, looking ready to blow.

"If I ever hear you call my granddaughter fat again, I'll ensure all your hair falls out."

I snort while she looks at all the men, glaring.

"Take your eyes off of my granddaughter; she is off-limits to you lot."

I go bright red and shake my head as Dead Shot shouts,

"I SECOND THAT."

Fucks sake, I sigh, then place a kiss on Cammy's cheek, who is grinning widely at me, making me narrow my eyes at her and making her chuckle. What is she up to? I check my watch, knowing I've got to head back to the bakery because Sandy's taking Tizzy to the vet again and also because I know these two women are up to something. I need to leave before their plan is put into place, whatever it may be. But alas, I'm not fucking quick enough when Cammy waves her hand.

"Axel, I want to introduce you to someone."

My eyes widen, and I look at Grams, who has a wicked smile on her face. Oh, no.

They're setting us up. Really?

He's a player, and I'm, well, me. Grams must see the look in my eyes at what I'm thinking because she narrows hers at me, and I look away from her quickly as Axel stops next to me. I swallow hard and clear my throat.

"So, you're the famous Axel?" What the fuck was that? My cheeks redden while Grams shakes her head at me, eyes full of disappointment, but I just shrug. She knows I have next to no experience with men, and David doesn't count; he was a tester and a failed one at that.

Axel smirks and holds out his hand, and I shake it.

"Logan, it's nice to meet you. Although I had no idea that you existed until a few days ago,

His voice is smooth and rich, fuck. I nod while everyone gasps. His parents and my Grams grin like loonies. I give them funny looks while Axel, no Logan, smirks again. Fuck, that's a good smirk; he even has a little dimple to the right of his cheek, dammit. I need to get out of here. I look at him and smile a small smile.

"Yeah, Grams was worried for a little while." I look around the room, and everyone is watching while a few of the women who are basically in their underwear glare at me, and the one who was on Axe, I mean Logan's lap, is staring daggers at me, and blue-haired Barbie looks ready to stab me with a knife.

OK, time to go. I look back at him and meet his intense stare; my body shivers with delight. Shit, I really need to go.

"Well, it was nice to finally meet you; your parents basically brought me up, so I hear a lot about you most weeks. I'll, um, uh, let you get back to your girlfriend before she burns holes into the back of my head." He furrows his brows in confusion and looks to see what I mean, but I don't pay any attention even when I hear Dead Shot mutter.

"Shit."

I quickly lean down and give Grams and Cammy a kiss on the cheek, who are both glowering, not happy that I'm leaving, and I state,

"I wish I could stay, but Sandy's taking Tizzy to the vet, so I've got to get back to the shop." I give them sad eyes, and they instantly know she's having him put down. Ever since 'Bubbles' aka 'blue-haired Barbie' kicked him, he's not been right in the head; he went to bite her yesterday. Whether it's because of that or the cancer just spread some more, I don't know, and neither does the vet, so hopefully they don't come into contact again anytime soon because, as far as Sandy is concerned, it's not the cancer. I smile awkwardly at Logan, who is now looking at me again, and I walk around him to head towards Dead Shot. When in reach, he pulls me in for a hug and kisses my head, but when I pull away from him to leave something that niggles in my gut, I'm forgetting something, but I just can't think what.

I shake my head and go to say bye to him when he gives me a serious look, making my eyes widen.

Oh, shit. What did I do? He raises a brow and asks,

"Did you get it sorted?" My face pales, and I can feel all the blood leaving my head, shit. See, gut instant, I knew I forgot something.

He sees my reaction, and he scowls at me and growls.

"Annalise Jessica."

Then he gives me the flipping look AGAIN. My eyes widen more, twice in one day. so-not-fair.

I hear Grams and Cammy gasp, and it hits me; he used my middle name.

Shit, I'm in trouble.

        I slowly walk backward, knowing I'm about to get my ass reamed and end up bumping into a hard body. I turn a little, look up, and see Logan standing there. He quirks a brow at me, his eyes showing how amused he is by my situation.

"What'd you do?"

I clear my throat and look at Dead Shot, who is glaring at me.

Oh crap.

I stutter, "I, uh, um, may have, sort of, kind of, um, forgottogetmysparetirechanged." I say the last bit all together, quickly hoping they don't understand it, but I fail because I hear a bunch of 'oh, shits.'

Cammy sighs,

"Annalise."

I hang my head in defeat. "I know, I forgot. I'm sorry. I promise I'll sort it today." I furrow my brows, trying to figure out my day before I continue, trying to look innocent. "Although I do have that cake to make, maybe tomorrow," I say sheepishly as Dead Shot sighs,

"Why won't you just let me buy you a better car sweetheart." Now it's my turn to glare at him while my grandmother and mother figure burst out in laughter. He brings this up every time he sees me in my car, and it's always the same argument. Apparently, I should have gotten a better car before donating the money, but I don't see anything wrong with the one I got; it was cheap and runs perfectly fine.

I place my hands on my hips, ready to fight him on this, when he walks over to me, where I tried to slink away before Axe, dammit, Logan intercepted me for his dad. I really need to get used to calling him Logan.

Deadshot and Cammy always called him by his road name.

Dead Shot kisses my head and murmurs, "Just think about it, sweetheart, ok? It'll give me peace of mind; you know we worry about you."

I sigh and nod my head, hugging him quickly and whispering, "OK. I'll think about it." He smiles and goes over to his woman with a triumphant look on his face. He makes Cammy stand, then takes her seat, forcing her back down on his lap, and I smile wide. I love their love; it's one for the ages. If I do give someone a chance, it'll be because of those two.

I go to walk around Logan when he grabs my arm, making me look up at him confused. I try my absolute hardest to ignore the electric spark I feel going through my arm.

What the hell was that?

He puts his palm out and states, "Keys."

I furrow my brows. "Why?"

He just smirks, "Because the club owns a garage, Flame will take your car and give it a full workover, including changing all tires, until you realize Dad buying you a car would be better for your safety and his sanity."

Dead Shot snorts, I don't even need to look at him to know it was him, while Logan continues to piss me off.

"And I'll take you to work. One of the prospects will bring it back to you when it's done.

I scowl and remove my arm from his hand, missing his touch instantly.

Traitorous body.

     I growl in frustration, "I don't need a knight in shining leather, buddy. I can get my car fixed by myself." I hear a couple of chuckles. He looks towards the women and says,

"You really did raise her, huh, momma." Cammy just grins widely, proud of the attitude that she instilled in me, while

Dead Shot's body shakes with silent laughter and the whole room erupts when someone mutters,

"Fuck, there's two of them." I shake my head and go to walk out when he grabs my arm again and whispers, "Please." giving me innocent eyes.

I narrow my eyes at him, then sigh in defeat when Dead Shot speaks up.

"Do as he says, Annie girl," in his threatening voice, no less.

I shoot a glare his way and slam my keys in Logan's hand, causing everyone to laugh again. He smiles, then hands the keys to someone before said someone puts his hand out to me to shake. I take it and look up as he speaks; his dark blue eyes sparkle.

"Names Flame, I'll make sure to have it done quickly for you."

I smile at him and give him a nod when a beautiful woman comes to stand next to him smirking at me. I grin, shaking my head, as her caramel eyes sparkle with laughter as she states,

"Fancy meeting you here."

I chuckle while everyone except Grams, Dead Shot, and Cammy look at us confused. She hugs me tightly.

"I take it; this is the guy I'll never replace as your top friend."

She giggles and nods her head as Flame's eyes sparkle with recognition. "You're the one she met a few years ago when she attempted to try a cooking class, and now you're stupid enough to teach her how to cook and bake?"

I laugh and nod. "That would be me; she really sucked beforehand."

Star narrows her eyes at me, and I just grin at her. She looks at Flame and says, "Remember, I told you I sold that painting. It was on her wall at the bakery."

He grins widely, and I say,

"Your work speaks for itself; I've told you this over and over." I look at my watch again. "Right, I have to go. I'll see you on Saturday. Try not to burn your kitchen down this time when you practice."

She scrunches up her nose. "Yeah, I'll admit, that one was bad. Flame had to come put the fire out before I called you."

I chuckle and hug her while Flame bites his bottom lip to stop the laughter. Then I go to walk out of the clubhouse after waving bye to 'blue-haired Barbie', making her scowl. She hasn't moved from her space, which is fucking funny.

Star giggles at my actions, making me grin.

As soon as I get to the door, I stop and turn to Logan and raise a brow. He just chuckles and shakes his head before following me out the door, and we come to a stop next to a motorcycle, a matte black Harley to be precise. I look at him with wide eyes.

"Oh, no, no, no," I say, shaking my head, and he chuckles.

"Get on, darling."

I shake my head again. "Dead Shot couldn't get me on his bike; he's been trying for years, and he's basically a father to me. Why on earth would I get on yours when I barely know you?

Plus, I know the rules; only old ladies are supposed to go on the brother's bikes." He ignores me and places his helmet on my head, making my eyes go wider as he lifts me up, causing me to shriek in surprise, and places me on the back of his bike while quickly getting on it himself.

Oh fuck no, I go to get off, but he quickly grabs a hold of my arms and says,

"Hold on tight, darling."

Oh, shit no, no, no.

He starts the bike, revving it, causing me to hold him tighter, and I swear I hear someone shriek.

"He's put her on the back of his bike; no fucking way." but he revs it again to block whoever said it out, then pulls out of his spot, heading towards the gates.

The prospect opens the gates, and he floors it down the road. I grab a hold of him tighter, placing my head against his shoulder blades. My body shakes. I was told another injury to my back could cause permanent paralysis, so I've made sure to never get myself in these kinds of situations until now.

My grip on Logan tightens, and my chest feels tighter, like I can't breathe. He must sense my distress because he slows down a bit, and then his left-hand grabs a hold of my calf, slowly moving his hand up and down, trying to soothe me. I try to stay calm, but it's not easy. He didn't know, but he also didn't give me time to explain why I didn't want to go on his bike, so that makes him an asshole too. He picks up speed again once he thinks I'm calm enough, despite my grip not loosening.

His hand only leaves my calf when he has to go around corners.

5 minutes later, we arrived at Sweet Treats. He gets off the bike first, then helps me off, basically lifting me and keeping a hold of me until my shaky legs can keep me upright. He helps me take off the helmet, and I give him a shaky smile.

"Thanks for the ride." I'm hoping my voice doesn't waver. He tilts his head and goes to open his mouth when the door to my bakery opens, and Sandy comes out.

She smiles when she sees me.

"Sorry, Annie, I've got to get going. Are you alright to take over, or do you need a minute?"

Ha, like a minute with this tall glass of water would be any good for me. I'm definitely not his type. Plus, he has a girlfriend, as in plural,

I look at her and say, "It's ok, Sandy, you go ahead."

She smiles and comes over. She places a kiss on my cheek, then one on Logan's.

"Don't be a stranger."

He smiles and nods his head as she walks away.

I clear my throat. "Well, thanks for the ride; I'll let you get back to your girl and the club."

Then I shakily walk past him, hoping he can't sense the fear and adrenaline still coursing through me as my anxiety peeks high and I head into the bakery. Once I get behind the counter, I look towards the door and see him sitting astride his bike. He smirks at me before starting his bike up and driving off. I sigh and slowly drop my elbows to the counter, putting my head in my hands.

My heart rate finally comes down.

I'm screwed.

Chapter 5

Axel

Fuck, feeling her on the back of my bike, having her tits pressed against my back and her hands gripping the front of my Henley t-shirt. I shake my head. My cock is rock hard—harder than it's ever been before.

I head back to the clubhouse, wondering why she had such a negative reaction to being on my bike. I mean, it's the first time I've ever allowed anyone on the back of it. It's a rule among brothers. Girlfriends and old ladies only ride bitch, I thought she'd enjoy it, but when she walked into her bakery, I honestly thought I was going to have to carry her. Her whole body shook.

Fuck, concern wracks through me.

I arrive back at the clubhouse a couple of minutes later, and the prospect lets me in. I put my hand up and then parked my bike before heading in to find Rosie. I need some answers, and I hate to fucking admit it, but momma was right with this match because she's mine; my gut is screaming at me to claim her. I head inside and go towards the ladies. I quickly kiss my momma's cheek and pat my dad's back before kissing Rosie's cheek and then taking a seat next to her.

I look at her in her gray eyes, raising my brow at her, and she sighs.

"Did she freak?"

I tilt my head and say, "Not in such a way; no, she stayed on but held onto me like I was her lifeline, and when she went to go inside the bakery, I thought I was going to have to carry her in. What am I missing here, Rosie?"

My dad smiles and says, "You did a hell of a lot better than I did, son. When I tried a few years ago, she had a full-blown panic attack, fucking scared the shit out of me, especially when I see her as my daughter."

I furrow my brows. "Why? Why does she have such a negative reaction? She was petrified. I knew as soon as she started saying no to getting on, I had to just crack on with it. There was no way I wasn't getting her on the back of my bike, but I wanted to know. I needed to know because I couldn't have her not on my bike; it's not the biker's way to have his woman driving behind him in a cage unless she's knocked up, so I need to know how to help her."

My mother and Rosie grin widely while my father smirks.

"Fuck, son, you know we're never going to hear the end of this now, right?" I just shrug and chuckle, then look at Rosie. I know she probably feels like she's betraying her, but if I'm going to pursue her like she wanted, then she needs to talk.

She sighs again, "You know what happened to her, right? Your dad told you?" I nod, clenching my fists. Grant's lucky he's locked up; it's not only Butch and Stormy who gave me the name Axel. It turns out I'm really good with Axe with enemies and traitors too.

Rosie clears her throat.

"Well, after she recovered, the doctor stated that if she has one more accident on her back, she could end up permanently paralyzed, and she's become OCD with being safe. We've been trying for years to help her overcome her fear, but she just seems to be getting worse."

I sigh and slowly close my eyes, shaking my head.

I hear a sniffle and look at my mother. I tilt my head and soften my eyes.

"I'll take it slow, but I'll help her, I promise. She's mine now; you got your wish." My momma smiles a watery smile while I smirk and shake my head. Just as I'm about to get up and head to my room to sort out my little problem down south—well, not little, but you know, thinking of my woman—has made me hard again, a hand comes around from my shoulder down to my chest, making both my momma and Rosie growl like fucking dogs. My dad bites his bottom lip to stop laughing, but his body still shakes, making Momma slap his head, and I snort.

"Hey baby, are you ready to finish what we started earlier?" Ginger rasps in my ear.

My eyes lock with Rosie's, and she looks pissed. I don't blame her; I just said her granddaughter was mine, and I can guarantee she wouldn't be happy with me straying from her granddaughter, even if Annalise doesn't know she's mine yet. I smile at the old bat, then move my hand onto Ginger's arm and remove it from my chest, causing her to gasp in surprise, then frown as I state loudly,

"I'm no longer available to any other woman. Go find another brother because I'm officially off the market and I don't share, so I wouldn't expect my woman to have to share too."

Ginger gasps in shock and stumbles back like I hit her before letting a few tears escape, but I don't pay them any attention, making her sniffle and huff before walking away when she realizes I'm not taking the bait. Then I look at the grinning maniacs and point to them.

"Congratulations! Your plan worked. Now focus on another brother. I don't need you two trying to help me win my girl around."

My father snorts while the brothers who are still hanging around pale at my words, making me chuckle while they narrow their eyes at me. They knew how bad momma's match-making skills were until she and Rosie decided Annalise was the right fit.

I turn my head towards the kitchen door when I hear a loud crash and a cry. I shake my head because that was probably Bubbles finding out I'm taking an old lady but tough shit; she's a sweet butt; she should have known a brother wouldn't make them old ladies.

Rosie puts her hand on mine before I go to get up and says gently, so only we at the table can hear her, "She's only ever had one boyfriend, and that was to get the experience; he cheated on her. Now she wasn't heartbroken, but she saw all men except for your dad, like her father. The only reason why I have a little bit of hope that you'll get through to her is because she loves your parents and has seen their love growing up. I know she wants something like that, but you have your work cut out for you." I nod my head in understanding, and I get the message loud and clear: She has next to no experience in all aspects of a relationship. Fucking good.

I smirk, making Rosie chuckle. "Get out of here and let us finish our luncheon." I smile and say, "Don't worry, I'll take it slow." She smiles as I kiss hers and then Momma's cheek before I head to my room at the clubhouse.

I need to take a cold shower.

As I get to the bottom of the hallway towards my room, I notice Bubbles standing outside of my locked door. Fucks sake. "Not now, Bubbles; go continue the work that we paid you to do." She scowls and refuses to move. I sigh, shake my head, and walk past her. I unlock my door and go to walk inside, but I stop halfway and hold my arm across the doorway when she tries to follow. I look at her and state,

"Go and do your work." Rage overtakes her face, and she screams,

"I'M MEANT TO BE YOUR OLD LADY."

I chuckle darkly, and I hear the common room erupt in laughter as I state, "First of all, if you were my old lady, then I wouldn't let another brother touch you. Second of all, no brother would make a sweet butt who has been with every other brother an old lady. Go. And. Do. Your. Work. Or get out of my clubhouse." She pales as tears run down her cheeks. I shake my head and continue going into my room.

I shut the door and locked it to her screaming, then banging on the wood, and I shake my head again, sighing.

I look around my room and furrow my brows. I put my hands on my hips.

The back wall is dark grey while the rest are light. I have a queen-sized wooden bed that's brown with a side stand that's black. a white wooden chest of drawers, a small walk-in closet, and a bathroom attached with just a small bath and a shower with a toilet on the left side of the door.

Hmmm.

Fuck.

I turn around and unlock my door, opening it, and I see Bubbles leaning against Dagger's door, staring at mine. Her eyes light up when she sees me, and I roll my eyes, then look down the hallway, and I shout,

"LIAM, MOMMA."

Bubbles eyes narrow, and my momma with Rosie and my dad right behind her and Liam tagging along behind him come down the hallway. They look between me and Bubbles, but I just wave a hand and nod my head toward my room, where they all enter.

Momma shakes her head at the room while Rosie snorts and Liam tilts his head. Yep, just what I thought. I look at my momma and Rossie and state, "Fancy redecorating?" I hear a gasp behind me as they squeal in delight, making both my dad and me chuckle.

I look towards Liam, who's smiling at their antics.

"You're still good with construction, right?" He grins and nods his head. "Good. I want a bathroom remodel, a bigger bath and shower, and maybe heated floor tiles. If we're to live in this room until I have a house built, then we need it comfortable for her too."

He nods. "On it, Pres., I'll grab a few brothers now to help me measure up." I nod my head in thanks.

We're patching him in tomorrow, and I think as a welcome to brotherhood, we'll help him start up his own construction company, his first big job, designing and building my house near my parents. I look towards my dad, and he grins, sensing my decision with Liam, and nods his head in approval. Then I look at the two grinning maniacs, and I say,

"You two know her best, and you know me best; do your worst."

They jump up and down, giggling like school girls, causing both my dad and I to chuckle again as they run out of my room to bother Flame for a laptop.

I look to Dad,

"I think I may have created chaos."

He just shakes his head and says, "Somehow I think the brothers will be happy that you are keeping them off of their backs."

I turn my head to look down the hallway when the clubhouse suddenly erupts in cheers, and we laugh, confirming my father's theory.

I turn when I hear a sniffle, fucks sake, "Didn't I tell you to go do your work more than once?"

She wipes her eyes. "You're redecorating for someone you don't even know. I thought you loved me like I loved you."

My dad snorts, seeing right through her game, and I get in her face, making her eyes widen, "You love me that much, yet you let Flame fuck your mouth two days ago. You let Slicer fuck your ass while Ink fucked your cunt; you don't love me; you want my patch. Now either get the fuck over it and do your work or fuck off out of my clubhouse." Her face goes red, and she turns to leave.

I grab her arm and sneer.

"If I find out that you were a part of the faulty condom drama, then forget fucking off; I'll have you down in the basement." Her face pales, and she nods before running off to complete her work as I state to my dad, "She needs watching."

He nods, then slaps my back before heading to my mother, and I go back to my room to take a shower before the brothers come to measure up, fucking happy that my hard-on is gone, no thanks to the Bubbles drama.

The next morning, I'm sitting in church, waiting for all the brothers to arrive. Liam is on bar duty until we call him, which he is unaware of. We just have to vote about a few things first. I take a sip of my coffee when my dad walks in first.

"Morning son." I smile at him as he takes a seat, then Stormy and Butch arrive next, both giving me head nods and taking their seats next to Dad.

Butch looks at me and says, "Remodel, huh?"

I just smirk and shrug, making the three of them chuckle as the rest of the brothers come in and take a seat, Dagger quirks his brow at me, I raise mine back, and he states,

"An old lady?"

I can't help the smirk that takes place as my dad states, "He's got to convince her first."

The rest of the brothers chuckle while I shake my head and bang the gavel. "Alright, fuckers, quieten down, or I'll leave you all to the vultures of my mother and Rosie that I have kindly put to work."

They all pale and sit up straight while the old-timers laugh their asses off.

"Alright, a couple of things on the agenda today. First off, I had to sack a stripper yesterday; she was dealing the Devil's Coke in our establishment." They all sneer, and I state, "I've already spoken to Snake, and he states he doesn't know what we're talking about. Well, he will today when we send their crate of coke to them in flames. It's time to send a message. We've been at peace since Star and her dad were run off the road, and they tried to help us find out who posed as them to start a war, but now it's time to act. What do you think?"

They all banged on the table in agreement. We've had a treaty with them for years, but since he's got some new brothers patched in, the treaty is looking less and less bleak. I know he doesn't want an all-out war, but he needs to get his new brothers in check before there is one; we won't back down. I look towards my SGT in arms, Hawk, and he nods, grinning. Then I look to Flame, who seems to be good with explosives and fire, and he's also grinning like a loon, causing us to chuckle.

"Next on the agenda, we need to keep a closer eye on Bubbles. She didn't handle yesterday very well, and let's not forget about the shit she tried to cause at Sweet Treats. She's been getting too comfortable expecting to be the first lady."

The brothers nod as Ink speaks up.

"Last week, she tried her fucking hardest to convince me to go bare with her. Like I fucking would."

The brothers sneer, and I nod my head.

"I'm 99% sure she's the ring leader about the faulty condoms; the 1% is the fact we have no proof. Now would it be easier to just kick her out? Yes but..." I trail off as Gunner finishes my thought, "But it would be easier to keep her close. She's the kind of woman who would go to your enemy and tell them your secrets."

I nod and continue, "She doesn't know anything, but she knows the layout of our land and our schedules. Now we could kill her, but I have a feeling she'll be more useful alive, but also something in my gut is pulling me like this isn't who she is and it's an act for security; I don't know, something just doesn't seem right, plus we need to know which others are trying to trap the brothers, and she can lead us to them."

They all nod as Butch states, "She didn't have a good upbringing, and to be honest, when she's fucking a brother, she doesn't look like she's enjoying it; it looks more like an obligation, well, except for with you, Axel."

We all nod again because it's true: "I think we need to keep her on the banned list for a while longer." I look around the table and I state, "Say aye if you agree." Every brother shouts, aye and I bang the gavel.

"Alright, last on the agenda, Liam. Who starts the motion to patch him in?"

Gunner stands first, bangs a fist on the table, and shouts,

"AYE."

I smile, and the rest of the brothers follow suit, all saying aye. They look at me, and I bang my fist and shout, "FUCKING AYE."

We all cheer, and Ink gets up to go get him, but I stop him, putting my hand up, and state, "First, before we get him, how would we feel helping him start a construction company? He has the skills, the degree, and the experience, and he's fucking good at it. I've already seen the design he has for my bathroom, and I think we could turn a profit. Do we all agree?"

My dad states first, "aye." I nod, and every brother around the room agrees. Daggers the last one as he states, "Aye, your house can be his first big project; Rosie and Cammy can help decorate, keeping them occupied a little while longer."

The men chuckle while I grin and nod my head, then bang the gavel.

Looking at Ink, he grins and opens the door.

"Liam, get your fucking ass in here." He growls, and we all hold in our chuckles.

Fucking love this bit.

Liam enters, looking a little pale, and stands near the door, his head held high despite the concern in his eyes. I stand while the brothers look down at the table, trying to look disappointed, but their eyes are failing, and I look at Liam and state in a growl,

"Get your fucking cut of prospect."

He pales.

This is his first test. I'm the Pres, I've given him an order; now is he going to fight me on it? He looks down and sighs, then slowly, very fucking slowly, takes his cut off and places it neatly on the table.

He turns to walk out, and we all grin as I state,

"Where the fuck do you think you're going, brother?" He whips around quickly, shock on his face, and looks around the table to see every man grinning at him. I grab his new cut and chuck it at him.

He catches it with ease, a massive smile shining on his face as I say,

"Welcome to brotherhood, buzz." He chuckles at his new road name. His hair is always cut short to his head, so it was a no-brainer. I looked around the room,

"Alright fuckers, party tonight at 8 p.m. to celebrate our new brother."

The table erupts in cheers, and I look towards Buzz.

"And you, brother, need to come up with a business plan." He furrows his brows, and I smirk. "For the construction company that you will manage, you will get 15% of the profits while the rest is shared with the rest of us and 10% placed in the clubhouse funding; that is how all the businesses are done. The managers get a higher percentage. This is your first big project—my home for when I convince my old lady that she's well, my old lady."

The men chuckle while Buzz grins widely.

"I won't let you down, any of you." We all nod, and I bang the gavel. "Alright, fuckers, fuck off."

Ink grabs Buzz around the neck and puts him in a headlock, making us all laugh, then leaves the room shouting,

"NEW BROTHER FUCKERS, WELCOME OUR BROTHER BUZZ."

The common room erupts in cheers, and I smile. I slapped Dagger on the back. "I'll be up to the club in a little bit, I've got a woman to see." He chuckles as I walk out, passing momma. I give her a kiss on the cheek, and she grins at me, and I head out the clubhouse door to my bike. I climb on and grin. I'm coming, beautiful girl.

Chapter 6

Annalise

I'm out front today after giving Sandy a few days off after she had to put Tizzy down yesterday. I've been up since 3 a.m. baking while Louisa, another baker who I hired a few months ago when I started making a profit, is in the back making some more brownies and cookies that we've run out of but is taking her sweet-ass time about it.

I'm tired; my body aches, and my shivers from getting on a death trap yesterday haven't gone completely. I sigh; he probably thinks I'm a freak, but that's not a bad thing, really. He's a playboy; I've heard the stories from his own mother, no less. This is better than him thinking I'm weird, yep, better. Geez, I hate when I get like this; my anxiety flares up badly and can keep me out of action for several days. My mind goes 100mph, and I need to snap out of it before it takes hold.

I ring up a customer when I hear a bike rumble outside, and I smile, thinking it is a Dead Shot, but my smile falters when Axel dismounts and heads towards my bakery. Shit.

I clear my throat. Ok, this is fine. This is totally fine. He walks in, placing his shades in the front of his black tight t-shirt. Shit, why did that look so hot. I clear my throat again and smile at him, and he walks over.

"Hey Axel, what can I get you?" I'm hoping I don't sound like a fucking idiot.

He smirks, "Logan, Princess." My cheeks heat up, making him chuckle. "Can I have a couple of your white chocolate macaroon nut cookies, darling?" I nod and get a few, placing them in the bag, then I look up and ask, "Are you heading back to the clubhouse?" He raises a brow and says, "No, I've got to meet my dad and Dagger at the club."

I nod, then get a couple of chocolate chip ones for Dead Shot and throw a mixture in for Dagger, not knowing which is his favorite, and hand them over to him. He raises both his brows.

"They're his favorites, and I don't know Dagger, so I threw a few different ones in for him. And it's on the house." I smile, and he grins back at me when the door to the kitchen opens and Louisa comes out with some more baked goods nearly two hours after going in there, fucking finally.

I grab the tray from her and start placing the items in the counter when I hear,

"Hey Axel, I haven't seen you in a while; I missed you." I look over my shoulder to see she's pulled her white crop top down, and I snort, going back to what I was doing. Of course, he's slept with her.

I hear Axel sigh and mutter, "Shit."

I stand straight after finishing placing the cakes in their rightful place, look between them, and state, "I'll head to the back to bake so you two can catch up."

Louisa nods frantically, her eyes sparkling. Yep, time to go. I look at Axel, and I say,

"It was good seeing you, Axe, er, I mean Logan. Tell Dead Shot I'll see him tonight for dinner at Grams; I think she's doing her lamb roast."

He grits his teeth as he goes to say something, but Louisa cuts him off.

"Annie, honey, you can't call him by his given name, only his old lady can." I raise my brows in surprise and look at him. He looks pissed, but I don't understand why; he's the one who insisted I call him by his given name. I look back at Louisa and smile, nodding my head, then wave bye to Axel before heading back into the kitchen. I scowl when I get in there and see the mess she's left behind. Shaking my head, I get started on the washing up. She may be able to bake, but the rest of her job details she sucks at. Sandy can't stand her either. I shake my head again, too tired of dealing with her theatrics. I hear a bike roar off a few minutes later, but I just shrug and continue cleaning before I have to make a new batch of sausage rolls.

About an hour later, I'm knee-deep in marzipan for the birthday cake I'm making when Louisa breezes into the kitchen and grabs her bag.

"OK, I've locked the front doors, and all customers are now gone. I have to go get ready for my Tinder date, so I'll see you in a few days." Then she leaves the backdoor without a single glance at the mess around me, and I scowl. Yep, she's being fired. I've given her more chances than I can count. After I've finished with the icing and I've checked the chocolate sponge cake that the parents requested to make sure it's cooling down nicely, I go out front to ring out the till and come to a halt.

You have got to be fucking kidding me. Cakes are still on the counter, not boxed away for the homeless shelter, and customers' plates and cups are still littered over the tables. I take a deep breath before I blow; my skin starts to feel itchy, and my anxiety heightens.

I go to the till to ring it out and curse up a storm when I end up $400 short.

Placing the money in the safe in my office until I leave for the bank, I sort out Louisa's severance pay to mail to her with a formal letter and evidence of her not doing her job as well as evidence of the 2 warnings she had already gotten because I am done with her lazy ass, and I ensure I leave out the $400 that she stole, which means she's only getting $48.67 because she hasn't worked the full month, and I ensure I put in writing that I have evidence on camera of her stealing from me because I do so she can't try and sue me, then I head back out front and start cleaning.

I box all of the cakes and place them on top of the counter that I've just disinfected, then grab the washing-up tub to put all the plates and cups in and take them to the kitchen. I wipe down all of the tables, place the chairs upside down on top, and then grab the vacuum before I mop the floors. I ensure the door is bolted and locked and the alarm is set before putting all the blinds down, then head towards the kitchen after grabbing the box of cakes and placing them in my office. I scrub all the dishes and place them in the two dish washers that I have before I go and finish the birthday cake that I need to drop off on my way to Grams' house. Once I place butter chocolate icing on the sponges and place them all together, I cut around the edges to make a Labrador puppy. I place the light brown marzipan over the cake, making sure to mold around the mouth and ears, then get the eyes, nose, and tongue that I'd already made yesterday and place them on the cake. Then I get my piped icing and write 'Happy 4th Birthday, Millie' before placing the cake in its box and in the deep freezer until I leave.

I sigh and check my watch at 5 p.m.

I shake my head.

The bakery closes at 1 p.m. Monday through Saturday and closes on Sundays. I've been cleaning and finishing the cake for 4 hours on my own. I shake my head again and start to clean the rest of the kitchen before emptying the dishwashers and reloading them. Once they're done, I put everything away and turn everything off.

        I grab the birthday cake and head to my office. It's now 6 p.m. and the banks are closed, so I place the money in the safe that only Dead Shot and I know the code for. I grab Louisa's mail, ensuring I've put two stamps on it, and grab the box for the bakery before I come to a holt and curse. I don't have my car. I hang my head in defeat, fed up with this day, my chest feeling tight.

Shaking my head, I go out the back of the bakery and lock up, about to head to my flat upstairs to call Grams, when I notice a black Ford truck sitting where my car normally does. My pulse spikes, fear entering my veins, until the person behind the driver's seat gets out, and I sigh in relief.

Axel.

He doesn't have his cut, which he looks weird without, but I know they don't wear them in cars. He walks over to me, grabs both boxes before I can protest, and puts them on the back seat. He opens the passenger-seat door and nods his head. "Come on, princess, I'm taking you to Rosie's tonight. Flame said there was a problem with your engine." I hang my head again—more crap to pile onto a crappy day.

Tears sting my eyes, wanting to fall.

I hear Axel shuffle over to me, and he places two fingers under my chin to make me look at him. He tilts his head, frowning at my glossy eyes. He rasps,

"Hard day, darling?"

I sniffle and nod my head.

He wipes under my eyes with his thumbs when some tears fall and guides me to his truck, helping me inside, and I rasp before he shuts the door.

"I have to drop a cake off to the Joneses and the large box off to the homeless shelter. Oh, and I have to mail this envelope."

He smiles and nods his head before rounding his truck and starting her up. I lean my head against the window, feeling exhausted, and just let him drive in silence. My head's spinning and my chest still feels tight.

Today's been too much.

He takes the envelope a few minutes later from my hands, then gets out of his truck and mails it. He then opens the door, grabs the tub for the homeless shelter, and takes it inside.

A few tears fall and I quickly wipe them away. I've never been good with stress, but I guess that's what happens when you live the first years of your life in an abusive household. When he comes back, he jumps into the truck and puts it in drive, heading to East Street. When we make it to Maple Drive, he gets out again, grabs the birthday cake box, and runs up the drive, knocking on the door. Mr. Jones answers and grins at Axel, who passes him the cake. He says a few words before they shake hands, and he jogs back.

He gets in the truck, puts it in drive again, and takes me to Grams' for dinner, and I whisper, "Thank you," while leaning my head back on the window. He takes hold of my hand and gives it a little squeeze, leaving it there holding mine tightly, which helps calm me a little.

When we pull into Grams', Dead Shot is standing on the porch with his arms crossed over his chest, his face solid like a stone. My tears finally fall seeing my protector, and I sniffle, causing Axel to look at me confused and concerned, but I ignore him, even if my body wants to jump into his arms, and never let him let me go. Instead, I do the more sensible thing, and I jump out of his truck and walk over to Dead Shot, who takes me into his arms and holds me tight.

I sniffle again as tears trail down my cheeks, and he squeezes me.

I feel Axel behind, watching as Dead Shot inquires,

"On a scale of 1-10, how's your anxiety?" I rasp out, "8," and he curses, helping me inside with Axel following. As soon as Cammy sees me, her face goes red, and then she takes me in her arms.

"I've seen the security camera, sweetheart, when you were running late, and I'll tell you when I get my hands on that girl."

I rasp, putting my arms tightly around her. "She stole $400 out of the till before she left, thinking I'd be too tired to notice."

Everybody stills, and Axel growls, "What exactly happened after I left this morning?"

I sigh and wipe my eyes, heading to the dining table. My stomach growls, and I realize I haven't eaten anything except a banana this morning. Shit; hopefully, Cammy and Grams don't notice.

I sit down as Grams passes me a plate full, giving me a knowing look, and I grimace double shit. Axel sits next to me, waiting for my answer, when Grams places a plate for him too. When everybody sits, I explain what had happened: how she barely helped all morning, taking over two hours to bake 40 minutes' worth of goods, the mess she left for me, finding the money missing, then realizing I didn't have my car, which sent me in a spin.

Cammy's face is red, and I notice Grams slowly start to stand, trying to grab Dead Shot's gun, and my eyes widen.

"Grams Sit your butt back down. I took the money out of her severance after I sent her notice of employment termination effective immediately; you are not going to shoot her."

My Grams scowls while the men chuckle as she sits down begrudgingly, and I start to eat, absolutely starving but nearly choked when Cammy states,

"Want to tell me why you haven't eaten today?"

I cough and take a sip of my water, and I stutter, "I, um, uh, well you see, I uh." Fuck. I side-eye Axel, and he's looking at me, his chin leaning on his knuckles, his eyebrows raised, and I scowl at him, causing him to smirk.

"Look, I was busy, ok? She left me in the lurch, and my anxiety spiked for the first time in months. You know how I get when I'm like that; food doesn't even come to mind, so please give me a break." I snap, and my eyes widen. Dead Shot raises his brow at me, awe crap, and I hear Axel snort, so

I elbow him in his ribs, causing him to grunt and Grams to chuckle while Cammy tries not to smile.

I sigh. "I won't forget again, ok, I promise. I'll set an alarm."

He nods like he's satisfied, then continues to eat while Cammy smiles at me, and we all follow suit and eat. A few minutes later, Axel groans and states,

"Fuck Rosie, why haven't I been invited to these dinners sooner?"

My body shakes with laughter as she points her fork at him. "You've had leftovers before, so stop the whining."

He scowls at her and says, "Not the same, and you know it."

I clear my throat. "She was worried about me, but you are always welcome now." He smiles gently at me, squeezing my hand, and nods his head.

After dinner was finished, I helped Grams clean up the kitchen. When she stopped me and placed her hand on my cheek, she said, "You're alright, my darling girl."

I smile and nod.

"It was just a long day."

She hums, "You do look tired. Get Axel to take you home Pumpkin and I'll see you in a few days OK." I nod and place a kiss on her cheek before heading to the living area. Axel and his parents are sitting on my grandmother's flowered couch.

When I enter, Axel stands and says, "You ready, Princess?"

I smile and nod, my cheeks heating up a little at his nickname, making him chuckle. He kisses his mother's cheek, then heads to the kitchen to say bye to Grams. I hug Dead Shot as he kisses my head, then hug Cammy and kiss her cheek.

"I love you," I murmur, and she smiles, placing her hand on my cheek.

"I love you too, my sweet girl."

Axel comes back with a tub, making me chuckle, and we head out.

We get back to my small flat above my bakery 10 minutes later, and he helps me out and then passes me the tub. I furrow my brows, and he just shrugs.

"she's worried."

I huff and smile a little, then state,

"Thank you for picking me up and dropping me off. Goodnight Axel."

He scowls. "It's Logan Lise; if I tell you to call me by my given name, then you call me by my given name."

I clear my throat, nod my head, and ask, "Lise?"

He just shrugs. "I want to be different." I smile and shake my head.

He leans down and places a kiss on my cheek, then places a gentle one on my lips, causing me to gasp in surprise. My eyes widen in shock at the electric shock I feel go through my body, and he rasps,

"Head inside, Princess; I'll leave once I know you are inside safely." I clear my throat again and nod my head before turning around and heading up the metal stairs to my front door. Once I'm inside and lock the door, I hear him drive off, and my heart pounds in my chest.

Holy crap, he kissed me. I place my fingers on my lips and then scowl when I realize:

He's gotten under my skin.

Dammit.

Chapter 7

Axel

I can't stop my grin, even if I try, as I walk into our strip club. I look at my watch. 8:15 p.m. I sigh, wishing I was heading back to my room to sort my hard-on out, but instead, I have paperwork to sort out.

I walk into the club and see Sunny hanging upside down on the pole, her fake tits hanging loose, nipples hard, with a bachelor party cheering her on. I sigh and head to my office. My cock is harder than before seeing part of the show; I can't help it. I'm only human, and spending time with Lise has already gotten me hard. When I get to my office door, Sugar is standing near it, waiting for me in only a thong and nipple pasties. She looks up when she hears me and smiles.

"Hey, Axel."

I give her a nod and unlock my door, letting her inside. I shut it and go around my black desk to take a seat while she sits on one of the black armchairs I have. The room is basically a replica of my office at the clubhouse.

I look at her.

"What can I do for you, Sugar?" I ask in a rasp, my rock-hard cock straining hard against my jeans, trying to think of anything else to help get rid of it.

Her sexy ass was sitting in front of me, basically naked and not helping.

"I just brought a swap shift request; I've got to take my mamma to her hospital appointment."

I lift my left hand, and she stands up, her tits swinging, passing me the paper and I read through it. She wants next Thursday off; I log onto my computer and bring up the shift to see who is on and whether I'd need to replace her, but it looks like I won't need to; she was just an extra in case it got busy, but if it does, I'll just call one of the sweet butts to come in; they like the extra cash. I sign her sheet and pass it back to her, and she smiles gratefully. She comes over to me and hugs me, shoving her tit's in my face.

Fuck, fuck, fuck.

She pulls back a little, then smirks at me and rasps.

"How about I repay you for your kindness." Before I can say anything, she climbs on my lap and grinds her covered pussy against my jeans-clad cock.

Fuck, that feels good.

My hands go to her waist, adamant that I'm going to lift her off, but instead, I pull her closer, my cock overriding my mind.

Annalise who?

I rip off a pasty with my teeth and spit the sticker onto the floor before I take her perk nipple into my mouth. I circle my tongue around it before gently biting it, then sucking hard, causing her to moan and grind down on me harder. I grasp the back of her neck, her dyed pink hair falling over her shoulders as her hazel eyes stare at me full of lust, and I kiss her, shoving my tongue down her throat.

She moans as I groan, and I move my hands between us. I quickly undo my jeans and pull my hard cock out, while my lips never leave hers. I blindly reach into my desk, draw and grab a condom, and sheath myself before I move her thong to one side and place myself at her entrance. She lowers herself down on me hard and rides me like her life fucking depends on it. I break the kiss and rip the other pasty off before I bite her nipple and suck it into my mouth.

Her cunt squeezes me. Fuck yes.

I grab her hips while I lift her a little to fuck her harder, I shove a hand between us and pinch her clit hard. Her cunt juices all over me, squeezing me tightly, and I groan, thrusting one, two, three more times before I quickly lift her and then come in the condom.

She leans down and kisses me sloppy before getting off of me, then drops to her knees and takes the condom off my semi-hard dick. Then I watch entranced as she empties the condom into her mouth, swallowing my cum. Fuck, that's hot. My cock starts to get hard again, and she leans forward, taking it into her mouth, making me groan.

She expertly deep-throats me over and over while her hand plays with my balls.

 Fuck.

I grab her hair with a tight fist, then start to fuck her face. She moans, causing a vibration around my cock, making me squirt my cum down her throat, and she swallows it all like a pro. I smirk when she gives my cock one last lick before she gets up.

She leans forward, and I tug on her nipple before giving her a kiss.

"Thanks for the shift swap, Axel. I can't wait to do this again sometime." I chuckle and lean back in my chair as she walks out of my office, but my smirk falls off of my face once she's gone. I feel my face pale when it hits me. fuck.

I sigh and scrub a hand through my hair before putting my cock back away, feeling like I just cheated, which is fucking ridiculous.

My door opens again, and my father walks in with a scowl.

Great.

He crosses his arms over his chest and raises a brow at me, and I sigh again. "What can I do for you, Dad?"

He shakes his head. "Maybe it's best you don't pursue this thing with Annalise."

I chuckle darkly, "Seriously. Last time I checked, I was your son. We're not together yet. Heck, she's still not at the stage of even considering giving me a chance, so if I want to fuck women to get my rocks off, then I will. Shame my fucking father couldn't be on my side."

My dad's eyebrows rise to the top of his head.

"Axel."

I stop him by putting my hand up. "If you haven't got anything club-related to speak to me about, then you know where the door is." Then I ignored him and started on my paperwork. I never talk to my dad like that, ever. I respect and idolize him, but I don't need him to make me feel any more fucking shitty than I already do.

      I know I should just walk away from Lise, especially if I can't say no to a woman who comes to me, but I can't. I'm a selfish bastard, and she's now under my skin. And as far as I'm concerned, I'm still fair game to fuck who I want until she realizes she's mine.

I hear my father sigh and turn to leave my office, but not before I hear shouting from the corridor. He turns to look at me, and we both go into action. We turn left, which leads to the back door of the club, where we can hear shouting.

"WHAT DO YOU MEAN THEY BLEW UP MY FUCKING COKE BITCH?"

When we round the corner, Starlight, who we just sacked, is pushed up against the wall while a Devil's member has his hand around her throat, and I smirk.

Well, hello, idiot.

I quickly remove my revolver from the back of my jeans and press it against his head. He freezes. I look around him to starlight and sneer, "Get the fuck off of our property before we decide to do something about you."

She pales and runs away with her tail between her legs, and I chuckle darkly.

"Now, who do we have here?"

The guy, who is roughly two inches shorter than me, has a bald head covered in tattoos and says, "Killer."

I smirk. Not so hard now, are we?

My father chuckles when I knock him hard over his head with my gun, knocking him out. I grab my phone and call Dagger; he answers on the third ring.

"This better be important, yes, fuck, right there, bitch, right there, don't stop."

I sigh and hold the phone away from my ear as some bitch moans out. My father laughs his ass off as I state to Dagger before hanging up,

"Get me two prospects and a cage out the back of the strip club; I've got a Devil coming home."

I head back to my office to grab my keys and lock up before we head to the clubhouse to question this idiot. When I get back outside, my father is leaning against the wall as our two prospects are dragging 'Killer' to the club's van.

Dagger walks over to me, "Where'd you find him?"

I just chuckled and explained how he was arguing with Starlight out here loudly and he burst out in laughter at the guy's stupidity.

"Alright, let's go get some answers."

Dagger smirks at me, then heads towards his bike, and I go to mine only to be stopped by my dad, who grabs my arm.

He growls lowly, "You're my son, and I love you fiercely. You always come first. But you have to remember, your mother and I raised that girl like our own since she was four years old. She was supposed to live with us. I only say you give up your pursuit because as soon as she finds out you just fucked another woman right after dropping her off after you spent the whole evening trying to butter her up, she'll walk away without a backward glance. Her father was a cheater and an abuser. Her ex-boyfriend just cheated on her. And I get it; you're not together yet, but you made it publicly clear to everyone at the clubhouse that you don't share, and you wouldn't expect her to. Pull your head out of your ass, son, because you will blow your chance if you haven't already."

I scowled at him, hating that he was right. It was a weak moment, and I gave into temptation, and I know I fucked up, but she won't find out. I'll fucking make sure she won't. I nod and go to walk again, but stop when he states,

"Think of it this way. As I left to check on her a little while ago, I walked in on her fucking some guy."

My whole body vibrates with rage at the thought of her with someone else, and I pick up the trash can, throwing it at the wall as my father chuckles.

"And now you'll know how she'd feel if she ever finds out; don't be a hypocrite, son."

Fucks sake, he played me.

I glare at him, then pale when he states,

"And I don't want to know what your mother or Rosie would say or do if they found out."

Fuck, I climb on my bike while he laughs his ass off at the look on my face. I sigh. They won't find out. I won't let them, because I happen to love my fucking balls. I quickly text the council brothers to meet me in the basement, then I rev my bike and wheel spin out of the car park, heading to the clubhouse with my father right behind me. Dagger had followed the van to ensure they got him in the basement safely and quickly.

It's a good thing he was in his office, fucking.

10 minutes later, we arrived at the clubhouse. The prospect lets us in, and we park up near the door and head inside. The music's blaring, and most of the brothers are fucking a sweet butt while others are just drinking beer and playing pool. As I start towards the basement, Bubbles comes up to me and places her hand on my chest. I quickly grab it, removing it, and she pouts while I raise a brow at her.

"I told you; I'm taken."

She just smirks and shrugs her shoulders, then goes off to another brother. Huh, that was easy. Too fucking easy. I look towards my dad, and he's also looking at her with furrowed brows. I smack him on the back, and we continue to the basement. We haven't got time for her fucking games; she knows she's on her last chance.

As we walk down the stairs, I chuckle, making Dad look at me with a raised brow. I just shrug. "Just remembering when I came down here when I was 8."

He chuckles and shakes his head. "Don't remind me, son, I had to fork out 50 bucks for a fucking game; pay you $10 extra a month, and your mother still fucking found out." I laugh. "Yeah, we should have known she was in the bar when I got up the stairs; she did say 10 minutes."

He just laughs. Momma flipped out that day, two sweet butts ended up in the emergency room, and dad, well, he ended up with blue balls for a month and sleepless nights on the sofa.

When we head through the metal door, I smirk. 'Killer' is stripped down to his boxers while his arms are chained above his head, feet dangling from the floor, and he's swearing up a storm.

"I swear to fucking God that when I leave here, I'm blowing this shithole up. This is our territory now, and there's nothing you or Snake can do about it."

He pales when I stand in front of him with cold eyes.

Ink, Gunner, Slicer, Flame, and Hawk are all leaning against the wall smirking. Butch and Stormy stand with my dad on the other side of the room, as well as the other old-timers.

I get in his face.

"So, you think you can take my territory and take over Snakes Club?"

He pales when he realizes he fucked up in anger, and I smirk when he tries to backpedal: "No, no, we'll take this club with Snake; yeah, Snake knows what we're doing."

I raise a brow, take out my phone, and call the man himself.

He answers after four rings.

"Snake here."

I smile when I notice how pale the man's gone. Fucking big-assed biker, my ass.

"Snake, it's Axel. I have someone here that belongs to you. He was also the owner of the crate we left on your doorstep burning."

I hear a door shut. "What are you talking about, Axel?"

He growls, and I grab my knife and stick it in the man's leg. He screams out.

Shaking my head, I say, "Say hi, Killer."

He spits at me, "fuck you asshole." I hear a sigh on the other end: "Axel, let my man go, and we'll talk this out." I just chuckled. "You mean the same man who just admitted that there's going to be a coup in your MC, then they're going to blow mine up?"

I hear a smash: "What the fuck are you talking about?" He growls, and I twist the knife in the man's leg, and he screams out,

"STOP, STOP."

I hear Snake mutter, "Fucks sake, what kind of pussy did my VP patch in?"

I just chuckled and said, "Come on now, speak up."

The guy has sweat dripping from his forehead. "Fine, w-we're better off without S-Snake. He d-doesn't deserve t-the title of p-pres."

Snake curses then states, "Fucking kill him, Axel. I have a clubhouse to clear out."

Then he hangs up while 'Killer' looks at me with wide eyes, but I just shrug and take a step back, making him visibly relax.

"I knew you were all just talking. Untie me, and I'll leave the county. I won't tell anyone, I promise."

I just chuckle and look at Flame who has an evil gleam in his eye. He picks up his blow torch, and the guy starts tugging on his chains. We all stand back while we watch him burn the guy alive slowly. He screams over and over as Flame starts at his feet, working his way up. By the time he reaches his hips, the guy passes out, so Ink throws cold salt water over him, making him wake up screaming, and Flame continues. An hour later, he's dead, and the prospects are rolling him up in tarpaulin, ready to take him to the funeral home. He'll be burned and then thrown away like the trash he is.

I turn towards the brothers and say, "Church at 8 a.m. tomorrow." They nod, and I head out to the spare room I'm staying in while mine is being decorated. Shit. I sigh, going into the room and locking the door behind me before leaning against it.

Fuck.

My mind caught up on what I did at the strip club with full force.

Guilt runs through my veins.

How the fuck does Flame deal with this every day?

I shake my head and quickly go to grab a shower. I wash away my evening before getting out and heading to bed, where my mind stays on Annalise's perfect face.

Fuck, I fucked up.

Chapter 8

Annalise

I'm clearing some tables when the door to my bakery opens and Bubbles walks in with an unknown woman who has pink hair.

Ok. I'm not going to judge, even if they're both in barely there outfits. They head towards the counter, and my eyes widen when I see Sandy grab a knife.

Shit.

I quickly rush over to the counter, bump her out of the way, and nod towards the back to check on the cakes that are in the oven. She huffs, turns around, and mutters, "You're no fun," making me smirk. I wait for the women to place their orders while keeping an eye out for her, but they seem more interested in chatting.

I sigh and wipe down the counter until they're ready.

"I mean, I couldn't believe it, Bubbles. I know you told me he says he's now taken even if the girl he wants isn't ready, but when I went into his office to swap my shifts, he was looking at me like I was a snack, so I thought I'd try my luck, and it paid off. I rode him until we both came and then I sucked him off until he became hard again and came again, which was so much fun. I even drank his cum from the condom; it tasted divine, and he didn't even look like he regretted it. When I leaned forward to give him a kiss goodbye, I half expected him to push me away out of guilt after what you had told me, but instead, he tugged on my nipple and kissed me.

Apparently, he's looking forward to next time." The unknown woman grins widely. I roll my eyes while trying to hold in my vomit because, gross, why can't they have this conversation after they've ordered? I really don't want to hear that crap, and I have to sort out the new coffee machine that arrived this morning.

Bubbles looks at me and sneers, but I put my hand up, not wanting to deal with her crap.

"You're in my bakery; you want to sneer at me fine, but don't even think about trying to start shit, or you know where the door is. Sandy had to put her dog down after you booted it, so be grateful it's me standing here and not her, and that I'm even willing to allow you in my shop to begin with."

Bubbles pales, guilt showing on her face, and she mutters,

"Shit."

Hmm, maybe she does have a heart after all. She clears her throat and says, "Can I have some white chocolate nut macaroon cookies, please?"

I nod, then ask, "Will you be seeing Dead Shot today?" The other woman looks at me with a frown while Bubbles nods her head.

"Yes, they're at the clubhouse with Cammy; why?"

Confusion is written all over her face, but I ignore it and grab the cookies she requested, then I grab another box and place Dead Shot's favorite chocolate chip cookies as well as Cammy's mini cheesecakes in it.

Then I hand her both boxes, and I state, "The bag is your order, which is $2.49; the box is for Dead Shot and Cammy, which is on the house."

Her brows shoot high, and the other woman looks down on me and sneers.

"And who are you to them, huh?"

I just smiled sweetly. "Like their daughter, seems as though they had legal guardianship of me growing up and basically raised me with my Grams." Her eyes widen, and she swallows hard, regretting being a bitch, and nods, then mutters,

"Sorry, people try to get in their good books, wanting to be with their son."

I raise my brows and nod not saying anything else while Bubbles places the exact amount on the counter for the cookies. I give her a smile, ringing the order up, and as they turn, I see a gleam in her eyes. The sweet woman who showed guilt is completely gone, as she says to the woman while they walk out of my bakery.

"So, come on, Sugar, just how hard did Axel fuck you last night?" and my stomach drops, then I chuckle.

Of course, he flirts with me all evening, acts like I'm all he sees, and then he fucks someone straight after he drops me off home with a goodbye sweet kiss, which Bubbles seems to know all about. What a fucking shocker!

This is why I don't want a man.

Sandy comes out at that moment to take over the counter while I sort the coffee machine out, ready to place it near the frappe machine behind the counter in the front of the shop.

I quickly turned toward her before going through the doorway. "Anyone, and I mean anyone, comes in to see me; I'm not here."

She nods her head toward the door. "Maybe they were lying?"

I just raise a brow at her, and she sighs, nodding her head, and I head out back. We're not together; I know that, but he was pursuing me. You don't fuck someone else the exact same day you pursue someone; it's tacky, and I hate tacky.

I sigh, feeling disappointed.

Dammit, I knew he got under my skin.

An hour later, I have the machine set up ready to take out front when I hear him say, "Hey Sandy, Lise in?" I still like the nickname—what a jackass! I get it, we're not together, but come on, don't go flirting, making out like I'm all you see, only to go fuck someone else and then show up at my workplace the next fricking day.

I hear Sandy clear her throat.

"Sorry, Axel, she just popped out."

I hear him sigh. "I heard Bubbles come in here this morning. She gave a box to my parents; I just wanted to make sure she didn't start crap."

More like you didn't want her to tell me you fucked her friend, I snorted, shaking my head.

"No, don't worry; she was respectable to her, honey; no problems."

I hear him tap on the counter twice: "Alright, let her know I stopped by, and I'll try and catch her later, maybe."

Then he leaves, and I breathe a sigh of relief.

Sandy comes to the back and shakes her head. "That man, you'd think he'd realize that things don't stay secret for long in this town."

I just chuckle even if I have a lump in my throat. He's the Ramirez's son, so I have to see him now; he knows I exist, but I'll just ensure he's aware that we're never going to happen.

He's the kind of man who can't live with just one woman.

I nod over to the coffee machine. "Give us a hand."

She looks at it, then me, then the machine again, and mutters, "Shit," making me chuckle, and we both lift the machine.

"Fuck, it's heavy." I curse while Sandy giggles, causing me to giggle, and we nearly drop it, making us giggle some more.

"What are you two giggling about?"

We both scream and nearly drop the coffee machine again when two large hands grab a hold of it. I turn to see the man I see as a father looking at us with a smirk and a raised brow, and I scowl at him.

"Not cool, Dead Shot."

He chuckles and places the machine on the back wall bench behind the counter for us while Sandy plugs it in, setting it up as he walks over to me and kisses my head. "Sorry, sweetheart, I thought you heard me come in."

I just chuckle and head out back with him on my heels.

I grab the money out of the safe that I still haven't managed to take to the bank and pass it to him.

"Thank you for doing this for me."

He smiles and says, "Of course, Annie, you know I don't like you taking the money to the bank."

I just chuckle, and then head to the kitchen. He leans against the counter as I start to make the next batch of brownies ready for the lunch rush, and he tilts his head, studying me.

"You know."

I just smile at him, and he chuckles as I state, "It has nothing to do with me who your son sticks his dick into."

He sighs and scrubs his face. "He regrets it, sweetheart."

And I just shrug, "Again, nothing to do with me."

He goes to talk again, but I put my hand up.

"Axel and I are never going to happen. You and Cammy are like my parents, and I love you both tremendously, and that's never going to change, but he's a playboy; he can't stick to one woman; he proved that last night. I'm sorry."

He smiles gently at me, knowing my mindset, then states, "You just called her Cammy."

I smile wide. "Have you noticed how pissed she gets when I call her Mrs. Ramirez?"

He full-blown laughs, then states, "But you don't want to call her either."

I shake my head as I pour the chocolate chips into the batter.

This man knows me too well.

"I don't want to call you Dead Shot either."

He smiles at me, then walks over, placing a kiss on my head, then nicks one of the brownies, making me chuckle, and he says, "When you are ready, sweetheart, we're your parents and we love you, so when you are ready."

I nod and hug him before he takes a few more treats and the bagged money heading to the bank, and I shake my head. Cammy's definitely going to be pissed when she realizes I let him have all that.

I chuckle.

A few hours later, after the rush hour has ended and both myself and Sandy have cleaned up the shop, I head to my flat when there's a knock on my door. Shit. I really hope that's not Axel. I go down the stairs and quickly peek through the peek hole to see Flame. I open the door, smiling at him, knowing there's only one reason why he'd be here. He grins and holds up my keys.

"Oh, thank you, thank you, thank you."

He chuckles, and I invite him in. I have two boxes full of baked goods, one of which he can have; Sandy already took one box to the homeless shelter, and the other is for Star, who should be here in 10 for a catch-up.

I'm just glad I remembered to bake more than normal today.

"How much do I owe you?"

He just chuckles. "A box of baked goodies would be good."

I just laugh, then hand him the box, making him grin.

He looks in the box and groans, "You're an angel."

I just chuckle and state, "You better share them with Star; she'll be pissed if she finds out you have a box full, even if she's got her own for later."

He full-blown laughs, nods, then sighs, his eyes full of sorrow, and I tilt my head, studying him when I see the look in his eyes.

Oh my, "you love her."

He looks at me with a raised brow and says, "Of course I do; she's my best friend."

I smile and shake my head. "That's not what I mean, and you know it."

He sighs and runs a hand through his black hair. "I do, so fucking much, but she deserves better than this life, better than me."

Oh, the poor, clueless man, "This life is all she wants, Flame—the number of times she's brought you up. She doesn't just look at you like you're her friend; she looks at you like you've hung the moon. She's been in love with you for years, and the more you sleep around to push her away, the more you're just hurting her."

He looks down in guilt, knowing my words are true.

"Just think about it, maybe you'll realize that seeing her with someone else would hurt too much. You both belong together, Flame." He nods before placing a kiss on my head, and I walk him to the door when I hear another knock. When I open the door, Star is standing there; she smiles, and when she sees Flame, her eyes sparkle, and I see the love he holds for her. Her smile widens into a grin when she sees his box in his hands, making me chuckle. He shakes his head and takes out a cookie, giving it to her, then kisses her forehead. He lingers, breathing her in, and I bite my lip to hide my grin.

When he pulls back, she looks at him with all the love that makes him smile.

He turns and kisses my cheek. "I'll leave you ladies to it; thank you, Annie." I smile, knowing it's not just the box he's thanking me for, so I nod my head, and then he heads towards a blue truck. We watch him get into it with a prospect sitting behind the wheel, and he passes him a brownie. We watch the prospect grin widely, and we both chuckle and walk up the stairs as she eats her cookie.

She sighs, "I want more." Then she pouts, making me chuckle.

"More what, goodies or 'goodies'" she laughs her ass off as I grab the other box and place it in front of her, and she grins, "YES, I knew there was a reason why we're friends, but to your question: Yes, to both. God, I love that man."

I full-blown laugh then make us both a coffee before we head to my small living area. She takes the brown comfy chair while I sit on the sofa, and once we're comfortable and she's taken a bite into a mini cheesecake, she gets right into it.

"So, you and Axel."

I just shake my head and say, "Nope, after he flirted yesterday and made out like I was all he saw, he went and fucked a stripper."

Her eyes widen in shock while I nod and then take a bite of a croissant as she scowls.

"Fricking MC men"

I chuckle and nod my head. "Yeah, he has heartbreak written all over him. I can't go there. I won't."

She gives me a sad smile, and I know she's thinking about Flame.

I clear my throat. "You know he's in love with you, right?"

She just smiles and says, "I know. I've known for a while now, probably since I was 16, but he just keeps pushing me away. Like yesterday, he decided to let Ginger sit in his lap, grinding on him while I was right next to him. After a few minutes, his hand started moving between her legs, so I got up and left and told him I had a piece to finish, which I didn't, but you know."

I shake my head. "What a flipping idiot."

She snorts, nodding in agreement, as she takes another bite out of her cheesecake. I take a bite out of a brownie.

"Have you ever tried to, I don't know, come on to him?"

She full-blown laughed, "Yeah, when I was 18, he pushed me away with wide eyes and stated he didn't want to ruin our friendship, yet as soon as another man pays any attention to me, he's instantly there to scare them away."

I snort, "Men."

She nods, "Men."

She takes a sip of her coffee, and we spend a few hours catching up before I help her make a casserole, which turns out perfectly if I do say so myself. She ended up ringing Flame to see if he'd be her little taste tester, making me laugh. She left about 10 minutes ago to meet him at her place.

I clean up my mess and eat the plate she left for me, sighing and feeling lonelier than ever.

About a week later my decision to stay away from Axel is cemented when Cammy somehow manages to get me to drop off some cookies and paperwork to him at the strip club.

Being lonely is a lot better than being hurt if only he got that message.

Chapter 9

Axel – one week later

I'm sitting in my office doing paperwork. Well, I'm trying anyway. My mind kept going back to a certain blonde bombshell who, if I didn't know any better, was ghosting me. I haven't seen her since the night I dropped her off after Rosie's family meal, and I fucked Sugar—not for lack of trying, though. Twice a day, I have shown up at her bakery or flat. She's either just gone out or not been in, and it's now pissing me off.

My phone rings and I bark answering it, "WHAT." The person on the other end chuckles and says, "Hello to you too, Axel." I sigh, "Snake." He just laughs and says, "Who pissed in your beer this evening?"

"Is there a reason you called, or did you just want to piss me off?"

"Alright, I wanted to call to thank you for the heads-up about the coup. I've gotten rid of most of the men who were in on it, but I still haven't figured out who the ring leader was."

"It wasn't a problem, Snake. If you need a hand, just give us a shout.

He hums, "I'll do that. I'll let you get back to your prissy mood."

I scowl as he hangs up laughing, asshole.

About an hour later, my office door opens, and Sugar walks in with a sultry look.

I sigh.

I haven't touched another girl since her last week, and I know my dick likes what he sees. Dark blue body suit lingerie paints on her body, looking fucking sexy. My mind and body are at war with each other.

Do I fuck up and fuck her over my desk, or do I man the fuck up and go find the woman I want?

But as Sugar saunters over to me, her high heels clicking on the floor, I know I'm about to give in. I move my chair away from my desk, and she straddles my lap, rubbing her pantie-covered pussy against my jean-clad dick, leaving a wet spot from her juices. I know I shouldn't, but let's face it: I'm a red-blooded male; sex is a part of life, and until I convince Annalise to give us a shot, I might as well still get my rocks off; it's not like she'll know anyway.

I slowly guide one hand up her thigh while my other traces her generous tits. I lean forward and lick between them where they're pushed up by her bra while my fingers lightly trace over her hardened nipple, causing her to moan. My fingers, on the other hand, move the fabric of her panties to the side and trace her wet cunt, and just as I'm about to lift her onto my desk to fuck her hard, a throat clears from my doorway that Sugar must have forgotten to close.

I slowly pull away but keep my fingers tracing her juicy pussy to keep her in the mood, and I'm fucking praying it's not my mother in the doorway. But when I look, it's my worst fucking nightmare, and I feel my face drain.

Sugar looks to see who interrupted us and she smiles wide, "Oh, it's you. I must tell you, your cookies are to die for." Annalise smiles gently at Sugar while I feel like my whole world is falling apart.

She looks at me, her face void of emotion, and she states, "I'm sorry to interrupt. Cammy asked me to bring a box of goodies for Axel and also some paperwork."

I flinch at her using my road name, but she ignores it and walks into my office, placing the box and the paperwork on my desk.

She then looks at Sugar, smiling.

"It was good seeing you again. I'm glad you liked my baked goods. I'm sure Axel will share them with you."

Sugar grins at her, and without even looking my way, she goes to leave, and I finally find my voice.

"Lise, have you got a moment?"

She stops and turns a little. "It's Annalise Axel, and sorry, but I've got to get back to the bakery for clean up; I'll let you two carry on." Then she walks out of my office, leaving me fucking fuming while she looks fucking unaffected. It's only then that I realize my fingers are still tracing Sugar's pussy as more of her juices gush over my fingers. Shit. I quickly removed them, grabbing a tissue.

I sigh and look at her, but she's busy looking at the box, which I don't blame; the fucking woman can bake.

"When did you two meet?" I was curious, but Lise has avoided me all week, and now I'm starting to realize why.

Oblivious to my anger, she says distractedly, "Last week, Bubbles took me to the bakery while wanting to have the details of what happened with us before she even ordered. It was weird, though, because she refused to know anything until we were near the counter. The owner is really nice, though."

I sigh. Fuck. She knew last week.

I help Sugar off of my lap and open the box. She squeals in delight and takes an iced bun and a few cookies, and I state, knowing she's about to be pissed,

"She's the woman I want to make my old lady."

She turns to face me and scowls, shouting, "ARE YOU FUCKING KIDDING ME YOU FUCKING IDIOT." I nod my head when the realization of what Bubbles did comes across her face, then she decides to smack me across my head, and I let her because, let's face it, I am a fucking idiot.

Shit.

She places her hands on her hips, which isn't easy with the food in them, and then she growls at me, "This is what's going to happen. I'm going to explain to her that nothing is serious with us, and you're going to fucking grovel. The woman is fucking sweet, Axel. I never realized Bubbles was fucking playing me. I mean, I knew you wanted someone, but I thought it was all talk. You're a fucking idiot. FIX IT." Then she storms out of my office, making me chuckle.

I pick up the paperwork Momma wanted me to have and see that it's the final changes to my room at the clubhouse. Fuck. Shaking my head, I lock my office and quickly rush out of the club, hoping she's still in the parking lot. As I rush out of the door, a few brothers that have stuck around look at me in confusion, but I ignore them, waving my hand to not worry as I rush outside.

When I get to the parking lot, I spot her right away.

"LISE!" I shout, like, Fuck, is she stopping me from calling her that.

Her shoulders drop, and I can hear her sigh from here.

"Yes, Axel,"

I growl, pissed that she's calling me my road name; now I know how Flame feels when Star uses his road name when she's pissed at him.

"We're not together."

Fuck why in the hell did I just say that. She raises her eyebrows high. Amusement shines through her eyes while I continue digging my own fucking grave. "We're not together, and you're acting like a scorned girlfriend." Ah, shit. I really just said that. I hear a giggle behind me, and I know it's most likely Sugar to watch me make an ass out of myself and say shit I know I shouldn't be fucking saying.

Fucks sake.

"I'm aware we're not together, Axel," I growl again, but she ignores me. "And I'm not acting like a scorned girlfriend. I mean, my ex-boyfriend literally just cheated on me, and all I did was walk away. If I were acting like a scorned girlfriend, I would probably burn your office down. You are aware of who raised me, right?"

I tilt my head; she has a point, but as I said, I didn't mean to fucking say that it's just what came out, "then why just walk out like that? Why not give me a chance? Because if you did, what you saw in there would never fucking happen. It's not like I haven't made it obvious that I want you, Annalise."

She just chuckles. "I walked out because you were busy, and I didn't want to interrupt, and I can't give you a chance because you're not a one-woman man." Ok, now I'm pissed. I know I just fucked up, but I wouldn't fuck up if I were with her. She places her hands up in an innocent gesture and continues, "What I mean is, you like sex way too much, and I know in my heart of hearts that if I see this through with you and we get into an argument and I decide to withhold sex for a while, let's face it, I am female and I can be a bitch. Your mother did raise me." I chuckle at that while Sugar snorts because it's true: "You'll most likely stray, and I'd rather be alone than risk our family dynamics. Your parents mean too much to me because they're mine just as much as they're yours."

I sigh and shake my head. I'm losing; I know I am.

"I think you should give me a little bit more credit than that, Lise. I think we could be great together. We have the spark; I know you felt it."

She just shakes her head.

"One chance, that's all I'm asking for."

She sighs. "Why? You literally just had your fingers, which I'm guessing you haven't even washed yet, inside someone else while I stood on the other side of your desk."

I winced while said someone else came out of the shadows and said, "We're not together, and to be honest, if I knew he was trying to win you over, I would have smacked him one for you." Lise chuckles while I shake my head. "I think you should at least try."

Lise raises her brow, "For me or for your dire need of baked goodies?" I snort while Sugar grins. "I'm not going to lie, probably both." Lise laughs at her, then looks at me.

"Please, Lise, one chance; that's all I'm asking for."

She sighs and looks up at the sky that's gotten darker before looking back at me.

"Ok, I'll give you one chance, but on one condition." Oh fuck, I do not like the evil gleam in her eyes. I clear my throat and cross my arms over my chest, bracing myself. "I think it's only right for Cammy to know why I've been full of avoidance this week, and not only with you."

I hang my head, my arms dropping down to my side, shit. I hear Sugar laugh her ass off as I shake my head. When I look at Lise again, she's smiling, and I tilt my head. This isn't a challenge; she thinks I won't do it; this is her way of me not getting my chance.

Fuck, well played, darling, but I want you too much.

I sigh, grab my phone out of my pocket, and twist it several times in my hands. Fuck, fuck, fuck. I sigh again and find momma's number; fuck, she's going to kill me. I press call, putting the phone on loudspeaker.

Lise's eyes widen in shock, and I hear Sugar gasp.

Fuck me, this is going to suck.

"Hey, baby boy." My mother's cheery voice comes over the speakers. "Did Annie bring the stuff around?"

I clear my throat. "Hey momma, yeah, she did; I just, uh, well, you see, I uh."

Shit, I never stutter, but with Momma, I shake my head; she's going to know I fucked up.

"what.did.you.do?" Oh shit.

                       Lise comes over and tries to take the phone, but I don't let her. Her eyes plead with me, but I just lean down and gently kiss her on her forehead, knowing she wouldn't want my lips on her after what she walked in on.

"I fucked a stripper last week and nearly did again today. Lise walked in on it."

I hear Sugar mutter, "Crazy fucking asshole." Even she knows who my Momma is. Lise's eyes widen in horror at the fact that I did it and that I actually told her.

The lines quiet for a few minutes when Momma finally spoke, her voice low. Shiiiit.

"Where are you?"

Lise's eyes widen in horror. Yep, momma definitely raised her. She knows about her anger.

I cleared my throat. "Currently at the club." Sugar stares at me in shock that I actually told her my whereabouts, but you see, I'm a motherfucking president; I'm not scared of death—just my tiny fucking mother.

"And I take it you wanted to tell me and your father before she did."

I clear my throat again, hoping I don't drop Dad into it because the fucker already knows.

"Actually, Lise gave me an ultimatum: tell you, or she won't give me a chance to prove myself. I'm willing to do anything to convince her otherwise."

I smile at Lise as she looks at me with shock. I hear Sugar sigh in the background, "Now that was romantic," making us both smile. Fuck, she has a beautiful smile. I run my fingers through her hair, moving it out of her face, making sure it was not the hand I had tracing Sugar's cunt with because I know for a fact she'll nut junk me. "So, whatcha say, Princess? Are you willing to try?"

She looks at me with so many emotions running through her eyes; she's scared, and I get it; I haven't exactly shown her I'm serious. She looks down for a few seconds, playing with her fingers, and my heart rate kicks up. Fuck, I hope she says yes; otherwise, I'm fucking kidnapping her and tying her to my goddamn bed. I hear her sigh, and when she looks up, hope fills my chest.

"Ok, one chance, but that's it."

I can't stop the grin that fills my face. I pick her up and spin her around, making her giggle. I hear a couple of sniffles. One from behind and one from on the line making me chuckle.

"Alright, I'll leave you two to it. Don't mess this up, son. Oh, and nice try trying to cover for your dad; we both know he knew. Love you both loads."

Then she hangs up, and I grimace and quickly text my dad while keeping one arm around Lise's waist while she watches me type.

Me—run, hide; she knows you know about my fuckup, code fucking red.

I press send as Sugar walks over to us, "Um, so, now that this is settled, I have a massive question." We both look at her with furrowed brows, "Can I have that box of goodies in your office?" Lise giggles while I shake my head. I was smart enough to lock my office before I ran out here because there was no chance she would get that box.

Lise moves away from me, making me frown, but she just shakes her head and walks over to her car. For fucks sake, I told Flame to blow the thing up. I'm going to have to have a talk with her about that; Dad's already ordered her an SUV. She comes back a few minutes later and passes another tub to Sugar as she squeals in delight.

That'll give you a headache if you stand too close.

She hugs Lise, then kisses my cheek before skipping. Yep, fucking skipping away. I shake my head and look back at my girl. "How would you feel going for a little ride? I won't go fast."

She stiffens, and I run my fingers through her hair, and I rasp, "I won't let anything happen to you; I won't crash, and I certainly won't let you fall. Come on, darling, take this step with me." She takes a deep breath and looks towards my bike, then gives me the tiniest of nods. I smile and take hold of her hand, leading her over to my bike. I place my helmet on her, and just before climbing on my phone,

Dad – too late, fucking ouch

He attached a picture of the lump on his head, and I grimaced. Yeah, Momma loves her pans.

Shaking my head, I hold my hand out to my girl, and she takes it, her body shaking like a leaf, but she still climbs on and wraps her arms around my waist, holding me tight.

        I start my bike, revving her, then gently pulling away. Lise's arms tighten around me, and I place my hand on hers, rubbing it before taking off down the road. I can't help the grin that spreads across my face as I take to the back roads, heading up to the lookout point. The road is curved, but it's a nice drive. I take it easy, and the longer I ride, the more relaxed my girl becomes. I place my hand on hers again and just enjoy the fucking ride.

20 minutes later, we arrive at the top of the cliff, and I help her off the bike before getting off myself. I take the helmet off of her, placing it on the back of my bike. I lean against the seat and bring her with me, putting her back to my front and wrapping my arms around her waist. I smile when she relaxes against me and sighs.

We don't talk.

We just look at the view of our town, the stars bright above us.

After a little, while I lean down, place my nose into her neck, and gently kiss it, I rasp, "I promise I won't let you down."

She lifts her head to the side so she can look at me, "We'll take it slow." I smile and lean down, placing a gentle kiss on her lips, then several more before I hold her close to me as we watch the view.

Fuck I feel content.

Chapter 10

Annalise – 3months later

I'm getting ready to leave for work when my phone rings. I frown because it is 4 a.m., so who in the hell would be ringing me this early?

I quickly grab my phone, and I can't help the smile that overtakes my face, so I answer it.

"Shouldn't you be asleep right about now?" He chuckles, and his voice sounds raspy and full of sleep when he answers me back.

"I should be, but my girl is up, and I wanted to hear her voice because I won't be able to see her today." I chuckled, a smile spreading across my face. We've spent nearly every day together or when we have time because of our different schedules.

"Let me guess, you are locking yourself in your office and hiding yourself from your mother all day."

He chuckles, "I swear she's driving me insane, Lise. There are only so many luncheons our brothers can take. But no, we have church this morning, then I'm off on a run. It's my turn this month, so I won't be back until late tonight, and I wanted to make sure I spoke to you beforehand just in case I don't get a chance later."

I can't help the smile on my face. "Be careful."

He chuckles, "Always princess. I'll let you get to work. If I get a chance, I'll call again; if not, I'll see you tomorrow."

I smile, and we say bye before hanging up. Sighing, I shake my head and go to my front door, ready to get this wedding cake baked and all the savory and sweet bakes ready for opening at 8 a.m. Logan and I have gotten quite close these last few months. We haven't slept together yet; he's going at my pace, which I'm grateful for, and I know I'm falling for him, but I just don't know if this is the right thing for me. I saw what my mama went through, and I can't live with that. Now I know he won't be abusive like my birth father because of who raised him, but I'm not 100% sure that he'll be faithful. Heck, I'm not 100% sure he hasn't slept with someone else since we started seeing each other.

I sigh and head into my bakery, trying to get out of my own head as I start switching everything on after ensuring the doors are locked. It doesn't matter if we're in a small town in Dallas; you can never be too careful.

I wash my hands before I start making the pastry for the pasties and sausage rolls, then place them in the freezer and start on the cake mixes for the wedding cake and cupcakes. Once I have them in the oven, I start on the meats for the pastry filling, then grab the pastry out of the freezer, roll it out, and start making the pasties and sausage rolls before placing them in the other oven I have. I check the cakes and see they're ready and quickly place them out on the cooling trays, then make a start on my brownies, then the cookie dough with flavors from white chocolate nut macaroon, triple chocolate chip, chocolate chip, and hazelnut. Once done, I place them in the oven and work on my mini cheesecakes, which range from raspberry swirl to galaxy chocolate to snickers.

I check the time and see I've been cooking for 2 hours so far; I have another 2 hours until Sandy arrives to open, so I need to crack on.

I really need to hire someone else.

I start making my rice crispy tarts before placing them in the oven and taking out my savory pastries, putting them on the rack to cool, and then I start making the icing for the cupcakes and then decorating them. Another hour later, everything is cooked and decorated except the wedding cake. I'll do that in a little bit. I've already molded the marzipan flowers, so it shouldn't take too long. The groom will be picking up the cake at 12.

By the time I have everything in the countercase and the kitchen cleaned up again, Sandy unlocks the front door, and I smile at her before I turn the coffee maker on. She flips the closed sign to open and then kisses my cheek before taking her bag to the staff room. The door opens again, and I look up but freeze, then roll my eyes at the clothes she's wearing.

Short shorts that her ass hangs out of with heels so high I'm worried she'll break her ankle and basically a bright pink bra—really, it's 8 a.m.

She looks down at me, but I ignore her attitude and wait for her to order, "a few white chocolate nut macaroon cookies." I nod and bend down to get them for her when my phone beeps. I open the message and smile. Logan has sent me a photo of himself; he's sitting at a gas station outside of Dallas. God, he looks hot with a bandana over his mouth and nose in his biker gear.

His bright blue eyes shine.

I shake my head and quickly set it as my cover on my phone before I grab Bubbles' cookies and place them on the counter. "$2.49, please."

She places the exact amount, then grabs the cookies, saying, "These are Axel's favorites; I can't wait to surprise him at the club with these in a little while." I nod my head, trying not to laugh; she's completely clueless and has been for a while now, which is how I think I'll keep her; she has no idea he spends most of his free days with me or how we're actually dating, and I know he won't be in town until tonight.

I smile and wave, "Have a good day." She huffs, pissed that I didn't take the bait, and leaves just as Sandy comes back out. I smile, then head to the back to start making more pastry before getting the marzipan cover for the cake done.

A few hours later, I had finally finished the wedding cake. I check the time quickly: 10:30 a.m., and I sigh in relief, placing the cake in the freezer until the groom picks it up. I start to wash up the pots and clean up the mess in the kitchen before I start making some more baked goods for the front counter when my phone rings. I wash my hands before grabbing it and smiling at the name.

I answered it.

"I thought you said you couldn't talk today."

"I wanted to hear your voice and to let you know Rosie called me." My eyes widen. Oh crap.

I clear my throat.

"Apparently momma decided to let her know how much of an idiot I am, and now I have to watch out for my life, which fucking sucks because it's been 3 months and you've forgiven me."

I can't help it; I burst out in laughter. I hear him grunt on the other end of the line, and I know he's rolling his eyes at me.

"I'm sorry, but come on, that's funny."

He chuckles. "Yeah, I guess. Fuck I wish I could just spend the day with you."

I smile at his words. "You're being sweet."

He hums, "Only to you, Princess."

My cheeks blush, and I shake my head. Someone in the background shouts his name, letting him know they are ready to roll out.

"That's my cue, darling. Talk soon."

Then he hangs up and I grin before I finish cleaning up my mess and making the rest of today's goodies, ensuring I made enough for the shelter too. By the time the groom had picked up his cake, I was exhausted. I clean the kitchen and start shutting everything down a little early then head out front to start cleaning up. There are only two people finishing up, so I send Sandy home and she hugs me tightly, even agreeing to take the goods to the shelter, making me chuckle. I wait for the couple to finish before I can close the till when the door opens. I look about to tell the person we're closed and sigh, great.

"Hey, baby." David says and I give him a small smile then grab my phone when it rings again from my apron, I clear my throat, "Just a second" he smiles his snarky fake smile, clearly not happy being told to wait for but tough shit, and I answer it without checking the ID.

"Hello."

"Did Bubbles pop by this morning?"

I smile, hearing Logan's voice.

"She did; she tried making out that you were at the clubhouse and she was surprising you."

He chuckles. "You didn't tell me before because?"

Oh dear, he sounds pissed, but I just chuckle while David narrows his eyes at me. Shit, I forgot he was there.

I clear my throat. "Because I didn't want to worry you while you were out of town. Besides, I quite enjoy pissing her off." He laughs, and I smile, which quickly drops when David crosses his arms over his chest, his face going red.

I sigh, not realizing I did it out loud.

"What's wrong, Princess?"

Shit, I clear my throat again. "Um, I, uh, have to go; David's here at the moment."

Logan growls, making me smirk. Yeah, not nice, is it, buddy?

"I'll speak to you later." I don't give him a chance to answer me; I hang up and look at David. His beady eyes were narrowing at me. I look towards the tables that did have people and notice that they are now empty. Shit. I'm alone with him.

I cleared my throat again.

"What can I do for you, David?" I try to be polite, but it's hard. I may not have loved him, but it didn't give him the right to fuck someone else. His cheeks are red, so I know he's pissed. I'm not sure why, though.

"Well, I wanted to come see my girlfriend, you know since I haven't heard from you in months." Both my brows rise to my hairline. Oh shit. He never actually saw me when I caught him with someone else; I literally just walked out of the restaurant bathroom and he was fucking the woman, which was 3 months ago. I laugh, like a full-blown laugh, making him narrow his eyes.

I try to calm down and place my hands up in surrender. "Sorry. That was rude of me."

He places his hands on his hips. His white shirt stretched more over his podge. "Want to explain where you've been, Ann?"

I cringe at his name for me; my father used to call me Ann, and I hate it.

I square my shoulders and state, "Well, I've been here, David, working while you've been fucking that woman behind my back in Dolly's restaurant."

His eyes widen before they narrow, and I just shrug.

"I found you with her; I literally just walked back out again. So, are you here to order something? If not, then I need to close and lock up because your showing up out of nowhere three months later is ridiculous." I say this as I walk around the counter and start to walk towards the door.

He grabs a hold of my arm making me stiffen as he sneers, "You don't get to say when we're over bitch. I don't care how long it's been; your fucking mine."

My eyes widen, and I burst out in laughter. "Well, tough shit, douche canoe, now get the hell off of me."

I twist my arm. I learned to use self-defense and get out of his grip, but he moves fast for someone so unhealthy. He grabs a hold of my bun and yanks me backward. I scream, and I fall onto my back on the floor, and he sits on top of me. My pulse quickens as memories from when my father did this enter my mind. He punches me once, then twice, in the face, making my head spin. I can taste blood. My instincts kick in, and I lean forward with my head as quick as I can and headbutt him in the nose. Blood squirts out of it, and he shouts, swearing, then hits me again. I start to lose consciousness; my head hurts.

Everything comes back to me from when I was just a small girl, wanting her mommy.

Just when I didn't think it could get worse, his hands go to my jeans, and my heart rate picks up, no, no, no, no.

I won't let him do that to me. He has his right hand keeping hold of both of mine above my head, and I quickly pull both my arms down, forcing him to let them go, and I start hitting him hard in the face. "FUCK!" he shouts as I hit his nose again, and he falls off of me. I twist onto my stomach and quickly get to my hands and knees, scrambling for the chair that's near us. Just as he grabs a hold of my foot, my hands grab the leg of the chair, and I swing it around, hitting him in the head. He screams in pain, then scrambles to the door when he hears people walk past my bakery as blood pours from his head, his breathing heavy.

He points at me and says, "This isn't fucking over, bitch," before making a run for it.

I crawl to the door and pull myself up by the handle. I lock it and bolt it before pulling the blinds. I try to walk around the counter for my phone but only get just past it when my legs give out, my arms are no longer able to keep a hold of the counter, and I fall to the floor.

Blackness starts in my eyes, and I pass out with Logan on my mind.

I don't know how long I'm out for, but banging on the front door to the bakery arouses me. Light shines through the blinds, so I know it could only be a few hours later or even in the morning. Then I heard his voice: "Lise, darling, you in there. Come on, Princess, open up. Mom and Dad are driving everywhere to try and find you, we're all worried. LISE."

The banging continues, but my body doesn't want to move. My face itches where the dried-up blood is.

He bangs again: "Annalise, if this door isn't opened in 2 minutes, then I'm knocking it down."

He's quiet for a few minutes until he curses.

"Fuck, I knew I should have popped by last night."

Suddenly there's a massive bang on the front door, and I know he's kicking it in, but blackness is trying to take hold again.

There's another bang and I hear someone say, "Brother, are you sure she's in there." I hear him growl, but I don't know what he says as I start to close my eyes.

Just as the blackness takes me, I hear a massive crash and then the roar of someone in pain.

Chapter 11

Axel

I'm aroused from sleep when someone bangs on my door. I look at the time: 7 a.m. What the fuck? I've only had 3 hours; we didn't get in until 3 a.m.

The banging continues, so I get up to open it in only a pair of shorts. When I open the door, I growl out,

"WHAT."

But my irritation quickly fades at the worried faces of my parents, and I instantly know—Annalise.

Fuck, I knew I should have dropped by hers when we got back into town.

"What happened? Is she okay?" I inquire as I grab my shirt and cut before changing into my jeans and getting my boots on. Momma has tears in her eyes, and my dad rasps,

"We can't find her. The bakery is closed, Sandy's out of town today with family, and her apartment is empty; her car hasn't been moved.

Fuck, I grab my gun and rush out of my room. The brothers are in the common room, and Misty, Trickster's old lady, is trying to console an inconsolable Rosie while I notice Ginger and Bubbles smirking, making me narrow my eyes at them. I walk over to Rosie, and she stands, throwing her arms around me as she cries out.

"You have to f-find her, p-please."

I nod against her head, then pull away from her after kissing her cheek. I look around the room.

"Alright fuckers, split up into teams of two, and tear this fucking town apart until we find her."

They all nod, knowing I've claimed her even if she isn't ready yet; she's their first lady.

I look towards the sweet butts and say, "Make yourselves fucking useful and clean this pigsty up, then make breakfast." They all look at me with their mouths open, but I don't give a shit. We don't pay them to lie on their backs and fuck brothers. This isn't a brothel. We pay them to fucking clean.

I look towards Hawk next and say, "You're with me." he nods once, and we both leave. When we get to our bikes, gut instinct has me looking towards Hawk, stating, "We'll try the bakery first."

He nods again, and we ride out at full speed.

I'm coming, Lise. I'm coming.

When we get to the bakery, the doors are locked and the blinds are down, but my gut is telling me this is where she is. I try the door, but it doesn't budge. Fuck.

"Lise, darling, you in there. Come on, Princess, open up. Mom and Dad are driving everywhere to try and find you; we're all worried. LISE." I bang again, but there's no answer. My blood boils, and I feel fucking panicked.

I bang again. "Annalise, if this door isn't opened in 2 minutes, then I'm knocking it down."

I wait to see if I can hear anything, but it's quiet.

I curse, "Fuck, I knew I should have popped by when we got back into town." I walk back a bit, then, using the bottom of my boot, I lift my leg and slam it into the door. The glass cracks a little, and I do it again. More cracking; fuck, this is good shit. My father probably.

I go to do it again when Hawk grabs my arm. "Brother, are you sure she's in there?"

I growl out, "My gut is saying she is." He nods, knowing my gut is never wrong, and stands next to me. We both lift our feet and together we slam them down on the door while people look on in shock. The glass smashes, and the door cracks open. I quickly go inside with Hawk on my heels when I see my girl lying on the floor, covered in blood.

I roar out in pain and run towards her while Hawk gets his phone out to call an ambulance. I kneel down next to her and gently move her hair from her face.

"Princess," I rasp.

She's still so fucking still. I check her pulse. It's there, but only just. Fuck, I look to Hawk and say, "The ambulance is on the way. I'm now calling your dad and then the sheriff to keep this under wraps."

I'm fucking glad we have the sheriff's office in our pocket. It helps that he's Stormy's blood brother.

I look back down at my girl, and my chest tightens with worry. I've only just found her. We haven't had time to live as one yet, and I can't lose her. I run my fingers through her matted hair and say, "I'm here, darling, I'm here."

5 minutes later, paramedics show up, along with brothers who stand by the door, keeping the nosy people of Parkerville out while my parents burst through the door.

Hawk pulls me back as my mother wails out,

"MY BABY."

Tears run down her cheeks, and my chest tightens. I walk over to her and grab her from my dad's arms, holding her tight while my dad wraps his arms around me.

I look at them and rasp, "The sheriff is keeping his men back; has Rosie been informed?" They both pale and shake their heads. Shit. I look towards the paramedics and see them about to lift her onto her back after placing a neck brace on her when I say loudly,

"Watch her back; she's at high risk of becoming paralyzed."

They both nod and slowly move her from her front. Her face is swollen and covered in blood, and rage overtakes my body. Her lip is busted, and her right eye is double the size. She has a massive cut going down the side of her right temple. My dad squeezes my shoulder as they walk past with her on a gurney. It's only then that I notice her jeans are undone, and I stagger back. My dad looks to see what got my reaction apart from the obvious, and he curses. We all follow out to the ambulance, where a crowd has formed, and as they get her inside, I rasp,

"Her jeans are undone."

They both pale and look, then nod as my mother pushes past us.

"I'm her mother; I will be going with you."

They nod again, and she gets inside but stops to look at me. Her mascara runs down her cheeks with her tears, and I know I can't fight her on this, even if I want to. I lean forward and place a kiss on her cheek.

"We'll meet you there." She sighs in relief and nods, and the paramedic closes the doors before getting in to drive off. I quickly ran to my bike but stopped to look at the brothers. Gunner, Trickster, and Buzz stand there looking pissed. "I need you to clean up the bakery and get some new doors. Box all the food for the homeless shelter, then have a look at the CCTV." They all nod, and I look to Gunner and say, "Ring out her till and bring it to my office at the clubhouse; Dad will take it to the bank later."

He nods and goes off with the others while my dad speeds off to the hospital. I sit on my bike and grab my phone, and with my gut churning, I call Misty. She answers on the second ring.

"Axel."

I clear my throat. "Put her on Misty, please." Her breath hitches at the rasp in my throat.

"Axel, have you found her?"

Shit, "We have. I need you to get one of the brothers to bring you to The General Hospital, Rosie."

She screams in pain, and Dagger comes on the phone and says, "Pres?" He knows I hate him calling me that, but he's in VP mode, so I ignore it.

I rasp out, "It's bad, brother; get her to the hospital."

Then I hang up and put my phone away before speeding off after the ambulance, hoping my girl makes it.

5 minutes later, I pulled up to the hospital, which should have taken 10 minutes. I quickly rush inside, about to head to the reception, when I notice my dad pacing. I rush over to him, and he pulls me into the waiting room where Momma is pacing. When she sees me, she rushes over and hugs me tight. I rasp, "Any word?" They both shake their heads, and I sigh, running a hand through my hair, when a doctor walks in with Doc, and I sigh in relief seeing him. He walks over to us with the other doctor at his heel.

"Pres," he doesn't get to finish when the other doctor, who is about to meet my fucking fist, opens his trap,

"I'm sorry, I understand that you're in a motorcycle club, but we can't dish out patient information."

My father growls, making the man's eyes widen, and he nods his head between my mother, him, and me.

"We are her parents by law, and she's his woman." The man nods, his head paling, while Doc scowls at the young doctor, who wishes he could just vanish. Shaking his head, he looks back at us.

"Sorry Pres. He is new. Ok, she's lost quite a bit of blood and had to have a transfusion; her eye socket is thankfully only bruised and not broken. I've managed to stitch up the laceration near her hairline by her temple. She has a grade 4 concussion that will be monitored in the hospital for a few days, but she got lucky."

I hear my parents sigh in relief, but I clear my throat, not wanting to bring this up, but I know I have to.

"Her jeans were unbuttoned when I got there."

My mother sobs while my father slowly closes his eyes, realizing he forgot about it with all the worry. Doc nods with a solemn look. "She's still not awake yet, but hopefully soon. We can't do a rape kit until we have her permission." I nod, and he pats my shoulder. "Someone can go and sit with her, but only one person at a time; she should hopefully wake in the next 12 hours. We have her on high-dose painkillers. A nurse will be with you soon."

Then he turns while the idiot doctor follows like a good little puppy.

I look towards my mother, give her a smile , and nod my head towards the nurse that's making our way, eyeing me and my father like fucking snacks.

"Go on."

She looks at me with concern, but I just smile at her and nod my head again, and she smiles and kisses my cheek before intercepting the nurse, who gives her a strained smile.

My father chuckles, "You just held off a war, son, because I know for a fact, you wanted to go in first."

I smirk and shrug. It was needed; we can't have Momma kicked out of a hospital. A few minutes later, Rosie rushes in with tears falling down her cheeks. I meet her halfway and hug her tight.

I rasp, "She's going to be okay."

She lets out a sob as Slicer and Ink hold back a little, both looking pissed that this happened to my girl.

Rosie whispers, "Find the bastard and put him 6 feet under."

I smirk, as do the brothers who heard her say, "I will." I promise.

The person who touched mine is going to wish he were dead. I pull back. ""Momma's just gone in there; Doc said only one person at a time." She just raises her brow, and we chuckle as she heads towards the desk. After a few minutes of tense arguing with the nurse in charge, she's taken to see her granddaughter, and we all chuckle. No one keeps their granddaughter from that woman or their daughter from my Momma.

10 minutes later Momma comes back out, "OK, you two quickly go in to see her before we get caught then me and Rosie will stay with her until you get back." We both go to protest, but she just puts her hands up and says, "Go find the bastard who did this to my baby." I nod while my father kisses her, and we head to see our girl. When we get into her room, Rosie is clutching her hand, and my father goes over to her while I freeze in the doorway. Fuck, she's covered in bruises and wires, with a bandage on her head and her face swollen. Pain like no other spreads through me, and I know, I know that she is my end, my world and that I am falling madly in love with her. With her smile, her laugh,

her kindness, and the quirky way she tries to tell a joke, she laughs all the way through it.

My father bends down and kisses her head. He whispers something to her, then looks at me, understanding in his eyes, "Come on, son." I just shake my head, rage flowing through my veins. My girl, someone did this to my girl.

Rosie looks at me, tears falling from her cheeks as she rasps, "You either get over here or I'll kick your ass for fucking another woman; I don't care how long ago it was or that you both are together now; I will do it." My eyes widen while my father snorts.

I quickly move forward, and Dad moves towards the door to wait for me. I run my fingers through her hair, and I lean down, gently kissing her forehead, cheeks, and lips.

I rasp, "I'll be back soon, Princess, and when I am, I expect to see your beautiful violet eyes."

I rub my nose along hers, then walk over to Rosie and kiss her cheek before both my dad and I head out of her room. My mother enters as soon as we leave and heads towards our bikes, going to the clubhouse with Ink and Slicer right behind us.

We arrive at the clubhouse 15 minutes later, a prospect lets us in, and we park up. It looks like all of the brothers are here except Trickster and Buzz. We head into the clubhouse, which goes deathly silent as we enter. The sweet butts look at us and pull their tops down even more, hoping to comfort us. Yeah, fucking right. We ignore them, and I shout,

"SWEET BUTTS FUCK OFF. CHURCH IS IN SESSION."

They all look at me with a mix of confusion and fury, but I don't give a crap. It's not every day I call for an all-out church. Once they're all gone to their rooms or outside, the 5 prospects go to all doorways to ensure they're not listening and stay clear, as I stated.

"Old ladies, can you please give us a moment for our meeting?"

I ensure I say it softly: these women don't try to stir shit up; they know their place when it comes to meetings. Unlike the sweet butts who don't give a shit, the old ladies have our respect.

They all smile at me, kiss their men, and leave to go outside. I look towards my club brothers,

"Sometime yesterday, my woman, Annalise, was attacked. She's lost quite a bit of blood and had to have a transfusion; her eye socket is thankfully only bruised and not broken, and she had to have stitches near the temple. She has a grade 4 concussion that will be monitored in the hospital for a few days. She was lucky." I see fury in every one of my brothers' eyes. I look at each one of them as I state, "I want this fucker found. I want his fucking head." The brothers bang their fists down on the tables, and Gunner stands up.

"I've found the CCTV footage but haven't looked at it yet. Flame is now connecting it to the TV."

I nod and then look towards the TV with everyone else. My heart rages in my chest as the video begins. I recognize the guy right away, and so does Flame, because he's the one who did a background check on the slimy fucker. I growl, "It's her ex-boyfriend David; he's up to his ears in debt; he was hoping she'd give him her inheritance after he heard the whispers around town of her mama having money before she was killed."

The men tense and growl. Then my body tenses as we watch him grab her hair when she goes towards the front door. We watch as he yanks her backward and sits on top of her. My hands fist as I watch him pummel into my girl's face, and pride swells when I see her try to fight back, making the brothers cheer her on as she leans forward and slams her head into his nose, but it doesn't deter him; he hits her again, his ring slicing near her temple, and you can see her body giving out; she's losing consciousness.

My breathing becomes heavy as my father picks up a chair and throws it against the wall when the soon-to-be dead man's hand goes towards her pants, undoing them while his other hand keeps hold of hers above her head. The brothers suck in a sharp breath before jumping up and screaming at the TV. Her fight or flight instincts kick in; she quickly pulls both of her arms down forcing him to let them go and she starts hitting him, hard in the face making him fall off of her as she twists onto her stomach and quickly gets to her hands and knees, scrambling but she's not quick enough because he grabs a hold of her foot trying to drag her back. I place my hands behind my head, my breathing heavy.

"COME ON, GIRL FUCKING FIGHT BACK."

Stormy shouts, rage erupts through his whole body, and my father's bent over, hands on his knees, as he watches the girl he sees as a daughter fight for her fucking life.

She manages to grab the leg of the chair and swing it around, hitting him in the head, and we all shout at the TV, fucking proud of her. You can see David scream, but we can't hear it. He points at her and says something before making a runner.

The fucking coward.

We all watch with pain on our faces as she crawls to the door, trying to pull herself up and lock it before trying to walk around the counter where she falls, blacking out. Flame stops the video and rasps,

"This happened yesterday at 12:30 pm."

My breathing picks up, we didn't find her until 7:30 this morning. Guilt builds in my chest.

"She was lying there in her own blood for 19hours," Butch growls, and I look towards my brothers as fury takes over me,

"Fucking find him. NOW."

        They all bang on the tables and leave to start searching and the women all trail back inside looking concerned, but I ignore them and head back to my bike. I needed to see my girl with my father right behind me.

Chapter 12

Annalise

My head feels fuzzy, and my eyes feel like they are glued tight. I try to move but groan out in pain.

My whole body is aching.

I try to open my eyes, but my right one won't, and I start to panic. I can hear beeping.

Am I in the hospital?

What happened to me?

My mind feels hazy. I feel a hand lift my left, a thumb stroking over it, and I slowly open my left eye, my right refusing to play ball. Looking around, I see I am in the hospital, and when I look to my left, I see Logan sitting in a chair, looking down at our joined hands.

He looks sad.

"L-Logan?"

His head shoots up, and relief spreads across his face as he stands and places a kiss on my forehead before placing a little one on my lips. He rests his forehead against mine, his eyes bloodshot, his hair a mess.

"Fuck Princess."

I place my hand on the side of his neck, rubbing it slightly with my thumb.

I rasp, "What happened?"

He looks at me with concern.

"What do you remember, darling?"

I furrow my brows and try to think hard: "I remember Bubbles coming into the bakery and you calling."

He nods, "OK, what else, darling, think hard."

I shake my head a little, instantly regretting it because of the pounding and dizziness making my hand tighten on his neck. He runs his hand through my hair. "I remember thinking of closing early. Then David..." I stop, my eyes widening, "He attacked me."

Logan nods and then kisses my head before pressing a button, making my hand drop. He comes back to the same position, sitting on the edge of my bed right next to me, and places my hand back on his neck, making me smile.

He smiles back.

"I got in at around 3 a.m.; I wanted to come see you, but I didn't want to wake you, and I wish I had." He shakes his head, guilt written all over his face, his brows furrowing. I move my hand from his neck and rub it, rasping.

"You didn't know."

He shakes his head again and takes my hand, kissing it.

"I don't care; I knew he was there because you hung up on me and I was pissed you had. I should have called back, but I just didn't realize he was dangerous. We didn't find you until 7:30 the next morning, darling. 19 hours—that's how long you were on your own—hurt. We saw the CCTV, and I've got to say, I'm fucking proud of you, my little warrior."

I smile a little, then state, "He said it's not over; he's going to come back."

He nods. "He won't be back."

His face is serious, and I know, without a doubt, he won't be back.

I sigh in relief. "You found him?"

He just smirks, "This morning, the fucker was hiding out at his latest flings house." I just sigh in relief, but then concern for the man who's turning into my universe churns through my gut. He must see the look in my eyes, well-left eye, because he leans his forehead against mine again. "I promise nothing will happen to me, and I mean nothing. He's in mountains worth of debt. His plan was to try and take the money your mama left you to pay some nasty people. They'll all think he ran out of town."

I nod as a tear falls. I did suspect that's what he was after before I caught him cheating, but then I just ignored him. I really wish I hadn't given the slim ball my virginity now. Another tear falls, and he kisses it away.

"You are safe, princess, I promise."

I nod and close my eyes, relishing in his comfort when someone walks into my room and clears their throat. We both look at a man who looks to be around Dead Shot's age; he has short brown hair and brown eyes with a tattoo showing just above his shoulders around his neck, but he has a kind smile.

"It's good to see you awake, Annalise. I'm Doctor Thomas, also known as Doc in the club, Hawks Dad."

I smile as he rounds my bed, the opposite side of Logan. He shines a light into my left eye, making me wince. He hums, then gently pries the right one open. It's all blurry, but he just hums again, making me scared, so I clutch Logan's hand while he does a check over me.

Once done, he smiles.

"Ok, you still have a concussion, so you'll need monitoring when you're discharged for about a week. Your right eye is healing perfectly. It will be a little blurry for a while, but it should heal with no problems.

I sigh in relief. "How long until I'm discharged?"

He smiles gently. "Two days, and I'll discharge you, but only in the care of someone. You can't be alone for a week."

Shit, I'll just have to stay with Grams. I know Logan and I are not ready for that yet, so I nod.

"Ok, I'll let you rest, and a nurse will be in to check you frequently." I nod again, sighing when he leaves. I look at Logan and see him smile at me. I scoot over, and he grins, climbing in next to me. I lay my head on his chest, his arms going around my shoulders, and I close my eyes.

He rasps, "Sleep Princess."

And I do, feeling safe and content, just like I have the many times he's snuck into my bed in the past 3 months.

I don't know how long I sleep, but I'm woken by some whispering while a hand runs through my hair. I slowly open my left eye, my right still not able to open yet, and I lift my head off of a hard chest, looking up to see Logan smiling down at me.

"How are you feeling, Princess?"

I smile a little and rasp, "OK." He nods and gently moves my hair out of my face.

I look towards the chair to my left and see Dead Shot sitting in it, relief spreading across his face.

"Hi, baby girl."

I smile, "Hi Daddy."

His eyes glisten with unshed tears while Logan squeezes me tightly, approving. We have had many conversations about what I should call his parents. He was all for me to give them the titles they both deserved, but I just didn't know. I thought maybe it might be weird because we're seeing each other now. Well, I'm trying to date anyway to see where it leads, but he just laughed when I mentioned it to him. As far as he's concerned, we didn't grow up together; his mother ensured we didn't because this is what she wanted—me and Logan together. And he is right; they do deserve the titles.

They may not be my parents by blood, but they're still my parents.

Dead Shot gets up and kisses my forehead before sitting back down. He grabs my hand and says, "It's about time, sweetheart." I grin at him and shrug, making him chuckle. I look around the room but don't see anyone else.

"Where's?" Logan doesn't let me finish.

"We sent them home, darling. You've been asleep for over 24 hours, and we were starting to get worried. Doc thought you may wake with memory loss; they needed rest."

I nod my head as guilt starts building up in my chest.

Dead Shot scowls at me, "None of that Annie girl. This wasn't your fault, so don't feel guilty about the ones who love you staying by your side; you hear me." I sniffle and nod my head again when the door to my room opens and my Grams walks in with Cammy right behind her. She comes to a halt when she sees I'm awake, making Cammy walk into her.

Dead Shot and Logan chuckle.

Her eyes swell with tears.

"Rosie, what on earth?"

Cammy stops mid-sentence when Grams rushes over to me and hugs me tightly.

"I'm okay, Grams."

She shakes her head and says, "You took 10 years off of my life, pumpkin." I squeeze her tighter, ignoring the dull ache in my head. I hear a sob as Grams pulls back, and I look towards Cammy. I tilt my head, my brows furrowed in concern, as she stares at me wide-eyed; it's like she's frozen.

"Momma, come here."

But she doesn't move.

"Cam baby."

Again, not moving, just staring at me with tears falling down her cheeks.

"Mom,"

I rasp, and I hear my grandmother gasp as Cammy sobs, snapping out of it and rushes over to me. She takes my face in her hands and kisses my forehead before hugging me tightly.

Logan continues to play with my hair while he rubs a hand down his mother's back. Once she's calmed down, she pulls away, her hand cupping my cheek on the left side. She smiles at me with her mother's smile, and I finally feel whole.

A few days later, I'm sitting on the bed waiting to be discharged and for Dead Shot to arrive to pick me up. Logan said he would, but he had some business to take care of, so I didn't argue with him. He's spent the past two days by my side, barely sleeping.

About 5 minutes later, Dead Shot walks in, waving my discharge papers, and grins at me.

"Ready to go home, Annie girl?" I smile and nod my head frantically, then instantly regret it. I don't get dizzy now, but my head still aches from time to time, and I can finally open my right eye, which stopped being blurry this morning.

Dead Shot grabs my bags, then helps me into the wheelchair, which is apparently necessary, and we head to the club's 4x4 truck and finally head home. I sigh when I sit in the passenger seat, happy to be out of the hospital. I lean my head against the window and watch the world as we drive by. After we've driven for 10 minutes, I get confused when I notice our surroundings and look at him.

"Dad, why are we heading to the clubhouse?"

He grins at his title and then states, "I just have to pick up some paperwork real quick, sweetheart."

Oh, I nod and go back to the world, watching until we pull up outside of the gates. The prospect lets us into the compound, then shuts the gates again, and Dead Shot parks up. He helps me out and keeps hold of my arm as we walk through the doors of the clubhouse, my legs still a bit shaky since being attacked. When we get inside, I notice Grams and Cammy at the same table they used when I was last here. I haven't been back since, despite dating Logan for the past 3 months. I thought it would be better without all the sweet butts around us trying to cause crap, though they still try, especially Bubbles. She likes to come into my bakery and try to get a reaction, and apparently, she also broke into Logan's room.

He had found her sitting on his bed naked. I really hope he burned those sheets.

Star rushes over to me and hugs me gently as tears fall down her cheeks. Flame tenses when he notices them and quickly pulls her back, putting his arm around her, making me smile while I rasp,

"I'm ok, I promise."

She nods and wipes her cheeks. "I know, I was told, but seeing you in person confirms it for me. I spoke to Sandy, and she's running the bakery for you; I'm helping a few hours a day too."

I smile and kiss her cheek in thanks when Logan walks over to us looking absolutely gorgeous in his jeans that hug his legs and ass perfectly, a tight Henley t-shirt and cut with his hair messy on top, causing my smile to widen, and he grins at me. He wraps his arms around my waist and gently kisses me in front of everyone, making me blush.

He chuckles, then rasps, "I have a surprise for you, darling."

I raise a brow at him as he bends down, placing an arm under my legs and another across my back so he can lift me, and I yelp in surprise, making everyone chuckle. He walks past the bar where most of the sweet butts are scowling at us, but we ignore them, and he heads down a hallway that has a few doors shut while my arms are wrapped around his neck. Coming to the last one, he unlocks the door and then enters, and my mouth drops open in surprise. It's beautiful.

Light gray walls with a midnight mural on the back wall that's clearly Star's work, it smells fresh too. A king-size box bed with a metal headboard and matching dark blue side tables on either side, a dark blue dresser, and a dark blue comfy chair sat near the window with a dark gray rug. He moves towards a door with me still in his arms and opens it—a large bathroom with a separate shower and what looks like a jacuzzi bath. Then he heads to the other door and opens it. A his-and-hers walk-in closet with... all of my clothes. I look at Logan in confusion, my hands still wrapped around his neck, and he clears his throat.

"I know I didn't ask, but to be honest, I thought you'd say no, but I want you to stay here to recover."

My eyes widen in shock as he walks over to the bed and places me on the edge of it. He kneels and takes my hands, rubbing his thumbs over the back of them, and smiles gently.

"I know you could go stay with Rosie, but honestly, darling, I want you here, with me, where momma and dad could help you if I'm not in or one of the brothers, and I know you're not ready to stay in your apartment yet. Please, Princess. Your Grams is okay with it; I just, I need you here." His eyes stare into mine so I can see his sincerity, but my heart rate quickens, unsure if it's the right move, especially with women here wanting to skin me alive.

I clear my throat. "Logan."

He shakes his head, knowing I'm about to turn him down. He leans forward and gently kisses me, rasping, "Please, Princess. In this room, I had Momma and Rosie redecorate it just so you'd be comfortable. I had the bathroom re-done. Please, I know it's only been a few months, but please." I sigh and lean my forehead against his, making him smile as he rubs his thumbs on either side of my jaw.

"Trial basis."

He grins wide.

"But if I feel uncomfortable, you will take me to Grams'."

Nodding his head, he kisses me, and I kiss him back, loving the feel of his lips against mine. I smiled into the kiss, making him smile back. He runs his fingers through my hair, frowning at my bandage.

"I'm ok."

He nods, then kisses the bandage. "You want to lie down for a bit, or do you want to go sit with Rosie and Momma?"

I smile at him and rasp, "Sleep. My head and right eye ache."

He nods, then lifts me up again, making me giggle.

                        He smiles at me as he pulls the dark blue covers back and lays me down. He takes my shoes off, covers me with the duvet, and kisses me again. "I'll come and check on you in a little while; sleep, darling."

I sigh and slowly close my eyes, falling into a deep sleep, feeling safe surrounded by Logan's smell of spice and wood, all while hoping I'm not making a mistake.

Chapter 13

Axel

I smile as I watch my girl fall into a deep sleep, wanting nothing more than to climb in beside her, but I have someone to finally get rid of. I make sure to lock the door after I shut it, not risking her safety.

Especially after I accidentally left it unlocked last week and Bubbles was sitting on my bed naked, I kicked her out and told Lise, knowing Bubbles would try to turn it around against me, and I know Lise could unlock the door from the inside if she wakes.

I turn and head to the common room.

My momma is sitting on my dad's lap while Rosie sits next to them, and I head that way, ignoring Bubbles' scowl. I swear I'm going to boot her out if she continues. I lean down and kiss Momma's cheek, then Rosie's, and state, "She's asleep and thankfully agreed to stay here on a trial basis."

Rosie smirks. "Does she know that you've basically moved her in permanently?"

I smirk back, "No, she does not, but she will. I've basically emptied all of her personal belongings from her flat; she'll notice them when she looks around our room. I just hope she doesn't run scared. I know it's only been a few months, but she's mine." I look toward my dad and smile. "Her cut should be here next week."

He grins wide while my momma squeals, causing everyone to look over with raised brows, and she shouts,

"MY BABY ORDERED AN OLD LADY CUT."

I chuckle as the clubhouse cheers while the sweet butts' mouths drop open. I shake my head. "Ready, Dad?" He just smirks, and I get up, placing two fingers into my mouth, and whistle, "Alright brothers, you know who you are; let's go."

Stormy, Dad, Buzz, Gunner, Flame, and Hawk all head towards the basement while all the other brothers grin and smirk. I follow getting antsy to finally end this fucker after what he did and then tried to do to my girl.

When we get into the room, I smirk.

David is sitting tied to a chair in his boxers. His stomach is hanging a little between his legs, and his red hair is a mess and greasy. When he hears us, he opens his eyes, and they glitter bright green with rage. "Release me, and I'll pretend this never happened," he rasps with fury, and we all just laugh.

I remove my cut, handing it to my dad before I stalk over to him and get in his face.

"Just like you'll pretend that you didn't nearly kill my old lady?" Fuck, it feels good calling her that, even if she doesn't know it yet.

He furrows his brows in confusion. "I don't even know your whatever."

I just smirked. "Really, I mean, the reason you wanted her was for her inheritance, right?"

His eyes widen, and he rasps, "Ann."

My father growls and walks over. I step back just in time when my father punches him in his already swollen nose. David screams, and blood pours as my father growls.

"Annie girl hates that nickname, so don't fucking call her that again." I raise both my brows, knowing now is not the right time to ask. I'll ask my girl later and look towards the soon-to-be dead guy, and I state,

"You see, after you cheated on her, my mother and her grandmother decided to set us up. I haven't looked back since. Now you have to pay for touching what's mine."

His body shakes. "I -I didn't hurt her badly, though."

I just snorted while Buzz growled out, "No, you just nearly broke her eye socket and gave her a grade 4 concussion that had her unconscious for hours. Oh yeah, and you also tried to rape her."

He shakes his head. "No, no, she's lying. I didn't try to rape her. I swear I didn't."

Panic overrides his voice, but I look at him with dead, cold eyes.

"We've seen it on her CCTV."

His eyes widen and he pisses himself. I shake my head in disappointment while the brothers chuckle. I haven't even started yet. I walk over to the far side wall, grab my axe, and grin wide, turning back to the piece of shit.

"So, you think you can hurt my girl?"

His body shakes from fear. "P-please, I'm sorry. I-I won't g-go near h-h-her again, p-please."

Tears run down his face, but I feel no sympathy, no guilt; he shouldn't have touched what's mine. I bring the axe up past my shoulders with both arms, and David starts screaming and shouting, but I ignore him, swinging the axe down and chopping it into his kneecap. I grin while he screams out in terror and pain.

I hear Buzz muttering in the background.

"I don't get it; his road name is Axel, yet his signature move is with an axe. Why not just call him Axe?"

I snort, shaking my head when Stormy responds.

"Because Axel sounds cooler than Axe."

                        I look in time to see Buzz nod his head like it makes sense, which it fucking doesn't. I mean, come on, Axel is what you use on a car; he just doesn't want to look like a prat that he'd gotten mixed up on his bloodlust when Butch called me it when I was 8 and they gave me my road name. Shaking my head, I turn back to the weasel to see he's passed out; fucks sake.

I roll my eyes and look towards Gunner, who's silently laughing at Stormy's logic, knowing he fucked up, and I nod to our 'guest'; he just smirks and grabs the saltwater in the bucket. I step back just in time for Gunner to throw it over him, shocking him awake, the salt water burning through the gash on his kneecap, and I grin. I grab the handle of the axe and yank it out of his flesh, and he screams again.

I get in his face, his eyes full of fear as I sneer.

"Now, how about we lose the hand that tried to unbutton my woman's jeans, shall we?" He shakes his head frantically, "p-p-please, p-p-please, I-I'm s-s-so s-sorry, p-please."

I just tsk at him, "Yep, so sorry that you made sure to tell her that you'll be back." His eyes widen, and I swing the axe again, chopping it through his wrist like it was butter. Blood spurts everywhere, and his eyes roll into the back of his head. I hear the men chuckle, but I don't turn around; instead, I end this early because I want to go check on my woman. I bring the axe up again, and I swing it, slicing through his neck, his head barely hanging on.

See you in hell, fucker.

"Fuck, that's gross." I hear Buzz gag out, making us all laugh.

I chuck the axe into the bucket of disinfectant and head towards the shower. I throw my clothes in the bin there and set it on fire before I shower quickly and change into fresh clothes. My dad's waiting for me when I get out of the changing area and hands me my cut, grinning like a loon. Buzz and Stormy are wrapping the body up while Gunner and Flame get started on bleaching the basement while my dad and I stay back to make sure nothing has been missed. After 20 minutes, two of our prospects come down, and with Gunner, they take the body out through the hidden wall we have to the right of the basement. It's a tunnel that goes under the town and comes out in the basement of the funeral home that we pay a fortune to keep in business in order to keep our dealings under wraps. They'll burn the body and collect the ashes, throwing them in the Hudson River.

The rest of us head back upstairs once the others have also showered and burned their clothes, all while Hawk bitches about not changing his shirt before coming down, making Flame snort in amusement.

When we get back upstairs, the sweet butts try to flock to us, but all of us except for Hawk ignore them. Apparently, Buzz has his eyes on someone, and Flame, well, he just goes straight over to Star, who's sitting with Momma and Rosie. I lock eyes with Rosie and give a subtle nod, and she physically relaxes. Then I pat my dad's and Stormy's backs before heading towards my room in need of seeing my girl. Bubbles tries to intercept me, but I just scowl at her and walk around the table near her instead.

Bitch needs to learn her place.

When I get to the room, the door is being opened, and my beautiful girl, full of bruises, black and blue, walks out wearing her pajama pants and one of my Henleys making me smile. She looks up in shock when she nearly bumps into me and my hands go around her waist, pulling her close. She looks up at me like I hang the moon, her eyes full of love, and I smile down at her,

"Hey, darling."

She grins and lays her head against my chest, right over my heart, her arms squished between us as she lets me hold her.

"Hi."

Her voice is raspy, full of sleep, and I lean down, placing my nose against the top of her head, breathing in deeply, loving the orange and strawberry smell.

"How are you feeling?"

She just shrugs and says, "Hungry, but I was also wondering why all of my pictures and little trinkets are in your room from my flat?" Her stomach rumbles to confirm her hunger, and I chuckle, ignoring her question while grinning like a loon at her, making her chuckle. She's onto me, but I don't give a shit. I lean down and pick her up, making her yelp,

"Lo, I can walk."

I smile at her nickname and hum in agreement. "Yes, but you feel so much better in my arms."

She giggles and shakes her head at me before leaning down and placing her nose in the crook of my neck, making my heart melt. It took us a few months to get to this point. When I fucked Sugar, I royally screwed up, and the fact she was willing to give me a shot makes me the luckiest asshole going. She brightens my day.

I carry her back to the commons but swerve off to the left and into the kitchen. A couple of the sweet butts are standing around yapping, and I clear my throat. When they notice me, they stand up straight and try to pose sexy, and I roll my eyes while Lise just chuckles silently. They still stand there despite seeing me with a woman in my arms, and I snap,

"OUT NOW."

Their eyes widen, and they run with their tails between their legs while Lise bursts out into cackles. Shaking my head, I place her on a chair at the table we have here.

"Alright, you laughing, Hyena, what do you fancy?"

She just grins at me, and I sigh, dropping my head. Anytime I cook, she only wants one flipping thing.

"a juicy burger?"

She chuckles, "Yes, please."

I grin at her and kiss her forehead.

"Anything for you, princess."

I get the frying pan out and place a drop of oil on it, letting it heat up. I go to our commercial fridge and grab four patties, some lettuce, and some tomatoes before getting the buns out of the storage cupboard. I place the buns under the grill for a few minutes before frying the patties. The smell instantly flows through the kitchen, and I can hear her stomach grumble again, making me smirk, but she doesn't notice.

She's too busy watching me move around the kitchen with a lazy smile on her face and love shining through her eyes. I think that's one of my favorite looks on her.

I flip the patties when the door opens, and my dad walks in with innocent eyes that don't fool anyone. I see my girl bite her lip to stop her laughter, then wince quickly, letting it go and making me glare at her. A little blood drips from her now-reopened split lip. I quickly hand the tongs to my dad, who places a few more patties in the pan as I grab some tissue.

I rush to her and kneel, gently placing the tissue on her cut. My brows furrow with concern.

She places her hand on my cheek and rubs my jaw with her thumb.

"I'm ok."

I just shake my head. I hate seeing her hurt.

"Should I call Doc?"

She just smiles at me gently, still rubbing my jaw. "I'll be okay, I promise. I just forgot is all." I sigh as she takes over, holding the tissue, and then smirk when she orders me around. "Go make me my burger before Dad burns them." I place a quick, lingering kiss on her forehead, then grab the tongs back off Dad because she's right, he always burns them.

"Can you get some more buns?"

He grins and rubs his hands together, making me and Lise chuckle as he rushes to the pantry.

10 minutes later, the burgers are done, and Dad takes four out to the common room. One each for Rosie and Momma and two for himself while I sit next to my girl. I place two on her plate, leaving two on mine, and whatever she doesn't eat, I will. I move my hand towards the inner side of her thigh and leave it there as I start eating. She grins at me, making me smile.

I lean forward and place a gentle kiss on her lips, then continue eating when we hear a groan of complaints about not getting some food, causing us both to chuckle. As she takes a bite, she moans out, causing my dick to harden, and I squeeze her leg in a warning. She looks at me wide-eyed, then blushes, making me chuckle as we continue to eat in silence.

It's the one thing I found refreshing.

She'd rather eat her food than gossip. Once we're both done, I make her a cup of tea and then clean up while she drinks it before I pick her up again and take her back to our room, completely ignoring everyone else.

When we get inside, I lay her on the bed before locking the door. I hang my cut up, then climb on top of her, resting between her legs as she puts her arms around my neck, and I run my nose along her cheek, making her smile. I ensure to keep my hard-on away from her. "I like having you here, in my bed, in my room."

"I like being here; I feel safe and at home, which I guess is a good thing, as it seems as if you've basically moved me in."

I grin and lean down, gently kissing her lips once, twice, and three times. Then I rub my nose along hers, still ignoring her questioning look, and she giggles. She pulls me closer, forcing the lower part of my body to hit between her juicy thighs, and she gasps as I groan.

"Darling, we can't; you've just gotten out of the hospital."

Fuck do I want to though, 3 months, 3 fucking months I've had to hold back. She smiles sweetly at me, then leans forward, kissing my lips gently once, twice, and three times before I take over the kiss. I lick the seam of her lips, and she opens for me, my tongue tangling with hers while my body, involuntary, decides to grind down, rubbing my jeans-clad hard-on against her trouser-covered pussy. Fuck, that feels good. I slow the kiss, knowing we can't go any further, but she bites down on my bottom lip, making me groan.

She rasps, "Please, Logan, I promise I'll tell you if I hurt. I want you." I groan again, putting my head in the crook of her neck and breathing her in before I decide, Fuck it. I know she's not stupid; she'll tell me if she can't take it, and I gently nip and kiss her there before slowly kissing down. I grab the edge of her shirt, moving my body a little so I can gently take it off of her. Her bare tits freeing; fuck, she hasn't got a bra on; how did I not notice that?

"Fuck, darling, your tits are perfect."

I rasp before I gently circle a nipple with the tip of my tongue and then gently suck it into my mouth. She gasps then moans, her hips moving for friction, and I smile before going to the other breast, giving it the same attention as the other one before slowly kissing down her flat stomach. I grab the edge of her trousers and look up at her. She smiles at me, making me grin as I gently lower her trousers, taking her panties with them. I go and stand at the edge of the bed, looking over this beautiful woman that I get to call mine.

She doesn't shy away from my gaze, but a blush coats her cheeks, neck, and chest, making me smirk before I lower myself back down again, spreading her legs as I go, settling my head between them. I press my nose against her pubic bone and inhale. Fuck, she smells so sweet. I gently kiss her there before peeking my tongue out and gently licking over her engorged clit making her hips jolt. I press my forearm over her lower stomach to keep her still and lick again, just touching her clit, teasing her.

She gasps.

I slowly circle her clit with the tip of my tongue before flicking it gently, then going back to circle it, teasing her again.

She groans, "Logan."

I smirk then suck her clit into my mouth. Hard. She moans, trying to move her hips, but my arm is keeping her still. I glance up as I keep sucking on and off. Her eyes are closed, her head is tilted back, and she looks glorious. Leaving my arm on her lower waist, I move my other hand and gently prod her entrance with my finger, pushing in a little.

Fuck, she's tight.

I pull my finger back all while still sucking her clit off and on, making her moan like crazy, my dick straining against my jeans. I push my finger in again, this time all the way in. Her cunt squeezes my digit, and I groan around her clit wishing it was my cock inside her.

Soon, once I get her off first.

I pull my finger back, add in two, and start to gently move them in and out. My sucking on her clit increases as I curl my fingers and start rubbing her G-spot harder and harder. She screams, her cunt tightening around my digits as fluid gushes out of her entrance, and she squirts into my mouth, her body shaking. Fuck yes.

I groan, making sure to get it all before pulling my fingers out. Once her body has stopped shaking, I move my mouth to her entrance to suck up all her juices. I stand up and suck my two fingers into my mouth, keeping eye contact with my girl.

She blushes while I smirk.

"You ready, Princess?"

She nods her head and spreads her legs wider, making me grin. Her glistening pussy is on display. She was fucking made for me. I strip my shirt, throw it on the floor, then unbutton my jeans, pull them down, boxers and all, stepping out of them while grabbing my hard cock, squeezing it. Her eyes widen a little, and I smirk before I slowly climb over her, kissing her pubic bone as I go. When I get to her face, I lean one hand near her head while I reach into the drawer for a condom with the other.

"Are you sure about this, darling?"

She smiles gently and wraps her arms around my neck, pulling me down for a kiss.

I smile into it.

While my tongue tangles with hers, I somehow manage to sheath myself and press my cock at her entrance. Our kiss heats up, and I thrust forward in one full push, making her gasp into my mouth, while I stop at the hilt so she can get used to my size. When she starts to wiggle her hips, I gently pull out before thrusting forward again, harder. She wraps her legs around my waist, and I grab her hands, holding them against the mattress on either side of her head as I make love for the first time. Yes, I fuck, but not this. This feels right—perfect, like I finally found my missing piece. I keep my thrusts up, going harder but keeping the rhythm slow. I tilt my hips, hitting her spot inside.

"Logan."

She gasps, and her pussy tightens around me, squeezing me. She's close again. I pick up speed while also making sure my pubic bone rubs along her clit on each thrust in while our connected hands squeeze together, not once breaking eye contact; it's intimate and fucking perfect.

      Our breathing picks up as her cunt squeezes me tighter, and in one, two, three, four more thrusts, she breaks eye contact as her head tilts back and she screams out in pleasure. I lean down and take a nipple into my mouth, biting it gently before sucking it hard as my thrusts piston into her, getting her through her orgasm. I can feel my cock swelling as I cum into the condom, groaning around her gorgeous tit. I go to the other side, paying just as much attention to the other one while I slow my thrusts.

I look up into her eyes, letting go of her hands; hers instantly wrap around my neck while I lean my forearms against the mattress on either side of her head, caging her in. My condom-covered cock was still inside her.

I rub my nose along hers and rasp,

"I'm falling for you, Annalise, hard and fast. You are becoming my world."

Her eyes glisten, and she leans up, kissing me lightly, and says against my lips,

"Same."

And I grin, kissing her hard while being mindful of her split lip. I feel my cock perking up again, so I gently pull out, causing her to gasp in the kiss, and remove the condom, throwing it into the bin next to my bed. I'll empty it properly tomorrow as a precaution. I can never be too careful with these sweet butts. I tell you, kicking them out and hiring a cleaning service and a full-time cook seems like a better idea every day if I knew the brothers wouldn't throw a hissy fit, especially Slicer and Hawk, who love easy pussy.

        I quickly grab another condom and sheath myself again, all while kissing her, my tongue tangling with hers, and I thrust back inside her, causing both of us to groan out in pleasure. I make love to her most of the night before we fall asleep with her lying on top of me, her nose in the crook of my neck.

Fuck I'm a lucky bastard.

Chapter 14

Annalise

I wake up lying on top of Logan, my head resting on his tattooed chest while my legs entwine with his. He has one arm wrapped around my waist, holding me to him, while the other is high above his head.

I rest my chin on his chest watching him sleep for a few minutes and smile. He makes me happy, and if you'd told me three months ago that this is where I'd be, I'd probably laugh in your face. He was a playboy; he couldn't really keep it in his pants even when he was trying to convince someone to give him a chance, and I definitely had my doubts when he asked me to give him a chance that night, but I'm glad I did. He always puts me first, and seeing his panic after what happened to me by David just proves what I mean to him.

I gently rub my forefinger against his lips, and I look at the time: 5:30 a.m. I slowly and gently get off of him and head to the bathroom, taking some clothes with me while looking around the room, noticing more of my belongings from my flat, and I shake my head. The slick bastard has actually moved me in.

I chuckle, then close the door to the bathroom.

I go to take a quick shower when I see all of my shampoos and washes and shake my head with a smile on my face. I love that man. I continue to grab some more of my bathroom necessities while I smile wider, remembering about last night, my body ached in all the right places. Never did I think sex could be like that, or I could even have an orgasm, because, as a fact, I never did with him, who will no longer be named.

Shaking my head, I get into the shower and quickly wash myself and my hair before getting out. I towel dry my hair, then place it in a messy knot, then put on some panties and leggings with one of Logan's Henley's and my Ugg slippers, leaving the bra off.

When I leave the bathroom, I smirk when I notice he's grabbed my pillow, holding it tight in his sleep, making my heart flutter, and I head out towards the kitchen, thinking of making breakfast for everyone. When I get there, I frown at the mess, which makes me sigh in frustration: plates littered everywhere, old food spilled on the floor, and grease fat stained behind the cooker. I quickly get to work to clean it up, which takes me roughly an hour and a half before I look in the pantry and then the fridge and see that I have all the ingredients I need to make blueberry muffins, pancakes, scrambled eggs, bacon, French toast, and sausages. I grin and get to work, ensuring I leave the scrambled egg to the very last. There is nothing worse than cold, soggy eggs.

About an hour and a half later, after I've put the coffee pots on, Dagger stumbles into the kitchen with Jingles I think her name is. Her black hair is a complete mess, her makeup is smeared all over her face, and her hazel eyes look extremely bloodshot. I quickly make a black cup of coffee and a white one, then clear my throat. Dagger's head shoots up in surprise, while Jingles looks at me with wariness.

I just smile and hold the two cups out.

"Coffee black for you, Dagger, and a white coffee for you, Jingles; I don't know if you take sugar, but I've already loaded it up on the table." Jingles looks at me in surprise, while Dagger grins wide at me. He comes over and takes the cup.

"Thanks, sweetheart."

He goes to kiss my cheek, but I quickly move back, causing him to shoot his eyebrows high into his hairline, and I clear my throat.

"This has nothing to do with what you decide to do behind closed doors, you know, each to their own and all that, but um, I, uh, don't want Jingles juices on my face."

His eyes widen in shock while Jingles snorts out a laugh. "I like you, Annalise."

I chuckle while I hand her the coffee as Dagger narrows his eyes at me. I give him a grim smile. "Would it help if I told you I made breakfast? Everything's in the heating tubs." His grin returns, and he rushes to the food. Thankfully, I was smart enough to place two plates covered off to the side for me and Logan; the rest is fair game, though. I look towards Jingles, who's biting her bottom lip, looking at the food, and I smile gently.

"There's plenty Jingles, help yourself."

She smiles gratefully at me and makes herself a plate, and as soon as she disappears and Dagger sits down with a heap full, making me chuckle, more brothers come into the kitchen and look at everything in surprise, then to me, and I just shrug. One by one, they all kiss my cheek before grabbing a plate, and I smile, realizing I made enough for the brothers and their old ladies.

The men drop their plates near the sink and thank me as they leave half an hour later, and I turn with a sigh, knowing it's supposed to be the sweet butts job to clean up, but I know for a fact it will annoy me just sitting there so I get to work. I wash everything up, and thankfully I was smart enough to wash as I went this morning when I was cooking, and I put everything in the two dishwashers before wiping down the sides. I then empty the dishwashers and smile at how clean the kitchen is.

I make two cups of coffee, one for me and one for Logan, then grab the two plates I had saved, placing them on a tray with the coffee. Just as I'm about to pick up the tray to surprise my man, Bubbles and Ginger walk into the kitchen.

Bubbles smirks, "Well, wasn't it nice of you to make us a tray of food? It seems as though you fed everyone else."

Ginger smirks, but I just give them cold stares.

"Touch this food, and I'll rip your fake hair out; that's a promise."

Ginger takes a step forward like she's about to grab the tray, and I stand in front of it and sneer.

"You really want to explain to Logan why his breakfast was eaten by you this morning Ginger?" She pales at my words and backs off. Then I look towards Bubbles, who's glaring at me.

"Look at me like that all you want; not only did I do YOUR job from last night and this morning while still dealing with a concussion, but I also just cleaned up the whole kitchen after I was up at 5:30 making breakfast for everyone. If you wanted to eat, then you should have gotten here before the brothers, who had two helpings."

She goes to say something to me but pales at the voice of my man.

"Why in the fuck is my woman doing your jobs? Jobs, I pay you to fucking do?"

I smile and blush a little when he walks into the kitchen, making his way over to me. He kisses my head, and I look up at him shyly, full of innocence, knowing I'm probably in trouble for cooking.

He narrows his eyes at me and says, "You're supposed to be resting, not cleaning the kitchen that should have been done last night, then cooking a feast for the brothers and their women, and then cleaning the kitchen again."

He growls at me, and I just quirk a brow.

"So, you'll be alright with Ginger taking your plate, then that I saved for you and kept warm." He just narrows his eyes, making me giggle. "Bacon, scrammed eggs, French toast, pancakes, and a blueberry muffin." His stomach rumbles as he groans, and he kisses me gently on my lips. "OK, you are forgiven about cooking, but you shouldn't have cleaned, princess."

Bubbles decides to butt in, "She's lying, Axel. I cleaned the kitchen last night, and then after she finished cooking. All I asked was if I could have a plate, and she bit my head off; she's crazy."

I see Ginger make her way out of the kitchen, and I snort, then look at Logan.

"Isn't that a camera there in the corner of the room?"

Bubbles' face pales a few shades of white,

"He doesn't have cameras in the clubhouse."

He just chuckles. "Actually, we do, and yes, the kitchen is one of them."

I hear her mutter, "Fuck," making me smile.

"Bubbles, it seems as though you've decided to try and cause shit with my woman this morning, your on-bathroom duty for the rest of the week." Her mouth drops open, but he ignores her and takes our tray with one hand, then wraps his arm around my waist and says, "Come on, darling, you're going back to bed to rest."

I don't protest; my body's aching, but it felt nice to be back in a kitchen, especially the clubhouse one. Stainless steel everything, like a professional kitchen, is awesome.

We go into the common room, and Logan whistles loudly, "Bubbles is on bathroom duty for the rest of the week, as she just tried taking credit for cleaning the kitchen last night, then just now after my woman had finished doing it herself."

Slicer frowns, "Who cleaned it if it didn't get done last night then because I saw it before I went to bed, and it was bad, Pres, I'm shocked we didn't get rats bad."

I bite my lip and look around the ceiling, not making eye contact, when suddenly Stormy growls, "Annalise?" making me look at him sheepishly. He raises his brow and gives me a fatherly, disappointed look, making me clear my throat and say as quietly as I can to try and make them think I'm intimidated, hoping they'll back off.

"I'm sorry, I just wanted to say thank you to everyone for making breakfast."

Their eyes all softened, and I nearly sighed in relief until I remembered Dead Shot was here with Cammy, who was biting her lip to try and conceal her laughter, especially considering she's the one who taught me that little move—shit,

"Annalise Jessica, these men might not know you well enough yet, but I brought you up. Your full of shit."

That does it. Cammy can't help it. A full-blown laugh comes out of her mouth, and the brothers look at me confused.

"Dammit Dad I fricking had them."

Logan's body shakes next to me with silent laughter as the men all glare at me, realizing my little play, and I stomp my foot—yes, me, stomping my foot, like a fricking child.

"Give me a flipping break; if you'd seen the state of that kitchen, you wouldn't want to even think of touching the food I cooked, let alone eat it; the place was disgusting, and the baker in me just couldn't let it go, OK."

Logan can't hold it in any longer. He bursts out in laughter with the men following him, and I screech in frustration before stomping my foot again, then head towards our room, all while hearing Dead Shot state, "That's more like the Annie girl we know and love."

Another round of laughter follows.

I stomp into the room and plop down on the bed with Logan following, still chuckling and making me glare at him, but he just shrugs and passes me a plate of food with some cutlery.

"Darling, you had to know dad would out you."

I snorted, "It's like the 4th of July all over again when I told Tommy Sling, a boy who decided to try and take my sandwich I bought with my pocket money from the Mason shop and pull my hair when I tried to take it back, that my dad would shoot him in his 'willy' if he didn't give it back, and dad decided to tell the boy he'll just tell his parents after he started hyperventilating." I sigh, shaking my head. "Such a letdown."

Logan full-blown laughs, "How old were you?"

I give him an innocent smile. "6."

That does it again; he's nearly on the floor, laughing and making me smile.

"That day you begged your parents to let you go water rafting with your friends, so they decided to crash mine and Grams' BBQ at the lake. It was a good day." He grins and leans forward, kissing me gently before whispering, "Morning, darling." I smile, kissing him back, and when he pulls away, he narrows his eyes. "As much as I love that you cooked for us all, next time wake me up and I'll help, okay?"

I nod, knowing full well I won't, and he sighs, knowing it too, before plopping down next to me and taking a bite out of his pancake.

He groans. "Fuck, darling, this is good."

I chuckle and start eating, starving after our late-night activities. A blush coats my cheeks again, remembering how open I was with my body to him, but I ignored it.

When we're finished, he takes my plate, and I clear my throat. "When can I go back to the bakery?" He sighs and sits next to me again. He moves a piece of hair that's fallen out of my messy knot.

"Are you sure you're ready for that, Princess? Maybe you better stay in bed for today."

Shrugging, I say, "There's only one way to find out, though Logan and I feel fine; if I didn't, I'd let you know." He sighs again and nods his head. He kisses me one more time. "Get dressed, then, darling, we'll take the truck." I nod, grateful not to have to deal with the fear of being on his bike. It's exciting and thrilling at the time, but there's always the fear of injuring my back permanently. I'll progress, just not today, not when I need to see if I can handle being in my bakery after my attack. I don't need my anxiety building up before we get there.

I quickly change into a pair of jeans, leaving Logan's shirt on, then comb through my hair before placing it into a neat bun, calling it a day. I put my boots on, then go to find Logan, but not before I grab the tray of our dishes and lock our door. When I get into the common room, Jingles takes the tray from me, giving me a smile.

"Thank you," I say, and she pats my back, taking the tray into the kitchen for me, and I head over to Logan. He doesn't look at me as he continues to go through the paperwork in his hand that Buzz gave him, but he does lift his arm as I get closer, wrapping it around my shoulders. I lean my head against his chest, sighing. He looks at me in concern, but I just shake my head at him.

"It's just a small headache. Doc said they'd come and go."

He still furrows his brows but nods anyway, placing a kiss on my forehead, lingering a little before going back to his paperwork when he randomly says,

"What would you prefer, Princess, an open kitchen, dining, and living room combo, or having the kitchen closed off?" huh, weird. I look at him like maybe he's taken something, and he just chuckles.

"Humor me, Princess. Buzz here is starting a construction company with the club, and he has a client who can't decide which one is best."

Hmm, fair point.

I nod and say, "Open all the way, but not the dining area. I would rather have that closed off with a wall between itself and the living area but having a large archway in between itself and the kitchen." He smiles and nods. "What about the kitchen and the living area?" I tilt my head and think for a minute, then smile, "a 3-seater breakfast bar to separate them, but you can still see in either. It'll especially come in handy if the people who are designing it are to have kids."

He grins at me, then looks at Buzz, who is also grinning.

"You're a lifesaver, Annie."

I smile back, "Anytime."

Logan passes the paperwork back before slapping him on the back, then guides me outside all while ignoring Bubbles' glare.

When will the woman give up? It's been 3 months, seriously.

Not long later, we're standing outside of my bakery, staring into the double glass doors that look the same, just different. Star and Sandy are both hard at work in the bakery, and gratitude fills me.

Logan wraps his arm around my waist, rubbing his thumb along my hips.

"Breathe, Lise, maybe we should try again another day?"

I clear my throat.

I didn't realize my breathing had picked up.

Shaking my head, I look into his gorgeous blue eyes, which are looking back at me with concern.

"I'll be okay, with you, always with you." He smiles gently and guides me towards the doors.

When we enter, Star gasps, then rushes around the counter and squeezes me tightly.

"I'm so proud of you." She whispers in my ear.

                I nod and hold her back just as tight when Sandy rushes out of the kitchen with some more baked goods. She looks stressed, and guilt builds up in my chest. She places the tray on the counter, as I state.

"You deserve a raise."

Her head shoots up, eyes watering, and she rushes over to me, grabbing me tightly into her arms. I feel tears soak into my shirt, well, Logan's shirt and I hold her tightly,

"I'm ok."

She nods, then pulls back, checking me over from head to toe, and then nods her head again. I look around the bakery, and people are smiling wide after seeing me in person, and I smile back at them. My heart rate is still going hard and fast, and memories of that day are flooding my mind.

Logan wraps his arms around me from behind, kissing my head, and I start to calm down, slowing my breathing.

I look towards Sandy and say, "It'll take me a while until I'm comfortable being here, but I'll do most of the baking at the clubhouse until I can stomach being back behind the counter, and maybe we should consider hiring a couple more people, one for the counter and one for the kitchen? And maybe a kitchen assistant; we can afford it now." She smiles at me with a sad smile and nods her head. I look up at Logan from behind me.

"Is that OK?"

He smiles at me and says, "Anything for you, darling. A prospect can even bring the food if you're not ready, or either myself, Dad, or Momma will come with you. Whatever helps bring you back to where you deserve to be, and we'll vet anyone you think is a good fit."

I nod and gently kiss his jaw, making him grin at me. I look towards Star and Sandy, and they are both also grinning.

I shake my head at them before looking around the bakery again. I know it'll be tough, but this is my life, I need to get back to it.

Chapter 15

Axel – 2 months later

I sit here in our chapel, trying hard not to roll my eyes.

Fucking Snake.

He's found 95% of the traitors in his club but can't seem to locate the last 5% or the ring leader. He thinks it's someone on his council and has contacted me and my club for recon help. He wants to set a few of his brothers up doing fake runs to see if anyone betrays him, but he doesn't trust his men doing recon, which is where we come in.

"I know this is a lot to ask. I want an alliance, and this would be the perfect way to show it. If I give you the time and dates, I'll just need a few of your men over the next 6 months to see which of my men are going to fail. With each run, I'll ensure only the brothers who are going know the drop-off points." I look around our table as Snake speaks through the phone that sits in the middle of the table. Most brothers are focused on the phone, while others, like my father and the other old timers, are smirking, knowing how difficult this must be for Snake. We don't ask our enemies for help; it's a sign of weakness, but he's desperate.

I clear my throat, and before speaking, I look at each brother, who all give me a nod in agreement.

"Alright, we'll help out; I'll spare two brothers on each run. They'll follow in a different cage each time and watch their cues, then report straight to you."

I hear him sigh in relief.

"Thank you, Axel; I'll be in touch." Then he hangs up, and I look around the room and ask, "Are you all still good with that?" They all nod while my dad speaks up. "That wasn't an easy call for him, but it'll help with an alliance, and we could probably ease back with the guarding shifts around our family members and friends in the future."

I nod, knowing he's right. It'll make things a lot more peaceful. I look at Ink.

"How's the financing coming along?"

He gets his paperwork out and looks over it with a big fucking grin. "We're doing good, 94% up in profits in the club account, and it would seem words have gotten out about the construction business we're starting for Buzz; several people have stopped him asking about a job or to do something for them on their homes."

The brothers all bang on the table, and I smirk, knowing it was a good direction with Buzz.

"Fucking good. Get with Buzz and start interviewing people. Make sure you send every file to Flame so he can get a thorough background check before each interview. Ink nods, and I then look at Flame and say, "You think Star will plan our next fundraiser? This one's for the children's hospital."

He grins, "Of course, she will, she's in her fucking element planning that shit and she loves it. Plus, it helps that we give her a stall for free for her art." We all chuckle. I look around the room and say, "I'll talk to my woman about baking stuff for it too; with her now having three new staff on board, it'll be easier for her. Any more concerns?"

Stormy raises his brow. "When are you going to give Annie her cut, I know you have it?"

The men chuckle while I try my fucking hardest not to flinch.

I clear my throat. "Soon, she's not ready yet. Any more questions?" He and my dad furrow their brows but stay quiet while everyone shakes their heads, so I bang the gavel, "Meeting finished then, fuck off, and we'll meet again next week unless I've heard from Snake." The brothers all get up, leaving just me and my dad. I sigh and scrub a hand down my face, feeling frustrated and fucking pissed off, but that's been me for the past month, no thanks to my blond-haired beauty.

"How's Annie girl, son?"

I just snort, shaking my head. "She's back at the bakery doing what she loves."

I sound bitter. I know I do, but I don't know where my girl has gone. The loving woman from two months ago seemed to have vanished. I woke up one morning, and it was like she couldn't stand to be near me. For the past month, she has been pushing me away, and I don't understand fucking why. If I try to touch her, she'll move away from me. The only time she lets me even fucking kiss her is around the brothers and parents. We haven't had fucking sex in a month. I mean, my balls are turning blue, and then she had the fucking nerve last week to accuse me of sleeping with Bubbles after she apparently cornered her.

Bubbles has denied it, and usually, I wouldn't believe her, but my gut is telling me Bubbles hasn't been near my woman for a while, and my woman is trying to start fucking trouble for no apparent reason than to make me end it with her. My father tilts his head and says, "Why do you sound pissed, son? The past month, you've been like a volcano about to erupt.

I just shrug. "She's been spending more time at her flat above the bakery."

My father furrows his brows. "Have you told her about the house?" I know what he's thinking. She's figured out about the house that we've all been asking her subtle questions about, basically, what her dream house is, what kind of living area she would prefer, how many bedrooms she would like when she finally owned one, and whether she would like a pool. Would she prefer a cottage-style house with a wraparound porch or one in Victorian style?

We've been building it a few doors down from my parents for the past 5 months now. I know he thinks she's found out and she's freaked out by it, but that's not it

I shake my head. "Nope, she isn't aware of it. For the past month, she's been pushing me away, bit by bit, to the point of accusing me of fucking Bubbles.

My father's eyes widen in shock, and I nod my head, looking down.

" Yeah, and I can't even think about why she's acting this way. We were fine—more than fucking fine. We were happy. I'd been helping build her confidence back up with the bakery, spending all my free time with her, cooking breakfast together, then it's like a switch has flipped." I look at my dad after basically talking to the table and say, "I don't know what to do, Dad. I feel like I'm losing her, and I don't even fucking know why. I mean, she'll only fucking let me even kiss her if the brothers are around; otherwise, she shoves me away."

My dad's face is full of concern: "I'll see if I can get her to open up, son; if not, your mother will, but don't give up on her; clearly something's up." I nod, then get up, heading out of the chapel, not wanting to talk about this anymore. I'll get to the bottom of this. I did originally think she'd found someone else, especially after the cheating claim, but I know that's bullshit. She loves me; she might not have said it yet, but she does. It's in her eyes every time she looks at me, and even when she's trying to push me away, you can see the pain it's causing her to try.

Something happened, and I will find out, one way or another.

Going into the common room, I sigh when I see Bubbles and Ginger giving me bedroom eyes. You'd think after 5 months of not touching them, they'd get the fucking message. Shaking my head, I decide to go to my office for a few hours and get some paperwork done from the strip club before I go find my woman and fucking have it out with her because if she thinks I'm going to walk away all because she's being a fucking bitch, then she has another thing coming; she's mine just as much as I'm hers. I lock my office door and sit behind my desk, cracking on.

I look at the clock a little while later, and my eyes widen. 5 p.m.

                        Shit. I've been in here for four hours. Fuck. I rub a hand down my face, and I sigh, turning my computer off. I managed to do at least three-quarters of the club's paperwork and all of the strip clubs, but I need to see my woman. I lock my office door before heading to the common room, and I notice a lot of brothers hanging around.

Some with old ladies, some with sweet butts on their laps, eating burgers that looked to be cooked by Lise. The brothers have been treated for the past two months. Every evening, my woman makes them a full meal, and on Sundays, breakfast. I look around the room and notice Momma on Dad's lap with Rosie sitting near them. I see them in deep conversation, and I curse inwardly. I knew I shouldn't have opened up to my dad, fucks sake.

Shaking my head, I go to my room, seems as though my woman is nowhere to be seen.

When I unlock our door and head inside, I come to a halt. My brows furrow in concern when I notice Lise sitting on our bed, legs crossed, looking down at some kind of stick. Tears run down her cheeks, which are red from crying, and when she looks up at me, it's like a punch in the gut at the fear in her violet eyes. I rush over to her, kneeling. I put both my hands on her cheeks, cupping her face,

"Princess, what's wrong? What's happened?"

She just shakes her head and lets out a little sob, and I suddenly think maybe Dad's right; she knows about the house.

Fuck, shit.

"Ok, look, I can explain, darling. I know I should have told you instead of having people come talk to you about the house, but I wanted it to be a surprise."

Her brows go to her hairline in surprise, "house? What house?" I slowly close my eyes, fuck. She didn't know. "Logan, what house?"

I clear my throat and look into her beautiful red eyes. "You, uh, um, aren't upset over a house, are you?"

She just raises her brow and says, "No, but you're going to tell me what you're talking about before I hurt your already blue balls."

I narrow my eyes at her little dig at our lack of sex life making her smirk. Sighing, I get up and take hold of her hand that isn't clutching a stick. I look at it with furrowed brows, but she just shakes her head. "Uh, uh, mister, tell me what you mean, and then I'll let you know what's wrong with me."

I narrow my eyes again; amusement shines through hers, and I mutter, "You're lucky. I love you." She sucked in a breath, so I know she heard me, making me smirk. We haven't said the words yet, but I think it's time we get some things on the fucking table. I drag her over to the window and stand her in front of it, and I point to the houses.

"You see the light blue Victorian house?"

She nods. "Yeah, it's your parents' house."

I nod, then point a few doors down to the next house that has a building crew tidying up for the day. "You see that house?"

She furrows her brows. "The gray cottage style with a wraparound porch where there's a building crew?" I nod. "What about it?" She looks up at me, and I smile, leaning down. I kiss her gently on the lips, and she finally fucking kisses me back, so I deepen the kiss before rasping against her lips. "That's our house, darling; everything you've told the brothers you may like in a house is right there."

Her eyes widen in shock.

I run both my hands on either side of her head, through her hair.

"Princess, I fucking love you. Did you really think I'd make you live in this room forever?" Tears fall from her eyes again, and I wipe them away with my thumbs.

"You really love me?"

I smile, "With everything in me."

More tears fall.

"You built us a house? With 5 bedrooms, 4 bathrooms, a conservatory for breakfast mornings, and a swing seat on the porch for evening cuddles?"

She sobs the last bit, and I wipe more of her tears.

"Yeah, darling, I did. I even put in the open concept with the living room and kitchen, with a breakfast bar seating three separating them, as well as the curved archway from the dining room to the kitchen. And I ensured you got your dream kitchen too."

She sobs out again and then throws her arms around my neck. I catch her with ease, holding her tight to me, then even tighter when she whispers, "I love you too, so much. I'm sorry, I've been crazy this past month."

I smile into her neck and rasp, "I missed you, darling."

She sobs again. "I've b-been s-s-so stupid. I-I tried to p-push y-you a-away; I-I thought y-you d-d-deserved better."

Fuck, my woman. I gently pull her back a bit and cup her face again with my hands, wiping her tears with my thumbs. "Darling, you are my fucking world; do you hear me?" She nods, then goes to her tiptoes and kisses my lips gently before standing back a bit. I furrow my brows, but she just shakes her head and places the stick in my hands, and when I see it close up, I realize it's a pregnancy test. I still, fuck, it's positive.

She's pregnant.

I look up at her face as more tears fall, and she rasps, "I suspected this past month, but I just couldn't make myself take the test. My birth mother." She shakes her head and says, "I don't remember her. I don't want to leave my child in this world without a mother."

Ah, fuck.

This makes perfect sense.

I wrap my arms around her waist and pull her to me. "Princess, you may have lost your mother young, but you still have two more. They brought you up to be kind, loving, smart, and generous, and let's not forget fucking gorgeous and crazy as fuck." She smiles, and I pale when a thought comes to mind: "Fuck, if it's a girl, I'm going to have to get more guns and hide her from my momma." She giggles, and it's music to my ears. I gently kiss her again. "You're going to be an amazing mother, Annalise, and I know because you are already an amazing person; you saved me from myself, and I couldn't think of a perfect woman to start a family within a house that I built for them."

She smiles gently as a few more tears fall.

"And while I'm buttering you up, do you fancy baking for our fundraiser? It's for the children's hospital."

She full-blown laughs, "Of course."

Her brows suddenly furrow in confusion, "I don't understand how this happened though. We used condoms." I tilt my head; she's right, and while they're not 100% foolproof, what are the odds of falling pregnant after only having sex for one month?

Shit, it hits me.

"Fuck," I rasp, "remember when I told you I found Bubbles in our room before your attack?"

Her eyes widen, realizing Bubbles wanted to fucking trap me. Lise's cheeks redden in anger, and her eyes burn with rage.

Oh, double shit, bulldog 2.0.

I go to grab her, but she dodges my advantage, rushing past me and out of our room.

"INCOMING!" I shout loudly, trying to warn the brothers as I race after my woman. When I get to the common room, I see my woman racing towards an unsuspecting Bubbles who is sitting on Flame's lap, smirking at Star, who's decided to pack her stuff up as Flame tries to convince her to stay longer, I shake my head.

What an idiot!

I look around the room and notice all the brothers staring at Lise with wide eyes, and I hear Gunner mutter, "Fuck. Bulldog 2.0" making me snort. I continue rushing over to my woman, just not in time. She grabs Bubbles' hair and yanks her off of Flame's lap, making Star grin.

Bubbles screams, "OUCH, WHAT THE FUCK, GET OFF ME YOU CRAZY BITCH."

She does as she's asked, but grabs her arm and turns her around. Lise pulls her arm back and punches Bubbles in the nose, blood spurting everywhere.

"Holy shit." Dagger gasps as she pulls her fist back again while Bubbles screams, trying to protect her already probably broken nose, but not well enough because my woman manages to punch her again, and this time, we hear a crunch.

"That's gotta hurt." Slicer Chuckles as Bubbles falls to the floor. My eyes widen as my woman then decides to jump on top of her, wailing down with her fists while my mother, Rosie, and Star grin with pride along with the other old ladies who are cheering her on.

Chapter 16

Annalise

I sit on my and Logan's bed in our room after I've just cooked homemade burgers and fries for the brothers, my legs crossed, while I look at the unopened pregnancy box in my hands. For the past month, I have suspected, but I haven't wanted to confirm it because then it means it's real; it means it's not only me in danger.

I think back to a month ago, when I was at the bakery. It took me a while to be comfortable there, and now it's tainted again, and the only reason why I go to work and stay in my flat above the shop is that I know if I stay with Logan, who has stolen my heart, he will also be in danger. Fuck, he's already on 'his' radar, and if something happens to him all because I get to call him mine, it will kill me. He's become my whole world.

I wipe away the tear that's fallen and zone off in my memories while my stomach churns with fear.

I'm in the back of the kitchen making the sausage rolls and Danishes, finally feeling back to normal. Logan has been my pillar this past month, helping me come over my ordeal.

Sandy is out front serving customers when I suddenly feel like I'm about to be sick. I furrow my brows. I've been feeling sick for about a week now. I quickly remove my gloves and wash my wash hands before I grab a hold of the counter, taking a deep breath, then slowly letting it out. I try this a few times, but when the smell of the sausage comes through my senses again, my eyes widen, and I rush to the bathroom off to the side. I make it just in time to vomit in the toilet. Everything I ate this morning comes up until I'm dry-heaving.

I wait a couple of minutes to make sure it's passed before I go to the sink and rinse my mouth. I grip the basin and look up at the mirror. My face is pale, and I furrow my brows when I notice my boobs are a little bigger. When I touch one, I wince; they're sore. My eyes widen in shock. Fuck, fuck, fuck. Sore boobs, sickness, and vomiting. No, no, no, no. I think back to when my last period was, doing the calculations in my head, and I gasped. No, no, no, my period is two weeks late.

No, this cannot be happening. We haven't been together long, and we've used protection. How did this happen? I start to hyperventilate, trying to breathe through it.

What if he doesn't want kids?

What if he ends things?

My breathing gets heavier. Shit, I need to calm down. I may just be late because of stress, yeah, stress. I'll probably get my period today or tomorrow. Yeah, that's it.

I take a deep breath, calming myself down because I won't lose Logan because I'm not pregnant. I'm not; it's stress.

I leave the bathroom.

I'll take a test in two weeks if it hasn't come. That's a good idea.

When I get back into the kitchen, I freeze when I notice a man leaning against my counter. Fear ran through my veins. He shouldn't be here; he should be in prison. Why isn't he in prison?

He smiles at me, "Hello Ann, missed me?" I flinch at the name, his brown eyes flashing with amusement. "Wow, you are a spitting image of your mother." I swallow hard. "What no hug for your dear old dad?"

My nostrils flare, anger seeping in. How dare he come here after what he did? "You're not my father; Dead Shot is. Why don't you cut the niceties and tell me what it is you want?"

His eyes flare with cold anger, but I don't let it affect me. He touches me, and Dead Shot will kill him. He knows this; it's why he's not approached me; he values his life. "Fine, the dickhead can have you for all I care. I want your mother's money, and I want it now."

I chuckle; I can't help it, making him narrow his eyes at me.

I just smirked and said, "What makes you think I still have it?"

He stood tall and chuckled darkly. "Honey, your mama left you over £500,000 when she died; there's no way you haven't got it."

I sneer at him. How dare he? "She didn't die, you asshole; YOU killed her right before you tried to kill me."

He just smiles evilly at me. "And yet, if I'd managed to get rid of you, I wouldn't be here trying to get what I'm owed."

Dickhead, "You're not owed fuck all. You were abusive, manipulative, and just downright cruel. That money was never yours and never would have been if you had killed me. I want to know why, Grant." He growls at me, but I continue, "Because she ensured if I didn't survive you, then the money, every single cent would have been transferred to a woman's abusive center, and you would have been homeless." His eyes flash with rage as his cheeks redden with anger, and I decide to give him a final blow. "And there is no money now."

He takes a step towards me, but I tsk at him, "Ah, ah, ah. I wouldn't if I were you; this place is riddled with cameras. If Dead Shot sees this, then I can guarantee that you'll be a dead man walking for going anywhere near HIS little girl, and let's not forget his wife, Cammy, who sees me as her daughter. Oh, and don't forget Grams; you remember Grams, right, your mother? Have you seen her yet? Well, I'm guessing not because you haven't got a shotgun hole in your stomach yet."

"Where's the money, Ann?"

I just smirked and said, "Really, ignoring the warnings about my parents and Grams." I shrug as he gets more pissed. "Your funeral. Anyway, the money, right, well, you see, I, uh, haven't got it anymore." I smile at him.

"What the fuck do you mean you haven't got it anymore? Where the fuck is it, Annalise?" Oh, he's mad. "Well, you see. I gave $100,000 to Dead Shot and Cammy because, well, they did raise me. I mean, you are aware that you're not on my birth certificate, right? Mama had everything planned; she'd already signed all parental rights over to the Ramirez's when I was an infant. Anyway, I also gave £100,000 to Grams, and, well, yeah, she hasn't got that anymore; she did a lot of refurbishing on her house, and the

rest, well, I gave it to the women's shelter just like Mama was going to." I lie through my teeth. Yes, I gave money to my family, and yes, I gave the money to the shelter, but not before I put myself through cooking school and bought my bakery and everything in it.

His face turns redder if that's even possible.

"You will get me the money."

I just chuckled, "Or what you going to finish the job?"

He sneers at me and says, "Yeah, I fucking will."

I just shrug and hold my arms out wide, ignoring the frantic beat of my heart. I play a good actress because I'm absolutely terrified.

"Then what are you waiting for?" As soon as the words leave my mouth, I regret them. I could be pregnant.

What about the baby?

He points at me and says, "You have 1 month to get me what is owed to me, or I won't come for you; instead, I'll kill that little boyfriend of yours."

My eyes widen, and then I just laugh. Is he stupid? "You mean the Ramirez's son, the president of the Untamed Hell Fires? Yeah, sure, good luck with that. Heck, he'd probably skin you alive. I mean, that's what he did to my ex."

He doesn't act scared; he just full-blown laughs, making the color drain from my face. "I have connections; the people I owe money to are the Devils. I'm pretty sure they'd kill him in a heartbeat just to get their rival, and that club of his will be fucking done for. One month, bitch, or I'll make you fucking watch it all as I tear your world apart."

Then he stalks out. My heart hurts, my breathing is shallow, and tears run down my face. I've heard of some of the problems with the Devils, and I know they'd love to have Logan's head on a stick. I sniffle, realizing I have to distance myself from him, maybe even end it just to save him. If he's watching me, which he is, then he needs to think Logan means nothing to me. Tears flood my cheeks as my hand goes to my stomach.

Tears fall down my cheeks.

For the last month, I have been pushing Logan away. I even accused him of cheating, which was horrible because I know he hasn't; I'm all he sees.

I sniffle again.

I was hoping he'd just end things instead, because I can't seem to let go. I love him—I do—so much, and the thought of him not being with me every day physically hurts. I let out a sob and tried to breathe through my tears. Taking a deep breath, I take the test and head to the bathroom. I've put this off long enough. If Grant finds out about this, then it'll be something else for him to use against me. I've seen him in the shadows; he's watching, and I know what I have to do to protect the love of my life, my family. I just hope I have the guts to go through with it.

                        I take the test, then sit back on the bed, crossing my legs and putting the test on the bed in front of me, and I wait impatiently, fear rolling through me for my love and this potential baby. I didn't care if it was just me; he could kill me for all I care, but it's not just about me; he's made sure I know it too. I wait a few minutes before I take a deep breath and pick up the test, turning it over, and my stomach flips as tears run down my cheeks.

I'm pregnant.

A sob climbs up my throat. How am I supposed to keep this baby and Logan safe from Grant? I sob harder when the bedroom door unlocks and Logan walks in. I look up, not bothering to hide my pain, fear, and tears. I've pushed so hard, but all I want is to be in his arms. I've missed him so much. He rushes over to me, kneeling, and cups my cheeks with his large hands.

I feel at home, and a sob comes out.

"Princess, what's wrong? What's happened?" I just shake my head, sobbing. His eyes look panicked. "Ok, look, I can explain, darling. I know I should have told you instead of having people come talk to you about the house, but I wanted it to be a surprise."

My sobs stop at his confusing confession, and I look at him in surprise and rasp, "House? What house?"

He slowly closes his eyes, making me narrow mine. What has he done?

"Logan, what house?" I ask firmer; my problems are well and truly forgotten, and he clears his throat.

"You, uh, um, aren't upset over a house, are you?"

I raise my brow and say, "No, but you're going to tell me what you're talking about before I hurt your already blue balls." He narrows his eyes at me, making me smirk. Yeah, darling, I know how much your balls must hurt; believe me, I've got lady blue balls too. Sighing, he gets up and takes hold of my hand that isn't clutching the pregnancy stick. He looks at it with furrowed brows, confusion showing in his eyes, but I just shake my head.

"Uh, uh, mister, tell me what you mean, and then I'll let you know what's wrong with me." He narrows his eyes again, making me want to laugh until he mutters, "You're lucky I love you."

My heart rate picks up, and I suck in a breath.

He loves me. Even after I tried to pull away, he loves me.

He smirks, but I ignore it; he loves me. We haven't said the words yet, but I've wanted to. I do love him so much that the thought of him leaving me in any way cripples me with fear.

He loves me!

I'm brought back out of my head when he drags me over to the window, stands me in front of it, and points to the houses. "You see the light blue Victorian house?"

I nod and say, "Yeah, it's your parent's house." And I love that house; it's full of family and memories, including pictures of my mama. I've been there a couple of times without the brothers knowing while Logan was away or with friends. He nods, then points a few doors down to the next house that has a building crew tidying up for the day.

"You see that house?"

I furrow my brows; it's beautiful, my dream home, "the gray cottage style with a wraparound porch where there's a building crew."

He nods,

"What about it?" I look up to him, and he smiles, leaning down. He kisses me gently on the lips, and I sigh.

Home, home, home.

I kiss him back, making him deepen the kiss before he rasps against my lips.

"That's our house, darling; everything you've told the brothers you may like in a house is right there." My eyes widen in shock, and he runs both of his hands on either side of my head, through my hair. "Princess, I fucking love you. Did you really think I'd make you live in this room forever?"

Tears fall from my eyes again. I've been pushing him away while his second family and his brothers have been ensuring to get my exact views on the perfect house I've always wanted. I sniffle, and he wipes my tears with his thumbs.

"You really love me?" I rasp; it's still the only thing I can grasp right now, and he smiles, "with everything in me."

More tears fall.

"You built us a house? With 5 bedrooms, 4 bathrooms, a conservatory for breakfast mornings, and a swing seat on the porch for evening cuddles?"

I sob the last bit as he wipes more tears.

"Yeah, darling, I did. I even put in the open concept with the living room and kitchen, with a breakfast bar seating three separating them, as well as the curved archway from the dining room to the kitchen. And I ensured you got your dream kitchen too."

I sob out again, then throw my arms around his neck, guilt building high and firm in my chest. I should have just told him about Grant instead of trying to put it all on my shoulders. I should have trusted him, and I will, but there's something else he needs to know first.

He catches me with ease, holding me tight to him, then even tighter when I whisper, "I love you too, so much. I'm sorry, I've been crazy this past month."

I feel him smile into my neck as he rasps, "I missed you, darling."

Guilt eats away at me, and I tighten my hold on his neck and sob, "I've b-been s-s-so stupid. I-I tried to p-push y-you a-away, I-I thought y-you d-d-deserved better.."

He gently pulls me back a bit and cups me with my hands, wiping my tears with his thumbs. "Darling, you are my fucking world; do you hear me?" I nod, feeling so stupid for not thinking he wouldn't be there for me. I go to my tiptoes and kiss his lips gently before standing back a bit. He furrows his brows as panic starts to build in his eyes, but I just shake my head to help ease his panic and place the stick in his hands, and his whole body stills making me hold my breath, hoping he won't hurt me right now, and tears fall again from my eyes in fear as he looks at my face with wide eyes and I rasp,

"I suspected this past month, but I just couldn't make myself take the test. My birth mother." pain over what Grant did to her and how much I lost not knowing my birth mother because of him and the knowledge I should have gained from her, "I don't remember her. I don't want to leave my child in this world without a mother."

He tilts his head with a sigh, wraps his arms around my waist, and pulls me to him. "Princess, you may have lost your mother young, but you still have two more. They brought you up to be kind, loving, smart, and generous, and let's not forget fucking gorgeous and crazy as fuck." I smile, knowing he's right. I had Grams, and I had Cammy. In all this pain and fear, I misplaced it. Guilt built again at not going to them when I suspected I was pregnant. I look up at Logan's face as it pales, making me furrow my brows.

"Fuck, if it's a girl, I'm going to have to get more guns and hide her from my momma." I giggle because I would love to see it. He gently kisses me again. "You're going to be an amazing mother, Annalise, and I know because you're already an amazing person, you saved me from myself, and I couldn't think of a perfect woman to start a family within a house that I built for them." More tears fall as I smile gently at him.

"And while I'm buttering you up, do you fancy baking for our fundraiser? It's for the children's hospital." I laugh, feeling honored to do it for the club.

"of course,"

I sigh and then furrow my brows, something that has really been niggling me for a few weeks now whenever I think about the possibility of being pregnant. "I don't understand how this happened, though. We used condoms."

He tilts his head and furrows his brows when suddenly his eyes widen in shock.

"Fuck," he rasps, "remember when I told you I found Bubbles in our room before your attack?"

My eyes widened; she was going to try and trap him. ARE YOU FUCKING KIDDING ME? My cheeks heat with anger, and my eyes flash with rage.

This bitch is done.

Logan can see the anger and goes to grab me, but I dodge his advantage by rushing out of the room to find the bitch. When I get to the common room, I see her sitting on Flame's lap. The fucking idiot, my anger burns brighter seeing Star packing her stuff up, trying not to fall apart, while Flame tries to convince her to stay while keeping the bitch on his lap. I stare daggers at him, and he looks at me with furrowed brows.

After feeling my glare, I shake my head at him and then focus on my opponent.

You're so done, bitch.

I hear a loud 'INCOMING' from Logan, making all the brothers look at me as I race towards the bitch who's too busy smirking at a heartbroken-looking Star. Flame doesn't fucking deserve her friendship when he's fully aware of how much she loves him, and he does this shit. I know I tried to push Logan away, but at least I was human enough not to sleep with someone else and shove men down his throat, especially when physically I couldn't. Just the thought of it makes me gag.

I hear someone mutter, "Fuck. Bulldog 2.0," but I don't pay any attention; I only have one person in my direct view. I grab Bubbles' hair and yank her off of Flame's lap, making Star grin. I give her a wink as Bubbles screams, "OUCH, WHAT THE

FUCK, GET OFF ME YOU CRAZY BITCH." I do as she's asked, but I grab her arm and turn her around. I pull my arm back and punch Bubbles in the nose, blood spurting everywhere.

"Holy shit."

Someone else gasps. I pull my fist back again as Bubbles screams, trying to protect her already bloody nose, but not well enough because I still manage to punch her again, and this time, we hear a crunch, making me smile. I hear Cammy whooping in the background as someone says, "That's got to hurt," while Bubbles falls to the floor, giving me great access to jump on top of her, wailing down with my fists on her already bloody face.

Fucking bitch thinks she can try to trap my man. Someone gently wraps their arms around my waist, pulling me back, and I instantly know it's Logan. "GET OFF ME, AXEL. I'M GOING TO FUCKING KILL HER." Everyone in the room freezes, but I ignore them. I know I never call him Axel, but I'm fucking pissed.

Ginger takes an uncontrollable Bubbles in her arms and glares at me, making Logan tense, but I just smirk evilly at her.

Bring it, bitch.

"You're fucking crazy and shouldn't be allowed in the clubhouse. I'm going to ensure she presses charges against you."

I chuckle darkly while the brothers still at her threat. It's not very smart to bring the law around bikers, and she knows this: "Go ahead, bitch, let's call the sheriff, and while we're at it, how about we explain to them how I ended up fucking pregnant?" Everyone gasps while I hear Star, Cammy, and

Grams let out a sob. Bubbles stops her whining about her nose, and both she and Ginger look at me with wide eyes.

"Funny how Bubbles was caught in our room right before my attack, and suddenly after I sleep with Logan, using the condoms in his dresser, I end up pregnant." Ginger swallows hard and lets go of Bubbles, shock written all over her face, and I smile wider. "Want to still call the law around these bikers? I mean, it seems as though she was so desperate, trying to trap a man who didn't even want her."

I look at Bubbles and go for her again, but Logan keeps hold of me and then gently rubs his thumb over my stomach as he rasps.

"Think of the baby Princess."

He made me take a deep breath, agreeing with him. Stress can't be good for our little bean, and I've been under way too much this past month. I look at Bubbles again. "What were you going to do, Bubbles? Drug him, get him plastered just so he'll fuck you and you can become pregnant." Bubbles pale, and Logan sneers at her. "I know you're not the only one trying to trap a brother, but you're on house duties only until further notice. You fuck a brother, then you're out. We'll discuss as a group church in two days whether we want to keep you around."

Tears fall from her eyes. "I'm sorry."

I growled at her. Sorry, my ass. My life's already in danger, and now, because of her, so is this unplanned baby. Just as I go for her again, Logan booms, "Trapping a brother is forbidden; always fucking has been. This is not a brothel; we do not pay you to fuck us; we pay you to cook and clean. The fucking is all down to you. If I see one more incident like this, then all sweet butts will be banned permanently."

They all pale while the old ladies smirk. Star comes over to us and hugs me tight, saying, "That was fucking awesome, and congratulations." She whispers so Flame can't hear her, but Logan does, and he snorts, getting Flame's attention as he rises, raising a brow at Logan, but he just smirks at him, then nods his head to Star. He looks at us, then towards Bubbles, who is currently sobbing, making me smile, then back to Star. Horror and guilt eat at his face, and I narrow my eyes at him, idiot.

As Doc goes over to Bubbles, trying to keep his face impassive when he wants to laugh, Cammy and Grams rush over to me and hug me tight, causing my tears to fall, making them hug me tighter, and I hear Dead Shot mutter to Logan, making guilt eat away at me some more. "Well, that explains a few things."

I see him nod in the corner of my eye, "She now knows about the house too, she's ecstatic."

Dead Shot grins but my fear and guilt are eating away at my soul.

I'll tell him, all of them, I will.

Chapter 17

Axel

I go to my woman after patting my father's back and pull her from my mother and her grandmother, making them both scowl, but I don't give a shit. I haven't had sex in a fucking month; my blue balls want emptying inside her; bare seems as she's already pregnant, which I must admit makes me fucking proud, and my dick wants his pussy.

I lean down and whisper in her ear,

"A whole month, Princess."

She bites her lip to try and control her laughter while her eyes shine with lust. I just shake my head at her. I'm already fucking hard after seeing her go crazy; now I want what's mine. I bend down and lift her bridal style, knowing I can't throw her over my shoulder and risk our baby.

"NIGHT FUCKERS."

I boom, and the whole clubhouse falls into a fit of laughter, and excitement fills me as my dick leaks from the tip. As soon as we're in our room, she's getting down on her knees. I want my cock in her sexy mouth, but as we round the corner, Ginger is leaning against the wall, waiting for us. Fucks sake. My dick can't catch a break. I don't put Lise down; I just look at Ginger with a raised brow.

She clears her throat.

"I wanted to apologize; I didn't realize what she had done."

Lise tilts her head and says, "I understand she's your friend, but you defending her without realizing the full story made you look bad. Next time, ask what's going on while trying to comfort her before snapping. She had a full plan in place, not realizing Logan and I were intimate, and now because of her, I'm now pregnant when I wasn't ready." I tense up at her words, but she ignores me. "I didn't want kids just yet; I wanted some time with Logan and, preferably, to get married before we started a family. She messed with our fate and our lives, trying to get what she wanted."

My heart drums in my chest. Does she see our future together? Because if she does, then fucking hell yes. Ginger bites her lip, but Lise continues, "I forgive you because you were sticking up for your friend, but next time don't get involved if you don't know the full story." My woman is full of heart.

Ginger looks at me, and I shrug. "My girls spoke, but I don't forgive as easily. You also are going to be on cleaning duty until the meeting." She nods her head solemnly, then smiles at Lise before leaving us, and I sigh in relief.

Lise bites my ear, making me growl at her, and she giggles.

When we finally get into our room, I lock the door and place her on her feet. I gently kiss her before I rasp, "On your knees, darling." She grins as a sparkle shines through her eyes, and she listens, slowly dropping down as her hands go to my jeans and she unbuttons them, taking them and my boxers down together with her, freeing my rock-hard cock that's seeping from the tip. She gently grabs it before squeezing tight from base to tip, making more pre-cum spill from my tip. I groan as she leans forward and licks it away, making my eyes roll to the back of my head. Fuck yes.

She lifts my cock a little then licks me from the base underneath all the way to the meaty triangle, moving her tongue backwards and forwards fast before licking around my tip. I moan and try to thrust my hips, but she just smirks at me and does the same thing again, from base to tip.

"Fuck, darling, put me in your mouth."

She obliges and gently sucks around the head of my cock, teasing me. I grab a hold of her blonde hair, gripping it tight, making her get the message. I want down her fucking throat. She slowly sucks me down until her nose presses against my pubic bone, and I hold her there, groaning as the head of my cock touches the back of her throat, causing her to gag, but she doesn't struggle; instead, she brings her hands up my legs. One goes to grip my ass while the other fondles my balls, rolling them between her fingers, and I lose it. I pull back, then slam forward with quick and hard thrusts. She squishes her thighs together, trying to quench some of her need, and groans around my dick, causing a vibration.

I speed up, and I make eye contact with her.

"Ready Princess? Don't swallow."

I breathe heavily, warning her, and she nods just as she squeezes my balls while sucking harder on my dick as I fuck her mouth, "FUCK YES." I shout out as I shoot my cum into her beautiful mouth. When I pull out, I grip her chin and say, "Show me," and she slowly opens her mouth.

I groan when I see my seed swimming under her tongue, and I drop onto the floor in front of her and say, "Swallow," and without breaking eye contact, she swallows it, and I grab the nape of her neck, kissing her with passion, tasting myself on the lips and tongue.

I slowly lie her on the floor, my body going over hers, not breaking the kiss as I kick my shoes, jeans, and boxers off completely. She moans into my mouth, trying to rub herself on me, making me smile as I break the kiss and slowly kiss down to her neck.

I suck hard, leaving my mark before I continue down.

I lean up and slowly run my hands up her stomach, taking her top with them and moving it over her head. I look down at her tits, which are covered by a black lace bra, and my mouth waters. They're fucking bigger. I can see her pebbled nipples pocking through the fabric, showing how turned on my woman is, and I lean down and suck hard through her bra. She gasps loudly as I gently bite it and suck again, then do the same with the other one before I reach behind her arched back and unclip her bra. I get it off of her and throw it across the room, then go back to her beautiful tits, sucking and gently biting each one until she's rifling under me.

She gasps, "P-please, Lo, p-please."

            I smirk again and kiss down to her stomach, spending a little bit of time kissing where our baby is growing before moving down her body. I unbutton her jeans and drag them down her legs with her black lace panties then, ever so slowly, I gently run the tip of my fingers up her legs on the inside, causing her to squirm and moan in frustration. As I get to her knees, I put a little pressure on her legs as I continue going up, forcing her to open her legs wider.

Her shaved cunt glistens with need.

Her thighs are drenched with her juices, and I lean forward, running my nose from her entrance to her clit, taking in her sweet and salty scent—fucking perfect. I take the tip of my tongue, circling her clit and flicking it, causing her to tilt her hips, before I gently lick down to her entrance, pushing it in a couple of times before I move my tongue further down and circle her asshole. She tenses, but I continue circling it. I'm taking this one today. I slowly move my right hand to her clit and put pressure on it as I stiffen my tongue and push it into her hole, making her gasp. I move my fingers from her clit and push them into her entrance, and I lap her asshole, gently pushing my tongue in and out, making her gasp.

I go back to her clit with my tongue and flick it a couple of times as I move my finger to her ass. I gently circle her hole with the tip of my finger and push a little, making her tense. She needs a distraction. She's not telling me no, but she's nervous, so I suck her clit into my mouth hard, and she screams in pleasure as her clit throbs in my mouth. I push my finger into her ass, thrusting it in and out before I add a second, all while I keep sucking her clit and my left hand has traveled to her tit, squeezing and pinching her nipple.

She cums, squirting her juices into my mouth, making me groan as I gently pull my finger out of her ass. I kiss up her body again, sucking each nipple into my mouth before I make it to her mouth, and I kiss her with passion, letting her taste herself.

"You ready, princess?"

She wraps her legs around my waist, my now rock-hard cock poking at her entrance. "Please, Logan." She whispers, and I lean down, kissing her hard and fast as I thrust forward, all the way to the hilt, and I swallow her gasp, not stopping our kiss. I fuck her mouth with my tongue at the same pace as my hips, which thrust hard and fast. I can feel her cunt starting to tighten on me, and I quickly pull out, making her groan in frustration, and I smirk, placing the head of my cock at her back hole.

She tenses, and I rub my nose along hers. "I want this hole today, darling; are you going to let me have it?"

She swallows hard, then nods her head, her eyes showing wariness but also excitement.

That's my girl.

I slowly push the head of my cock into her ass, making her gasp.

I lean down and gently take her nipple back into my mouth as my tongue circles it before I gently bite it and then suck hard. I put my hand that's not supporting my weight between our bodies, and I strum her clit. She's completely distracted as I push in some more, pushing through her tight ring of muscles, her pain forgotten by my distractions. She cums again, screaming my name, and I push all the way in. She tenses, and I hold still.

Fuck, her ass is tight.

I lean my head down and gently kiss her lips before I poke my tongue out, pushing past the seam of her lips to tangle it with hers. I groan as she moans. then finally she moves her hips a little, and I slowly pull out, leaving only the tip in before I gently thrust forward, and she moans again in pleasure, so I do it again, but a little faster and a little harder, not giving a shit that I'm getting carpet burns on my knees. By the time I'm fucking her ass hard and fast, her whole back arches, pleasure vibrating from our bodies. I go back to sucking and biting each tit as my hand goes between us again, and I shove two fingers into her tight cunt. I fuck her with them as my thumb finds her clit and I press down hard on it.

She detonates, her pussy squirting for the second time tonight. Her cunt and ass pulsate, squeezing my dick and fingers, and I groan as I cum in her ass, squishing my dick in as far as it'll go before I place my head into her neck.

"Fuck, darling."

I rasp, and I can feel her smile against my head as she runs her fingers through my hair, and I pull up and kiss her gently as I slowly remove my still half-mast cock from her ass, making her wince, "Sorry, darling, wait right here, ok." She nods her head, her eyes looking into mine, full of love. I lean down again, kissing her before heading into the bathroom.

I plug the bath plug in then start running her a bath with her favorite lavender bath bombs, then I grab a flannel and wet it up, taking it to her. She's where I left her, on the floor, and I lean down and gently wipe her ass and cunt. My cock hardens again seeing our juices mixed together. Fuck, I need her again. I throw the flannel into the washing basket before I pick my woman up and take her to our bathroom. I place her on the counter so I can check the water and its temperature before I pick her back up and place her in the bath. I get in behind her and pull her back to my chest before I get a washcloth and squirt her vanilla body wash onto it before I gently wash her body, causing her to groan in pleasure. When I'm finished, I cup her flat stomach and rasp,

"Our baby."

She twists her head and smiles wide at me.

"Our baby."

I lean down, kiss her hard, and force her to turn around onto my lap. Once she's straddling me, I kiss her again and find her entrance with my now-hard cock again, and I grip her hips, pulling her down and making her impale it. We both moan, breaking the kiss, and she starts to fuck me slowly, never breaking eye contact, making love and fuck if it doesn't do something to my chest. My right-hand grips her on the back of her neck, forcing our noses to touch but continuing with our eye contact.

Fuck her violet eyes are perfect, shining with love. She goes faster as her orgasm approaches, and I trust up harder: "Come for me, darling, let me feel that tight cunt squeezing me." I reach down and pinch her already sore clit and she screams, "LOGAN." With her head tilted back, giving me perfect access to her tits that I suck on generously before I cum inside her, thrusting into her high and staying there until it's all gone.

I gently move her hair out of her face as she drapes her arms around my neck, keeping my dick snuggly tight inside her cunt, and I rub my nose alongside hers. "Do you know how much I love you?" she smiles, "not as much as I love you."

Smiling, I kiss her gently before I rasp.

"Be my old lady."

Her eyes glisten. "Are you sure that's what you want?" I narrow my eyes at her, making her giggle, and I groan as her cunt futters around my now-hardening member again.

Fuck, it's going to fall off at this rate. But what way to lose it!

"Darling, you are my everything and my home. I couldn't ask for a better old lady."

She sniffles and nods her head, making me grin wide as she rasps, "I love you, Logan Ramirez."

I kiss her hard on her lips before I rasp, "I love you too, Annalise Lawrence."

She gives me a watery smile, "Take me to bed Logan." I grin at her and stand, my dick falling out of her. I help her dry before I dry myself, then I pick her up under her thighs, causing her to wrap her legs around my waist, and I state, "You may want to let Sandy know you're going to be late for work tomorrow because I'm about to spend the whole night fucking you then making love to you while you wear your cut that I had made."

She grins wide, and I drop her onto the bed before grabbing the cut that arrived three weeks ago. It has our emblem like what's on our church table: a massive hawk with its wings on fire on her right breast side, and on the back, it states, 'property of Axel' and as soon as she has it on, I do exactly as I said I would.

Ensure she can feel me for the next week.

Chapter 18

Annalise

I wake up groggy the next morning and know instantly I'm in bed alone, making me sigh.

I feel emotionally drained. This past month has been hard.

I find my phone charging on the nightstand to check the time when I notice a message, and I swallow hard.

Unknown – tick tock, your time is almost out; two days or kiss goodbye to that precious boyfriend of yours. The president of the Devil's is already intrigued by my connection. $500,000, no less.

My heart beats faster in my chest. I need to tell Logan and Dead Shot.

I'm so fucking stupid.

How did I think I could deal with this alone?

Tears start to well up in my eyes and I sniffle, fed up with the stress. Shaking my head, I get up and quickly shower, ensuring my hair is up and out of the way. I use Logan's wash because it smells divine and woodsy. I'll blame the pregnancy on that one. Once I'm out, I go to the walk-in closet and dress in one of Logan's shirts, a pair of jeans, my sneakers, and my new cut before I head to the common room, ensuring I lock the bedroom door. These bitches have no limits, apparently.

When I get to the common room, only a few brothers linger, eating breakfast that Ginger and Bubbles have made. And when the bitch walks out of the kitchen in barely there clothes, face full of makeup to hide her bruises, and a carefree smile like she hasn't fucking caused shit in my life, like she didn't unknowingly put an innocent child in danger, I fist my hands down my sides as my anger returns tenfold and go to take a step forward when a heavy arm goes over my shoulders, making me growl.

I look up to see Slicer's beautiful hazel eyes looking down at me with amusement, and I cross my arms over my chest in a huff.

He's no fun.

"Easy there, fighter. Think of the baby." I growl again, catching Bubbles' attention, and her smile drops. Clearing her throat, she places the food on the table and hightails it back into the kitchen, and I can't help the smirk that appears on my face, causing Slicer to full-blow laugh, making my smirk turn into a smile.

I love making these big bad bikers smile and laugh, especially when it comes to my food.

He guides me over to a table where Dead Shot is sitting, and I smile wider seeing him as Slicer pulls out a chair for me and kisses my head. "Alright Annie, I'm going to get you some food because I promised Axel I'd look out for you until he gets back from his errand, and I don't trust you anywhere near Bubbles right now. Not that I blame you." I frown while he looks at Dead Shot. "Keep an eye out will yah? She just tried to go for her again."

I narrow my eyes at him for grassing me up, making him and Dead Shot chuckle.

When Slicer isn't in earshot, I turn to the man I see as a father and ask, "Fancy helping a girl out and distracting him?" He chuckles and shakes his head while I pout and whine.

"Dad."

But he just shakes his head again. "Annie girl, she's not worth it, and the stress isn't good for my grandchild." I can't help the tears welling in my eyes as a big smile takes over my face, making him smile as Slicer returns. He pales at my wet eyes and looks at Dead Shot, his own eyes widening and his voice full of panic.

"Whatcha do?"

I giggle.

"It's just hormones; relax, Slicer."

He nods like he understands when we all know he doesn't, then places a plate that's filled to the brim with pancakes and syrup, making me raise a brow at him while Dead Shot's body shakes with silent laughter.

"What? Axel said, make sure you eat because you're eating for two."

I groan and go to bang my head on the table, but I think otherwise when I remember the syrupy goodness sitting in front of me.

Too much syrupy goodness, though.

I sigh. "I'll eat what I can, but I won't be able to eat it all. Now off you go, warden; mama's hungry."

He nods once with a smile then heads back to one of the sweet butts making me roll my eyes. I think he's the biggest man whore here and that's saying something. Axel said he wasn't like this once upon a time. A few years back, he met someone on a run for the club; apparently, he fell hard, but she wasn't there when he woke the next morning after spending the night together.

I watch him sit down and pull the sweet butt onto his lap, running his hands towards her breasts, and I shake my head. I take a bite of my food and groan at its goodness. They're not as good as mine, but they're still good enough to eat.

I look up after taking another bite to see Dead Shot smirking at me.

"What?" I asked after I swallowed and took a drink of some juice.

He just shakes his head. "You finally look more relaxed. This past month, you've been off and distant, and I don't just mean with Axel." I sigh and look down, knowing I have to tell him. When I look at him again, concern retches all over his face, and I look down again and clear my throat. "Do you know when Logan will be back?"

"No, sweetheart, why?"

I sigh again and look around the room. A few sweet butts are staring at me, and I know I need to have this conversation in private. I look at him again and ask, "Is there anywhere we can go to talk in, uh, private? And maybe bring Dagger if he's around."

Dead Shot leans back in his chair and looks at me with a cold look. It doesn't scare me; I know this is his way of controlling his emotions because he knows that not only is what I have to say important, but it will involve the club and most probably my life. He stands, nodding his head to the side to get me to follow, which I do without saying a word but making sure I take a few more bites of pancake first. He taps Daggers and Gunner's shoulders.

"Follow me, brothers."

They both furrow their brows but do as he asks, and we head into their meeting room. I can feel my heart beating wildly in my chest. I don't want to get them involved, but I know I have to. He's threatening Logan, and not only that, but I have to think about our baby too.

When we head into the room, whispers erupt in the clubhouse, but we ignore them, and I look around when we enter the room. It's dark but also manly, I guess. I don't know; the walls are like the common room, but with lots of pictures and memorabilia, and there's a massive table in the middle of the room with their logo carved into it.

Huh. It's like the knight's table.

The men all sit opposite me as I stand at the edge of the table near the door. Dead Shot sits to the left of Dagger, who is VP, so I guess this is his show while Gunner sits to his right. I clear my throat, nervous, while I fidget with my fingers.

Dead Shot softens his eyes, knowing my anxiety is starting to flare up.

"Annie girl, it's just us."

I nod, then start to pace as I start to ramble. "I didn't know what to do; I thought distancing myself from the people I love would help, so I pushed Logan away. I even accused him of cheating, which is flipping ridiculous. But I didn't know what to do; I didn't want him to get hurt; he's my world; then I thought, Well, if Logan is a target, then so are you and Mom, and I couldn't."

I shake my head, the pain too great to think of losing the two people who are basically my parents. "I can't lose you two as well; I just can't, but then I finally had the courage to take a pregnancy test, and what do you know? It's positive, no thanks to that bitch and her meddling, so it's not just me that's in danger now, is it? It's me, the baby, Axel, you, Mom, and the club."

Dagger stood during my rant, but I didn't notice until he banged the gavel, making me scream out in fright, looking at him with wide eyes.

He winces, "Sorry, sweetheart, but you were rambling. Why will any of us be in danger?" His eyes are soft, and I keep mine connected with his, knowing Dead Shot is about to fly off the handle, and I rasp.

"Grant Lawrence has been released from prison and wants what is owed to him."

Dagger's eyes widen in shock while Gunner stands, ready to fight, but Dead Shot reacts calmly, which scares me more than anything, and his voice is void of emotion. "What is it he thinks you owe him, sweetheart?"

I clear my throat as tears well up in my eyes, and I look at the man I see as a dad, hating to be bringing this to his doorstep: "The money mama left me, the inheritance."

He nods calmly. "Continue, Annie girl."

The tears fall as I rasp, "He showed up in the kitchen a month ago at Sweet Treats. I told him I didn't have the money, and if he touched a hair on my head, he was as good as dead. He says he owes money, and I'm to get it for him; otherwise, I'm dead as well as L-Logan." I sobbed the last bit, the weight of the pressure that was crushing my chest lifting a little, but the guilt of putting my problems on them building. "He said h-he owes m-money to the D-Devils and-and that t-t-they were-were interested in his c-c-connection to Logan, and they w-w-would love to have his-his head."

I break down fully as Dead Shot now rages in the room, throwing chairs at the wall while roaring out in anger, and Dagger rushes over to me, catching me before I fall to the floor as my legs give out.

The door to the room slams open, and Ink, Flame, and Slicer all run inside before slamming it shut again, then freeze when they see me in tears in Dagger's arms and their old Pres losing his shit. Gunner and Ink grab Dead Shot, holding him so he calms down. He struggles for a little while but finally stops, breathing hard. His hard eyes soften when he sees me basically being held up by Dagger, and he shrugs the men off him, rushing to me.

He takes me from Dagger's arms and holds me close in his as I sob into his chest.

"What the fuck is going on?" I hear Flame snap.

Dead Shot's chest rumbles as he speaks, "You need to call Axel now. Emergency church for all brothers."

Flame and Slicer curse while Dagger gets his phone out to call Logan, and the guilt builds in my chest, feeling like I can't breathe.

Dead Shot runs his hand through my hair as he murmurs, "Annie girl, you should have told me the same day."

I shake my head, hiccupping, "I didn't want to be a burden."

He leans me back so he can look me in the eyes, "You can never be a burden, do you hear me?" More tears fall as I nod my head, and he pulls me back into his chest when there's a knock at the door. Slicer opens it, and Cammy rushes in. When she sees the state I'm in, her eyes narrow, but Dead Shot lifts his hand and then states,

"He's been released."

Tears automatically fill her eyes as she gasps, and then she rips me from Dead Shot's arms, taking me in hers. "I'm taking her back to her room." She doesn't wait for anyone to say anything as she helps guide me towards the back hall by passing the common room. We bump into Bubbles, and she looks at me with furrowed brows, but we ignore her.

As we get to mine and Logan's rooms and Cammy unlocks the door with my key, we hear Dagger shout, "EMERGENCY CHURCH, SWEET BUTTS, AND OLD LADIES OUT NOW."

She shuts the door as we hear women complain, but we ignore it all as she sits me on the bed and cups my face.

"How long, baby?"

Tears fall faster in "one month."

She slowly closes her eyes; disappointment crosses her face and I sob. She takes me in her arms and says, "You silly, silly girl. You are our daughter. My son loves you deeply. You should have told us straight away."

I nod, "I'm s-s-sorry."

She nods her head against mine and says, "It'll all be ok, I promise." I nod again and hold her tightly as my eyes start to droop. More tears fall as my eyes start to fall shut and I fall asleep on Cammy, feeling safe and loved as she whispers, "You are safe, baby, sleep."

If only that were true.

Chapter 19

Axel

I get out of the club-owned truck because mine is in the club's garage and grin as I reach for the box holding a little present for my woman. As I get the box out, my phone beeps and I quickly juggle the box to see if it's Annalise. I forgot to leave her a note this morning, but I did tell Slicer to make sure she ate.

I grab my phone to take a look and furrow my brows in confusion.

What the fuck?

Dagger – EMERGENCY CHURCH ALL BROTHERS

I quickly rush inside with the box and stop dead when I see only brothers in the common room and the prospects at the doors. What makes me pause, though, is the look on my father's face. Anger, rage, and worst of all, fear—which means this is either about my mother or my woman—and I boom.

"WHAT THE FUCK IS GOING ON?"

Dagger clears his throat as all the brothers look towards me, most in confusion, but it's my father who speaks up in a void of emotion, "Where have you been?"

I tilt my head at him. He's angry I get it, but right now, I'm not his son; I'm his Pres and he needs to remember that. I scowl at him, and he closes his eyes with a sigh when he realizes he overstepped.

"Not that it has anything to do with you or the brothers; I went to book Lise in for a scan tomorrow morning. Make sure our baby's growing okay, then I decided to get her a little present, which could backfire on me yet."

My father's eyes shoot open as everyone looks at me in confusion, until a little bark comes from the box, making me move my eyes around, looking at the ceiling in an innocent gesture.

Dagger and Flame burst out in laughter as my father bites his lip to stop his from coming out.

"Please tell me you at least got her a good dog and not a tiny chihuahua."

The men all bark out a laugh at Hawks's question as the puppy's head bounces up, opening the box's lid, "Holy shit, you got her a German shepherd puppy?" Gunner's mouth drops open, and I grin. "Yep, a pure black one; she'll make a great guard dog for my woman and child, don't you think?"

The brothers laugh, except for my dad, Gunner, Ink, Flame, Slicer, and Dagger, worry etches their faces, and I tilt my head again.

"what's happened?"

My dad clears his throat as Dagger speaks, "Grant Lawrence has been released from prison. He sought out Annalise a month ago at her bakery and threatened her.

I freeze, and my breathing picks up as my whole body vibrates with rage. A whole month, and she didn't fucking tell me? I place the box on the table as the puppy jumps out to sniff her new surroundings, but I don't take my eyes off of my dad. He slowly closes his eyes, taking a breath before making contact with mine.

"He wants her inheritance even though she no longer has it. He used the only leverage that would scare her into complying."

I growl as my body vibrates with rage as I flip the nearest table that, thankfully, is nowhere near the new puppy as it comes back to me.

a month ago.

She's been pushing me away for a month. Fucks sake. I push past the brothers and grab Flame's laptop, and he lets me, knowing no one could stop me, and I bring the security footage from the bakery. We updated it after the whole David incident. I scroll through the footage until I reach the date she started pulling away, and I start it from the time she opens, then move it to the big TV, pressing play.

It starts off with her baking as normal, but after a few hours but only minutes for us, as I skip through, I play the footage when she drops her head and grips the counter, trying to breathe.

I smile a little. Morning sickness, I realize.

She takes off to the bathroom, and about 3 minutes later, her back door opens, and in walks a scruffy, overweight Grant strolling in like he owns the place. Both me and my dad growl as we watch the scene play out. He leans against her counter, and as she walks out of the bathroom, she freezes, noticing him.

Flame leans over and turns up the audio.

"Hello Ann, missed me?" I see her flinch at the name as my dad growls. *"Wow, you are a spitting image of your mother; what no hug for your dear old dad?"*

My nostrils flare as my dad shouts at the monitor, "YOU'RE NOT HER FUCKING FATHER, YOU CUNT."

I see Lise's eyes flash with anger, and she snaps back, *"You're not my father, Dead Shot is. Why don't you cut the niceties and tell me what it is you want?"* His eyes flare with cold anger, but he doesn't move to hurt her; he's not that stupid. *"Fine, the dickhead can have you for all I care. I want your mother's money, and I want it now."* She chuckles darkly and smirks at him as pride shines through my chest at her for not backing down. "What *makes you think I still have it?"* He stands tall and chuckles darkly. *"Honey, your mama left you over £500,000 when she died; there's no way you haven't got it."* Lise looks down at him. Good girl, darling. *"She didn't die, you asshole; YOU killed her right before you tried to kill me."* He just smiles evilly, proud-like, making me fist my hands at my sides as the puppy sits on my feet, nuzzling its nose into my legs. "And *yet, if I'd managed to get rid of you, I wouldn't be here trying to get what I'm owed."*

Fucking asshole,

"You're not owed fuck all. You were abusive, manipulative, and just downright cruel. That money was never yours and never would have been if you had killed me. I want to know why, Grant." He growls as she continues, *"Because she ensured that if I didn't survive you, then the money, every single cent, would have been transferred to a woman's*

abusive center, and you would have been homeless, and there is no money now." He takes a step toward her, making me growl.

I hear Slicer mutter, "Fucking hell, we've been here before." He shakes his head, concern all over his face, and I know what he means. It wasn't that long ago that we watched her take a beating from her ex.

"Ah, ah, ah. I wouldn't if I were you; this place is riddled with cameras. If Dead Shot sees this, then I can guarantee that you'll be a dead man walking for going anywhere near HIS little girl, and let's not forget his wife, Cammy, who sees me as her daughter. Oh, and don't forget Grams; you remember Grams, right, your mother? Have you seen her yet? Well, I'm guessing not because you haven't got a shotgun hole in your stomach yet."

Sarcasm drips from her lips, making me fucking hard and pissed off at her for goading him at the same time.

"Where's the money, Ann?" She smirks, *"Really, ignoring the warnings about my parents and Grams, your funeral. Anyway, the money, right, well, you see, I, uh, haven't got it anymore."* I watch her bait him some more and smile, making me shake my head. I'm going to fucking tan her hide. "What *the fuck do you mean you haven't got it anymore? Where the fuck is it, Annalise?"* Fuck, he's pissed. *"Well, you see. I gave $100,000 to Dead Shot and Cammy because, 'well, they did raise me. I mean, you are aware that you're not on my birth certificate, right? Mama had everything planned; she'd already signed all parental rights over to the Ramirez's when I was an infant. Anyway, I also gave £100,000 to Grams, and, well, yeah, she hasn't got that anymore; she did a lot of refurbishing on her house, and the rest, well, I gave it to the women's shelter just like Mama was going to."*

I look at my dad and smirk, making him grin, while the brothers goad him, calling him a lucky fucker, not realizing he gave it all to me. Then I laugh when she lies through her teeth, leaving out how she paid for her school and bakery. However, the rest did go to charity.

We watch as Grant'' face goes red, worry flashes through his eyes, *"You will get me the money.."* She chuckles, *"Or what you going to finish the job?"* she goads, and he sneers back, *"Yeah, I fucking will."*

She shrugs, holding her arms out wide making my breath come short, fuck, no, *"then what are you waiting for?"*

I shout at the TV while the brothers roar in outrage, "WHAT THE FUCK YOU DOING LISE."

She's fucking pregnant, and she knew that then.

His eyes flash with irritation that his threat didn't work, and he points at her and says, *"You have 1 month to get me what is owed to me, or I won't come for you; instead, I'll kill that little boyfriend of yours."* Her eyes widen before she laughs. *"You mean the Ramirez's son, the president of the Untamed Hell Fires? Yeah, sure, good luck with that. Heck, he'd probably skin you alive. I mean, that's what he did to my ex."* She says it so proudly, but the fucker doesn't even flinch, just full-blown laughs. She starts to look panicked, which means she didn't notice the terror that shone through his eyes. The fucker is scared of me but doesn't want her to know it. *"I have connections; the people I owe money to are the Devils. I'm pretty sure they'd kill him in a heartbeat just to get their rival, and that club of his will be fucking done for. One month, bitch, or I'll make you fucking watch it all as I tear your world apart."*

Then he stalks out as we watch my woman slowly fall apart at the threat against me and my club.

My dad kicks a chair while I ball my fists, planting them on my hips, angry as fuck and blindly knowing there's a fucking puppy sitting on my feet, so I can't hit something without hurting her. I look towards Flame and say, "Get me fucking Snake on the phone now." He nods, his face full of rage, and gets his phone out. He puts it on speaker, and we listen to it ring four times before Snake answers.

"Axel, what can I do for you?"

I take a deep breath. "Grant Lawrence, how much does he owe you?"

I hear him clear his throat, "$750,000 in debt; he states he can get me $500,000 tomorrow so he can keep his legs; why? What's he to you?"

I see my father throw another chair. "He's my old lady's biological father. He's currently trying to blackmail her into getting you your money for him, using me as collateral against her."

He curses. "Are you fucking kidding me?"

I go to speak, but my father beats me to it, and rage takes over at his words.

"Snake, it's Dead Shot. Annie girl came clean today about his blackmail. Apparently, you are very intrigued by his connection to our club. He told her you're going to kill her old man and destroy our club, so she tried to distance herself from him and our club over the last month. She's pregnant, Snake."

We hear something break in the background.

"The fucker is either out of the loop or our little traitor has decided to play games, and if he is, then it looks like he's after your club too." I look down and see the puppy looking up at me, making me sigh. I bend down and pick her up, stroking behind her ears as I state, "When are you supposed to be meeting him?"

"In two days."

I nod. "Keep the meeting, and we'll ambush him, but don't tell anyone in your club."

I see my father nod.

"Ok, I'll send the details of the meeting to this number; get some extra men around your woman and unborn baby Axel as a precaution." Then he hangs up, and I take a deep breath, trying to control my anger while still stroking the puppy behind her ears.

I look around the room and say, "Trigger and Jizz, you're on Annalise duty until this is over; be ready to leave in the morning at 8:30 am for her appointment; I'll take her in the club's truck." They both sit up straight and nod, then I look towards the rest of the brothers and say, "Annalise will not be cooking tonight; just order takeout, and the prospects can go and pick it up."

They groan but nod, and I feel a little bit bad because, well, I love her cooking too, so I sweeten them up a little.

"I hear Sandy has given Star the leftovers from the bakery; she should be here any minute." They all cheer, making me chuckle, and I look towards my father and ask, "Can you make sure some food is sent to my room, Dad? We won't be leaving it much."

He nods his head in understanding. My woman has some explaining to do.

"Alright, fuckers, meeting over."

They all nod, and the prospects open the doors as Flame puts his laptop away. The front door opens, and Star walks in with perfect timing, holding three large boxes of baked goodies. I grin when the brothers make a beeline for her, and she screeches.

"ZAYNE."

He rushes over to her like the unknowing, whipped idiot that he is and grabs the boxes, but she keeps one. The brothers follow Flame like animals as Star comes over to me, and when she spots the dog, she squeals, "A puppy," and I chuckle as I hold the dog in one arm and Star shoves the box in my other arm, trying to take the dog.

Flame quickly comes back and picks her up from behind.

"Zayne, no, the puppy; I want to see the puppy."

We all laugh at her antics.

"Oh no, you don't; you'll dognap her."

The men laugh harder, and I raise a brow at her and say, "OK, Star, you can see the puppy once I surprised my old lady with her." She sighs and stops struggling. "OK, fine. That box is for you and Annie, by the way. Her cooking lessons came in handy over the past few months." I grin wide while Flame complains, "Hey, not fucking fair; I'm your best friend." I shake my head and say, "Alright, you two; I'll see you later; I've got a woman to surprise and confront." I hear a load of 'oh, shits' while Star asks what I mean.

Flame will tell her the basics. We don't like the woman knowing too much unless it's necessary.

I get to our room and try to balance the dog and the box while unlocking our door, which is not fucking easy, and I head inside. I place the box on the bedside table and look at my woman sleeping on our bed, and my heart picks up. Fuck, I love her, but I'm so pissed at her for not telling me right away what was going on.

I look at the dog, then at my woman, and I grin. I place the fluff ball on the bed, and the dog instantly goes over to her and sniffs her hair and face. She scrunches her nose up, making me grin wider, and when the dog puts her wet nose against my woman's, her eyes open wide in shock as she gasps.

And her eyes instantly turned wet.

Chapter 20

Annalise

My eyes spring open in shock as something wet hits my nose, and I gasp. A beautiful pure black German Shepherd puppy with bright brown eyes stares back at me, and my eyes turn wet.

She's absolutely beautiful.

I gently lift my hand and let her sniff it before I pet her. Her fur is so soft. "Hey, pretty girl, what's your name?" I rasp, and the bed dips, making me look, and I see the whole reason why I breathe: looking handsome with his hair messy on top, wearing a black Henley that's tight across his chest and muscular arms, his cut covering it, and his dark blue jeans hugging his thick thighs. He pats the dog's head as she tries to nuzzle my neck, making me giggle.

Logan's eyes sparkle. "What would you like to call her, Princess? It seems as though she's all yours."

I gasp as my tears fall, and I look at the dog again as she pulls back to see what the noise is out of my mouth.

"Mine?" I whisper, and he nods, looking at me, full of love, and a sob is released from my throat.

This man.

"Diamond, because her eyes sparkle like them."

He grins and nods his head as the puppy goes over to his side of the bed, snuggling into his pillow, making me giggle, but when I look back at Logan, my smile drops at the look on his face—disappointment and anger.

He knows.

A few tears leak from my eyes as I sit up properly, and I rasp, "I'm so s-s-sorry."

I can't help the sob that escapes, and he sighs, pushing my hair out of my face. "Annalise, you never should have kept this from me. I will protect you. That is my job. My life. You are my life."

I shake my head. "But who p-protects you?"

He sighs again before lifting me onto his lap, so I straddle him, and his large, tattooed hands cup my cheeks. "Darling. I have over a dozen of my chosen brothers who have my back. I love you so much, and I love that you want to protect me, but Lise, your trying to distance yourself from me only hurts me more than any bullet wound could."

My tears fall hard and fast and guilt eats up my body, "I-I'm so-so sorry." Sobs wrack my body, and he holds me tight to him, placing my head in the crook of his neck, his scruff of a beard brushing across my temple as I inhale deeply, taking in his musky wooden scent and cologne as I try to control my tears until I can calm myself enough to talk.

"You are all I want. You've become my world, and when he threatened you, I-I didn't believe him at first because you were you, but then he mentioned the Devil's and I panicked. I-I-I...." Another sob comes out, my tears soaking his neck. "Darling, I understand how scared you were; I've seen the footage, but you need to trust me. You can't hide something like this from me, and you certainly cannot try to push me away because, as I'll tell you now, Princess, it wouldn't have worked."

I sniffle and nod my head into his neck, sniffling again. "If anything ever happened to you, it would kill me." I rasp, and he holds me tighter. "Nothing will happen to me, not with my brothers at my back, okay?"

I nod again, snuggling tighter into him and holding him tight. "I love you," I whisper,

"Not as much as I love you, darling."

He pulls me back a little bit and cups my cheeks. "I made you an appointment for tomorrow morning; we get to see our baby."

I grin wide, then launch myself at him, kissing him passionately before I whisper against his lips, "Thank you."

He grins. "Anything for you, darling."

Then he kisses me again before gently lying me on the bed sideways, away from the diamond who's snoring away. He lays over me, then rubs his nose against mine before kissing me again. I wrap my legs around his waist, smiling against his lips when I feel his hard-on rub against me.

Hmm, yes, please.

He glides his hands up my jeans-clad thighs before unbuttoning them. He grips them, bringing them and my panties down with them, then gliding his hands back up my thighs again, spreading them as he goes up before placing his head right where I love it. He breathes against my clit before he slowly licks over it, then flicks it with his tongue, causing me to gasp.

"Logan."

He sucks my clit into his mouth before he pushes one of his thick fingers into my entrance, pulling it back, then adding another.

"Fuck, you feel tight, darling."

I start to flutter around his digits as he curls them, then rubs my magic spot.

Black spots dance around my eyes as I moan out a scream. "That's it, Princess. Squeeze my fingers and cum in my mouth." His mouth goes back to sucking my clit into his mouth. My stomach squeezes as I gush all over his face. He drinks up my orgasm before he slowly kisses up my body while his hands glide up my sides, lifting his shirt that I'm wearing along with my cut with them. He lifts the fabrics over my head, placing them next to us, before leaning down to kiss me, and I can taste myself on his tongue.

I moan as he groans before he stands up. He takes his cut off, grabs mine off the bed, then places them on the hook by the door before taking his Henley off, throwing it on the floor, his abs on show making me bite my bottom lip, and he smirks. He unbuttons his jeans and shoves them down his legs; he's not wearing any underwear, so his rock-hard cock juts out before he grabs a hold of my ankles and twists me over onto my hands and knees, making me squeal and then giggle. He grabs a hold of my hips, pulls them up, and rubs the head of his cock against my clit, bumping it a couple of times before sliding his hard cock down to my entrance, where he circles it and then gently pushes in. He puts his hand on my shoulders and gently runs his fingers down the middle of my back, then grips my hips. "Ready, darling?" he rasps, and I nod my head before he slams into me in one thrust.

We both groan as he holds still.

I wiggle my hips, wanting him to move. "Please, Logan, move."

He chuckles before rubbing his hand along the side of my ass and then slapping it, causing me to gasp. Then he pulls out slowly, only leaving the tip in before thrusting back inside me hard. I moan as he groans, picking up his tempo. I go to fuck him back, but he grips my hips, keeping me in place, hitting my G-spot. He snakes his right hand around my body and finds my clit. He pinches it hard before rubbing it furiously, making me squeeze his member hard.

"Fuck, yes, that's it, Lise; squeeze me tightly; cum on my cock, darling."

And I do. I scream out as my eyes roll into the back of my head. I can feel myself gush all over him, and he groans, thrusting, one, two, three, up to eight more times before he pushes himself right into me, holding me in place as his warm cum spurts out into my body. We stay like this for a few minutes before he leans over me, linking our fingers near my head, and he kisses the crook of my neck as he rasps, "How'd you feel about spending the evening in bed with takeout and a box of goodies from your bakery? Just you, me, our unborn baby, and Diamond."

I grin as I turn my head to the side to kiss him and rasp against his lips, "sounds perfect to me." He smiles against my lips before he gently pulls his still-half-mast member out of me and tells me to stay where I am. He gets a washcloth and wipes his cum that's dripping from my entrance before throwing the cloth in the washing basket. I climb into our bed, not disturbing the puppy. My eyes widen as I look at Logan when he climbs in next to me, "We had sex with her right there."

I can't keep the shock out of my voice, and he bursts out in laughter before kissing my head. I can't help but smile, nuzzling into him.

The next morning, I'm grouchy. I was woken up a few times during the night with Diamond after Logan, and I spent the evening making love, and now I'm exhausted. Logan woke me up at 7 a.m., thrusting into me and giving me a blissful orgasm before he brought me breakfast, which I of course threw up, making him panic. So far, everything hasn't gone according to plan, and now we're standing in the common room, where we're arguing in front of everyone who's looking at us with wide eyes.

"I DON'T NEED TWO BABY SITTERS LOGAN."

Yes, I'm shouting, but did I mention I'm grouchy? I haven't had enough sleep, and he won't let me have a coffee even though I'm allowed a little a day, and now I'm being told I have to be watched whenever I'm off clubhouse grounds. I'm fucking pissed.

He sighs and shoves a hand through his messy hair while Cammy smirks, holding the puppy. Dead Shot is glaring at me, but I just glare back.

"Annalise."

My eyes shoot to Flame, and he gives me a gentle smile. "It's not for long, sweetheart. It's just until Grant is no longer a danger to you and the baby. We're just trying to keep you safe."

I huff, then look at Logan, who's now glaring at Flame, and I poke his chest, causing him to look at me and say, "Why couldn't you just explain it like that instead of telling me I had to have two men stay with me at all times?" I raise a brow at him while the brothers burst out in laughter, and he narrows his eyes at me, making me smile.

He shakes his head. "I'm sorry, darling. Next time, I'll explain better. Now let's go see our baby, yeah?" I grin wide and nod my head as he guides me over to the door with Trigger and Jizz following, who are chuckling at our little entertainment act this morning.

Assholes.

20 minutes later, we arrived at the clinic. All three men flank me, and I roll my eyes. I understand it's for my safety, but come on. Surely this is overkill, right? I shake my head and go to the reception, ignoring the looks the men are getting, but I will admit that if this receptionist doesn't stop staring at my man like he's a piece of meat, then I'm going to scratch her blue eyes out.

Logan walks up behind me as I reach the desk and wraps an arm around my waist. I clear my throat, making the receptionist look at me instead. I give her a sweet smile, and she quickly sits up straight, trying to act professionally like she wasn't just eyeing my man, "Annalise Lawrence."

The woman clicks on her computer and then clears her throat as she speaks out in a squeaky voice, "Yes, take a seat, and the nurse will be out to get you soon." I nod and then go to take a seat, Logan right on my heel, but before I can sit, he sits first, then drags me into his lap, and I smile at him, putting my nose into the crook of his neck, causing Trigger and Jizz to chuckle. I hear the receptionist sigh and then mutter, "Lucky woman."

And yes, she's right, because I am.

A few minutes later, my name is called, and we both go with the nurse, leaving the other two with all the women staring at them, making them uncomfortable. I guess the brothers don't like attention from pregnant women as much as the sweet butts.

I laugh while Logan shakes his head.

We get taken into a side room, and I'm asked to do a urine sample before the nurse takes my height and weight. She then brings us to another room, where I'm sitting on a reclining chair near a monitor. The walls are covered in posters about women's bodies as well as pregnancies, and I look at them while the nurse takes my blood.

Logan doesn't let go of my hand, rubbing his thumb over the top of it.

"Ok, the doctor should be in momentarily."

I smile and thank her, then look at Logan, who leans down and gently kisses my lips. "I love you, darling."

I smile and say, "I love you too."

He smiles back as the door opens again, and a lady with white hair and green eyes walks in, looking to be in her late fifties. She smiles kindly at us and says, "Well, hello, you must be Annalise and Axel. I'm Dr. Murphy." We shake her hand before she takes a seat next to the monitor. "Okay, your urine test came back positive for pregnancy, so let's take a look and see exactly how far you are. I'm going to step out of the room for a moment. If you could get your pants and underwear off, then place that towel over your lap."

I nod and smile as she walks out. Logan helps me off the seat before I remove my jeans and panties then I do as she asked. I look towards Logan and see him readjust his jeans, making me snort at him.

"What? I can't help it, darling. My dick loves your pussy."

Oh my god, he did not just say that. My cheeks heat up while a giggle shoots out of my throat, making him smirk when the door opens and Dr. Murphy walks back in, causing me to narrow my eyes at my man in warning to behave, but his smirk just gets bigger. "Ok, Annalise, I want you to lie back and scoot your bum down until it's near enough to hang off the edge of the seat and lift your legs onto the stirrups here."

I nod and do as she asks, not feeling comfortable at all while Logan frowns. She gets out the wand, putting lube all over it before placing a condom on it, adding more lube, and placing it at my entrance.

Logan stands and says, "Hang on a second; what are you doing with that?"

I try, I really do, but his eyes are wide with panic, and he looks like he's about to be sick, and the laughter, well, doesn't want to stay in. Even the doctor is trying not to laugh. She clears her throat, saying, "Because she may not be far along, we have to do an internal vaginal scan. This wand will enter her, and I should be able to get a more accurate picture of the baby as well as maybe the heartbeat, depending on how far she is. Next time will be a stomach scan."

He nods like he understands, but his face is still pale, so I grab his hand, concerned he'll faint, which I must admit would be hilarious.

She looks at me and says, "OK, you're going to feel some pressure, but it won't hurt; you'll only feel a little uncomfortable." I nod and take a deep breath as she pushes the wand inside me.

It doesn't take long when there's a sudden whoosh-whoosh sound echoing in the room, and I look at the doctor with wide eyes. She smiles and says, "That would be your baby's heartbeat."

I let out a sob as Logan leaned down and kissed my tears away. "Thank you, darling, for this gift." He rasps as more tears fall from my eyes, "OK, it looks like you are 8 weeks + 3 days and everything looks good; congratulations, you two. I'll print you off some pictures, then I want you to book an appointment for 4 weeks' time, OK?"

I nod, feeling emotionally happy, and say, "Thank you."

She smiles wide as she removes the wand and gives the pictures to Logan. "Of course, get yourselves dressed and book the appointment with the receptionist on your way out." She shakes our hands and then leaves the room. I quickly dress as Logan stares at the pictures with a little smile on his face, making my heart flutter. He takes hold of my hand when I walk up to him, kisses my lips lightly before wrapping his arm around my waist, leading me back to the receptionist, and when we get to the room, I have to stop at the scene in front of me.

Trigger is sat down, eyes wide, as four pregnant women crowd around him while Jizz is flirting with the receptionist. I look back at Logan and say, "We can't take them anywhere." And he burst out in laughter, causing both brothers to shoot their heads our way. I grin at them. Trigger narrows his eyes at me while Jizz grins like a loon, making me shake my head. I make my next appointment and go to leave with all the men following.

I hear the receptionist call out, "Call me." and my laughter escapes as I walk to the club's truck.

"You can't go just a little while without a woman, Jizz?" Logan asks while Jizz grins madly. I shake my head again. "Alright, you three, let's go; I've got baking to do."

Logan grins, helping me into the truck while the other two head towards their bikes, and they take me to my bakery.

When Logan helps me out of the truck after we get in front of my bakery, he gives me a passionate kiss, long and hard, before he speaks, "You sure I can't convince you to just come back to the clubhouse?"

I snort, "No, I need to bake, and you have some paperwork to do. Now go, and I might make you some of your favorite cookies."

He grins then kisses me again. "Alright, darling, those two will stay in the front of the bakery because I know you don't want them crowding you; if there's a problem, then just shout them alright?"

I nod my head and then go inside my bakery, knowing he won't drive off until I'm safely inside.

I smile at Sandy and say, "God, it smells good in here."

She grins wide as she serves a customer. "It's your pregnancy smell kicking in."

I giggle and shake my head at her words as I head to my office, ready to sort some inventory out before I have to start baking the birthday cake that's being picked up tomorrow, but just before I can unlock the door, someone stabs a needle into my neck, and everything goes black as worry for my baby enters my mind.

Chapter 21

Axel

I can't keep the smile off my face as I walk into untamed girls. Finally, things are going well, and as soon as Grant is dealt with, life will be near perfect. Well, it will be once my girl accepts my proposal.

I grin again as I walk through the bar, "well, look who's happy." I turn to the voice and smile at Sugar. "Of course I am. I have my woman, who's carrying my baby, accepted to be my old lady, and hopefully, she'll accept my proposal too."

She squeals in delight, and when I think she's about to hug me, which, let's face it, I'm going to have to push her away because of our history and my jealous pregnant woman, Sugar holds her hands out and I raise my brow. "Give me, give me, give me," she chants, and I tilt my head in confusion like a fucking dog. And she sighs, rolling her eyes. "One, I want to see the ring, and two, I want to see the baby."

I chuckle and get the scan picture out first and show her; her eyes instantly get wet. "Oh my, I'm so proud of you, Axel, so proud." She sniffles, and I smile at her. Then I get the exceptional Edwardian, Colombian Emerald, and Diamond Ring, and her eyes go huge, "holy shit. Now that is what I call a ring; fuck me, Axel, it's perfect."

I grin wider, "Yeah, but we can thank Star for this. She helped me pick it out yesterday morning before she went to the bakery." Sugar grins wider as she passes me the ring and scan photo back.

"You did good, Axel. Now get your butt in your office. Dagger says you've got a shit ton of paperwork and emails to sort."

I groan while she cackles as she walks away from me, the evil woman. Hanging my head, I walk to my office to start on the paperwork, and when I get inside, I groan again when I see the pile sitting on my desk, and I know straight away that Dagger has given me some of his pile, knowing I'll do it because he fucking hates it, the shithead.

    Shaking my head, I go and sit behind my desk, placing the ring in the draw before leaning the scan photo against the picture of my girl smiling wide in a beautiful sundress, sitting on my matte black Harley. I grin, then get to the paperwork.

Hopefully, I can have most of it finished before I go get my Lise.

It couldn't have been more than 5 minutes when my office door opened and Flame, Dagger, and Dad walked in.

I scowl and point at Dagger.

"You."

He smirks at me while my dad and Flame look between us, then to the pile on my desk, making them both try to hold their laughter in.

"It's not fucking funny; I have plans tonight, and they don't fucking include the extra paperwork on my desk."

Dagger just shrugs. "I'm sure your old lady would wait until tonight for you to fuck her."

I narrow my eyes at him while my dad smacks him on the back of his head. "Shut up, that's my fucking daughter."

Flame tilts his head, "Is it incest if technically you had legal rights over her growing up?" I feel my face go pale while Dagger's eyes widen.

My dad sighs and shakes his head before hitting all three of us on the back of our heads, making us all grunt, "No, you dipshit. She's not blood-related, and they didn't grow up together; it's all fucking normal, but she is still my daughter, not because I technically brought her up but because she's now Axel's old lady." Then he looks at me and says, "If you're about to tell me Dagger's insinuation is correct, then I'm going to beat your ass."

I smirk while the others laugh at him.

Shaking my head, I get the ring box out of the drawer and open it, setting it on my desk. They all look at it, then me, then the ring again with wide eyes. "Actually, I was planning on taking her and Diamond to the lookout point at Hudson Lake, where I first took her, to convince her to give me another chance after I fucked up with Sugar. I was thinking about putting it in Diamonds collar."

My dad's eyes have gone misty while Flame looks at the ring and furrows his brows.

"Star helped me pick it out."

He looks up at me and nods his head. I can see his pain in his eyes; he wants what I have with my woman, with Star. He's wavering; you can see it in his eyes, and hopefully, it won't be too late when he finally decides to claim his girl. Dagger stands up and goes to the pile of paperwork and takes half of it, snapping Flame out of his head. We all look at him with raised brows, and he shrugs. "What? He's going to fucking propose; I'm not stupid enough to get in the way of that.

Bulldog is getting everything she ever wanted. A daughter-in-law who happens to be her daughter in every way except blood, a grandbaby, and now a wedding—I value my balls. Thank you very fucking much."

We all burst out in laughter as he walked over to the door when my phone rang.

My chuckles die down when I see Trigger's name pop up. My heart starts to beat fast. He wouldn't be calling unless it was an emergency.

My dad furrows his brows. "Axel?"

Dagger stops and turns to look at me while Flame stands ready for anything.

I clear my throat and answer my phone, putting it on speaker.

"Trigger?" Everyone in the room freezes.

"Fuck, Pres., FUCK."

I stand when he shouts; I can hear screaming and crying in the background; it sounds like Bubbles: "I tried to stop him; I tried; I'm so s-s-s-sorry." She wails, and I tense even more.

"Trigger, talk to me," I say, trying to keep my voice calm.

"Pres? It's Jizz; fuck, someone took Annalise. Bubbles witnessed it. The guy shoved Annie into the trunk of an old sedan, and when Bubbles tried to stop him, she got a punch to the face for her efforts before she stumbled through the front of the bakery. We ran out straight away, but, fuck, fuck. They were already fucking gone; oh, fuck, we lost her; we fucking failed."

Jizz breaks down while my whole body freezes momentarily. Fear for my woman and fear for my unborn child run through my veins. I look up to see my father fall to the floor on his knees, tears filling his eyes, worried for his daughter, while Flame and Dagger seem frozen too. I snap out of it; I can't think like a partner right now or a father-to-be; I need to think like the president of an MC, and I boom through the speakers, "EMERGENCY CHURCH RIGHT FUCKING NOW."

I hang up, send out a mass text, and then rush out of my office. It snaps the others out of it, and they race to follow me. The brothers that were at Untamed Girls rush out after us to our bikes, and we speed off down the road to the clubhouse.

When we rush into the clubhouse five minutes later, it's in chaos. My mother is breaking things while Stars sits on the floor by the wall near the pool table with tears running down her face. Flame rushes over to her. One of the sweet butts, Ginger, tries to intercept him, but he dodges her and goes straight to his girl, and jealousy like no other fills my chest.

His woman is right there, and he won't get his head out of his ass while mine is fucking missing.

Fuck.

I look around the room again and notice Lise's grandmother is absent, which means she doesn't know yet. Bubbles is sitting at the bar, Doc has an ice pack on her right cheek, and the sweet butts surround her while Trigger and Jizz sit on the floor near the bar with their heads in their hands. I see tears running down Jizz's face, and I know I can't blame them for this; they were told to stay out front; they were following orders; fuck, they're going to take this badly. Shaking my head, I boom above the noise.

"SWEET BUTTS OUT NOW, EXCEPT FOR BUBBLES."

They all look at me wide-eyed but don't argue well, except for Ginger, of course. "I'm not leaving Bubbles here with you and your temper."

I go to walk towards her, my patience running thin; we haven't got long to try and find the scent, so to speak, and she's wasting precious time.

My mother beats me to her, though.

She grabs her by the hair and then drags her out the backdoor, all while Ginger screams.

"When the Pres says fuck off, you fuck off." Momma grunts the last bit as she shoves her out the door.

            I turn to look back at Bubbles; she looks at me with fear, and I soften my voice. "Are you ok?" Tears fill her eyes, and she shakes her head. "I should have gotten some-someone instead of trying to-to get her my-myself."

I sigh and go over to her, pulling her into a gentle hug. "I am grateful you tried." She nods her head as I pull back, then I point at my two brothers and say, "Stop beating yourselves up; I gave you an order; you stuck to it."

They both shake their heads, and I sigh. They're not going to forgive themselves until we find her. Yeah, you and me, both brothers, this is my fault. I should have ensured a brother stayed right next to her, but I didn't want to piss her off; her hormones are everywhere at the moment.

I look towards Flame, who has an arm around Star. "We need the surveillance video, brother." He nods, and kisses Star's head, who flinches a little, making me furrow my brows. I've noticed her pulling away from him recently.

Shaking my head I watch as Flame gets up to grab his laptop. He connects it to the TV before finding the footage we need. He starts off with the kitchen after the time I dropped her off, and we all watch as fucking Grant walks in, heading towards her office. Flame switches the camera over, and we see my woman grinning, a hand rubbing her stomach, making mine clench with fear. She's completely unaware as Grant comes up behind her, and it's too late for her to try and fight him because he's sticking a fucking needle in her neck, and I growl.

I pick up a chair and throw it against the wall as Flame moves to the outdoor cameras, ignoring my outburst, and we watch as he drags, fucking drags, my woman by her hair to his car. We watch as her body bumps down the steps before he picks her up and throws, fucking throws her inside his trunk, locking her in.

Fuck, the baby.

My pulse rages, and I try to breathe through my panic, shaking my head, knowing I can't think about that right now. My main concern has to be getting my woman back. Yes, I want this baby, but we can always make another; we can't make another her.

I look back at the screen, ignoring the feel of eyes watching me, most probably my parents. We watch as Bubbles rushes over, trying to open the trunk, when he grabs her arm, spinning her around as he pulls back his left fist and punches her hard to her right cheek, making her fall. He kicks her for good measure in the stomach, making us men growl, then quickly gets into the driver's side as Bubbles gets on all fours, trying to get up. She stumbles towards the bakery, struggling to get it open before she's inside. Not even two minutes later, you see Jizz and Trigger running outside the bakery with Bubbles clutching onto Sandy, just as the car with my woman stuffed into the trunk turns in the distance around the bend. Jizz and Trigger get on their bikes and fly after them while Sandy clutches a screaming and distraught Bubbles.

Flame turns the monitor off, and everyone is quiet except for Momma's, Bubbles', and Stars' sobs.

All the men are still looking at the TV.

I take a deep breath, needing to act like a president. I'll break when I'm alone. I look towards my grief-stricken mother. "Momma, I need you to go to Rosie's, fill her in, and please keep her from having a fucking heart attack before bringing her back here; we can't take any chances that he won't try and hurt her too; take four brothers with you; no arguing."

        Momma nods as tears run down her cheeks, kisses my dad on the lips, then my cheek before heading out the clubhouse with two prospects, Ink and Thunder, and then I look towards the man I look up to who is trying his hardest to stay calm.

"Dad, I need you, with the help of some brothers, to start making calls to every bed and breakfast, motel, hotel, and hostel you can think of. Start asking around to see if anyone knows where Grant is."

He nods as Trigger and Jizz get up and walk over to him. I guess they're on his team. I look towards Dagger and say, "Call Snake, explain the situation, and see if he has any intel."

He nods and heads to his office, his face set like stone. I look toward Flame next. "Flame, you and Star, get on your laptop, start trying to find the model of the car; see if it's registered; he may be just stupid enough to keep it in his name and check her old house; see if it's sold; he could have taken her there; if not, try and check through the town's cameras to follow the sedan; then collaborate with Snake and call the Sheriff; update him on the situation."

They both nod and sit at a table, while Flame keeps an arm around her shoulders.

Then I look to the rest of the brothers and say, "Ride out, brothers; scan the streets and the neighborhoods."

They nod, banging on any surface they can find before heading out while I head to our room, ignoring Bubbles' stare. I unlock the door and pick Diamond up as she rushes to my feet before heading inside and shutting the door again. I slide down it, sitting on my ass as the smell of my woman takes over my senses and hits me hard. My tears start to fall, and I sob into the dog's fur while she nuzzles my neck, whining.

I sob for my woman, and I sob for my baby, who I don't know is strong enough yet to live through this.

Chapter 22

Annalise

I struggle to open my eyes; my head is pounding, and I feel sick.

Oh God, what happened?

I can feel myself dragging myself back to unconsciousness again when a sudden throbbing pain hits my stomach and I gasp, my eyes opening as someone grabs my hair tight, making me look up, and I see those angry brown eyes of the man who fathered me.

"Well, about time you woke up, Ann. Got me my money?" He sneers, breathing on my face, and I try not to gag. He stinks of rotten eggs, and I can't help my sassy comeback, hoping he'll move away from my face. "Does it look like I have it on me?"

He narrows his eyes at me before he punches me in the face.

I blink several times.

Wow, that hurt.

My cheek throbs on my left side, and I can feel the blood dripping from my lip, shit. I blink a couple more times when he gets in my face again, and I try to hold my breath; otherwise, I'm going to puke on him. "Okay, maybe I should have spoken to you before knocking you out. Where is it, and I'll go pick it up?"

Geez, is he thick or something?

"With the woman's abuse center, like I told you."

He growls and shoves my face back, making me fall to the floor as he starts to pace, and it's then that I notice how filthy he actually is. His dark t-shirt barely covers his gut, while his jeans look like they've been peed on several times. I quickly look around to see where he's keeping me, hoping I don't throw up, and I gasp.

We're in my old bedroom; I recognize it from some of the photos Cammy showed me of Mama; I don't have any with both of us. The pink walls are moldy and dark, while my old princess bed has bugs all over it with my teddies torn on top, like someone put a knife through them all, and I swallow hard.

I look towards the white nightstand that's now basically black and tears well in my eyes. It's a picture of me and my mama smiling wide. I don't have any of us together, and there one sits, only a few feet away. She should be here in person; she should get to meet the man I've fallen for, her best friend's son; she should get to meet her grandchild; and this monster took her from me. I look at him again, determined that he won't take anything else from me.

"Did you really think I'd fall for your bullshit?" He snaps his head back towards me, narrowing his eyes, and I smile at him. "Axel is one hell of a man—a dangerous one at that. He has over 15 brothers at his back, and you thought you'd be able to get to him with the Devils?" I chuckle as he makes his way over to me. He grips my hair again, but I don't let him talk. "You are pathetic; you only know how to hit women. Try to take someone your own size, and I bet you'd be dead in 5 minutes flat, you weak bastard."

He punches me hard again before kicking me hard in the stomach, and my eyes widen. No, no, no.

Not my baby, NO.

I try to secure my stomach with my arms, but he still manages to kick it three more times. I hear a crack, and immense pain shoots through my ribcage.

Oh cow.

I gasp while he chuckles, grabbing me by my hair again. "Who's weak now, bitch?"

I would roll my eyes if I didn't think I'd vomit, "still you jackass, woman, man. Do the math." I gasp out, and he sneers, "Let's see how cooperative you'll be, shall we?"

I furrow my brows in confusion, but he just shoves me away before leaving the room, slamming the door behind me. I cough, then groan out in pain as I slowly get on all fours and crawl on the filthy, moldy, used-to-be white carpet. I grip the nightstand and try to slowly pull myself up, biting my already-cut lip to stop the scream that's lodged in my throat, and I grab the picture frame that's on there. I quickly undo the back to grab the picture without him noticing, but I see a silver key first. I furrow my brows but quickly shove it in the side of my bra before carefully folding the picture in half and placing it with the key. Then I crawl back to where he left me after shoving the frame under the bed.

Just as I get back to where he left me, the door opens again, and he shoves someone in—no, not someone, "Grams." I gasped as she fell down next to me.

He kicked me again in the stomach, and I wasn't prepared. No, please. I gasped out a cry,

"STOP, LEAVE HER ALONE."

Grams screams out. I look at her and see she is covered in bruises, and my tears fall.

Grant gets in her face and says, "You see, mother, dearest, I can't; I need the money. Now she says she hasn't got it anymore, but I do know about the key, so fess up, old woman, where'd you hide the key the bitch gave you?" oh no. I try to calm my beating heart. "What key, Grant? I-I wasn't given a bloody key."

He doesn't like her answer, but instead of going to her, as I feared, he grabs the golf club next to the door.

How in the hell did I miss that?

He walks over to me, where I'm lying in pain, and whacks the club hard into my stomach. Oh God.

My baby.

Grams screams as he gets in her face, "The key Lucy gave you. The one that opens a safe in the bank where all her parents' jewelry that's worth over a million dollars, as well as another $500,000 in cash."

My eyes widen in shock, and as I look at Grams, her eyes are wide as well. "I didn't know-know about any key; the lawyer didn't-didn't say." He growls but turns to me when I gasp out a cry as a sharp pain, like period pain, just more intense, hits my lower stomach. When I look down, I see red staining my jeans, and I sob as realization kicks in.

My baby, my baby.

I hear Grams scream out in pain as Grant stands over me, "You dirty fucking bitch, couldn't keep a tampon in your cunt or something."

Tears stream down my face as I look into his cold eyes, mine turning colder, making him step back a little in confusion. "No, this is your grandchild that you just killed. Good luck when Axel finds you, because whether you kill me or not, you're a dead man walking."

My voice is void of any emotion, his eyes widen, and he starts to sweat, but I don't pay any attention to him as I place my palm against my stomach and whisper,

"I'm sorry, baby; I'm so sorry."

More tears fall from my eyes as I cry out again, and another pain shoots through my stomach. I bend my knees to my chest as the pain keeps shooting through me, the pain in my ribs and face all but forgotten.

I feel more blood gush from my entrance as more tears fall.

My baby, my baby, my baby.

Grams screams out as she gets up to attack her son. She grabs his hair and yanks it hard. He shouts out before grabbing her, and throwing her onto the ground.

"GRAMS."

I scream out as he kicks her hard in the head, causing her to black out. Then he looks at me, anger and fear covering his face. He bares his teeth at me before he storms out of the room, slamming the door before I hear a click.

He's locked us in.

I take a few deep breaths before slowly crawling over to Grams; the blood trickles on my legs inside my jeans each time I move, and more sobs release from my throat. As I get to her, I move her short white hair from her forehead before checking her pulse.

I sigh when I feel it.

"Grams?"

I rasp, but she doesn't move.

I try again, shoving her shoulder a little, and she groans out in pain, her eyes slowly opening as more tears fall from mine.

"Grams?"

I rasp again, and she sits up slowly before looking at me. Her eyes fill with unshed tears when she sees my bruised face, but when she notices all the blood, she sobs.

"Pumpkin." I shake my head and sob some more, "The-the baby's g-g-gone Grams, gone; I-I can f-feel the blood." She wraps her arms around me, hugging me when I start to feel faint and putting most of my weight on her.

She gasps and slowly lays me down, putting her hand on my cheek.

"Annie?"

My eyes feel tired, and I know I've lost more blood than normal because of my miscarriage. "Oh God, you're losing too much blood." Her tears fall from her eyes as I shush her. "Grams, I-I have the key. The one-one he wants, it-it was in a-a picture frame on-on the nightstand, it's-it's in m-my bra." Her eyes widen. "Don't tell him; you hear me, Annalise; you do not tell him; no matter what he threatens, that bastard isn't getting anything that belongs to you and your mother."

I slowly nod my head.

"Grams?"

She wipes my tears. "Yeah, baby."

"How-how do I-I tell Logan?"

Tears fall from her eyes. "Gently, but he'll stand by you, and you'll both get through this; I promise, pumpkin, you will. You are both strong."

I shake my head. "I-I wanted this-this baby so much. At-at first, I-I was scared but then I-I became happy. I-I wanted-wanted this b-b-baby." My sobs wrack my body, sending pain shooting through me as Grams cries with me, trying to help soothe me, but it doesn't work. I want Logan so much. My sobs subside a little while later as I finally give into the darkness.

"Annalise, open your eyes, ANNALISE."

I can hear the panic in her voice, but right now, I just want to die.

I don't know how long I blacked out, but I semi-wake when I hear Grant come back in. My eyes don't want to work, though, so at least there's that.

"Wake her up, now."

I feel Grams run her fingers down my cheek as she rasps, "I-I can't," he growls, "then allow me."

I feel my body being dragged and my body hurts, badly, making me groan but my eyes still won't open. He kicks me in the stomach again. I groan, but again, my eyes don't open. "Wake the fuck up, bitch." He growls as he punches my face again. I hear a crack as my nose throbs.

"STOP." My Grams shouts, "SHE CAN'T WAKE YOU IDIOT, SHE'S LOST TOO MUCH BLOOD, HER PULSE IS WEAK."

The hitting stops: "FUCK." I hear him shout as my body is dropped to the floor, "FUCK, FUCK, FUCK." He chants, and things go completely black again.

"Where's the key, Mother? A little birdie told me the $500,000 wasn't the whole fortune, so I know she must have told you where she hid it."

I wake to Grant's growl again, but I still can't seem to get the energy to open my eyes. I know Grams needs me, but I can't; my body feels weak, and my heart is broken from my loss.

My baby, my baby, my baby.

"I don't know. I-I didn't even know-know it existed until you-you said, "

Grams is gasping for air, and I can feel panic build in my stomach, but I still can't seem to open my eyes. I can feel myself slowly fading away while my grandmother is being hurt.

I blacked out again.

This time, I'm woken up by banging. I manage to open my eyes a little to see a man kick my old bedroom door in.

"What the fuck?"

Grant curses as he turns around, fear showing all over his face when he sees who's standing there. The man is tall, about 6"2 like Logan, but he has no hair; his whole head is tattooed, and there's a snake tattoo on the side of his neck. He's wearing a cut, but it has a devil logo on it instead of a hawk like the Untamed Hell Fires. This must be the Devils.

"Snake, just the man; I-I was going to call you."

The man nods his head and takes in the scene. When his eyes land on me, his nostrils flare with anger while his eyes travel down my body, and he visibly stiffens when he sees the blood all over my jeans. It doesn't take a genius to figure out why it's there. He looks back at Grant and tilts his head, getting his phone out and putting it on speaker as my eyes start to close again.

The man, Snake, looks at me for a second, and his eyes shine full of concern while mine fill with relief when I hear who answers the phone after it rings only twice.

"Snake? What did you find out?"

Tears run down my cheeks as my grandmother sobs.

Grant pales.

"I found them; he has the grandmother as well in what looks like a room your woman used to use at her old house."

I hear commotion on the other side of the phone, lots of feet stomping before a dozen motorbikes roar over the receiver. Grant takes a couple of steps back but stops when Snake pulls a gun out, pointing it at his head. "Axel, bring your Doc and hurry."

"FUCK." He shouts. "We'll be a few minutes tops."

Then the line cuts off as blackness takes over again.

Chapter 23

Axel

I kick the club's chair.

We're all at our bar in town, Untamed Fire, to see what everyone has, and so far, no one can find her or the fucking Sedan.

Leah rushes over to me, one of our barkeepers; she's been with us a while now and is always nice and never flirts with the brothers, despite the rumors that one of our brothers, Razor, had stated several times. Apparently, they were involved and she cheated, yet we all went to high school together and grew up together, and not once had he mentioned her.

Something doesn't sit right with me or the whole situation, which is why I've been monitoring it.

Her white, blonde hair with blue streaks sits on top of her head as she shoves a glass into my hands. I raise a brow at her, but she just shakes her head at me and says, "Drink, now." I sigh and toss the whiskey back before she snatches the glass back, heading over to the bar to continue doing inventory. I notice Gunner's eyes follow her, but I shake my head. I can't deal with that just yet; I need to find my woman.

Flame rushes in with Star right behind him, his hand in hers. "The house—Annalise's old family home—never sold. It's just sat there for years." My eyes widen, and we all crowd around his computer, and he points at the documents on his screen and says, "See, it's still in Annie's name. She owns it but never knew; I don't even think Rosie knew. I've spoken to Snake; his clubhouse is closer, so he's going to take a look; we're 10 minutes out from here."

I take a deep breath, trying not to get my hopes up, when my mother bursts through the doors, her face covered in tears. The brothers and prospects who went with her to get Rosie follow her, looking worried, oh fuck. My father catches her as she flies into his arms and cries out, "Rosie's gone; her house was ransacked."

I slowly close my eyes, then look towards Thunder. "There was blood on the kitchen floor."

Oh fuck, I grab the chair closest to me, ready to throw it, but it's snatched out of my hands.

I turn and scowl at the pixie-sized woman.

"Leah."

She shakes her head. "No, I know you're mad; I know you want to break things, just not my bar, and yes, I said MY bar. I'm the one who has to clean up. If you want to hit something, get into a ring."

Then she turns back to the bar while the brothers all bite their lips to hide their laughter. Heck, if I weren't so wound up, I would have laughed too. I shake my head and start to pace.

We're at a dead end unless Snake can find something.

Not even 5 minutes later, my phone rang, and I answered it on the second ring when I saw Snake's name on the screen,

"Snake? What did you find out?"

Everyone stands quickly, looking at me, and I put the phone on speaker. "I found them; he has the grandmother as well in what looks like a room your woman used to use at her old house."

Leah's head shoots up from behind the bar, eyes full of worry.

Fuck,

We all run out of the bar to our bikes and start them up. "Axel, bring your Doc and hurry."

"FUCK." I shout, getting everyone's attention again. "We'll be a few minutes tops." And I hang up and shout, "DOC, WE NEED YOU."

The men all curse as we head out of the bar's parking lot, all of them in formation behind me in pecking order, and I pray. I fucking pray my woman's ok.

Not even 5 minutes later, we arrive at a run-down, two-story gray house that looks like it used to be white. I park next to Snake's dark green Harley and rush into the house.

      Dagger, Ink, and my father follow with Doc on their heels while the rest wait outside. We rush upstairs, where I hear sobbing and my heart beats faster; it doesn't sound like Lise.

Rosie, it must be her.

As we round the corner into a bedroom, following the sobs, we see Snake with his gun trained on the soon-to-be dead man. I see Rosie sitting on the floor, black and blue, with blood on her head, sobbing while holding my woman's head in her lap.

Fuck, no.

My woman.

Her hair is full of blood; she has two black eyes; her nose is bleeding and swollen; and she has a fat lip.

I end up gripping my father, who's trying to keep me up, when I see all the blood between her legs.

The baby, fuck, she's lost the baby.

I rush towards her with Doc close behind, "Annalise, darling." I rasp as I place one of my hands on her cheek and the other on her stomach, where our baby was supposed to grow.

I look at Snake, who's looking at us with sorrow, and I swallow hard.

The baby's gone; I know it is.

I clear my throat as Doc starts checking my woman over, and I rasp, "Dagger, call for a van, then call your uncle; we can't have the law involved with this. Ink, grab that piece of shit, and take him to the basement at the clubhouse. Snake, you are welcome to follow them."

Ink grabs him hard and says, "No, wait, please. I just wanted the money, WAIT, I DIDN'T KNOW SHE WAS PREGNANT,

PLEASE I DIDN'T KNOW, YOU CAN'T DO THIS TO ME, I'M HER FUCKING FATHER, SHE'LL NEVER FORGIVE YOU FOR HURTING ME." He shouts, and Ink drags him by his hair like he dragged my woman. Snake nods his head, his eyes showing concern and worry for us, then follows them out. I look back at my woman and shake my head.

I gently kiss her forehead and say, "I'm sorry I couldn't save you before you lost our baby."

I hear Rosie sob while my father helps her; tears well in my eyes, but I hold them in.

It is not the time to fall apart just yet.

"Axel, we need an ambulance. She has a concussion, two broken ribs, and a broken nose, but my main concern is the amount of blood she's lost from the miscarriage, which I believe she has had. I'll need to do a scan to be sure, but if we don't get her to the hospital quickly, we could lose her. Her pulse is already weak."

   Rosie sobs some more as my heart rate picks up, and I nod my head, but my father butts in, "There's no time for an ambulance; we'll take that piece of shit's car; I'll call a couple of prospects to collect our bikes."

His voice is raspy and full of emotion, and I nod my head, not being able to say much with the lump in my throat.

Both me and Doc go to lift her when Rosie shouts,

"WAIT."

We look at her, and her eyes are on me. "In her bra, there is a picture and-and a key to a safe at the-the bank; it's the rest-

rest of her mother's fortune, Grant; he-he wanted it; someone told him about it." My nostrils flare, and I quickly pat the side of her breast. I feel it on the right side, and I grab the key and photo, placing them in my cut. I nod to Doc, rasping,

"Ready."

He nods back, and we both lift her again, gently, because we don't want to risk her any more than she already is. By the time we get to the front door, half the brothers are still here, while the other half left with Ink. They all growled in fury at seeing my woman. Two prospects wait near our bikes, and as soon as I get Lise into the back seat, I throw my keys to Billy while my father throws his to Shane.

Dad gets in the driver's seat while Rosie gets in the passenger seat, and I climb in the back with my woman, placing her head on my lap. My hand goes back to her stomach, and a few tears spill from my eyes as I lock eyes with a few brothers.

All their eyes widen when they realize she's lost the baby because, with this amount of blood, there's no way it survived.

We head to the hospital with roughly eight bikers surrounding the car, breaking all traffic laws. Doc had already sped ahead, and when we got to the ambulance bay, he was already there with a gurney and several staff members. A doctor takes Rosie, making her sit in a wheelchair to get checked out; her eyes don't leave Lise until she's out of view while the doctors and nurses all try to safely get her onto the gurney, and we're rushing after them when I remember about her last injury from Grant.

I quickly grab Doc's arm, and he twists to look at me as I rasp, "Her back, brother." His eyes widen. "Fuck," he says, then rushes after them while a nurse escorts us all to the waiting room.

My dad, Flame, and Dagger look at me with wide eyes, and I slowly close mine before sliding down the nearest wall, sitting my ass on the cold floor, placing my head in my hands as tears fall from my eyes.

I don't know how long I sit here before a nurse finally comes in. I shoot to my feet and walk over to her, but her eyes are on Dagger, making me roll mine. I clear my throat, and her cheeks go red. "Sorry, uh, um, I was sent out to give you an update." Her eyes slide back to Dagger again, who looks ready to snap her head off and shout at her.

I growl. "For fucks sake, he'll fuck you in a minute. Now tell me about my fucking woman. NOW."

I shout the last bit, making her eyes go wide while Dagger smirks at her.

"Sorry, right. He wanted to let you know that he's taking your wife for an MRI."

I nod my head and try not to laugh in her face, my wife? I bet she doesn't even know her name. She looks at Dagger again, who looks furious, coming to the same conclusion as me, and I decide to put my theory to the test: "Is she awake?" She startles, looking back at me. She clears her throat again. "I, uh, I'm not sure; she didn't say."

I tilt my head at her. "She? Hmm, that's funny because Doc is definitely a male. You weren't sent in here, were you?" She stiffens but shakes her head no. "Let me guess, another nurse was supposed to give me an update, but you wanted to because of my brother here but didn't get all the details you were supposed to give to me."

Dagger growls, narrowing his eyes at her, and she clears her throat again. I shake my head with a sigh, "Send the nurse in who was supposed to come in and fuck off before I report you."

She sucks in a deep breath. "It'll, uh, be a little while; she's, uh, gone to see one of my patients."

I growl, and she quickly turns to go out of the door, but not before looking over her shoulder at Dagger one more time before going out of it. I sigh, running a hand through my hair, sitting on one of the chairs while Dagger saunters off, making my father shake his head.

I can't help the evil smirk that takes over my face too, because he won't let her get off for her stunt; he's about to punish her the only way we men punish women.

The door bursts open 10 minutes later as Star rushes in with Ink and jumps in Flames, awaiting arms.

She rasps, "Misty is sitting with Rosie; she has a concussion but is going to be okay. Any news?" She looks at me, and I shake my head, causing tears to run down her cheeks.

I go to her and take her into my arms.

"She's a fighter."

She nods against my chest then goes back to Flames, awaiting arms, while Ink states, "Subject contained with Hawk, Gunner, and Snake, I sent the rest of the brothers back to the clubhouse that was outside except for a couple of prospects that are with Misty and Rosie; your momma is on route."

I nod and take a seat again grateful for Ink but needing to be alone. I put my head in my hands when someone sits next to me, and I sigh. Sitting up, I look to see a pale-looking Dagger.

Ink, Stormy, Butch, and Dad come over to see what's up with him while I look at him with a raised brow. "What she do, bite your dick or something?"

The men chuckle while he looks at me with wide eyes and rasps,

"I think I found my one."

Both my brows go up while Stormy, his dad snaps, "Not the ditzy fucking nurse who shoved another nurse aside who actually knew about our girl's update just so she could get to you? Because if so, I'm divorcing you as my blood."

Dagger doesn't even bite his head off instead instead he just rasps again, in shock while I try not to laugh, "Nope, I was fucking said nurse in a storage room when she walked in and-and I opened my big fucking mouth without thinking while my hips were still thrusting into the other fucking nurse I was about to leave hanging."

My mouth hangs open.

"What do you say to her?" I look at my dad, wondering why he would ask that, but he just shrugs, clearly wanting a distraction plus a good story to tell Momma. Dagger clears his throat. "Hey, beautiful, what's your name?"

Flame and Star have now joined us as he continues while Ink and Stormy look at him like he's the biggest idiot on the planet, "and she said, 'not Hers, please continue' before grabbing some blankets, then walked out; she didn't even look back."

I can't help it; I fucking laugh my ass off while Ink falls to the floor full of laughter. Stormy looks at his son with raised brows, and Dagger just sits there, shell-shocked that a woman didn't want to know him while he was fucking someone else. I shake my head at the idiot while the rest of the brothers try to calm down when the door opens again and a petite woman who doesn't look any older than 24 or 25 walks in. She's slim in her nurse's dress, has brown curly hair in a messy bun on top of her head, and her blue eyes look remorseful when we make eye contact.

I know this is the nurse who was supposed to come in.

She looks at Dagger briefly, her cheeks going red, and I curse under my breath, another one only wanting a brother instead of doing her job.

Fucks sake

I go to get up when she starts to walk towards me, but Dagger grabs my arm, stopping me for a moment. "Fuck, that's her."

My eyes widen. Well, that explains why she blushed.

I bite my lip to stop the laughter while the other brothers clear their throats, turning away. I shake him off of me, shaking my head, and meet her halfway; she doesn't break eye contact with me, so it's a plus, I guess, as she fiddles with her fingers in front of her.

"Are you Axel?" Her voice is soft, and I swear I hear Dagger sigh, the fucking idiot.

"I am. Do you have news about my woman?"

Yeah, I'm testing her, I learned my lesson from the last one.

She gives me a gentle smile; I see her fingers tremble a little.

She's nervous.

I can feel my brothers at my back, so I can understand why. She clears her throat. " Dr. Thomas asked me to give you an update on Annalise Lawrence." I give her a gentle smile when she gets my woman's name correct as Ink steps beside me. He also gives her a gentle smile: "Just tell us, sweets; I know we look scary, but we are not; rip the band-aid off."

She gives him a small smile while Dagger growls under his breath at his brother's nickname for the woman he's by the looks of things, claiming.

"Ok."

She looks at me again, eyes full of compassion, and my heart picks up. Worry churns in my gut.

"After we got her into her private room, she coded, and her heart stopped beating." Ink and Dagger quickly grab a hold of me before I collapse on the floor. I hear Star sob while my father is extremely silent with the other brothers. "We gave her CPR, managing to get her heart started again." She gently puts her hand on my arm, keeping eye contact with me. "She had lost a lot of blood and had extensive trauma to her lower stomach, and I'm so sorry, but after a scan, a heartbeat was not found and her womb was empty; it was determined that she had lost the baby."

The brothers curse in the background, but this woman doesn't take her glossy eyes off of mine, her compassion shining through them. I knew she lost it, but having it confirmed was like taking a bullet to my chest. I couldn't breathe as a few tears fell from my eyes.

"The good news is that her womb is still intact. No permanent damage was done; she'll still be able to carry more children if she chooses to do so in the future." I slowly close my eyes as more tears fall, and she gives my arm a squeeze before letting me go. I open my eyes when she talks again: "Dr. Thomas believes her ribs are only cracked, but he wants to make sure. About half an hour ago, she was taken for an MRI scan to determine his diagnosis, but also to check her spine. We need to ensure she hasn't received more damage to her back due to her previous injuries, and it'll also show any internal bleeding. He is also taking her for a head CT as a precaution due to the extensive injuries to her face and nose. Her head has received some trauma, so we want to ensure she has no bleeds on the brain. She does have a concussion and will need monitoring for a few nights. Dr Thomas will keep her admitted for the duration."

I nod and rasp, "Thank you." She nods. "Is she awake? I mean, does she know about our..."

I can't finish the sentence, but she smiles gently at me. "She hasn't woken since being admitted; she doesn't know as of yet that we are aware of. During the incident, she may have already noticed; I'm just not sure how awake she was during her trauma."

My heart breaks at the thought of her being alone, realizing our baby's gone. The nurse squeezes my arm again before turning to leave. Dagger clears his throat, making Ink snort while I sigh, not wanting to deal with this but knowing she most likely won't answer him if he asks because, well, he was just fucking another nurse, then tried to hit on her during the act.

"What's your name?" I rasp.

She turns and gives me another gentle smile: "Melanie Wilson. If I hear anything else, I'll come to you straight away, but otherwise, if you need anything, I'll be around this area." I nod again and say, "Thank you." She smiles again, then walks out without so much as looking at Dagger, who groans and sits down on the chair while I stare at the door.

Star comes and stands by me; she takes hold of my hand.

"Axel?" she whispers.

"My baby's dead." It's all I can think to say: Our baby is gone, killed by Grant. My tears fall. "How am I supposed to tell her?"

I hear Dagger mutter, "Fuck," before he grips the back of my neck, pulling me to him while Star squeezes my hand tighter, sobbing.

My father stands next to me on my other side, gripping my shoulder, and rasps, "You hold her close. She's going to struggle for a while, son; she'll need you now more than ever, and you don't fucking let her push you away. We both know she will; she'll blame herself, but you don't let up; give her some space for a few days, then go all fucking in."

I nod against Dagger as he, my father, and Star drag me over to the chairs where we sit and wait for some more news.

Axel: An MC Romance

Chapter 24

Annalise

I hear beeping.

It's absolutely annoying.

Where am I?

Am I in a hospital? Again?

I slowly start to open my eyes but wince because of the light before I take in the white room that smells of antiseptic. I feel a squeeze against my right hand, and I look to see Logan sitting in the chair, both of his hands gripping my one tightly, his red-rimmed eyes filling with unshed tears, his hair a mess. "Hi, darling." I look into his eyes as my memories flash through like a movie.

Grant, Grams, the baby, blood, and pain.

I move my left hand to my lower stomach, which aches, and his tears fall. "I'm sorry, darling, so sorry." He lets out a sob, but I can't seem to move properly. I want to scream; I want to cry and shout and tell him he's wrong; I want to tell him he's not sorry because our baby is fine, yet all I feel is numb.

So goddamn numb.

I look towards my flat stomach that's covered by a hospital gown and blanket and just stare at it as visions of the blood fill my mind. No, not blood; my baby being flushed from my body.

The door opens, but I don't look up; I just stare at my stomach. "Annalise?"

I recognize the voice; it's the clubs Doc, but I can't seem to look up from my stomach.

He clears his throat. "OK, Annalise, I'll just get right to it."

I feel myself nod, but I still don't look up. I don't know what I expect to see, yet I can't look up.

"On arrival, you had lost a lot of blood and your heart had stopped; we had to give you CPR." He pauses, and I know he's expecting a reaction, but all I can focus on is my stomach. Maybe they should have just left me and let my heart stop.

My father had already taken my mother and now my baby, so why not take my life too?

I nod my head like I'm listening and not picturing no longer being here and how at peace I feel about that notion, and he continues, "Unfortunately, you had extensive trauma to your lower stomach, and I'm so sorry, Annie, but after a scan, a heartbeat was not found and your womb was empty; you've lost the baby." He stops again, and I know I should react, but I'm not. Why am I not reacting?

Am I broken?

Did he break me?

He clears his throat. "The good news is that your womb is still intact. No permanent damage was done through the trauma; I was concerned about some scarring, but all scans have come back clean. You'll still be able to carry more children if you choose to do so in the future."

Future?

More children?

I'll probably kill them too.

I can't get my thoughts together; I can't seem to be able to speak; I'm just staring at my stomach. "You've had an MRI scan to determine that you only had three cracked ribs and not broken ones; they'll take a few weeks to heal. We also did the MRI to check your spine, to ensure you haven't had any more damage to your back, and also to ensure you didn't have any internal bleeding."

Right, yeah, the last time Grant laid hands on me, he nearly paralyzed me.

I hear Logan sigh and squeeze my hand, but I don't look up from my stomach.

Am I being rude?

I feel like I'm being rude.

Doc continues, though: "Your MRI was clear, your spine is intact, and no further damage has been done. You don't have any internal bleeding. It's mainly bruising and your ribs that you're suffering from. We also took you for a head CT as a precaution because of the trauma to your face. You do have a concussion and will need monitoring for a few nights now that you are awake. You also had a broken nose that has been reset. You've been unconscious for nearly two days, so we'll keep you admitted for another two, and then you can go home. Do you have any questions, Annie?"

I don't answer him.

What is wrong with me?

Why am I not screaming and crying yet?

"Axel, can I have a word out in the corridor, please? Annie? I'll come check on you in a little while, OK?"

I feel myself nod, so that's good, right?

Why do I feel so numb?

They both leave the room after Logan kisses my head, whispering, "I'll be back in a minute, Princess," but they forget to shut the door fully, so I hear their conversation.

"How concerned do I need to be, Doc? She hasn't said a word since I confirmed we lost the baby; she just stares at her stomach."

"I don't know; she seems to be in a catastrophic state. She's in shock, and by her reaction, she was definitely conscious when she lost the baby, so she could be suffering from PTSD."

"Fuck."

"She's going to need time, Axel. Try to get her to talk. Let her know about Rosie."

I hear Logan sigh.

"What do we do if she doesn't speak? Doesn't react?"

"She will, Axel; it may not be now, tomorrow, or even this week. She'll talk randomly, but when she does, she'll also fall, and she'll need you, Axel, more than ever. She's gone through some major trauma. Just give her some time. I'll pop by later, OK?"

I hear the door shut and boots shuffle, but I still don't look up.

Logan takes his seat again before grabbing my hand and squeezing it tight. "Darling?" I don't look up, and he sighs in frustration but keeps his voice calm. "Your Grams, she's doing okay; she has some bruises, but her memory of the incident is non-existent. After being admitted, it's like it vanished. Doc says it's her body's way of healing."

I still don't react; I just stare at my stomach. I don't feel anything except numbness, but I should feel relieved, though right?

Why don't I feel relieved?

He squeezes my hand again. "Look at me, princess. I need to see those beautiful violet eyes." He sighs when I continue to stare at my stomach. "We'll get through this, darling, I promise."

He shouldn't make promises he can't keep because I don't know how I can survive this. I mean, this is my fault. I lost the baby because I didn't agree to someone with me at all times. He was trying to support my decisions, and now I've lost my baby, our baby.

My fault, my fault, my fault.

The door opens again, but I don't look up, even when someone gasps. I hear a quick shuffling of feet when someone wraps their arms around my neck. "My baby, thank the heavens you're awake."

Cammy.

I thought I'd break hearing her voice, but I still felt numb.

"Momma, just let up a bit."

I feel her loosen her arms a little, and I can feel her eyes on me, but I don't move.

"Annalise?" She sounds concerned, but I don't react. Blood swims into my vision as I look at my stomach, my blood, my baby, our baby.

I think I'm broken. I mean, am I?

The door opens again, but I don't react yet. I can hear Cammy's breathing; it's picked up.

"Annie Girl,"

Dead Shot.

He sounds so relieved; why am I still not reacting? Maybe I need my Grams; she can snap me out of anything. "Pumpkin, it's about time you woke." Ok, maybe not. "Annalise?" Come on, Grams, snap me out of this; I don't want to feel like this, please.

"Axel, what's wrong with my granddaughter?"

I feel Logan squeeze my fingers tighter, and I hear the concern in his words as he speaks, "Doc says she's in a state of shock."

"How long did he say it'd last?" Dead Shot sounds calm, but I know he's not. He's worried, and I hate worrying him—all of them—but it's like my body has shut down.

My baby, my fault.

"He's not sure, but she'll speak when she's ready; when her mind has caught up, then she'll probably fall." His voice is raspy, like he wants to cry.

"Has she said anything at all since she woke? Or even looked at anyone?" Gram's voice is stern. I like the stern voice of Grams. It's the 'I get shit done' voice.

"She looked at me when she woke, but as soon as I confirmed that we had lost the baby, she hasn't looked up from her stomach since or reacted to anything." The more he talks, the more concerned he sounds. I don't deserve him; I killed our baby, and I didn't protect it.

Soft hands gently grip my chin.

Grams.

She gently turns my head to look at her.

Her eyes fill with tears when she looks into my eyes. I know they're empty; I don't even blink; I'm broken.

My baby, my fault.

"Come back to us, baby girl." She rasps and I hear Cammy sniffle, but I don't react.

My baby, my fault.

Chapter 25

Axel

I sigh, scrubbing a hand over my face, feeling frustrated. I'm sitting in the club's common room at the bar with my laptop in front of me, trying to get the payroll sorted for the Untamed Girls, but I'm struggling to focus my mind on my woman. She hasn't spoken in two days, and if you don't move her face physically, then she'll just stare at her stomach.

I scrub my hands down my face again. I feel so fucking drained; I've barely slept since finding out Lise was taken, and I can't get the look of her emotionless eyes out of my mind, fuck. With a sigh, I go back to my laptop.

It's about an hour later when I feel a hand glide from the middle of my back to under my arm and around to my chest, and yet again, Bubbles decides to outstay her fucking welcome in my clubhouse because we all know she's the only one stupid enough to try and make a move on me.

"Hey baby, you've been really stressed lately; why don't I help relieve that for you?" She whispers, and I growl, grabbing her hand and yanking it from my body, but she pushes again, gripping my arm. "Come on, Axel, you've been miserable for two days; she doesn't deserve you; I mean, she doesn't even talk to her own family."

I spin around about to fucking blow at her for talking about my woman that way when she has no fucking idea what Lise went through when Star rushes up behind Bubbles and yanks her back by her hair, making her scream, and my mouth drops open in shock.

"What the fuck?" Flame gasps as he walks out of the kitchen with food for, I'm guessing, the little hell cat here, right as she yanks Bubble away from me.

"GET OFF OF ME." Bubbles screams out, but Star doesn't let her go; she continues to drag Bubbles over to the other sweet butts who are looking at Star with new eyes. She shoves Bubbles onto the floor, then gets in her face and says, "You spoilt selfish fucking whore."

My eyes widen, and I look at Flame and say, "Holy shit, she just cursed."

He nods his head in shock, his eyes never leaving the scene in front of us, and half of the brothers who haven't gone to work yet stare with their mouths wide open because Star never curses; she doesn't like the language, or well, she didn't.

"You know that baby, the one that you hoped was yours when you decided to poke holes in the condom?"

Oh shit.

I sigh and scrub a hand down my face. Only the brothers are aware of the full situation and Lise's immediate family and friends, which really only include Sandy, Star, momma, dad, and Rosie.

Bubbles' brows furrow,

"Yeah, bitch, she had that baby booted out of her when she was kidnapped, so if my girl wants to hide herself away in her own head to try and deal with that kind of trauma, watching blood soak her jeans knowing there's nothing she could have done because the attacker was a psychopath, then she gets that fucking right, so do me a favor and stop hitting on HER man."

Bubbles' eyes widen as she speaks while my heart breaks realizing Star is right; Lise deserves this right now; it's been only two days, and she was excited for this baby once she finally decided to face it head-on; it was a part of her and me, our baby.

Star shoves Bubbles down and then walks away while half of the sweet butts look on in shock, and the other half have tears running down their cheeks as they stare at me. I may have only just found out about the baby, but I wanted it; we were going to be a family.

Star walks up to me and kisses my cheek, whispering, "Sorry."

I give her a gentle smile. I'm not mad; she spoke up for her friend. She goes over to Flame, who's still looking at her in shock, and she takes the bacon sandwich out of his hand, kisses his cheek, and then sits down next to me, eating as if nothing happened. I chuckle, shaking my head, before getting back to the payroll before I bring my woman home this afternoon, but before I start, Flame sits next to me and asks, "How are you doing, Pres?"

I growl at him, making him chuckle. I can't stand my childhood friends calling me that, and he knows it: "I want my woman back."

He sighs, "You'll get her back, Axel; it'll just take time. I know you're hurting, but she is too, and she can't think about your hurt right now because all she can see is the blood. It's why she keeps looking down at her stomach; she sees the blood even though it's not there."

Fuck, how did I not put two and two together?

Fuck.

"Don't beat yourself up, Axe; you weren't to know."

I scrub a hand down my face.

"I know, Star, but I should have connected the dots."

She smiles at me while Flame pats my back.

"Just give her time, and hopefully she'll snap out of it, but at least she's safe now." I sigh and nod my head.

Dad, Dagger, Ink, and Snake dealt with Grant. I wanted to, fuck me did I want to watch him die slowly but I couldn't, Annalise needed me more, so I gave the ok for them to go ahead. Dad ensured he was tortured well before he died, including paralyzing him like he nearly did to his own daughter. He had a nice and slow, antagonizing death while crying for mercy.

But where was my woman's mercy, my baby's?

I get back to payroll while Star and Flame keep me company, ensuring I've eaten like mother hens. I do appreciate it though; things are hard at the moment. I've just finished the last pay when my phone rings, and I frown when I see it's the hospital.

"This is Axel."

"Hi Axel, it's Melanie Wilson. I'm calling because even though Annalise checked herself out this morning, she left her medication. I asked if she'd wait the 10 minutes until I had the script ready for her, and she nodded, but when I got back to her room, she was already gone. I tried calling her mobile, but it just rang out."

My heart rate quickens. Why the fuck has she signed out when I'm supposed to be picking her up?

I cleared my throat,

"Her mobile is at her flat; we found it the day she went missing, so she hasn't got it on her; one of the brothers will pick up her medication; is that OK, Melanie?"

Dagger walks out of his office just as I say her name, and he rushes over to me. If my heart weren't full of concern right now, I would have laughed, but I can't because my woman isn't where she's supposed to be right now.

"Yes, that's not a problem, but uh, um, Axel, can you ensure it's not the brother I caught in a storage room, please?"

I bite my lip to hold on to the laughter that wants to finally escape, making Flame, Star, and Dagger look at me weirdly.

I clear my throat. "I'll try. Thanks again, Melanie."

Then I hang up and chuckle looking at Dagger,

"Seems my woman decided to check herself out this morning and didn't pick up her meds. Melanie is asking if I could grab them for her, and I told her a brother would as soon as possible."

He grins wide, which quickly falls at my next words, making me swallow my chuckle.

"She asked for it to not be you."

Flame snorts, then coughs to hide his amusement, while Star just laughs in his face.

"That fucking woman, if she thinks I'm not getting Annie's meds, then she has another thing coming; she feels this between us; I know she fucking does; I'll fucking show her; she's mine whether she likes it or not, the damn stubborn woman."

He curses and mumbles all the way out the front door, and we all burst out in laughter, but mine quickly dies down when my phone pings.

Princess — I'm sorry, I just need some time. I know you are hurting too, and you need me, but I can't be there for you when I'm dying inside. I need to come to terms with everything before I can help fix you too. Just give me some time. I'll text back if you text me, but that's all I can deal with right now. I don't want any visitors, and I'm closing the bakery until further notice. I've already contacted my staff; please just give me some time. I love you so much. XX

I can feel Flame and Star looking at me with furrowed brows, causing everyone in the room, including my father, to look at me, so I read the message out loud, and the men curse while the women, including the sweet butts, sob. Bubbles' eyes widen and guilt shines through them, but I can't be assed with her right now, with anyone, really.

I clear my throat. "I'm, uh, going to head to the house for a bit."

I don't wait to hear what anyone has to say. I close my laptop down and head out of the clubhouse, walking in the scorching heat to my nearly finished house.

When I walk through the door, Buzz frowns. "You ok, Pres?" I clear my throat and nod my head. "I, uh, came to work." He nods, his eyes showing understanding, then nods towards the dining area.

The table needs to ascend perfectly.

It only takes me half an hour to assemble the dark oak dining table, and I move on to the kitchen cupboards before I help finish the deck with Buzz, before I know it, four hours have passed and the sun is starting to set.

I take a seat and look out to the trees behind the garden fence when I feel someone sitting next to me. I don't have to look to know Dagger as he passes me a beer.

"How'd it go with Melanie?"

"I swear to fucking God, that woman is difficult. When she saw me arrive, she fucking gave the medication to the dozy idiot I fucked."

He shakes his head, and I snort out a laugh. The girl is good; I'll give her that.

"You were fucking the nurse when she first saw you, Dag; she seems sweet, not the kind of girl to hit it and quit it. She's innocent."

I try to make sure he realizes what I mean; now I'm no expert, but she gives the 'I have barely any experience' vibe like my woman did. Dagger furrows his brows before his eyes widen.

"You mean?"

I shrug. "I don't know, but she blushed like mad when she saw you in the waiting room and stuttered when she asked for you not to be the one to show up today; now I don't think she's a virgin; she's too pretty to not have any experience." He growls at that, but I continue, "But I don't think she's very experienced with men."

He nods his head, still agitated by her being with someone else, which makes him a massive hypocrite.

I sigh and scrub a hand down my face.

"Are you doing okay, Logan?"

Slowly closing my eyes, I nod my head, then shake it, knowing I can't lie to him when he talks to me without our club titles or our road names.

"She messaged me, Trav. She says she needs space and will be closing the bakery until further notice. She doesn't want anyone to show up at the apartment above her shop. She says she'll answer me if I message, but that's it for now, and I know she needs this. Fuck, I know she's dying inside because I am too, but how in the fuck am I supposed to leave her to deal with everything on her own? It just isn't in me. I need her; I need her like I need air to breathe."

I shake my head and take a swig of my beer, still looking ahead.

"You give her 2 weeks." I look at him with furrowed brows.

"2 weeks to herself before you show up at the apartment and bring her home, here to this home you built for her. I spoke to Buzz on the way in, and he said it should be finished by then, so you help him out. I'll take the slack at the strip club while trying to convince Mel that she's mine, and you stay busy. Once Buzz gives you the okay, you go get your girl and help her through the trauma she's lived through, and you both help each other with the loss of your baby."

I nod my head. I know he's right.

"Ok, I'll give it a go, but you're going to have to take her medication to her because if I do, I won't just post them through the door." He grins at me.

"Already thought of it; Flame and Star are taking it before going to the bar for their 'friend date'."

I snort when he quotes 'friend date.'

"Those two really need to get their fucking acts together; they both love each other, but not in a friendly way. And the sooner, the fucking better, because it won't be long when someone looks at Star."

Dagger bursts out in laughter because he knows it's true. Star's a beautiful girl and also fucking talented, anyone would be lucky to have her.

I sigh again, running a hand through my hair. Fuck, I miss my woman.

"Two weeks, brother, two weeks."

I nod.

Two weeks.

Chapter 26

Annalise

I'm sitting on my sofa, staring at the wall.

What day is it? What time is it?

It's not very light out, so maybe it's early?

When did I come home from the hospital?

Was it yesterday or last week?

Have I showered today? I know my hair is wet, or is it grease?

I'm losing track of the day and time. Have I taken my medication today? I can't remember; I think they were antibiotics.

My baby, my fault.

I feel like I'm missing a piece of myself, like I can't breathe without it. I turn my head to look outside the window; the skies are a lovely orange, pinkie; it must be evening.

Maybe I should bake? It might help bring me back.

No, I shouldn't bake. I don't deserve to bake good things when I couldn't even save...

My baby, my fault.

My phone pings. I look at it but haven't picked it up yet. Logan has been messaging me, but I haven't always answered him. He deserves better than someone like me; I couldn't even save...

My baby, my fault.

My phone pings again, so I pick it up.

My heart – I miss you, darling. XX

Dagger – you are missed, sweetheart. Your man needs you; please message him back. The club wants their queen back.

I put my phone down again and don't reply. I don't deserve any of them. Why should I be happy when I can't save...

My baby, my fault.

I stare back at the wall again, my mind going a million miles per hour.

If only I fought harder, if only I agreed to have someone watch me closer, if only Grant had succeeded all those years ago, then I wouldn't have brought pain to people's lives.

He killed Mama because of me. He hurt Grams because of me. He...

My baby, my fault.

Bake. I need to bake. Baking's good. I have to bake...

My baby, my fault. I'm sorry, baby.

Axel: An MC Romance

Chapter 27

Axel

I can't sleep; it's 3 a.m., but I just can't.

It's been two weeks, as Dagger suggested. I waited, and I was going insane. I want to go get her now, but it's early. We finished the house and furnished it to Lise's liking, and I ensured the baby room that I had started to paint was changed into a guest room for now until she's ready to try again. I've kept myself busy, just not busy enough to notice she hasn't messaged anyone back since she asked for space, including her grandmother.

Fucks sake.

I throw the covers off and quickly dress in my dark jeans, my dark long-sleeved Henley, and my biker jacket with my cut over it. Maybe a ride to the lookout point will help.

Half an hour later, I'm sitting astride my bike, looking at all the houses in our little town, the lake a mile to the right just shining through the trees, but all I can still think about is my woman and how she's doing.

I'm scared.

I'm scared of what I'll find when I go to the apartment today. I know she needed this space. Well, I know she thinks she needs this space, and I had to give it to her. I promised I would, but now I'm done. My gut is telling me she needs me, and my gut is always right.

I stay watching the view for two hours before I make my way back down the hill towards the clubhouse. I want a quick shower before I drag my woman home, where I'll never let her leave my sight again. It doesn't take me long when I pull back up to the clubhouse, but I frown at the car sitting just outside the gate. I park my bike and look at the car, but the driver isn't looking at me; she's on her phone, and the prospect on guard nods his head, saying all is well. Huh. I shrug and then head into the clubhouse, but come to a stop when I bump into a disheveled-looking Star. I tilt my head when she looks at me with wide eyes full of fear. Now why would a woman who has looked at me like a brother figure for years look at me like that?

Her hair is a mess, there is makeup all over her face, and her clothes are ripped a little.

I raise a brow at her when I realize what has happened. They've finally given in to one another, yet she's doing the walk of shame.

"Star?"

I question: This isn't her; she's been in love with Flame since she was 10 years old. If they've finally slept together, which it's obvious they have, then there's no way he would let her walk out right now, which means she sneaked out. I know I haven't been around the past two weeks because of my own shit, but that doesn't mean I haven't noticed her absence at the clubhouse. Even now, as I look at her, I can see a difference in her. She's lost some weight, and her eyes are emotionless and hardened. Something's happened, and she has kept it to herself.

I go to walk towards her, but she steps back away from me, and I lift my hands up in surrender to show I'm not going to hurt her. The fear oozes from her body: "Star? You know I'd never hurt you, right?" Tears fill her eyes, and I go to walk towards her again, but she shakes her head at me.

"I know you wouldn't, but please stay there." I furrow my brows and say, "Please, Logan."

I tilt my head when she uses my legal name; she's scared.

"What happened, sweetheart?"

She shakes her head again as her tears fall.

"I'm leaving."

I nod. "OK, I'm not going to stop you, but I would like to know what's going on with a woman who I see as a sister."

She shakes her head again. "No, Logan, I'm leaving Parkerville."

My eyes widen. She's leaving her home and her family. No, this is not the Star we know and love.

"Star, this is your home; you've finally got Flame; why would you…" I trail off, studying her.

She looks broken. That's when I noticed her bracelet was gone. The one Flame bought her when she turned 10 had a tracking device built into it.

"Why would you leave Star? What happened?" My voice hardens, and her tears fall as she rasps.

"Hairy says hello."

A sob leaves her throat, and the color drains from my face.

"When did the Devil's VP talk to you, Star?" My voice commands answers; I'm no longer her pseudo-brother but the president of an MC.

She shakes her head and sobs.

"Two weeks ago, when Flame" spits his name with venom, making my stomach drop, she's using his road name, "decided fucking Ginger on our friend's date was a better idea than spending it with me. H-He grabbed me by-by the toilets." My heart rate picks up; I can feel it beating hard against my rib cage. Please, no, don't say it.

"H-He dragged me outside, and-and, oh God." Her whole body trembles and I can't stand here any longer. I go to her and wrap my arms around her, placing her head into my chest and holding her tight. "He-he said F-Flame killed his-his cousin, and I'm-I'm his punishment."

My body tenses, Killer.

"What did he do, sweetheart?" I rasp against her head, and she steps back out of my hold, her face full of disgust as she rasps,

"He-he raped me."

My breathing picks up as I bend forward, placing my hands on my knees.

"Fuck, no, no, no."

She sobs again, and I stand up again, looking at her. She's rubbing her arms as if she can still feel him, and I realize,

"This was your goodbye to him, wasn't it? You slept with him as a goodbye, but you can't stay and fight because you don't think you can forgive him."

She shakes her head again as she rasps,

"The women constantly thrown-thrown at me was killing me slowly, Logan, but this time he left me for someone else again, and I-I-I." She can't say the words again, but she looks me in the eyes and states, "It's all on CCTV. He made sure to do it in front of the camera. I need to leave; please let me leave."

I slowly close my eyes, pain shooting through me. When I open them again, her eyes are pleading with me; she needs to go, just like when Lise needed her two weeks, so I nod, and more tears fall from her eyes as I rasp, "We will always be your family, you hear me. You are my sister in every way but blood. He will try to find you though Star; he might not have shown it, but he loves you more than life itself."

She walks up to me and places a kiss on my cheek before whispering, "Just not enough to choose me. I love you, Logan; you are my family always, but make sure you always choose her; she needs you."

Then she walks out towards what I'm now realizing is the car out front, which must be an Uber. I quickly shoot a text to my dad, telling him to meet me in church, then run up the stairs towards Flame's room and bang on the door continuously until he opens it with a scowl and sleepy eyes.

"Get fucking dressed and meet me in church right fucking now, hurry."

Then I run to church, leaving a shocked Flame in his doorway. I get the club's laptop and log onto our security system, finding the exact day and time, because, well, it's the same day my woman asked for space. Just as I start going through the footage from the time they arrive, Dad and Flame rush in.

"Axe, is this going to take long? I need to call Star."

I shake my head, hating I'm about to tear his world down. "She's gone; you won't find her. Last night was her saying goodbye." No point sugar-coating it. Flame freezes in shock while my dad furrows his brows.

"What do you mean, son?"

I clear my throat when I find the footage of Flame going off with Ginger and the utter heartbreak on Star's face, and I switch on the screen on the right side of the room, linking the footage. Flame's face goes pale when he sees his arm around Ginger, while Star looks like she's about to cry, but before I play it, I look at the two men.

"Brace yourselves, especially you, Zayne." His head shoots my way when I use his legal name, and I clear my throat. "She said Hairy says hello."

"Hairy? As in the Devil's VP?"

I nod to my dad's question, but my eyes don't leave Flames, who's looking at me in confusion, until I state,

"Killer's cousin."

Now he looks like he's about to be sick. And I play the footage, and we watch.

We watch as tears start to fall down her cheeks while Flame walks off without even looking back, and he makes a pained sound in the back of his throat. We watch as she gathers her belongings before heading to the ladies, so I switch the camera. We see a hand come out from around the corner near the fire exit and grab her roughly, putting his hand over her mouth and then dragging her out of view. I look at Flame again as my eyes well up.

My father gasps when he realizes what she must have gone through. Flame, though, is in denial.

"No, she wasn't; I know she wasn't." I sigh. "No, Logan, she wasn't; she was a virgin; I took her virginity last night." I hear my father sigh in relief, but I can't; she told me she was raped, which would mean

Oh, fuck, fuck, fuck. No, no.

I feel bile climb up my throat as I rasp.

"She told me she was raped." and I switch the cameras to the alleyway where we see him shove her to the floor, making sure her face digs into the concrete ground while smirking at the camera. He whispers his message into her ear. Then we watch in horror as she tries to fight to get away from him, trying to put her legs flat on the ground as he pushes her skirt up.

"NO, HE DIDN'T FUCKING RAPE HER; I TOOK HER VIRGINITY LAST NIGHT."

Flame screams as my father's face pales when he realizes what I have. He grips Flame's shoulder as we watch Hairy grip the panties, ripping them off. You can see she's screaming, but no one comes to her aid. He pulls his jeans down a little, then shoves himself inside her.

Her whole body jolts with pain as he rips into her hard and fast.

You can see blood starting to drip down her legs, and my tears fall as we watch this man anally rape our club princess.

"No, n-no." Flame sobs as he falls to the floor, my father gripping him into his arms as tears fall from his eyes too.

We failed her; we didn't protect her, just like Annalise.

We watch as her body goes still. She's gone numb, and Flame sobs some more when he sees she's given up the fight. After about 7 minutes, the soon-to-be-dead man pulls out and cums all over her ass. She doesn't move as he chuckles and pulls his jeans back up. He spits on her and walks off onto the street. Star doesn't move for about 5 minutes; we can see the tears trailing down her cheeks, and she stares forward, not moving. When she does move, she uses the wall to help herself up, leaving her underwear. She grips the wall and uses it to guide her to the street.

I switch the camera again, this time to the street. We watch as she makes sure to stay away from the door, then flags down a driver on the road, and I scowl. She speaks to them through the window, and we see their eyes widen before they nod, and she gets in the backseat.

The car spins, doing a U-turn, heading towards the hospital.

I look towards Flame.

"Do we call Doc? Or do you want to hack the hospital for her records?"

It is up to him whether or not he can handle it.

He clears his throat as my father helps him stand. He comes towards the laptop, and myself and dad watch on the TV as he hacks into the hospital data. It only takes a couple of minutes, and he finds her folder, clicking on it.

My father reads it to us.

"Ok, she had been raped—raped anally. She had extensive tearing and, a minimum of a few weeks to heal. She had scrapes and bruises but nothing more extensive than that. Her blood work and HIV tests came back clear and was offered counselling and for the law to be called in, she refused both."

Flame throws a chair across the room and then looks at me, "Call Snake, now."

I nod and grab my phone. Finding his number, I press on it. He answers after 6 rings,

"Axel, do you have any idea what fucking time it is?"

I clear my throat. "Hairy is your traitor."

Chapter 28

Annalise

I'm sitting on my shower floor while the warm water cascades over my body.

My baby, my fault.

Two weeks—that's how long I've kept everyone away.

I was hoping I'd manage to get back to myself, but I can't. How do you get over losing a baby you never realized you wanted so much?

My tears start to fall again. I miss Logan.

I don't think being away from him has helped with my guilt. I've baked more than my kitchen and bakery can hold, but that's it. I haven't spoken to anyone or even gone outside; the ingredients all came from my bakery.

My baby, my fault. My baby, my fault.

I start to sob as the water goes cold, but I don't move. I deserve to be punished for not protecting our baby.

I don't know how long I stay sitting here with the cold water running over my naked body while I keep muttering to myself when my bathroom door opens and Logan looks at me with heartbreak in his red-rimmed eyes. "Darling," he rasps, and I let out another sob. He rushes over to me, switching the water off before wrapping a towel around my body and picking me up.

I shove my face into his neck as I sob.

"I'm-I'm sorry, so s-s-s-sorry."

He squeezes me tightly as he sits on the edge of my bed.

"It's good to hear your voice, Princess."

His voice sounds scratchy, like he's been crying, and I sob harder.

"It-it was a-a-all my fault, my fault, I'm so-so sorry." I feel his tears fall onto my shoulder, and he cries with me, making me sob harder. "I'm sorry, so, sorry, please forgive me, please, please. My baby, my fault, my fault."

"It wasn't, darling; it wasn't your fault; it was his. He killed our baby, not you."

My body shakes with my violent sobs. "I wanted to-to go with it; with our-our baby, I didn't want to be here anymore, how-how can I live with myself when I couldn't protect it?"

He squeezes me even tighter, his hand cupping my head.

"I wouldn't have let you leave me, Lise. You are my life. You're not allowed to leave me because I need you. Where you go, I go; remember that; you can't leave me, darling; you can't because I'd fucking follow you."

I sob again.

With my guilt building high in my chest from the pain I've probably caused him in the past two weeks, I gasp for breath.

"I've been so-so selfish."

I hear him sigh as he runs his fingers through my wet hair, and he mumbles against my head, "You haven't, darling. I know you wanted me here, but I also knew you needed time to process what had happened. You were kidnapped and tortured by the man who was supposed to love you, and HE killed our baby, but he will never hurt you again. I promise, no one will, princess."

I sniffle and rasp.

"Did he suffer?"

"Paralyzed before they killed him. I stayed with you because you were and are all I need. We also found the person who gave him information about you. It was an old neighbor who overheard a lot from before your mama was killed, Grant offered them $50,000 for any information they might have had over the years; we're not sure who the neighbor was working with to find you so quickly, but we're looking into it. The guy also suffered."

I nod my head and breathe in his scent.

"I missed you."

"Not as much as I missed you, darling. Never again are we doing this. You're not staying here anymore; I'm having this place gutted because we're going home with all the fucking baked goods you've been baking the past few weeks. I knew I should have come and gotten you sooner."

I giggle a little before sighing, staying quiet for a little while before a little sob comes out.

"I really wanted our b-baby."

"Me too, princess, me too."

And I continue to sob, with the man I love holding me tightly, trying to take my pain. A little while later, we've moved, and I'm covered by the Henley shirt that he was wearing. My whole body covers his while he lies on his back, head on a pillow, with my face in his neck.

"I want to get a tattoo."

His hand pauses on my back, where he is rubbing up and down.

"OK?"

I clear my throat. "I want to get the date we lost our baby with 8 weeks next to it so I never forget."

I feel him kiss my head.

"I think that's a good idea, darling; I'll get Ink to set it up."

I nod my head, and he sighs.

"I have some more bad news, Lise." I rest my chin on his chest and look into his beautiful, bright blue eyes, and they shine with heartbreak, making me tense. He runs his fingers through my hair again. "Star, she was; she was raped anally two weeks ago; she can't deal with being here. She's left town."

I quickly sit up and look at him wide-eyed. His eyes fill with unshed tears, and I quickly get off of him completely to find my phone. It takes me a few minutes to find it, but when I do, I notice several messages and missed calls, but it's the ones from Star two weeks ago that have a sob building in my chest.

Star – I need you; can we talk, please?

Guilt like no other takes over.

While I've been self-pitying, my best friend needed me. I quickly press on her name and listen as it rings on the other end several times before it goes to voicemail. I tried it again. Please, Star, please. It goes straight to voicemail, and I can't help the sob that releases from my throat.

"Darling." Logan rasps as he takes me back into his arms.

"I'm so-so selfish; she-she messaged me two-two weeks ago, and I never replied; she-she needed me."

My body's shaking with how badly I'm sobbing. She needed me, and I wasn't there for her.

"You didn't know; none of us did." He cups my cheeks with his large hands so he can look me in the eyes. "She slept with Flame last night as a goodbye. He didn't know." I furrow my brows in confusion, then gasp when he continues, "It was their friend's date, and he went off with Ginger. She went to the bathroom because she was crying and-and a Devil's biker, a traitor to their club, grabbed her and-and.

He did it in front of the cameras, so we knew. She blames Flame and can't forgive him, so she said goodbye the only way she knew how."

I slowly close my eyes as I rasp.

"She gave him her virginity." My tears fall again, and he wipes them away with his thumbs.

"She did, then she left him as punishment for leaving her."

I shake my head and sniffle. "Where has she gone?"

He shrugs. "After we'd seen the footage, we sped down the highway for over three hours and couldn't find her; she's gone, and I don't think she's going to be found anytime soon; just give her time, darling."

I sniffle again and nod as he moves my hair out of my eyes and gives me a gentle smile before I feel his soft lips against mine, gently at first, then he traces my lips with his tongue, and I grant him access instantly. His tongue tangles with mine as I wrap my arms around his neck. His hands glided down my sides before gripping my ass and then lowering to my thighs. He grips them and then lifts me up.

I wrap my legs around his waist, causing his shirt to lift a little so my bare pussy sits on his naked lower stomach. He groans, feeling my heat, before laying me down on the bed, his body covering mine as he does, while our kiss never wavers. He keeps a hold of one of my thighs, keeping it lifted, while his other hand goes between us. He runs his fingers over my pussy making me gasp while he groans again at how wet I am for him, and he quickly unbuckles his belt and unbuttons his jeans, freeing his rock-hard cock.

Never once stopping the kiss, he places the head of his cock at my entrance before he slowly pushes in. He doesn't stop until he bottoms out; only then does he break the kiss. We're both gasping for air as he brings his forehead down, leaning it against mine, our eyes staying connected, his full of love as he pulls out slowly before pushing back in with a little bit of a flex, hitting the right spot. No words are spoken as he moves his hips, keeping them at an angle all while his eyes stare into mine, and I fall even more in love with him as he makes love to me, minding my cracked ribs.

It doesn't take long for an orgasm to build. My lower stomach tightens with need as my body tingles. Keeping his left hand holding my leg, he moves his other and starts slow but hard circles on my engorged clit, black spots appear in my vision as my orgasm washes over me.

Logan groans as I moan out in pleasure while squeezing him tight inside me. He presses in one more time before he cums inside of me before he leans down and kisses my lips gently, one, twice, three times before placing his head in the crook of my neck, keeping his dick deep inside of me, not once worrying about contraception, but thankfully I'm now on the pill and next time we'll be using condoms.

I don't think children are in my future anymore.

"I love you, darling."

He rasps in my neck, and I sniffle, causing him to look up with concern.

"I love you too, Logan, but please, can you take me home? I want to go home."

He smiles gently at me, relief shining through his eyes.

"Course I will, darling, and this way, I don't have to throw you over my shoulder, kicking and screaming."

I giggle, making him groan, and I giggle harder, which soon turns into a moan when he pulls his hips back and then slams into me, mindful of my ribs.

"I think we should go home tomorrow because I have missed my girl and I need the whole night with her. Diamond can have her time tomorrow because she misses her too."

I smile. I do miss my puppy and my man.

The guilt builds again in my chest, but I push it down as he slides out of me before thrusting forward again.

And that's how we spend the rest of the night, catching up with each other's bodies in between kissing and talking while I pray Star is doing okay and my guilt over losing the baby and not being there for my friend will eventually fade because I don't think I can live with that kind of guilt anymore.

Chapter 29

Axel

I stand leaning against the door frame, watching my woman brush her wet hair, putting it in a messy knot on the top of her head. Fuck, she looks beautiful. She looks at me through her mirror and smiles. It doesn't hit her eyes, but there's love shining in them, so there's that.

I smile back at her as I walk over and lean against the dresser.

"I have something I wanted to talk to you about." She furrows her brows but doesn't say anything. "You've struggled, darling, a lot after losing our baby. You feel guilty for surviving and not being able to protect and save it." tears shine in her eyes, and I kneel in front of her, taking her cheeks in my palms, wiping away her tears as they fall. "Darling, you've lost so much weight, and the guilt is eating you alive. I want you to see someone."

She sniffles and goes to shake her head, but I squeeze her cheeks, "Annalise, your falling and I can't lose you, I can't. I need you like I need air to breathe; please, darling, I need you to do this so I don't lose you to survivor guilt or guilt at pushing me away." She lets out a sob, then nods her head, and I sigh in relief, taking her in my arms. I stand, holding her close as her legs wrap around my waist and her head goes into my neck.

I rasp, "How about we go home, darling?"

She nods her head but doesn't let me go, making me smile. I hold her tighter, then walk through to the living area towards the front door, happy that she's wearing jeans with my shirt that she stole a few months ago. I'd already turned everything off when she was getting ready.

When I get to my bike, I run my hand down her back and kiss her head.

"Let's get you on the back, darling."

She slowly unhooks her ankles from my back and slides down my body reluctantly.

"What about my car?" She asks, looking up at me, and I smirk, making her slowly close her eyes and shake her head. "Dad bought me a car, didn't he?"

I just shrug and grin before I give her puppy dog eyes. "Do this for us, please."

She growls at me before hopping on the back of my bike in a huff as I put a helmet on her, making me chuckle. I climb in front of her before she wraps her arms around my waist, placing her head on my back as I start my baby. Lise holds me tighter as I pull out of the alleyway and head towards the clubhouse, where it'll be mostly quiet. Most of the brothers are working while Flame tries to find Star and Hairy, who've gone underground, but I know Momma, Dad, and Rosie will be there, ready to pounce.

When we pull into the clubhouse, the prospect grins wide, seeing Lise on the back of my bike, making me smile.

My woman's loved.

I park up in my designated spot near the door and help Lise off the bike before taking the helmet off her, and I grin.

"You're getting better, darling."

        She grins back before going on her tiptoes, kissing me gently on my lips, and I grin wider. Fuck, I love this girl. I grab her hand and pull her towards the clubhouse, and I fucking pray everyone's given up waiting to see if I'd bring her home today and leave. I haven't messaged them to let them know; I just want some time with my girl.

Unfortunately, my wish was not met.

As we walk into the clubhouse, Mom, Dad, and Rosie all rush towards us, making Lise's eyes widen as they all talk at once.

Fucks sake, she doesn't need this right now.

"Are you okay, pumpkin? You had me so worried, sweet girl."

"What were you thinking, cutting us off like that?"

"How selfish could you be doing this to us and to Axel? He needed you, and you ran away, leaving my son in even more despair. Did it not come to mind that you're not the only one who suffered?"

Momma's face is red with anger, and she fucking overstepped.

I look toward Lise.

Yep, momma definitely overstepped. Lise's face pales at her comment, and hurt shines through her eyes. She sees momma as her mother, and instead of taking a step back and seeing her side, she instantly stands up for her son, and for the first time ever, I snap at my mother.

"MOMMA, ENOUGH."

Her eyes widen in shock while my father looks at me with murder in his eyes, but I match his glare. I'm fucking pissed; she's already admitted to wanting to go with our baby. I don't need this to set her back, especially now that she's looking at Mom with new fucking eyes.

Shit.

Dad must see the seriousness in my eyes because his widens as he looks at Annalise, who hasn't moved a muscle. I can see Bubbles out of the corner of my eyes smirking, and I shoot a glare in her direction, making her smirk fall off and stiffen before looking down. Then I look towards my mother, and she has her eyes on my girl, concern and guilt shining through them.

"Momma." I wait until she looks at me, and I continue. "She needed time; she still needs time, and she's struggling with guilt. I don't need you making it worse right now. I understand your upset, but not as much as she is, and you basically stood by me and ditched the woman who you brought up, who you saw as a daughter."

Tears fall down Rosie's cheeks as she looks at my mother with disappointment, while my mother's eyes widen more with each of my words, while Lise stiffens more and more, and then I look at my dad, who hasn't taken his eyes off of me.

He shakes his head like he's disappointed in me, really?

"I'm not going to fucking coddle you, Annalise Jessica Lawrence; you scared the shit out of us, and you were out of order. We're your family; you lean on us, not run away like a coward; we brought you up better than that. I'm so disappointed in you. I had to watch my son drown while you hid away. How fucking dare you do that to him, to my son. You were not the only one who lost a child."

I slowly close my eyes with a sigh, really hoping I don't kill my own fucking father; he has no idea what he's just done.

When I open my eyes again, I see my father's face pale. Lise has tears running down her cheeks, and I'm about to blow when she says coldly,

"I'm sorry, I'm such a d-disappointment. Next time someone kicks my-my baby out of me, I'll ensure to put everyone else's feelings before m-mine when all I want to do is die right along with it, but don't worry Dead Shot, I'll m-make sure to speak with you and Cammy first."

My father's eyes widen before she shoves past him, going to our room. I sigh again—shit, it looks like they just lost their titles. I look down for a minute while placing my hands on my hips before I state,

"When I went to the apartment yesterday, I found my girl sitting in a freezing cold shower, muttering, 'My baby, my fault,' I don't even know how long she was in there, but her lips were blue. She blames herself and has survivor's guilt. She wanted to join our baby, and you all gang up on her as soon as she walks through the door after I fucking convince her to come home."

I look up to see Rosie and Momma crying, then I look towards my father, his eyes full of guilt and unshed tears.

"You just called her a coward when she's the bravest person I know. She lost our baby. Her biological father booted it out of her body, and there was nothing she could do but watch as it left her body through her blood.

She didn't just shut you out, Dad; she shut herself out; she couldn't live with the guilt of not saving our child, and she couldn't look me in the eyes because she blamed herself; she still does, and I've only just managed to convince her to see someone."

Tears fall from his eyes, and I shake my head before going off after my girl. I pass Bubbles, who has tears in her eyes, making me want to roll mine, but I just manage not to. I think we need a full church to discuss her place here; she's become too clingy, and I think I've finally got footage of her poking the holes in the condoms. It's the proof we've been trying to find.

As I pass the bar, I look towards Bill, our prospect, and state, "Go to the apartment above the bakery and collect all the food Lise has baked over the last few weeks; take some to the shelter; then bring the rest here for everyone."

He nods and turns to leave as I head down the corridor.

When I get to our room, I find my girl lying on our bed on her side, facing away from the door, with Diamond curled up against her stomach. I smile gently before shutting the door and heading over towards her. I lay down behind her, placing my arm over her waist and squeezing her to me before stroking Diamond on her head behind her ears, and I placed my face in the crook of Lise's neck, breathing in her sugary scent.

"I love you, Princess."

She sniffles and whispers, "I love you too."

"You know he didn't mean it, darling; they both didn't; they were just scared, and they took their fear out on you in the wrong way; they love you."

She nods her head while stroking Diamond's paw.

We lay like this for a little while before I speak, hoping to distract her.

"I think it may be time to kick out Bubbles."

She tenses before looking up at me, and I gently move her hair from her face while she bites her bottom lip. "I understand wanting to; believe me, I do, but I just..." she sighs.

"Darling, you have a heart of gold, but too much crap has happened; she won't stop."

She nods her head, her eyes full of love and understanding. "But I just, I think it's all an act, Logan. I think she's desperate for security, and this persona is just a way to hide her vulnerability. I also think Ginger is her little fly in her ear, praying off her vulnerability."

I take a deep breath and nod because she is right; I've said for months that something with Bubbles was off.

"Maybe I could try and talk to her. Make her aware that she may be kicked out, and see if I can get through to her before you make a club vote regarding her future here."

I smile at my woman, proud of how kind she is, even to a woman who has tried to destroy and sabotage our relationship. I nod my head in agreement, then hold her close to me again while she strokes Diamond.

About an hour later, after feeling content with her in my arms, I finally rasped, "Want to go see how the house is coming along?" She looks back at me and smiles, nodding her head and making me grin. I lean down and kiss her gently before I get up, then help my girl up. Diamond jumps up, and I pick her up, holding her as we walk to the door, my hand still firmly in hers.

As we open the door, Dagger walks past, heading to his room on the opposite side, muttering,

"Goddamn stubborn woman thinks I'll just run away, then she's fucking crazy; she'll learn one way or another that she's mine."

I clear my throat; amusement flashes over my face while Lise tilts her head. Dagger's head lifts up, and his eyes brighten at the sight of my girl.

He grins and kisses her cheek.

"I missed you, girlie."

She grins at him. "Missed you too, Dag; now what stubborn woman?"

I chuckle, making Dagger narrow his eyes at me in warning.

Ha.

"You see, darling, while you were in the hospital, Dagger here decided to fuck a nurse and then leave her hanging for an orgasm after she shoved another nurse out of the way who was supposed to give us an update on you just so she could see Dagger here; she didn't even know your name...."

I trail off as Dagger sighs while Lise raises a brow at him.

"Fucks sake, fine, another nurse came into the storage room as I was fucking this stupid bitch, and I decided stupidly while fucking said bitch to hit on the other nurse." Lise's mouth drops open, but Dagger continues, "But, fuck, she's the one; I know she is; I can fucking feel it; it's like someone hit me in the gut, but I fucked up by hitting on her mid-fuck with someone else; I wasn't even fucking thinking; it was like I was mesmerized, and my hips didn't get the fucking memo to stop moving." He's pacing now, and Lise has to bite her bottom lip to stop her giggles, but her eyes are full of laughter. Well, it looks like I owe Dagger a few beers later for that.

He continues to pace.

"God, why is she so fucking stubborn?"

I chuckle, then look at Lise and say, "It's the same nurse who turned out to be the one the other nurse shoved aside just to get to Dagger; she also handled your medication."

Lise furrows her brows, then growls before slapping Dagger across the head, making my mouth drop open.

"Ouch, what the fuck, Annie?"

"You're the douche canoe who hit on Mel while fucking someone else?"

Oh shit, I can't help it. My laughter comes out in full force, and Dagger clears his throat.

"Mel?"

I shake my head while trying to calm down. What an idiot!

She growls again.

"Melanie. She is sweet, kind, and caring. And she was especially sweet to me, even though I never said a word. She was so embarrassed walking in on you with that nurse, although I think she only told me because she was hoping to get me to talk. Now if she had said your name, I would bet my bakery I would have shouted my denial that you'd do something like that."

Lise shakes her head then grabs his cut, pulling him at eye level, and my laughter gets louder while he looks at her scared shitless,

"Don't you dare hurt her, or I'll skin you alive." Got it?"

His eyes widen before he nods his head, then stands straight, looking at me with wide eyes.

"Bulldog 2.0, and she's your woman."

I nod. "Yep, I'm definitely screwed."

Lise rolls her eyes and starts walking towards the common room, saying over her shoulder,

"If you two don't want me telling Cammy all about her nickname, then I suggest you show me how the house is coming along."

Both our eyes widen, and Dagger dashes into his room, locking his door out of fear, while I run to my woman and grab her hand, squeezing it in a warning and making her giggle. It's only then that it hits me; she called momma Cammy instead of mom again.

When we get into the common room, my father quickly walks towards us from where he was standing, near the table where Momma and Rosie are sitting with matching frowns.

"I love you, Annie girl. I didn't mean everything I said; it's just that we were all so worried. You gave us no contact, and I've never seen Axel worry that much about someone."

He sounds so sincere, and I hope Lise can forgive him and Momma. She crosses her arms over her chest, and I swallow, unsure of how this is going to go. She loves dad a hell of a lot; hell, he's her dad in every way except for blood, but she hasn't got the fatherly love in her eyes anymore. He chose sides without realizing the guilt she was dealing with; he went with his blood, both he and Momma did.

She tilts her head at him.

"You bought me a car behind my back?"

My eyes widen, and I sigh.

She's not going to forgive; she's changing the subject.

My father's mouth drops open, then he clears his throat. "I, uh, um, well, you see, your car is, uh, um..." He trails, and he sighs, running a hand through his short hair. "Fuck." He looks into her eyes. "Call it even," he asks, holding his hand up. She thinks for all one second before she takes it, and they shake on it, making me smile, but I know it didn't reach my eyes.

She didn't hug him, and she made sure to change the subject.

I shake my head, then take her hand again.

"Come on, darling, it's time to show you what we've done."

My dad grins, but his eyes show concern because she's held back while Rosie and Momma stand. They want to see her reaction to the house, plus I have another agenda to do too, which I did want them involved in, but now I'm not sure it's a good idea. Fuck, my hands feel sweaty and my heart is racing, things are not going according to plan.

When we get to the driveway, Lise gasps and then looks at me, and I grin and say, "Welcome home, Princess." Tears well in her eyes, and we head inside. It's exactly how she wanted it. There is a grand staircase to the left, curving around to the upstairs rooms, while the kitchen is straight ahead, with a breakfast bar separating the rooms. The walls are white on top and dark gray on the bottom, which are connected by a black border.

We have a look around for the next half hour, and I show her everything, including the room that was supposed to be the baby's, and I whisper, "When you're ready, or even if you ever are, this will either stay a guest room or become a baby's room."

She nods her head and then rasps sadly, "A guest room," and my heart breaks a little. She may change her mind, but I don't think she will.

She doesn't want any more kids. Fuck.

I give Momma sad eyes. She, Rosie, and Dad have followed on our tour and are all now looking sad. I know Lise is enough for me; I just don't know if not having a grandchild is enough for momma, and by the look on her face and the anger that shines through, I'm guessing not. I sigh and take Lise's hand before Momma opens her mouth again and ruins my plans. I lead her to the fireplace, ensuring she sees the mantelpiece, and she gasps when we get closer and notices the beautiful picture of her mother and her when she was a baby, the one she saved when she was losing our baby.

Tears fall from her eyes as her fingers trace her mother's features, which are so much like her own. They could be twins, right down to the violet eyes. Her fingers trace the key, and I rasp,

"We have a meeting at the bank tomorrow, and your counseling session is next week, which I set up for you earlier."

She nods then furrows when she notices the ring box. My father sucks in a breath while I pull her closer to me. I grab the box and twist it in my fingers with one hand while keeping my other on her lower back, her front touching mine, before I look Lise in the eyes.

"I love you; you know that?"

She nods, still looking confused, and I smile.

"You've become everything to me, my whole world. When you were taken, I thought—I thought—I was going to die. My whole heart was tearing in two because, I know without a doubt, that there's no world without you in it. I need you like I need air to breathe."

I look into her eyes which are glistening with unshed tears and I get down on one knee, in our new living area. It's not how I wanted it, but it's the next best thing—our first memory in our new home with Diamond at our feet and our family looking on with her mother watching over us on our fireplace.

She gasps, her hands covering her mouth and her tears falling. I can hear sobs coming from the other two women as well, and I would bet my left nut, my dad, is recording this.

"Will you, Annalise Jessica Lawrence, make me the happiest man alive and become my wife?"

I open the box, and her emerald ring shines through.

"Marry me, darling."

Chapter 30

Annalise

"Marry me, darling."

My tears fall fast and hard as I stare at the most beautiful emerald green ring; it's gorgeous.

More tears fall as I look into his eyes, which shine full of love, and I rasp,

"Yes."

He grins as his eyes fill with unshed tears. He places the ring on my finger before taking me into his arms. I wrap my legs around his waist and my arms around his neck as he kisses me hard while our family claps and cheers. I try to block them out, not wanting to ruin our moment. I know I hurt them, but I can't help them when I'm basically dying inside, and unfortunately, they've just shown that when push comes to shove, their son will always come first, as he should. I just thought I earned their respect over the years for them to talk to me first before turning nasty, especially when they've stated several times over the years that I'm their daughter, but obviously not.

When we break the kiss, I lean my forehead against his, letting out a watery laugh. "I love you."

"I love you too, darling."

He kisses me again before he helps me down, and my Grams rushes over to me, hugging me tightly.

"I'm sorry, Grams."

She shakes her head and squeezes me tighter. "All's forgotten, Pumpkin. I knew you needed time, and I made sure you got it. I love you, sweet girl."

I sniffle. "I love you too, Grams."

Cammy and Dead Shot interrupt and grab me in a hug, squeezing me tightly, but I tense up a little before Logan takes me back into his arms, and I smile wide at him, glad for him to read my signals, ignoring the looks of concern from his parents. I also notice anger in Cammy's eyes; it's been there since I commented on the room. More kids just aren't an option for me, and I hope Logan understands even if his mother does not.

Pain spreads through my chest, and I feel like I've lost my parents all over again. Grams looks at me with concern, but I just shake my head at her while Logan kisses my head, and I squeeze him tightly around his waist, happy to be in his arms again—my fiancé. We spend the rest of the evening cooking together after his parents and Grams leave, and then we spend the night loving each other, and I keep my mind from going into the dark spaces.

The next day, after spending our first night in our master room, which's full of dark blue and light grays, in a massive king-sized bed, we headed back to the clubhouse for breakfast. I want to catch Ink before he heads to work. I look at Logan as we walk to the clubhouse and smile a little. He's been very attentive since I've come home.

He looks at me.

"Are you doing okay, darling?"

I give him a small smile.

"I am." Guilt builds in my chest again. "I haven't exactly made sure you're ok, though, have I? I'm not the only one who lost our baby."

He sighs and stops for a minute, placing his hands around my waist. "Darling, yes, we both lost our baby, but you, you experienced it on your own, no less. Yes, we lost our baby, but I could have lost you too." He sighs before rubbing his hands down my arms. "We can make another baby princess, or we can live with just us for eternity, but we can't make another you."

I nod my head as some tears fall before I press my face into his chest.

"I love you, Logan, so much."

He runs his fingers through my hair as he rasps, "I love you too, princess. Come on, let's go get some food."

I nod my head and take his hand and we head inside the clubhouse. When we enter, the whole room erupts in cheers, making me jump and Logan chuckle as everyone shouts congratulations. Flames is the first one to come towards us; he's smiling, but it doesn't reach his eyes. I go to him and meet him halfway, hugging him tightly before whispering,

"We'll find her, I promise."

He nods his head and hugs me tighter before the rest of the brothers come over and hug me, congratulating us both on our engagement and making me smile. From the corner of my eye, while I was hugging Trigger, I saw Ginger try and wrap her arms around Flame, but he pushed her away and then walked off to his office down the hallway, making me smile a sad smile.

He's finally learning, but maybe just a little too late.

When Ink comes to hug me, I grab his hand and pull him toward the wall, making him furrow his brows.

I clear my throat. "Is it possible for you to fit me in for a tattoo?"

His brows shoot high in his hairline, and he nods. "Of course, why don't you come in after breakfast if you know for certain what you want?"

I smile and hug him, saying, "Thank you."

He smiles back as Logan wraps an arm around my waist.

"Make that two brother."

I look up at him in surprise, and he just smiles at me. Ink chuckles and states, "Anything for my Pres," making Logan growl at him, and I giggle. He hates his childhood friends calling him Pres, even though that's what he is. I shake my head and kiss Ink on the cheek before heading into the kitchen for some food, keeping my distance from Dead Shot and Cammy. When I get in there, Bubbles is standing over the stove with a frown on her face, and I sigh. She looks at me and scowls.

It looks like we're having this conversation now.

I walk over to her and lean against the counter, making her scowl harder. "What?" You want to take the kitchen now too; taking my man wasn't good enough for you?"

I raise my brows and give her a look before I state, "Let's get this right first, shall we? He was never your man. Men don't want a woman who has slept with half of his brothers, the men they see as family. You know this, so your being territorial over my fiancé is getting ridiculous." Her eyes fill with unshed tears, but I continue. "You don't want him because you love him, Bubbles; you want him because he could provide you with security, especially with his position. Whereas I cannot breathe with the thought of him not being near me."

Her tears fall when she realizes I saw right through her. She may be a bitch, but her eyes give her trauma away just like mine do. I wipe her tears away for her, and she lets me. I know Logan is now in the room but is staying back so I can speak to Bubbles. I can feel him like I always do; it's how I know he's the other half of me.

"They want to vote you out of the club, Bubbles."

Her eyes widen, and she gasps.

"You're poking holes in condoms to trap the men, mainly the president; you're trying to ruin and sabotage relationships all because you want security, but you don't realize you have security living here anyway. Don't try to settle and trap one of the men out of fear of being alone or wanting a sense of security you've probably never had. Because you do have it now anyway; you've had it since you started working here; sleeping with the brothers was never part of the deal. You never had to go down that path, and every brother here would have told you that if you had questioned it."

She lets out a sob, and I grip her hand.

"I'm here talking to you to try and help you now before they decide to kick you out. I know you have nowhere else to go, and I also know you love living here, so I convinced Logan last night to let me speak with you. I don't want to see you homeless."

She nods her head.

"I'm-I'm sorry."

I give her a little smile and say, "I know; I want to help you; we all do."

I give her a hug, and she squeezes me before letting go when Logan comes up behind me, pressing his front to my back.

"I'm sorry, Axel, so sorry."

Her tears fall some more, but he smiles at her. "I know you are Bubbles, but things have to change, alright?" She nods her head. "And if you don't want to fuck the brothers, don't. You have our protection and security because you are employed by us; sleeping with us doesn't change that; you are a part of the club."

She nods her head and clears her throat.

"I don't want to be called Bubbles anymore or try to be with a brother or be a bitch to everyone, trying to take another woman's man. I want Amy back, and I want me back."

We both grin at her; this is her no longer wanting to be called a sweet butt, and pride fills my chest.

"That's a much better name."

We both giggle as she nods, and she hands me a plate full of pancakes and bacon. "Thank you."

She nods. "You've lost too much weight; you need to eat more."

I smile at her and kiss her cheek before taking a seat at the dining table. She hands Logan a plate next before he squeezes her hand and then takes a seat next to me. I nod my head to the spare chair for Bubb, I mean Amy, to sit in, and she smiles wide and takes a seat with some food for herself.

"I have a question for you, Amy." She raises her brows while Logan smiles. "What's your passion? What is something you really wanted to do?"

Her cheeks pinken a little. "I always wanted to be a florist."

I smile at her and nod my head, then look at Logan, who grins at me before facing Amy.

"I know a woman called Daisy Harris; she owns a florist shop in town. Would you like me to give her a call?"

Her eyes widen, then she whispers, "But what about the club?"

He smiles at her while I squeeze her hand in reassurance.

"You can still work weekends here, cleaning or cooking, if my woman hasn't tried to take over the kitchen until you've got yourself on your own two feet; we'll help however you need us to." I poked my tongue out at him, causing Amy to giggle. Dagger and Flame come in at that point quickly, grabbing a coffee and raising their brows at us, but we don't say anything.

Logan gets up and kisses my lips gently.

"We've just got a quick church, then we'll head to Fire's Ink." I nod my head as he looks at Amy. "I'll mention what was said this morning at church, alright?"

She nods her head, and appreciation shines through her eyes as they all walk out. Then she looks at me and clears her throat.

"I'm sorry. For everything. Ginger was in my head, and I took things too far. I mean, fuck," she says, shaking her head before she squeezes my hand. She rasps, "I was in his room. But I didn't break in. There was a note on my bed, but I don't know who put it there. It said Axel wanted me in his room naked. I didn't even know the condoms were faulty.

My eyes widen in shock; her eyes are genuine and full of concern. "Who do you think left the note?"

She clears her throat as fear enters her eyes too. "Ginger. She wants Flame badly, and I think I was the diversion." I nod. I've been getting a bad vibe from Ginger for months now. "Just be careful and watch her."

I nod. "I will, and I'll make sure Logan is aware."

She nods and raps again, "I am so sorry."

I lean forward and hug her tightly. "It's ok."

I try to reassure her, but she just shakes her head before clearing her throat when we pull apart.

"Do you, I mean, this weekend, could-could you go shopping with me ready for Monday?"

I smile wide at her. "I'd love to, and you know what? I think Jingles would love to come as well."

She grins nodding and we get to talking while waiting for the men to leave church. It turns out she's actually quite amazing now her persona is gone, and it doesn't take long until we're laughing.

When the men leave church, most of them head into the kitchen, and one by one they kiss Amy's cheek, making her eyes shine, and I grin. Logan comes up to me,

"You ready, darling?" I nod my head and get up before squeezing Amy's hand. Logan looks at her. "It's agreed that you will be starting Monday morning at 8:30 am, the shops three down from the bakery that will be re-opened again on Monday as well."

He gives me a pointed look, and I smile, nodding my head despite the aching feeling in my stomach.

Re-opening feels like moving on and forgetting our baby.

Can I do that?

He looks back towards Amy, oblivious to my thoughts: "If you don't want to fuck a brother, then don't. It's as simple as that. We're not evil, Amy; we don't expect sex in payment for helping you; we just expect you to do your job correctly. We'll help you get on your feet, alright."

She nods with tears running down her face before she hugs him. We wave bye as we head out to his bike, which, I must admit, I love going on now. I want to live my life, not live it in fear. Losing our baby showed me that. What a sucky way to realize something, though.

When we get to Fire's Ink, I'm still clutching Logan's shirt on the back of his bike. I may love being on his bike, and I may be trying to overcome my stupid fear, but it doesn't go away overnight. Logan gently pries my fingers off his shirt before climbing off the bike and then lifting me off too. He removes the helmet from my head and kisses my lips gently.

"You're getting better, darling."

I smile at him before he takes my hand, pulling me into the back door of the shop, straight into Inks room. He smiles when we walk in, then pats the big black chair for me to take a seat, then waits for me to tell him what I want done.

I cleared my throat,

"I would like the date 09/06/22 on my right wrist, please, with 8 weeks underneath it."

My eyes start to tear up, and Ink nods his head, then looks at Logan. "I want the same, but on my chest plus what we discussed on my neck."

My tears fall, and Ink wipes them away.

"I'll quickly do a design; you let me know if it's good, alright?" I nod my head and grip Logan's hand as Ink gets to work. Not even 10 minutes later, he shows me what he's come up with, and my tears fall again, and I nod my head.

In the beautiful script he's written,

Our fallen angel

09/06/22

8 weeks were made.

I nod my head, and he takes my wrist, cleaning it before getting his ink gun ready. I grip Logan's hand tighter as Ink says, "Distract her Pres."

Logan growls again, making Ink smirk before he starts the tattoo.

Wow, that hurts.

I gasp and clutch Logan's hand tighter, then look at him. He smiles gently.

"I noticed you called momma by her name, and you changed the subject to dad."

Ok, I think I'd prefer the pain of the tattoo.

Logan smirks when he sees my train of thought after I look at my wrist while Ink snorts.

I sigh, "It's hard because, to me, they are my parents, they brought me up. And I know they feel the same way about me; I'm their daughter, but when push comes to shove..."

Ink finishes my thoughts: "They chose to side with the blood child even though he wasn't asking them to because he was always on your side."

I nod my head while Logan's eyes drown in sorrow, but I just shrug my left shoulder, so I don't move my right arm.

"Grams instantly knew I needed time; you knew I needed time, but they couldn't accept that despite knowing me, my tics, and my anxieties because they saw you in pain, and I will forever hold that guilt, but how was I or am I supposed to help you when all I want to do is die? I can't, and I couldn't. They turned on me despite knowing how badly I had been destroyed. I didn't just lose our baby that day. It was torn out of me by my own father, the man who took my mother from me and nearly killed me, but how I felt the last two weeks never came to mind. Instead, I was accused of being coddled and basically dramatic by the people I saw as my parents. I don't know if we can get back what we had after yesterday. I love them; I always will, but I don't know if I can forgive them fully."

Logan slowly closes his eyes and nods his head in understanding.

"You'll get there, Annie; just give it time. Now we're all done."

I turn and look at my wrist, and I smile while Ink goes over how to look after the ink until it's healed, then he wraps it for me before Logan takes the seat after he takes off his cut and black t-shirt that I'm currently holding. Ink starts with his chest, putting the same tattoo as mine directly over his heart before Ink moves to his neck. I can't see what he's done because of the angle, so instead I play with Logan's fingers on his right hand while I tell the men about what Bub, I mean, Amy said they were tense but agreed to look into Ginger.

It only takes an hour before Ink says he's all done. Logan stands and shows me his neck, and tears instantly fall.

Annalise

I gently kiss him on the lips and whisper against them, "I love you."

He smiles wide, and we break apart, thanking Ink. I hug him tightly, and we both leave him for his next client. When we get out near his bike, I look at him and clear my throat.

"I, um, uh, was wondering after we went to the bank if we could, uh." I can't stop stuttering, and he looks at me with his brows furrowed, "I don't want a wedding."

Crap, that came out wrong, and the look in his eyes proves that as he stares at me with hurt in them and I clear my throat again,

"I was, uh, wondering if we could just go to the courthouse today?" and I hold my breath, waiting for his answer.

Chapter 31

Axel

I look at her with my mouth hanging open while she plays with her fingers nervously.

I cleared my throat,

"You don't want a big wedding with all our friends and family?"

She shakes her head. "We could always have a party at the weekend or something, but I just, I just want it to be me and you, and maybe Dagger as a witness seems like he's your closet friend."

I tuck some of her hair behind her ear.

"I just want to marry you, only you. I don't want a packed ceremony, just us."

I smile at her in understanding. She's never been big on attention, and now that she's distancing herself from my parents, which is heartbreaking to watch, she doesn't have someone to walk her down the aisle. I mean, Dad would still do it in a heartbeat; he still sees her as a daughter, but she's kind of lost faith in him and Momma.

I gently kiss her on the forehead, then get my phone out.

Me- stop stalking the nurse and meet me at the courthouse in an hour. Don't tell anyone and call the judge; tell him to expect us.

I show her the text, and tears start to fall as she flings herself into my arms, holding me tight, so I hold her tighter, feeling fucking happy that the judge is in our pocket, before letting her go to help her on the bike. I kiss her lips softly before putting her helmet on. The bank is just down the road, but I love feeling her wrapped around me, and the more she's on the back of my bike, the more comfortable she'll get.

I climb on in front of her just as my phone pings, and I grin, knowing it's Dagger.

Dagger – ok, it's not fucking stalking when she knows I'm here, and I know she knows because of the fucking glares she keeps sending me. I'll see you in an hour.

I snort and show her the text, making her laugh, before putting my phone away in my cut. I rev my girl up as Lise's arms wrap around me tightly, and we head off down the road to the bank to see what her mom had hidden there.

It only takes us two minutes before we pull up in front of the building on Banks Street, and we head inside with Lise's hand clutching mine. I know she's nervous, but she's got this, and if she hasn't, well, I'm right here for her.

When we get to the desk, Mrs. Lionel smiles at us.

"Hello, you two. Come on through to the back, and I'll let Mr. Stafford know you're here."

We smile at her and head through to the back office. We don't even get a chance to sit down before the door opens and Mr. Stafford walks in. He holds his hand out to Lise first, then to me, and we both shake it.

"Annalise, Axel, please come through to the vault. Do you have the key?" Lise nods her head as we follow him. "Good, good. Your mama was a little concerned your father would find it before you could, but we made sure to have precautions in place if he had, per your mama's request, Annie. She was a lovely woman and is missed dearly by others.

I squeeze my girl's hand as her eyes water. "Thank you, Mr. Stafford."

She rasps and he smiles at her. We head into a big metal room full of wall safes and pull out a large black one with the number 7685 embroiled on it. He looks to Lise and says, "The key, please Annie." She nods and places the key in his hand. He places his fingerprint on the safe, which unlocks one door before it comes to another one with a keyhole. Mr. Stafford inserts the key and then unlocks the door but doesn't open it.

He turns to us.

"I'll give you a little while to have a look through it, and as per your mother's request, Annie, there is already an account where whatever cash is in this safe can be placed into. We already have the amount typed up; we're just waiting for your okay."

She nods while my eyes widen in shock. If he's known her for so long, why hasn't he come to her? Mr. Stafford smiles when he sees the look on my face.

"Unfortunately, Lucy did not want us to explain to Annie about the safe as a precaution because of

Grant; she had to be the one to come to us unless she turned 35. If anything was to happen to Annie before then, then everything in the safe would have been donated between 4 charities unless Annie had any children."

I nod my head in understanding as he squeezes Lise's arm gently.

"I'll come back in half an hour."

She nods and thanks him as he leaves before looking at the safe. I wrap my arms around her from behind, leaning my chin on top of her head. "You ready, darling?" I rasp, and she nods her head before walking forward.

She pulls the safe open and gasps, and I peek over her shoulder, my eyes widening,

"Holy shit"

"There must be thousands worth of jewelry in here, Logan."

I blink. Fucking hell, she's got that right, plus all the fucking cash. I cleared my throat,

"I'll go get Mr. Stafford back; he may know the exact amount."

She shakes her head and looks at me.

"Grant rambled when I was in and out of consciousness, and I remember him mentioning how the jewelry is worth over a million dollars and that there's another $500,000 cash, but I thought he was just insane and going crazy."

I blink again. "So basically, my future wife's fucking rich. Do we need a prenup?"

She smacks my chest, her eyes showing amusement.

My smile dies when I see an envelope.

"Darling,"

I state and nod to it. She looks, her smile leaving her face too, and she grabs it gently as if it'll disappear. It has her name written on the front.

Annalise

"Do you want me to read it to you, Princess?"

A few tears fall from her eyes, and I wipe them gently as she nods her head, passing me the envelope.

I sit on the chair and pull her into my lap, where she curls up, placing her head into the crook of my neck, taking a deep breath, I clear my throat while opening the envelope. I place one hand around her waist, holding her close while my left-hand keeps a hold of what looks like a letter.

My dearest Anna Banana, I smile at the nickname.

If you're reading this, then I'm no longer with you, and I'm so sorry for that because it would mean you were only 3 years old when you lost me. I had a plan to up and leave your father, taking all the money in the safe as well as the money I left with the lawyers as a precaution, and run. I was going to run far with you in my arms, and I'm so sorry for failing you, for not keeping you safe like a mother should.

Lise lets out a sob, and I squeeze her tighter. We lost our baby, and this hits home for my girl because she blames herself for not saving our child. I can't fucking wait for her counseling session next week. I clear my throat again and continue.

I loved you so much, so much so that I tried to make it work with Grant. I really did, but he was just, he was using me, and I knew it. My parents tried to warn me, but they suddenly died in a car accident, and I was all alone. He played on that, and I felt like I owed him; I just didn't realize he was the one who killed them to get their money. I had my suspicions, but the police didn't want to listen, so I stayed with him, hoping to find proof, and thankfully I wasn't stupid enough to let him get his hands on the money. I know what you're thinking: why not leave him after the first time he hit me when I refused to give him the information he needed to pay off his debts? Well, I couldn't, because I had come to realize I was pregnant with you, and I hoped he would change because, despite everything, I had come to love your father dearly. But once you were born, he only got worse. When he started threatening your life, my love started to die, and that's when I made a plan to leave.

I'm just sorry it didn't work.

I hope you have had a good life. I ensured Cammy and Dead Shot (I still can't get used to calling him that; he'll always be Bruce to me). I ensured they had legal parental rights over you when you were just so small. They have a son, Logan, who is an amazing little boy, so I know they'll do right by you. Cammy used to joke about you two becoming an item; I hope her wish came true.

I grin while my girl giggles. Momma's wish definitely came true. I kiss Lise's head before continuing.

I never placed your father on the birth certificate but still had to give you his last name as a precaution, so he didn't demand to see the certificate. I know my dear friends would love you like their own, and I know they would make sure you were safe, but my darling girl, you are my whole world, the light of my life, and I want you to know just how much I love you.

If I were a betting girl, I would bet that you made sure you got to where you needed with the inheritance I left you before giving some to your new parents and most likely your Grams, because if I knew Rosie, she would have had a hand, a massive hand in raising you right, but I would bet you donated the money and most likely to a women's refuge center because of what I went through. So in this safe for you, darling girl and I mean for you, not for charities or the people who raised you but for you and your hopefully growing family, a million dollars worth of jewels. Sell them, keep them, hand them down to your children, and do what you please with them. You also have another $750,000 in cash.

Both I and Lise open our mouths in shock. Fuck, $750,00. I shake my head.

Mr. Stafford will ensure that an account is ready-made, all you have to do is give the OK, and the money will be in the account for you, and he will log the cash into the bank.

Make something of yourself, darling girl. Fall in love, get married, and start a family. Live, my darling girl; live for me and for yourself; live for a family I hope you have. I love you so much and cannot express how grateful I am to have a daughter like you.

Tell Rosie it's okay; she tried to help as much as she could, but there's only so much a person can do, and she did so much for me. Tell her I love her like she was my own mother, and I'll always be grateful for her and watch over her.

Tell Cammy and Bruce, thank you. Thank you for taking such good care of my little girl, my light. Tell them I love them dearly and to take care of the gift I've given them in you because you are a gift, my gift, and now their gift.

And tell the person who you have fallen in love with, who I hope you someday have (hopefully Logan), to cherish you, because that would mean you'll be their gift just like they'll be yours. Tell them thank you for me being there for you when I can't.

I have to go now, sweet girl. I need to make our plans final. I hope you don't have to read this so that I can tell you about it instead, but if I don't, know I'm always with you.

I love you so much. You are my brightest light on my darkest days.

I love you always.

Mama xx

Lise's whole body shakes with sobs, and I wrap my other arm around her, holding her tight to me.

"I'm so sorry, darling." I rasp, and she sobs harder. I hold her, I hold her tight until she can breathe again, until her sobs die down, she's only hiccupping, and her grip loosens a little. There's a knock on the door a little while later, and Mr. Stafford comes in. He gives us a sad smile before taking the chair opposite us, his gray hair neatly combed back and his hazel eyes looking at us with compassion.

"I would like you to take the cash, p-please Mr. Stafford, and set up the account."

He nods his head and hands her a card with her name on it, and she passes it to me. I place it in my cut with the letter that I already folded up, and I know Momma and Dad will want to read it.

"Already done, sweetheart. The money will be available in the next 24 hours."

She nods her head, then looks at the safe and rasps, "Do we have a safe in our home?"

I smile at her and say, "Yeah, Princess, we do."

She looks at Mr. Stanford and says, "Can you bag up the jewelry, please?"

He smiles at her and says, "It would be my pleasure."

He hands her a piece of paper, and she takes it in her shaky hands. "This is the list of jewelry that you have and the worth of each item; it's in your mama's handwriting; we went through it together when Grant was out of town with friends." She nods and says, "It'll take about 10 minutes to bag it all up; they are already in individual bags."

She nods again.

"Thank you,"

He smiles at her, squeezing her hand before patting my back. He calls an assistant through, and I stay sitting here watching them gently place the items, roughly 37 of them in a satchel, as my girl places her head into my neck again while I rub my hand up and down her back.

Roughly 15 minutes later, after he's double-checked each item, he comes over to us with one of the little bags in his hand and the satchel. I help Lise off of my lap, and we both stand as he places the bag in Lise's hand, and then gives me the satchel.

"This was your grandmother's wedding ring; I thought maybe you'd like it for when you get married, especially since I know you two are engaged. If you have any questions, then give me a call, day or night.

Lise gives him a gentle hug, and I shake his hand, thanking him, before we head to my bike. When we stand next to it, I place the bag in my saddle, which only just fits; we'll have to take it to the courthouse with us. I then take the bag out of her hand and take the ring out, smiling. It's white gold with an emerald and green diamond in the middle, like her engagement ring, and little black and white ones going around it. It's fucking perfect, and I grin wide. I grab her right hand, not wanting to jinx it, and push the ring on her third finger, and it fits perfectly.

Nodding my head, I take it off again and put it in the bag, placing it in my cut, ready to marry my girl.

Chapter 32

Axel

We get to the courthouse not even 10 minutes later and park up next to Dagger, who's looking at us with a raised brow after placing his shades on his head while we climb off my bike.

I grin at him.

"Lovely day for a wedding, don't you think, brother?"

His eyes widen before he whoops, punching his fist in the air and making Lise giggle as he jumps off his bike. He kisses Lise's cheek and grins before looking around. Then he furrows his brows, and I smile a little at Lise.

"It's just us three, brother; we'll have a party this weekend to celebrate."

Lise clears her throat.

"It also doesn't feel right without Star to have a big wedding; I just want to marry him with no fuss, and I thought you'd be the perfect witness. Although I'm a little disappointed you didn't kidnap Mel."

His face goes from loving to a scowl within seconds, causing me to chuckle and Lise to giggle before she grabs both our hands to drag us into the courthouse. I quickly pull my hand back, making her look at me as I get the pouch.

"I can't leave this out here, darling."

She nods her head as I pass the bag to Dagger. "Don't lose that, brother; it's worth a million dollars."

His eyes widen and his face pales as he gently grabs hold of the bag, swallowing hard. "This is what was in the safe?"

I nod. "And another $750,000 with a letter from her mama."

His eyes widen further before he nods, making me chuckle. We all walk into the courthouse, and I smile wide, placing my arm around her waist, happy that my girl's about to marry me.

An hour and a half later, we're walking towards the clubhouse after putting the satchel into our safe in my office at home and collecting Diamond, who's currently being held in my wife's arm, her grandmother's wedding ring shining next to her engagement ring on her wedding finger as we walk. I look at mine while I hold her hand tightly.

"It looks like I'll be seeing Ink again tomorrow."

        She looks over to me and sees where my attention is, on my ring finger with no ring, and I look at her just as she grins, making me smile at her. I let go of her hand and wrapped my arm around her shoulders, bringing her closer to me as we kept walking.

"I love you, wife."

She grins wide.

"I love you too, husband."

And I grin back at her as we continue walking.

When we walk into the clubhouse, it's full, and I know that's was Daggers doing so we can make an announcement.

Amy runs over to us, her hands out towards our puppy, as we pass the doorway. "Gimme, gimme, gimme."

Lise giggles and hands our puppy over, and Amy takes her when she suddenly squeals and grabs Annalise's left hand and says, "OH MY GOD."

Her eyes are on my woman's left hand while she grips it, and I grin.

Everyone is now looking at us, causing Lise to go red, and I chuckle before clearing my throat. "Brothers, old ladies, prospects, and sweet butts, I believe you all know my WIFE Annalise Ramirez?"

The whole clubhouse quietens for exactly 3 seconds before everyone erupts in cheers while Amy inspects my wife's wedding ring,

"It's absolutely gorgeous."

Lise smiles a small smile. "It was my mothers, mother's wedding ring."

Amy smiles, then kisses her cheek before kissing mine.

"I'm happy for you two; you deserve all the happiness in the world."

We smile at her as she kidnaps our dog, making me shake my head as she goes into the kitchen with her, which means she'll be feeding her treats. She's been extremely different today since opening up, and I hope this is the real her because, I must admit, we all like this side.

Rosie, who seems to be staying here more frequently, walks over to us, tears in her eyes, and I really hope it's of happiness because this is the last woman I ever want to upset other than my mother. I hold my breath when she gets closer, then sigh in relief when she grabs us both in a group hug.

"The best news ever."

I furrow my brows when we pull apart and say, "You're okay that we basically eloped."

She snorts, "Boy, I was expecting it. Have you met my granddaughter? Your wife?"

I chuckle, nodding my head, because it's true; she doesn't like to be the center of attention. I look at my wife as she grabs Rosie's hands and squeezes them. Tears shine in her eyes, and I smile a sad smile as my woman rasps.

"I wanted to pass on a message for you from someone who loved you dearly; she says, 'It's ok, you tried to help as much as you could, but there's only so much a person can do, and you did so much for her; she loved you like you were her own mother, and she'll always be grateful for you' and mama will always watch over you."

Rosie's tears slide down her cheeks as she removes her hands from Lise's before grabbing her hands this time. She looks at her wedding ring and lets out a sob, "Sheila's wedding band, you went to the safe."

We nod, and I grab the letter and pass it to her.

"This was left in there for Lise."

She takes it with a shaky hand while keeping a hold of Lise's left hand, rubbing her thumb lightly over the band as the brothers stay back while we have a moment, but I can see momma in the corner of my eye; she looks pissed, and dad looks heartbroken, and I hold in my sigh. After Rosie's read the letter, she passes it back to me, and I kiss Lise on the head, then Rosie. I leave them be and let them talk. I know they need a little time to discuss things. As I head to my parents, the brothers all pat my back while I lift my ring finger to Ink, who nods before grabbing his sketchbook, and I grin—he'll design something awesome. I notice Flame by the bar, and I pat his back as I walk past. He gives me a head nod.

I know this must be hard for him; he misses his best friend, as we all do.

"You got married without us, without your father walking her down the aisle, without me going dress shopping with her? We never got to watch our son marry or plan his wedding. It's bad enough she won't give me any grandchildren, and now I don't get a wedding. How could you?"

It's the first thing momma says when I get closer, and this time my sigh comes out; she's spitting mad.

"She's barely said two words to us; she hasn't forgiven me, has she? or your mother?"

I run a hand through my hair; it's getting longer, and I think I'll have to get it cut soon.

"She's forgiven, I just don't think she sees you as her parents right now, given the things you both said."

I sigh, shaking my head at the hurt in my parents' eyes, but they should have seen this coming; they turned on her in her hour of need. Yes, I'm grateful they love me so much that they'll disown people, but not the woman they brought up as their own. "Yes, I'm your blood son, but you raised her, and she finally called you mom and dad. Then the world caved in on her, and the guilt ate her alive. Still does, she hides it well.

You turned on her because you saw me depressed without her, but you never saw how broken she was when I picked her up yesterday. She was destroyed; you can see it in her eyes now. When she laughs, it's forced. When she smiles, it doesn't reach her eyes; marrying me today is the only thing that made that smile reach her beautiful eyes before they turned sad again. She's drowning, and instead of looking at her like parents, comforting her, and helping her through the trauma and ordeal of losing our child, your grandchild, you treated her like a girl who hurt your son."

My mother lets out a sob, and I take the letter out of my cut again and hand it to my dad.

"Have a read; we found it today in the safe that her mama left for her." My momma squeezes her eyes tightly before looking over at the letter. My father sniffles while Momma openly sobs, and I take the letter back after they've finished reading it.

I need to frame it and place it with the picture on the fireplace.

"She trusted you to take care of her daughter. I love you both more than life. But you failed her yesterday. Was I hurting? Fuck yes, my girl needed me but also needed time to deal with what had happened. I knew that, and I dealt with it. Rosie knew that and dealt with it. She never pushed me away; she just struggled to look me in the eyes.

Momma goes to talk until the clubhouse quietens and my wife speaks up, breaking my heart.

"My baby, my fault."

Shit.

I turn to look at her, and the pain in her eyes breaks me. I'll admit, I'm mad at my parents for doing this today, our wedding day.

"That's what is running through my head every day. I answered back to him, gave him sarcastic comments, and all I could think about and still do think about was, maybe; maybe if I kept quiet, maybe if I didn't try to fight back, would I still be carrying our baby?

Maybe if I allowed a brother to stay with me in my office, would I still have our baby? or would the brother be dead? Maybe if I just stayed at the clubhouse, would I still have our baby, or would more people be hurt because he wanted me and was going to get me one way or another?

My baby, my fault."

Momma sobs while my dad looks like he's ready to fall to his knees. I hear the woman sniffling while Rosie also sobs.

I go to walk to my girl, but stop when she looks at me.

"Maybe if I'd just listened to you and done everything you asked me to for my own protection, I would still be carrying our baby. But instead, I tried to negotiate, and I made it easy for him to grab me. I lost our baby because I couldn't defend myself like I was taught. Then I hid away because I struggled to live with the pain and the constant memory of the blood—so much blood that I can still feel it every day on my legs, no matter how much I scrub them—and I left you alone to deal with it instead of helping you because I felt like dying. Our baby, my fault."

All the brothers drop their heads while Lise turns and walks out of the common room to the backyard. Flame follows her while I look at my parents, who look devastated, before following them outside.

When I get to the benches where they've sat with my parents hot on my heels, I hear her speak.

"She messaged me that the night she was, was. Anyway, I thought you had a right to know. I didn't see the message until Logan told me, and I checked it. If I'd answered instead of drowning in self-pity, maybe she'd still be here now."

She shakes her head while Flame puts his arm around her.

"You can't be blaming yourself over this Annie girl. You are barely holding on; she understands; I know she does."

She nods again.

"When's your counseling session?"

I tilt my head, listening.

"Next week, Logan's taking me. I-I was thinking of asking him to-to come in with me, so he knows where my head is."

I smile, feeling proud of her. Momma and Dad stand next to me, also smiling at her answer, pride shining through their eyes.

"I think he'll fucking love that idea, sweetheart."

She smiles at him, and it actually reaches her eyes before placing her head on his shoulder. I walk up behind them and wrap my arms around her waist while Flame smiles at me.

"I'm so fucking happy for you two."

I nod as Lise says, "I know everyone wanted to celebrate a big wedding, but honestly, I just wanted to marry Logan. I didn't want the fuss. Grant killed my mother. He killed my-my baby. He has nearly killed me twice now, not including all the times he put bruises on me when I was little." I squeeze her tightly as she continues, "I've fallen out with Cammy and Dead Shot, Mom, and Dad. I needed them, and they pushed me aside despite raising me. It's a lot of pain, and I didn't want that to cloud our day when we got married. And it didn't feel right without my best friend, who would have been my maid of honor."

She clears her throat when she locks eyes with my parents before looking at Flame, then back at me.

"I was wondering when we find her, and we will find her, and when my head is not full of stuff I don't want it to be full of, maybe we can do a ceremony out here. Maybe I could go dress shopping with Mom, and Dad could go tux shopping with Logan, then walk me down the aisle like I dreamed of growing up."

I smile wide as momma sobs, nodding her head. Both my parents grab her in a hug as Dad rasps, "I know it'll take time, but remember this: we love you so much, and you are our daughter. We'll never push you aside like that again, I promise."

Momma sniffles, squeezing Lise tighter. "We both promise. I'm so sorry, sweet girl."

Lise lets out a sob, and I look at Flame. We both smile wide, and I finally fucking start to feel at peace, which will hopefully strengthen after her counseling session.

Once they break apart, Flame breaks the silence.

"I say we go and fucking party to celebrate your marriage, which, by the way, I will be having words with you two about why Dagger was a witness and not fucking me."

I snort while Lise's eyes widen before she slowly gets off the bench and backs away, then makes a run for it back inside while shouting over her shoulder.

"I'LL LET LOGAN EXPLAIN." leaving me in the lurch, and I can't help the laughter that burst out along with everyone else.

Fuck I love that girl.

Epilogue

Annalise – 6 months later

I sit on our bed with tears running down my face, staring at the pregnancy test, which just so happens to be positive, and instant guilt fills me. It's only been just over 6 months since I lost our baby; it just doesn't seem right to be carrying another. This shouldn't have happened. More guilt builds because of my line of thought.

I sniffle and pick up my phone, debating whether or not to call Tate, my counselor. He's helped me a lot over the months, and Logan has been with me for every session, holding my hand tightly as I got everything off my chest, from my childhood to the attack and the loss of our child. I started off with three sessions a week and now have one a month. I don't think of ending things anymore, and my guilt has started to ease over the months, until now.

I wipe my eyes as I dial a number—the same number I call once a week, hoping she picks it up but never does. It rings several times before her voicemail hits, and I sniffle again.

"Hey, this is Star; I can't get to the phone right now, probably hanging with Flame, but leave me a message and I'll get back to you."

I wipe my eyes again and rasp after the tone,

"Hi, it's me. 6 months, Star. That's a long time without my friend. My best friend, I don't care what Flame says. He misses you and hasn't stopped looking for you either. I sniffle again. "My guilt is building up again. I tried the exercises Tate suggested, but it's not working this time. That's why I've called you; leaving these messages helps."

I let out a sob,

"I feel like I'm back in my old childhood room with the blood soaking my jeans as Grant kicks my baby out of me."

I let out another sob.

"I feel so guilty for not being there for you, and I miss you so much, and now-now, I-I, I'm pregnant. I-I don't know w-what to do-do. It-it can't be ok to have a baby after not keeping the last o-one safe." I take a deep breath, trying to calm my shaking body, and sniffle. "Next month would have been my due date, and now-now I'm pregnant again, but I shouldn't be; I'm on the pill, and-and we've been using condoms. I don't know what to do; I can't go through that again; I can't lose another one; I said I didn't want any more kids; I-I don't deserve them; I-I don't. I need you, Star. I need my friend, p-p-please."

I sob again before hanging up, my tears staining my cheeks as I sob violently, my guilt burning my chest, eating me alive.

My phone rings seconds later, and I check the ID, gasping for air. I answer it instantly,

"St-Star."

Her gentle voice comes over the speaker: "Breathe, breathe, breathe."

I sob again, still gasping. "Breathe for me, Annie, in and out, nice slow breaths. That's it, nice and slow."

I do as she says, calming myself down.

"That's it. I'm here. I'm here. Keep breathing."

My heart rate slows as I hiccup, and she keeps doing this until my breathing becomes normal again.

"You just scared the crap out of me; are you okay now? please tell me you're okay now."

I giggled a little. Gone is the calm woman, replaced by the panicked friend.

"I miss you."

She sighs and lets out a sniffle. "I'm sorry, I just need time."

I sniffled next. "I understand; I understand more than anyone."

"You're doing good, Annie. And this baby is so lucky to have you as a mama, do you hear me? What happened six months ago was not your fault; it was Grants. I want to hear you say it. Say it now."

I sniffle again and rasp, "It wasn't my fault; it was his."

"Good, and keep repeating that in your head; do not go back down that hill. I've kept up with your voicemails, Annie; you're doing better. Hearing you fall apart just now, I couldn't stay silent. I know you needed me, and I'm here. I am."

I sniffled again and let out a small sob. "But you needed me, and I wasn't there for-for you."

She sighs, "Annie, you've been there for me these past 6 months with these voicemails, they've kept me going. You kept me going. When I called you and texted you, I knew you wouldn't answer. I think I just wanted to tell myself. I tried to tell someone before I left to ease my guilt about leaving my family. You were going through so much; you needed me, and I left. So, let's call it even because I miss my friend and I want a gossip catch-up."

I giggle a little on a hiccup.

"Now tell me again about Bubbles' transformation to Amy." I laughed this time. I've kept her updated in the voicemails with all the brothers that are settling down, including Dagger's torment over the years and the surprise Slicer got. I didn't want her out of the loop, so to speak.

We get to chat for the next hour about anything and everything, even though she never tells me where she is, just that she's safe. When we quietened a little, I decided to bite the bullet.

"Are you doing okay—for money, I mean?" She sighs, probably wishing she had never told me about her sister and mother spending the inheritance her dad left her behind, as well as the money he left them.

"I'm getting by."

I clear my throat. "I have an account for you; it has the sales for the artwork you left in the storage room; there are thousands in it; I had to put it in Flame's name because, well, your mom keeps asking for the sales, but it's there."

I hear her sniffle before sighing, "Can you just keep it in there for me? please?"

I furrow my brows. "Of course I will, but Star if you're struggling?"

"How about, if I really need it, I'll let you know?"

I sigh, the stubborn woman. "Fine."

She chuckles at my answer. "Look, I've got to go get ready for work, but I'll call you every Saturday; how does that sound?"

I smile wide. "Promise?"

"I promise." Her voice sounds sincere, and I smile.

"It sounds perfect because I miss you."

I bite my bottom lip before I clear my throat, wanting to ask but worried she won't call.

She must read my mind, though.

"You can tell him, but I don't want him around when I call, and I've turned my tracker off so he can't find me. I'm just, I don't know if I'll ever forgive him. Annie, he was my best friend, and he chose to sleep with Ginger instead of sticking to our friend's date. He was supposed to be keeping my mind off of you, so I didn't worry, but instead, he broke me in more ways than one. It's because of him and the club that I was raped, and I know I shouldn't have slept with him, but in my mind, it was a goodbye I knew I would regret if it didn't happen."

I hear her sniffle, making me sniffle, she's hurting so much. My tears fall when the bedroom door opens, making me quickly hide the test under my leg. Logan furrows his brows when he sees my puffy red face.

"Logan's just walked in. Do you want me to put you on speaker?"

I hear her clear her throat, and Logan walks right up to me quicker, tilting his head.

"No, I'm not ready, but tell him, tell him I love him, and I'm grateful he's my pseudo-brother. I'll speak to you on Saturday, and I expect every single count of Logan's reaction to your news. Tell him, Annie, I love you."

Then she hangs up before I can say anything else, and more tears fall. Logan wipes them away.

"Darling?"

I sniffle. "She loves you, and she's grateful you're her pseudo-brother, but-but she's not ready to talk to you yet."

He sucks in a breath.

"Star?"

I nod my head as he moves my hair out of my face. "I've been leaving her voicemails for months, keeping her up to date. It turns out she's been listening because she heard mine today and called me not even two minutes after I left it and got me out of my panic attack after I fell apart on the voicemail."

More tears fall, and he kneels in front of me.

"Okay, let's start with why my wife was having a panic attack to begin with."

I wipe my tears before grabbing the test from under my leg. Logan sucks in a breath and takes it.

"You're pregnant?"

I nod. "I don't know how; we've doubled up on protection, but I am. And I felt so guilty because we've not long lost our baby, and we shouldn't be having another one. Then I felt guilty for even thinking that because this baby is innocent."

I let out a sob, and he quickly took me in his arms, lifting me bridal style before sitting on the bed with me still in his arms. He keeps one arm around my back with the test still in his hand while his other hand cups my face.

"My darling wife. We were doubled up in protection, which means I think this baby was meant to be. It wanted you as a mama, and who knows, maybe it was a gift from the child we lost. This is a precious gift, and I'm thankful I get to experience it with you. Don't cry, Princess."

More tears fall as he gently kisses me.

"I love you, darling, and we'll get through this because this baby will be the light of your life, like you are mine. I promise the guilt will fade, and you'll get excited. We'll never forget the child we lost, but we will celebrate the one we get to cherish. Shall we call Tate and set up an appointment? Would that be better?"

I shake my head at him, and he furrows his brows, "Star helped me. She brought me back from the ledge when I needed her most. I love you and I love this baby, just as much as-as I loved our l-last one and-and I'm s-sorry." I sob, and he holds me tighter, rocking me gently while whispering sweet nothings in my ear.

When I've calmed down, he gently moves my hair from my face.

"So, Star?"

I smiled a sad smile at him.

"For months, after I had the missed call and text from her, I've been calling her. I leave messages about once a week, keeping her updated on life and trying to get her to call home. Today was the first time she called me back.

He nods his head then clears his throat, "Flame?"

I sniffle a little. "She doesn't want any contact with him; she can't seem to forgive him for the pain he put her through over the years and what happened to her. She blames him, Logan; she blames him and the club. I don't think she'll ever allow him back into her life or feel comfortable here again."

He squeezes his eyes shut cursing.

"We need to tell him, darling; I know you feel obligated not to, but he needs to know."

I nod. "She's okay with us letting him know she's fine, kind of, but she doesn't want to speak to him." He nods again before kissing my forehead, but furrows his brows when he pulls away.

"What do you mean, kind of?" concern shows all over his eyes, and I sigh, shit,

"I asked if she needed money, and she said she was getting by but would let me know if she needed any. She's promised to call me every Saturday."

He furrows his brows in confusion. "But what about the money her dad left her? I mean, her momma said she wasted it but I thought she was bullshitting."

I clear my throat, not wanting to go behind my friend's back, and Logan raises a brow at me, and I mutter, "Shit."

Causing him to stand and place me on my feet, crossing his arms over his chest, double shit.

"You see, she, um, well." He raises his brow again.

"Fine, her sister and mother spent it all behind her back. I don't know how they managed to get access to it, but they did, and they spent all of theirs as well."

Logan's face goes red, "MOTHER FUCKER." He shouts before storming out of our room, oh fucking shit. I ran after him,

"LOGAN."

But he doesn't stop. Instead, he storms out of our house towards the clubhouse with me hot on his heels.

"FLAME!" he shouts as he slams the door open, all the brothers looking at him in shock.

Oh, crap, he's pissed.

Flame looks at him with concern and stands.

"Pres?"

I swallow hard.

"When was the last time you spoke with Shayla?"

Flame furrows his brows. "Last week, she called distressed, still not knowing where her daughter is; it's killing her; she keeps asking if I've found her yet; why?"

I bite my lip as Logan snorts, "So distressed that she stole all of her daughter's inheritance that Bones left her as well as the money he left them."

Flame's face goes red.

"What the fuck are you talking about?"

I clear my throat, and the brothers all look at me, and I fidget, hating the attention. Logan notices my anxiety coming through and quickly wraps his arm around my waist.

"She, um, she was working in a café in the next town over, giving half her wage to her mother for bills. It's why she was trying to sell her artwork at the bakery; she's basically their meal ticket, and it's probably why they want to find her so badly. They've actually come into the bakery several times asking if I have the sales money for the artwork, but I just shrug them off, telling them the money automatically goes into an account for Star that only she has access to. It pisses them off, especially since I've actually sold 14 more since she left. I have loads in the storage room and put them up once a week. I opened an account in your name,

Flame, with her sales; she has roughly over $57,000 in the account."

Flame's eyes go wider with my words.

"Why didn't she tell me?" He sounds so hurt, and my eyes go soft.

"She mentioned not wanting to rely on you, and she finds it difficult because you slept with Emma."

He slowly closes his eyes but opens them when Logan places his hand on his shoulder.

"Brother, maybe we should go talk in my office."

I swallow again as Flame looks at me with furrowed brows. He looks at my eyes and notices they are red. Panic hits him, but I quickly shake my head, reassuring him.

"She's ok; she's ok." Everyone stands and looks at me, but I don't take my eyes off Flame.

"I, uh, for months, I've been leaving messages on her voicemail, you know, to keep her updated with the brothers who are settling down and stuff like that, and today, well, today I was having a meltdown; let's say, I couldn't breathe, and I needed my friend, so I called like I normally do and fell apart on her voicemail." I sniffle, causing Flame to walk over to me and take me into his arms. "Why were you falling apart, sweetheart?"

I sniffle again and look at Logan; he nods, and I whisper,

"I'm pregnant."

Flame squeezes me tighter as the brothers tense, knowing how hard this is for me. I can hear a couple of sniffles, and I know that it's most likely Mom, Grams, and the old ladies, but I just lean my head on Flame's chest, and I rasp,

"The guilt was eating me alive, and I hung up trying to breathe through my panic attack when my phone rang."

He tenses then pulls back looking into my eyes as my tears fall, while hope fills his.

"She called me Zayne, she called." He covers his mouth as the brothers' mouths all drop open, they know she left, they just don't know why.

Logan clears his throat,

"I walked in as she was on the phone with her. Star didn't want to talk to me but agreed to call every Saturday to speak to Lise."

Flame puts both his hands behind his head, taking deep breaths.

"She's ok?"

I nod. "She is, but she's struggling a little financially, which is when I had to tell Logan about her mom and sister. She doesn't want the money just yet in the account I made her; she said she'd let me know, but um, Zayne, she, uh."

I can't say it; I can't break him, but he gives me a sad smile.

"She doesn't want to talk to me, does she?"

I shake my head as more tears fall, and he hugs me again.

"It's ok; it'll be ok. I know she blames me, and I know she blames the club." Most of the brothers look at him confused; only a select few know why Star left and what happened to her, but he continues, ignoring the curious looks. "I know she thinks she can't forgive me or the brothers, but unless she's around us, then she'll never know. We'll get her home; her talking to you is the first step."

He kisses my head,

"This baby, it's a miracle, and you're going to be an amazing mama. Do you hear me?"

I nod and let out a sob, causing him to hug me again before Logan takes me into his arms.

Flame gives me another smile before turning to leave the common room, heading to his office, no doubt to try and call Star again. I know he leaves messages for her, just like I do. When he rounds the corner, the brothers all flock to us, congratulating us on the pregnancy. Grams, Mom, and Dad wrap their arms around us tightly in a group hug, smiling wide. I smile and excuse myself before heading into the garden. I take a seat on one of the benches and look up at the night sky, the stars shining bright, and a few tears fall.

Two strong arms wrap around me from behind, hands splaying on my stomach as a nose rubs along my neck while Diamond wags her tail sitting in front of me, her tongue out, and I smile, leaning back.

"The baby will always be with us, darling, always."

I nod my head because I know he's right. I knew for a while before I confirmed the pregnancy last time, and I was so scared for the safety of that baby, but it never felt right, and I think even though the guilt kills me, it just wasn't meant to be.

"I think the baby just wasn't meant to be; it never felt right, and I think that's why the guilt ate me alive when I couldn't save it like I wished it were gone, and I know that's silly, but I couldn't wrap my head around it, but this baby, this baby feels right, like it was meant to be."

His arms tighten around me.

"I'm proud of you, darling, so fucking proud."

I smile through my tears and rasp,

"I love you, Logan."

"I love you too, Annalise."

I smile again, then look back up to the stars, finally feeling at peace for the first time in 6 months in the arms of my husband as our second baby grows in my stomach, being watched over by the one we lost.

Dear reader

Thank you so much for reading the first book of my second series! I hope you consider leaving a review to let others know what you thought of this book, this is the first book of the series, and I thoroughly enjoyed every second of writing it. This story is based on fiction places.

Book 2 Daggers story next.

If you haven't yet, please check out my first series, Bound Mafia Series which is made up of three books that can be read individually but better reading altogether.

About the author

C L McGinlay is a full-time mum to two boys, but also a full-time carer for her youngest who was born with a medical condition and requires more care than the average child and had to leave her job in order to care for him.

Writing is something that she's always wanted to do but never had the courage to pull through with it, she's loves to read and creating stories is a passion. With much self-doubt she didn't think she could do it but with the support and encouragement from her husband and her family she decided to try and write to see what she can come up with, and the bound series was born. When she's not taking care of her family or spending quality time with them then she's reading, then writing in the evenings, hopeful a career might be born with her stories and people can fall in love with the characters and laugh and cry with them just like she does when she reads books.

Printed in Great Britain
by Amazon